"Has he inquired about your intentions toward me?" Bobby asked Jenna.

Her eyes widened. "My intentions?"

"My father has been looking for a wife for me for some time now. He doesn't think I'm capable of finding one on my own."

One look at the undaunted merriment in King's eyes had her reconsidering the sharp retort on the tip of her tongue. She grinned at him.

"For the right deal, I might be persuaded to let him court me. I couldn't make any guarantees about his success, though."

King hooted at her quick response.

Bobby frowned at her. "Jenna, stop encouraging him."

"Okay," she agreed cheerfully. "Let's hear *your* best offer."

Bobby stared at her. "You're playing us against each other?"

"Sure. Apparently you each have an agenda where I'm concerned. If the price is right, maybe I could be persuaded to ignore your father."

"What's your price?" Bobby asked, looking resigned.

Jenna didn't hesitate. "Another meeting once I've roughed in some sketches of what we saw today."

Bobby sighed heavily. "Done," he agreed.

Jenna turned back to King to find that he was regarding her with more respect than her own father had ever displayed.

"You'll do, young lady. You will most definitely do."

Dear Friend,

Welcome back to Trinity Harbor, Virginia, where there are always unexpected things just around the corner, but none more so than what happens to Bobby Spencer in *Ask Anyone*. Little does laid-back Bobby know that his life is about to be turned completely upside down by the arrival of Jenna Kennedy, a woman on a mission to prove to everyone that she no longer deserves the label of monumental screwup that has been pinned on her by her family.

Of course, with King Spencer as a father, Bobby knows a whole lot about trying to win parental respect, but his sympathy toward Jenna's plight may not be enough for him to make the kind of major commitment she's hoping for.

Once again, Anna-Louise Walton is around to lend a sympathetic ear and to provide the kind of moral guidance that you'd expect from a minister with a huge heart. And, of course, you'll get to catch up with Daisy, Walker and Tommy, as well as with Tucker, whose compelling story is coming soon from MIRA Books—the title is *Along Came Trouble*, and it's scheduled for release in December.

So come home with me to Trinity Harbor once more. I promise some laughter, maybe even a few tears and, of course, some wonderful new friends to welcome into your heart.

All best,

Sherryl Woods

Sherryl Woods

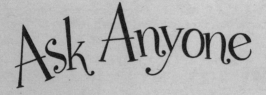

Ask Anyone

MIRA®

ISBN 1-55166-901-3

ASK ANYONE

Copyright © 2002 by Sherryl Woods.

MIRA and the Star Colophon are trademarks used under license and registered in Australia, New Zealand, Philippines, United States Patent and Trademark Office and in other countries.

Visit us at www.mirabooks.com

Printed in U.S.A.

Ask Anyone

Prologue

His son was making a spectacle of himself. Robert "King" Spencer had just hung up on the Trinity Harbor mayor, who was outraged not only by what was going on over at Bobby's this morning, but by just about everything Bobby had done lately. He had a list, and King had been forced to listen to every fool thing on it.

"Fine people ought to be getting ready for church at this hour on a Sunday morning," Harvey Needham had groused in conclusion. "Instead, they're over at your son's gawking like a bunch of tourists at an amusement park. This has to stop, King. The man's out of control. And I'd like to know what you intend to do about it."

"Not a blasted thing," King had told him, and slammed down the phone.

He sighed heavily. It wasn't as if this was the first time one of his children had stirred things up in Trinity Harbor. His daughter, Daisy, had almost given him a coronary when she'd insisted on letting that stray boy and his uncle into her life last year. The gossipmongers had had a field day, almost costing Daisy her teaching job in the process. Now, thank the Lord, she and

Walker Ames were respectably married and Tommy was on good behavior, which meant it was time for King to turn his attention to his younger son and namesake.

Unfortunately, Bobby was proving to be as difficult to control as Daisy had been. King had almost laughed when Harvey had asked him to step in. As if Bobby would pay an iota of attention to anything his daddy had to say! He seemed to have the idea that he was too old to take advice from his father. So far, that hadn't stopped King from offering it, but he was beginning to think he was wasting his breath.

What his son—both of his sons, for that matter—needed was a good woman in his life. King had been searching high and low for someone who fit his criteria, someone with a little spunk and a lot of class. So far the search had been in vain, but he hadn't given up. Of course, once he succeeded in finding a likely candidate, there was no guarantee Bobby would cooperate. More likely the opposite.

The sad truth was that Bobby was stubborn as a mule. King had no idea where he got the trait, but it was a blasted nuisance. Any other man would get at least a token amount of respect from his namesake, but not King. When he tried to advise his son, Bobby merely regarded him with tolerant amusement, then went right out and did what he darn well pleased.

The rebellion had started ten years ago, when Bobby went away to college. King had expected him to take business management or maybe even animal husbandry, something that would serve him well when he took over their Black Angus cattle operation at Cedar Hill, the farm the family had owned for generations.

Instead, the doggone fool had gotten his heart broken by his childhood sweetheart, and in an act of pure spite toward his daddy had signed up for cooking classes. As if that weren't bad enough, he'd topped it by dropping out his sophomore year and heading to France to take some fancy course in preparing gourmet food. When King had put his foot down and refused to pay for the trip, Bobby had gone out and earned the money himself. He'd worked at a fast-food joint over in Richmond for six months, putting every cent toward an airline ticket. King had never been so humiliated in his life…at least not until Bobby had come home with a diamond stud in one ear.

What kind of real man wanted to learn to cook? That was the question that stuck in King's craw. Wasn't that why they paid a housekeeper, so they'd never have to set foot in the kitchen except to raid the refrigerator? And if a man had to cook, what was wrong with a damned fine steak prepared on a grill or taking a wooden mallet to a pile of steamed crabs? That was the only kind of food preparation King wanted any part of.

Now Bobby owned the yacht center in town, spent his nights cooking in the club's restaurant and devoted his daytime hours to trying to drive his daddy into an early grave by upsetting all the town fathers with his big ideas about developing the waterfront. If he had a specific plan in mind, Bobby hadn't shared it with his father, but it must be a doozy if old Harvey was in such an uproar that he was trying to drag King into the middle of the fray.

Harvey didn't like turning to King for anything. The fool liked to believe he was his own man, but when push came to shove, who did he ask for help? That's right, King Spencer, the man whose family had settled Trinity Harbor way back when. Even Harvey was forced to admit that the Spencer name still counted for something in this part of Virginia.

Not that King didn't relish a good fight from time to time. Nothing made him happier. He just hated having to publicly side with outsiders against a member of his own family.

He had two choices. He could head on over to Bobby's and add his two cents to the commotion outside, or he could bide his time and say his piece over Sunday dinner. For once in his life, King opted for discretion.

Besides, he didn't really want a lot of witnesses around when Bobby told him to mind his own damned business.

1

There was a merry-go-round in his front yard. Okay, not a whole merry-go-round, just one lavishly carved, brightly painted carousel horse, but it was enough to make Bobby Spencer's jaw drop. He hadn't seen anything like it since a trip to the Santa Monica Pier years ago on one of the rare occasions when his father had deigned to leave his beloved Virginia.

That white-and-gold horse was also enough to have drawn most of the neighborhood kids out on a steamy Sunday morning to stare at it in fascination. The only thing that seemed to be keeping the curious youngsters from climbing onto that horse was the presence of a beefy uniformed security guard lounging in a rickety lawn chair about two feet away.

He had a merry-go-round horse *and* an armed man in his front yard. Bobby was pretty sure he'd awakened to stranger scenes in the past twenty-eight years, but he couldn't remember when. It was almost enough to make him regret moving away from the family estate at Cedar Hill, where the nearest neighbor was half a mile down the road. Of course, then he would have had King to contend with, and that would have been much worse than this innocent little spectacle.

Only after he'd been standing there, slack-jawed, for

a full minute, the morning paper absentmindedly clutched in one hand, did he realize that he was wearing nothing but a pair of boxers, and that any minute now, he was going to become part of the sideshow on his front lawn. Already Sue Kelly and Frannie Yarborough were ogling him with appreciative glances that Bobby might have found flattering if the two spinsters hadn't been at least seventy and, even worse, the two biggest gossips on the block.

Just when he was about to dart inside to put on something halfway decent and maybe drink enough caffeine to come up with a way out of this crazy situation, a police cruiser rolled to a stop at the edge of the lawn. The county sheriff—his own brother—emerged grinning.

Tucker's arrival was followed in short order by another cruiser. This time it was Bobby's brother-in-law, Walker Ames, who got out, cast one look at the scene and, displaying even less restraint, burst out laughing. He and Tucker exchanged an amused look, then strolled toward Bobby, making a pretense of looking somber and official. If he'd been armed, Bobby would have shot 'em both on the spot. No jury on earth—or at least around these parts—would have convicted him.

"Where's the cotton candy?" Tucker asked, barely containing another grin.

"Very funny," Bobby snapped, in no mood for his brother's wit.

"You got a permit for starting up a carnival in a residential area?" Tucker continued, clearly undaunted by Bobby's sour attitude. "We've been overlooking

Frannie's fortune-telling, but this is a little harder to ignore.''

"You don't have to enjoy this quite so much," Bobby said.

Tucker's grin spread. "Sure I do. Best time I've had all weekend."

"So where'd it come from?" Walker asked, his fascinated gaze fixed on the horse with its prancing feet and bejeweled harness. Someone had taken great care with the restoration. It was in like-new condition.

Bobby's scowl shifted to encompass his brother-in-law. "How should I know?"

"It is in your yard," Tucker pointed out.

"So are you, but I sure as hell didn't invite you," Bobby retorted.

"Seems cranky," Tucker observed to Walker.

"Downright irritable," Walker agreed.

Bobby studiously ignored the ribbing. They'd tire of it eventually. Besides, if he was going to get to the bottom of this unexpected gift horse, he needed their help. They might be acting like idiots at the moment, but they both had halfway decent investigative skills, and the authority to go along with it. Without a jolt of coffee, he couldn't even think.

"Maybe I should call Daddy and get him over here," his brother said, his expression innocent. "He might have some ideas."

Bobby frowned at Tucker, who could be an annoying son of a gun on his best days. "You do, and you're a dead man. Leave Daddy out of this. Besides, I'm sure someone has called him already. People always love to report to King when one of us is causing a scene. Who called you, by the way? Never mind, let me guess. It was the mayor, right?''

Sadly, his nemesis lived just around the corner, close enough to keep an eye on everything that Bobby did. Not that Bobby was prone to wild parties or overnight guests in his restored Victorian house facing the Potomac River, but Harvey was always lurking around, probably hoping for something he could use against Bobby. Bobby had actually caught him outside with a ruler measuring the grass one day, checking to see if Bobby was in violation of the town's overgrown-lot ordinance.

''Harvey did express some concern that you were desecrating the Sabbath, to say nothing of violating several zoning ordinances,'' Tucker admitted. ''Though he lacked confidence that I'd handle it with deliberate speed.''

''Which is why I'm here,'' Walker explained. ''Backup, in case your brother doesn't follow the letter of the law about arresting the people responsible for public nuisances.''

''This is not my damned nuisance,'' Bobby retorted. ''Oh, forget it. If you'll excuse me, I'm going inside to put my pants on before Sue and Frannie faint dead away over there.'' The two women were fanning their flushed faces ineffectively, their gazes locked on him as if they hadn't laid eyes on a partially clothed man in decades. The truth was, they probably hadn't. He waved, clearly flustering them. He'd no doubt have tuna casseroles waiting on his front porch for the next week because of this. They seemed to think a man on his own was likely to starve, despite the fact that Bobby cooked for a living.

"What do you want me to do about this?" Tucker asked, looking none too eager to do a blessed thing.

"Make it *go away*," Bobby said emphatically. He gestured to encompass the entire scene. "All of it."

"Don't you even want to know how that horse got here?" Walker asked, clearly overcome with curiosity himself.

Walker probably wanted all the details to relate to Bobby's sister, who was bound to have a million and one questions. In fact, Bobby was somewhat surprised Daisy hadn't beat her husband over here.

Bobby was actually pretty sure he knew what the arrival of the horse was all about. Maybe not the specific person who'd sent it over, but that fancy carved horse was clearly part of someone's bid to get his attention focused on a proposal for the boardwalk development he was planning. He'd had half a dozen unsolicited calls requesting appointments to make presentations since he'd announced a few weeks ago that he had signed the papers to buy the last parcel of riverfront land he needed. In his only public comment on the acquisition, Bobby had made the mistake of mentioning that he intended to get the project started this fall in the hope that it would be completed by the following summer. Eager developers had been crawling out of the woodwork ever since.

"I'll leave it to you two crack lawmen to figure out who's behind this. You have my permission to take the person responsible into custody for trespassing. And with all these other people crawling all over my lawn, that ought to help you meet your arrest quota for the month,'' he said, throwing it out as an irresistible challenge. Tucker really hated being accused of having quotas of any kind. ''Meantime, I'm getting dressed and making coffee. Join me once you've solved the mystery and gotten rid of this circus.''

Unfortunately, he had a suspicion *that* wasn't going to be as easy as he'd made it sound. Just as well. He'd have plenty of time to whip up a fluffy omelette and some hash browns before the two of them made it inside. Something told him he was going to need a lot of sustenance to get through the rest of a day that had started out this badly.

Jenna Pennington Kennedy was a royal screwup. Ask anyone, especially her father, who was giving her one last chance to prove herself with this boardwalk-development proposal for Trinity Harbor, Virginia.

Okay, he hadn't *exactly* given her the chance. She'd read about the prospect in the Baltimore newspaper and come after it on her own, without saying a single word to her domineering father or her brothers. They would have snatched the opportunity right out from under her, either by going after it themselves or simply by squelching her initiative with hoots of derisive laughter.

Unfortunately, though, her sneakiness seemed to have been for naught. The man she'd been told to contact—the one who owned the riverfront property and was looking to develop it—was steadfastly refusing to see her. His secretary claimed he wasn't seeing anyone yet, but Jenna suspected it was because she was a female. In the development business, she ran across a lot of macho males who ignored anything a woman had to say unless it pertained to sex. Since sex had been nothing but trouble for Jenna, she had no intention of indulging again, at least not in the foreseeable future. Better to concentrate on things she understood, like riverfront development.

Whatever the real story was behind Bobby Spencer's refusal to see her, this morning she had taken steps to snag his attention. She'd sent the man an extraordinarily rare carousel horse, part of an elaborate 1916 Allan Herschel carousel with a Wurlitzer organ that had cost her every penny of her savings and the entire trust fund her mother had left her. She'd considered it an investment in her future. Given the current state of the stock market, it probably wasn't as risky a decision as it seemed.

If all else failed, she assumed she could auction off the carousel—currently under lock and key in a Maryland warehouse—and at least get her money back. If she succeeded, it would become the centerpiece of this project, and Bobby Spencer would pay handsomely for it.

Of course, in an attempt to prove to her father that she could be sensible when necessary, she had also sent along a guard to protect the expensive antique from the sticky fingers of curious kids and the remote possibility that a knowledgeable thief would try to make off with it.

The whole plan had been a stroke of genius, if she did say so herself. Too bad she'd had to keep it from her father. He might have been proud of her, for once.

Jenna sat in her car down the block and happily watched the crowd on Spencer's lawn growing, despite the halfhearted attempts of two policemen to get it to disperse. Heck, if she'd thought to open a concession stand on the block, she could have sold enough lemonade on this hot July morning to pay the guard's salary.

She'd give it another half hour, let Bobby Spencer begin to see what a draw an old carousel could be for the town, then she'd seize the moment to demand an appointment to make her complete presentation.

Despite years of being regarded as a second-class citizen in her own family's company, Jenna had complete confidence in her design for the Trinity Harbor boardwalk. In her favor, she had an abiding nostalgia for all the old-fashioned beach towns she'd ever visited. People could get gaudy seaside entertainment in Ocean City. They could find more elaborate amusement parks just down the road from here at Kings Dominion or Busch Gardens. What a quaint little town like Trinity Harbor required was charm, and nobody understood charm better than a woman who'd spent her whole life with a bunch of men who were clueless on the subject.

But despite her self-confidence about the end result, Jenna resented the fact that she'd had to go to such an extreme just to put herself on Spencer's radar. What kind of businessman ignored the overtures of an expert? His behavior didn't bode well for their working relationship, but she was desperate. She'd work with the worst CEO in corporate history for this chance.

More dispiriting, though, than being dismissed by a stranger was having to jump through such elaborate hoops to prove to her father that she understood the business as well as he did and that she deserved to be more than decoration for the front office. If she'd been another son, he would have taken these things as a given. Dennis and Daniel had never had to prove themselves. They just showed up and made a pretense of working. As long as beachfront condos went up and didn't fall down, her father was content. It annoyed the daylights out of Jenna that he never saw her brothers' flaws—and never forgot hers.

Not that her father didn't have more than ample reason to distrust her judgment, she conceded reluctantly, but he bore some of the responsibility for her disastrous elopement himself. Randall Pennington had been an overprotective single dad who'd never had the first inkling about how to raise a daughter. After Jenna's mother had died, he'd settled on boarding school and tough love for his only daughter, while his sons had stayed at home under his watchful but indulgent eye.

As a result, Jenna had abandonment issues. She also had control issues. Big ones. She'd never had to consult a shrink to figure that out. A couple of episodes of *Oprah* had done it.

In an act of pure rebellion—and teenage lust—she had married the most irresponsible boy on God's green earth. To this day, he hadn't held a job more than the six months it took for boredom to set in. She shouldn't have been surprised that his attention span for women was no longer.

But to an eighteen-year-old girl who'd lived a sheltered boarding school life, Nick Kennedy had seemed wild and sexy and dangerous. His ability to make her father see red just by walking in the door had been one of his primary attractions.

Nick had also been a helluva kisser, which had led to her second mistake in judgment. She'd gotten pregnant so fast, it must have set some kind of a record. Her only consolation was that it had been after the wedding ceremony, not before. Nick was already straying before their daughter's birth, which had provided Jenna with her second dose of abandonment issues.

Now she had a precocious nine-year-old who was the spitting image of her daddy in looks and temperament. If Jenna had allowed it, Darcy would be pierced and tattooed in every conceivable spot on her plump little body. Jenna shuddered at the thought of what might happen the next time Darcy went to visit Nick, whom she could twist around her little pinky. Discipline and good sense were not among Nick's strengths. And in recent years he'd been given a tab at his neighborhood tattoo parlor.

But the final nail in her coffin as far as her father was concerned had been her divorce. He didn't believe in divorce. Not ever. Mistresses were just fine, apparently. It was an odd set of moral values, in Jenna's opinion, but there it was. Leaving Nick was another black mark on her record with dear old Dad, even though he hated the guy. Another incomprehensible incongruity, to Jenna's way of thinking. Trying to keep up with all of them gave her hives, but she did try.

She could have moved out of her father's house—

where a housekeeper was now looking after Darcy—
and away from Baltimore, struggled to find some kind
of work for which she was qualified and probably lived
happily ever after, but Jenna was stubborn. She still
craved her father's approval and her rightful share of
the company. Hoping for his love after all these years
was probably a wasted effort, but she even harbored
hopes of that, which was why she was still living under
his roof and accepting the paltry, nonliving wage he
used to keep her there.

She had worked for Pennington and Sons for the
last seven years, ever since her quickie divorce in
Reno. She was bound and determined to make her father regret that he'd only acknowledged the existence
and contributions of her two worthless brothers in
naming the business. She knew more, worked harder
and had more vision than Dennis and Daniel com-
bined, but all she got was a paycheck and the occasional patronizing pat on the head when she saved their
sorry butts after they'd overlooked some little detail
that could have cost the company a fortune. In fact,
she was just about the only person in the firm who
actually seemed to read and comprehend the fine print
of their contracts.

This Trinity Harbor job was her chance to prove
herself creatively, and no male chauvinist jerk was going to deprive her of it. If she had to take Darcy out
of her current school come September and move down
here so she could get in Bobby Spencer's face 24/7
until he caved in and gave her the deal, then that's
what she'd do.

And after seeing him on his front lawn in his boxers,

his body bronzed and his brown hair bleached by the sun, a rakish diamond glittering in his ear, the prospect promised to be a whole lot more entertaining than she'd envisioned when she'd driven away from Baltimore towing that antique horse in a trailer behind her beat-up Chevy.

She'd been thinking arrogant, crotchety old man, and, instead, she was going to be going toe to toe with a body—a *man*—so gorgeous he could make her forget her long-standing resolution not to even think about sex again until she hit menopause. Given her history of mistakes in judgment, her luck was not necessarily taking a turn for the better.

2

Bobby stared at the fancy little gift card that Tucker had brought inside. The guard had apparently handed it to him.

"'There's more where this came from,'" he read aloud, then looked at his brother. "What does that mean?"

"I think it means you'd better keep an eye on the front lawn or you'll wind up with a whole amusement park out there," Tucker said. "Won't be any need to develop the boardwalk. You can just invite folks over here, put a few burgers on the grill and make a fortune without ever leaving the house. There won't be another town in the entire state that can compete with that kind of down-home atmosphere. They'll be writing this place up in *Southern Living*."

Bobby shot a sour look at him. "The card's not signed," he noted.

"I imagine that's to keep you guessing," Walker chimed in with another of those annoying grins.

"Looks to me like a woman's handwriting," Tucker added. "Thought I smelled a trace of perfume, too."

"Is that the kind of top-notch investigative work the people of this county can expect from the sheriff?" Bobby inquired. "I could figure out that much."

"Any time you want to sign up to be a deputy, let me know," Tucker retorted.

Bobby scowled at him. "Didn't the guard have any idea who'd hired him?"

"As a matter of fact, he did, but he wasn't inclined to share it," Tucker said, snatching Bobby's cooling food from in front of him and shoveling it down.

"Hey," Bobby protested, "what do you think you're doing?"

"Having breakfast," Tucker said blandly. "The mayor rousted me out of bed, and I'm starved. Besides, you weren't eating it. This is the least you can do after spoiling my day off."

"I'm not the one who called, and I was going to eat that myself," Bobby countered.

Tucker shrugged. "It would have been too cold. Fix yourself something else. Last I heard you were a professional cook."

"I'm a chef, dammit, and that's not the point." Bobby sighed heavily. "Aren't the two of you on duty? Isn't it your job to find the woman who sent this card?"

"Actually, I'm not *officially* on duty. As for the rest, sometimes the smartest, most efficient thing a cop can do is nothing. I'm thinking the woman behind all this will find you," Tucker said. "Got any bacon? I'm in the mood for some nice, crisp bacon."

"Fix it yourself," Bobby said, then looked toward his brother-in-law. "Since my brother is more interested in filling his stomach than using his brain, what about you? Do you have any bright ideas about this?"

"Tucker's right. If someone went to this much trouble, they're going to show up to see how it turned out," Walker said, then added, "Damn, I'm sorry Daisy's missing this. Your sister would have to pick this weekend to take Tommy off to Williamsburg for an educational adventure."

"Thank God for small favors," Bobby grumbled. He'd forgotten about that trip. It was the only reason his sister wasn't in the thick of things. "Having the two of you here is bad enough. I don't need Daisy putting in her two cents. And Tommy'd be out there right now trying to charge people to take pictures. That boy has a true entrepreneurial spirit."

Finally thinking of something to smile about, Bobby said to Walker, "By the way, I'll bet you twenty bucks that those two haven't done an educational thing since they got to Williamsburg—unless you consider riding the roller coaster at Busch Gardens to be some form of higher education."

"That's a sucker bet," Walker said. "No question about it."

Just then the doorbell rang. Bobby frowned and didn't make a move to answer it. He'd had about as much unwanted company as he could take this morning.

"Well?" Tucker prodded when it rang again.

"Well, what?"

"Aren't you going to answer it? Remember what I said, that mysterious woman is likely to come looking for you. That could be her. Your mystery could be solved right here and now."

Bobby considered the possibilities. Tucker could be right. Or, more likely, it could be his father, urged to interfere by the mayor. It could even be some kid with a bunch of unanswerable questions. Or his buddy Richard, wanting some kind of a comment for this week's edition of the Trinity Harbor paper to go with the pictures he'd no doubt snapped of the chaos outside. When news happened in Trinity Harbor, Richard's journalistic instincts kicked in within seconds. He wouldn't miss this.

Bobby wasn't interested in dealing with any of them, not even the woman responsible for disrupting his peaceful Sunday morning.

"Nope," he said, and poured himself another cup of special blend French roast coffee. He was beginning to feel almost human, and he wasn't about to ruin it.

Whoever it was leaned on the doorbell.

"I can't stand it," Walker said finally. "I'll get rid of them."

Instead, five seconds later he returned to the kitchen looking vaguely bemused by a voluptuous redhead wearing a power suit and slinky three-inch spike heels. The dichotomy wasn't lost on Bobby. Clearly the woman hadn't gotten sidetracked on her way to church. She looked like a cross between a politician and a hooker.

When she teetered on those heels, he was forced to reconsider. He began to lean toward the image of a kid playing dress-up. There was something vulnerable in her eyes to back up that opinion. He really, really hoped this was not the woman responsible for that horse. He was a sucker for female vulnerability. His protective instincts rushed into action, overriding every defense mechanism he worked to keep in place.

"Nice job," Bobby said to Walker, who merely shrugged over his inability—more likely, disinclination—to get rid of the interloper.

"You must be Bobby Spencer," the woman said, offering her hand and a dazzling smile.

Bobby's gaze narrowed. Reluctantly, he shook her outstretched hand. "I am."

"I'm Jenna Kennedy of Pennington and Sons."

"Nice to meet you," Bobby said, recognizing the name of the Baltimore-based company that had been pestering him for a week now for an appointment. His secretary hadn't been happy about his repeated refusal to talk to the woman. Maggie had thought she sounded sincere. Maggie was an annoyingly soft touch, which was why Bobby frequently wound up in meetings he didn't want to have.

He forced a stern expression. "Sorry you wasted your time," he told her. "But I don't conduct business in my kitchen, especially not on a Sunday morning. Call my office."

To her credit, she didn't turn tail and run at the lack of welcome. "I would, but it's the funniest thing. No one there seems to be able to give me an appointment without your say-so. Either you're a control freak, you're stonewalling me in particular for some reason or you're just generally rude and bad at business."

"Or maybe I'm just busy," he said mildly, not liking her accusations one bit. Especially the one about rudeness, since it seemed to echo Maggie's assessment. He prided himself on being a gentleman. Good manners was one of the things King had drilled into all his children, right along with respect for their Southern heritage.

Of course, the truth was, he *had* been stonewalling Jenna Kennedy. Though he hadn't settled on a specific plan for his boardwalk project, he knew one thing for certain—he didn't want to deal with a woman. Not that he had anything at all against women. His sister was one, after all. And some of his best friends were females. But ever since his childhood sweetheart had run off with his best friend, he hadn't been inclined to get close to another woman. He had trust issues galore, according to Daisy.

Once burned, twice shy. That was the expression his sister used when she was scolding him about being skittish and telling him it was time to get over it and move on. She also added a lot of hogwash about his obsessive compulsion to take over the town being a bid to prove that he would have been the better choice for his old girlfriend. Like he really gave a rat's behind what that traitorous female thought of him, especially after all these years.

"Not every woman you fall for is going to go running off with your best friend," Daisy usually pointed out.

"Especially now that he's already married to my former fiancée," he generally retorted.

He frowned at Ms. Jenna Pennington Kennedy. "Look, I'm assuming that carousel horse was your idea."

"It was," she said.

"It was a nice touch, but I really don't think this will work out," he said.

"Why? You haven't even heard our proposal."

"It just won't," he said flatly. "Walker, could you show Ms. Kennedy out?"

Walker looked as if he wanted no part of this, but he dutifully said, "Ms. Kennedy," and stepped back to give her room to pass. She didn't budge.

In fact, she scowled first at Walker, then at Bobby, and planted her sexily shod feet a bit more firmly on the floor.

"Not just yet. Mr. Spencer, I don't know what your problem is, but it's my understanding that you want the kind of riverfront development that will put Trinity Harbor on the map. I can give you that."

"Really?" Bobby said, not bothering to hide his skepticism. His attention kept drifting back to those shoes and her well-turned ankles. He almost missed the rest of what she had to say.

"You don't want gaudy," she said with impressive confidence. "You don't want Ocean City. You want something that won't overwhelm the size of the community, something with charm, some green space and a sense of the town's history. Am I right?"

To Bobby's deep regret, she had intuitively pushed all the right buttons. "Yes," he conceded with a great deal of reluctance. "But if you understand that, why is there an antique horse on my front lawn disturbing the Sunday peace and quiet?"

"I had to get your attention," she said reasonably. "I thought that would do it." She grinned. "And it worked, didn't it?"

Walker and Tucker were watching him expectantly. What the heck? he thought with a sigh of resignation.

She was here. He had to start talking to prospective developers sometime. Besides, Ms. Jenna Pennington Kennedy was obviously the persistent type. She wasn't going to go away until she'd said her piece. He could see her in the morning and have her out of town by noon.

"Okay, I'll see you tomorrow," he told her. "In my office. Ten o'clock. If you're late, I won't be waiting."

A dazzling, relieved smile that could fell a stronger man than Bobby spread across her face. "You won't regret it," she said, reaching for his hand and enthusiastically pumping it.

Bobby sighed as the seductive scent of her perfume wafted through the air. He already did.

King slid into his favorite booth at Earlene's first thing on Monday morning. He'd almost stayed home today, but he wasn't going to let a little thing like being publicly humiliated by his own son keep him from the pleasure of seeing his friends the way he did every single day of the year, rain or shine.

It was bad enough that Harvey had been the first one on the phone on Sunday, but the chatter had kept up all the livelong day. He hadn't had a minute's peace. Worse, first Bobby and then Tucker had called to cancel out on the family dinner. Neither one of them had stayed on the line long enough for him to get a straight word out of them about what was going on. He'd been left with enough fried chicken to feed an army and enough indigestion to keep him from touching a single piece of it. It was damned annoying. He looked forward to that chicken all week.

Which was why, the second dusk fell, he had driven past Bobby's to see for himself what all the commotion was about. That merry-go-round horse that had gotten Harvey's drawers in a knot was still sitting out there. Half the neighborhood kids were still hanging around gawking at it, too, along with what looked like a dozen carloads of adults. Since all the locals had probably been by right after the word spread at church that morning, these had to be out-of-towners drawn by word of the rare antique that had sprung up on his son's front lawn.

To top it off, King had spotted Richard Walton snapping pictures for this week's edition of *The Trinity Harbor Weekly*. He was accompanied by his wife, King's very own pastor, Anna-Louise. Irritated, King had forgotten all about his intention to drive straight by without making his presence known. He'd pulled up to the curb and rolled down his window.

"Woman, don't you have better things to be doing than poking around out here like a tourist?" he'd grumbled. "Why aren't you over at the church, saving souls?"

Completely unintimidated, Anna-Louise had turned one of her placid smiles in his direction and strolled right on over to look him squarely in the eye. "Should have known you'd be skulking around here somewhere," she commented. "Why don't you park and walk on up to your son's front door if you're so curious about what's going on? I'm sure Bobby would be happy to see you. He could probably use some moral support about now. I imagine it's been a trying day."

"I doubt he'd be interested in anything I have to say. He never is. Besides, do you honestly think I could get a straight answer out of him?" King had scoffed. "Not likely. He stayed away from Cedar Hill today, because he doesn't want to tell me a blessed thing."

"Richard interviewed him a few minutes ago. You'll be able to read all about it later this week," she said, looking smug. She knew perfectly well how King felt about that nosy husband of hers poking into things, especially things that had to do with the Spencer family.

"You know, Anna-Louise, for a woman as well-versed as you are in God's word, you have a nasty habit of forgetting all about it when it suits you," he'd charged.

She'd leveled a look at him that would have wilted a lesser man. "Oh?"

"Whatever happened to honoring thy father? Isn't that one of the Ten Commandments?"

"It is," she'd agreed.

"Well?"

"I'm not sure of the relevance," she'd said, then reached into the car to pat the hand clenching the steering wheel. "King, I really don't think this horse has anything to do with you. Believe it or not, it's Bobby's problem, not yours."

"He's my son, dammit. What he does reflects on me."

"Oh, for goodness' sakes," Anna-Louise had snapped impatiently, "he's not the one who put the horse here. In fact, from what he said to Richard, I gather that he's every bit as anxious as you are to make it go away. Now either go inside to lend him your support or go on home and sulk.''

King had gone home to sulk. He'd spent the whole evening trying to figure out why everyone—himself included—was so stirred up. It was an awful lot of hoopla over one itty-bitty piece of a kid's amusement-park ride. Anna-Louise was right about one thing. The whole situation would be over with and forgotten in no time. He just had to go about his business and ignore it.

Which was why he was in his regular booth at Earlene's awaiting the arrival of his friends. A rousing conversation about the price of beef would get his juices stirring.

Pete Dexter was the first to arrive. ''Oh, boy,'' he murmured with a shake of his head as he slid in opposite King. ''Bobbby's gone and stepped in it now.''

King regarded him with a lofty look. ''I have no idea what you mean.''

''Harvey's out for blood. He claims Bobby is trying to stage a coup and take over the whole blessed town.''

King gritted his teeth. So he wasn't going to be able to ignore this after all. ''Where would he get a numbskull idea like that? Bobby's not interested in taking over anything. That boy doesn't have a political bone in his body.''

''Then why did he go and buy up all that property? Whoever develops it is going to set the direction of Trinity Harbor for decades to come. And Harvey's bound and determined that it's not going to be your son. He says Spencers have been in charge for too long as it is, that it's time for fresh blood to take this town into the future.''

King clung to his temper by a thread. "Just how does that pompous fool propose to stop Bobby?"

"The way I hear it, he'll tie him up with zoning regulations and red tape until Bobby gives up and walks away from the whole deal. Then I imagine he'll try to snap up that land for a pittance and do whatever he wants with it. You ask Will what he thinks when he gets here. I heard a rumor he sold a couple of parcels to the mayor a while back before Bobby could snap 'em up. My guess is Harvey would like to see condos all along the waterfront. Next thing you know, none of us will be able to stick a toe in that river without being charged with trespassing."

King stared at his oldest friend. "Harvey told you this?"

"Not about the condos, that's Will's idea. But Harvey told a whole roomful of people about the rest at lunch yesterday. I was eating crabs over at Wilkerson's at Colonial Beach. Harvey was holding forth like a preacher. He was talking so loud and his face was so red, I thought he was going to keel right over onto the seafood buffet."

"Did you set him straight?" King asked.

"Me?" Pete looked baffled. "What was I supposed to say?"

"That no son of King Spencer's would ever walk away from a fight, for starters," King declared fiercely. He might not be entirely in tune with Bobby's plans, but no upstart like Harvey Needham was going to sabotage them. "Did you tell him that?"

"No," Pete admitted.

"Then you're as big a damned fool as he is," King

said, sliding out of the booth and tossing some money on the table for the coffee he'd never touched.

"Now, King—" Pete began.

"Don't you try to placate me, you old coot. I thought loyalty still counted for something in this town. Guess I was wrong."

He stalked off to the sound of Pete's sputters of protest and the hushed whispers of everyone else in Earlene's. The way things were going, the entire conversation would be reported in *The Weeky,* right alongside that spread of pictures Richard had taken over at Bobby's.

Once King got outside in the hot, muggy morning air, he sucked in a deep breath and tried to calm himself down. He was going to kill that boy of his with his bare hands. He didn't have time to waste an entire morning on this kind of nonsense. He needed to get home. Somebody had to run that Black Angus operation that his sons didn't give a hoot about.

But first, maybe he'd go on over to the Social Services office and see if Frances could spare him a little time. The woman had been driving him up the wall since she'd stolen first place in a spelling bee from him a half-century ago, but she had a level head on her shoulders. In the last year, he'd begun to count on that.

Frances had kept him from strangling Daisy and given him some sound advice and pleasant company along the way. Maybe if he offered to take her out to play bingo tomorrow night, she'd keep his mind off of Bobby until his temper cooled down. The last place King wanted to spend his golden years was a jail cell.

And Tucker would slap him in one, no question about it. He didn't bend the rules for anybody.

When King arrived at Social Services, Frances was on the phone. The blessed woman was always on the phone, but he'd finally learned better than to try to interrupt her. She got downright feisty. He sat down and waited with what to him passed for patience. Fortunately, Frances didn't test him beyond his limits.

"I imagine you're here to talk about Bobby," she said with a resigned expression when she'd finally hung up.

"You heard," he said bleakly.

"Not only heard, I went by there yesterday. It was quite a scene." A wistful look passed across her face. "Seeing that carousel horse took me straight back to when we were kids. Remember? We used to have a carousel right here in town. And a skating rink, miniature golf and bingo on the boardwalk. I wish we could have all that back again. Kids need to know there's more to life than video games and computers."

King had a dim recollection of those days, but bingo and an old carousel were the least of his concerns. He sighed and regarded Frances with a plaintive look. "What am I supposed to do about all this nonsense Bobby's mixed up in?"

"Nothing," she said emphatically. "I know that goes against your nature, but Bobby can handle whatever's going on. Besides, I don't know what you're so upset about. I thought you'd be pleased as punch."

King stared at her. "Pleased? Why the devil would I be pleased?"

"Because the way I hear it, the woman responsible

for that horse turning up on Bobby's lawn is gorgeous and single. She's from a good family. Of course, she's from Maryland, not Virginia, but you can't afford to be picky if you want him to start providing you with some grandchildren to dote on. On top of that, she's already proved that she knows how to get Bobby's attention.''

That certainly put a new spin on things, King decided thoughtfully. ''Gorgeous, you say?''

''Yep, and a redhead,'' Frances confirmed. ''I ran into Tucker later in the day and he said Bobby's tongue was just about hanging out. He also said Bobby would probably deny that with his dying breath.''

King's spirits brightened considerably. ''Is that so?'' An idea popped into his head, one that required immediate action. He jumped up and headed for the door.

''What's your hurry?'' Frances asked. ''You heading back to Earlene's?''

''No time,'' King said. ''I've got something more important to take care of.'' He whirled around, went back and planted a solid kiss on Frances's mouth. ''Thanks.''

Cheeks pink, she regarded him with a startled expression. ''What did I do?''

''Same as always,'' he said with a grin. ''Put things in perspective.''

She laughed. ''Glad to help, though I have a feeling Bobby might not see it that way. Am I right?''

King gave her a bland look. ''Frances, I think you're a treasure. Remember that.''

''I'll remind you of it,'' she said.

She would, too. Over and over. But that was okay,

King thought, as he rushed out of her office feeling more upbeat than he had in months.

Let Harvey Needham rant and rave. Let Bobby try to keep him in the dark. King had a plan. Nobody could get the better of a man with a solid plan and the determination to implement it.

3

The God-blessed car was out of gas. Jenna pounded the steering wheel in frustration. Naturally, to make matters worse, her cell phone was dead. She'd used up the battery the night before trying to convince her daughter that it was absolutely not okay, much less necessary, for her to dye her hair purple. Darcy had cried and pleaded and accused Jenna of ruining her life. If Darcy was this difficult at nine, what would she be like she hit her teens? At any rate, Jenna had been so exhausted by the long-distance battle that she hadn't thought to recharge the phone.

It was 9:52 a.m. She had exactly eight minutes to get to the yacht center. In her running shoes she might have been able to do it. In three-inch spike heels, she didn't have a prayer.

Maybe Bobby Spencer wasn't quite as much of a tight-ass as he'd seemed yesterday. Maybe she could be a few minutes late and still catch him.

Yeah, right. The man had looked at her as if he'd rather be dealing with the devil. He'd obviously seize any excuse at all not to consider the Pennington and Sons proposal.

She stripped off her shoes, thanked heaven that her skirt had a slit in it and grabbed her briefcase off the seat. She hit the sidewalk at a dead run, grateful that she'd taken up jogging as a way to relieve stress.

Pounding along the pavement, praying that she'd gotten through to Darcy, praying even harder that she would not miss this appointment and blow her one and only chance to earn a little respect from her father, she concluded that this particular run was not likely to reduce her stress one iota. If anything, she was getting more anxious with every painful step she took.

Seven minutes and thirty seconds later, she reached the yacht center. She had runs in her hose, blisters on her feet and her hair no doubt looked as if it had been styled in a wind tunnel, but she was on time.

Bobby Spencer, however, was nowhere in sight and not even expected.

Jenna stared at the secretary. "He's not here," she repeated incredulously, certain she had to have misunderstood.

"Never gets in before eleven," the young woman said, clearly working to contain her curiosity over Jenna's disheveled appearance.

The woman's own attire consisted of shorts that showed off her long legs and a crisply pressed blouse with one too many buttons left open to display an ample amount of cleavage. Obviously Bobby did not stress professional decorum, or maybe at a yacht center, this was the appropriate uniform, Jenna concluded. She was probably the one who was seriously over-dressed…or had been when she'd left her car, anyway.

"Never?" she echoed, still certain that she had to be missing something.

"Not once in the year I've worked for him," the woman said. "Are you sure he said to be here at ten?"

"Oh, I am very sure he said ten," Jenna said, gritting her teeth. Her temper, which she usually worked really, really hard to contain, began to simmer. "Are you saying there has never been one single occasion when he's been here before eleven?"

"Not that I can recall," the woman said blithely. "He works late at night. Besides, he's just not a morning person. Believe me, you don't want to see him at this hour. In fact, if you'd like a little advice, I'd suggest you come back around two. He's pretty cheerful by then, especially if the reservations are up for dinner."

"Look…what's your name?"

"Maggie."

"Okay, Maggie, here's the thing. I saw Mr. Spencer yesterday. He told me to be here at ten. He made a really big deal about it. My car broke down, but I busted my butt to be on time. Could you get on that phone and track him down and tell him that I'm here and getting more aggravated by the minute that he's not?"

Maggie grinned. "You really want me to tell him that?"

Jenna sighed. "Okay, you can leave out the part about my attitude. Just try to hurry him along. I need to get back to Baltimore. I hadn't intended to stay overnight in the first place." In fact, she'd planned to be sitting cheerfully at her desk this morning with a contract in hand. Obviously she'd been overly optimistic about her powers of persuasion.

"Maybe you could think of this little delay as a blessing in disguise," Maggie suggested. Then she added tactfully, "You know, and use the time to kind of put yourself back together. Not that appearances are everything, but you look kinda like you tangled with a wrestler or something. I've got a sewing kit right here I could loan you."

Jenna stared at her blankly. "A sewing kit?"

"Your skirt," Maggie said, then gestured. "And your jacket."

Jenna looked down. The slit in her skirt now extended almost to the waistband. Any movement, she concluded with a horrified stare, revealed way too much of her lower anatomy. Two buttons on her jacket were hanging by threads, which left a gaping space across her chest featuring an even more ample display of skin and lace than Maggie herself was sharing with the world. No wonder she'd encountered a series of astounded stares and heard several cars skid to a stop en route to the yacht center. She was lucky that brother of Bobby's hadn't come along to arrest her for indecent exposure.

"Oh, God," she murmured, collapsing into a chair with a heartfelt moan.

"Now don't get upset," Maggie said, bouncing up at once. She was as refreshingly eager as an accommodating kid as she rummaged in her desk. "Here's the sewing kit." She glanced worriedly from the array of tiny spools of thread to Jenna's outfit, then grabbed the stapler. "Come with me. We'll have you fixed up in no time. It might not be pretty, but you will be decent."

"What if the phone starts ringing or Mr. Spencer comes while you're away from your desk?" Jenna said as she dragged herself out of the chair.

"Nobody important calls in the morning," Maggie assured her. "They all know how Bobby is. And you don't need to worry about him, either. He's a sweetie once he's had his coffee. You should see him. It's like this ritual the way he grinds the beans, then hovers over it as it brews. It's a little compulsive, if you ask me, but the coffee is way better than the instant kind I make at home. Anyway, once he's had his first cup, he's a doll."

"Really?" Jenna regarded her skeptically as Maggie led the way into a nearby bathroom. Jenna stripped off her skirt and jacket and they went to work with needle, thread and stapler.

"Oh, sure. Everyone knows that," Maggie said. "Everybody in town loves Bobby. Well, except for the mayor, but he thinks Bobby is a threat to his power. As if Bobby would ever want that job. He has all the power he needs just being a Spencer. Did you know that his ancestors founded this town? They came over from Jamestown. Not that Bobby flaunts that. I think it embarrasses him when I tell people, but I think it's just so cool. People should know, don't you think?"

"You admire him?" Jenna concluded.

"What's not to admire? He's nice. He's gorgeous. He works hard. He's from a great family."

Since Maggie was a young, attractive woman with no wedding band on her finger, Jenna asked, "Are you more than his secretary?"

"You mean like a one-woman cheerleading squad

or something?'' Maggie asked, then paled. ''Or do you mean is there something going on romantically between us? Good grief, no.'' She paused to consider the idea. ''He's kind of sexy, I suppose. That earring makes him look like a pirate. But he's way older than me.''

''He can't be more than thirty,'' Jenna pointed out.

''Twenty-eight, actually, but I'm only nineteen, and I'm not going to get seriously involved with anyone for years and years—and then it won't be with Bobby Spencer.''

More curious than she ought to be, Jenna asked, ''Why not, especially if he's such a paragon?''

''Because we're friends,'' Maggie said simply. ''He treats me like a kid sister. Heck, he used to baby-sit my brother and me.''

''And you've never had a crush on him? Not even a little one?''

''*No way,*'' Maggie claimed emphatically. ''He's really nice, if you know what I mean. I want a man with more of an edge. A guy who's a little dangerous.'' Her expression turned dreamy.

''Trust me, dangerous is highly overrated,'' Jenna told her. ''Nice is a better alternative.''

Maggie's gaze narrowed and her expression turned thoughtful. ''So, what do *you* think of Bobby? I heard about the commotion at his house yesterday. I would have given anything to be there to see his face.''

''Actually, he looked a little ticked,'' Jenna confided as Maggie stitched and stapled her skirt back together, while Jenna herself worked on the buttons on her jacket. The designer suit looked as if it had been pieced together by drunken elves.

Maggie's expression brightened at Jenna's description of Bobby's reaction. "To tell you the truth, that's a good thing," she declared. "We've all been saying for a long time now that somebody needs to come along and shake up that man's life. He's in a rut, emotionally speaking, that is. Not that he listens to me. He just rolls his eyes and walks away as if a kid my age couldn't possibly have anything intelligent to say about love."

Jenna didn't give two figs what kind of rut the man was in. She wanted to sell him on this proposal and get out of town with a signed contract in hand. She had to get back to Baltimore before Darcy defied her and dyed her hair purple. Even if Darcy used something temporary, like a powdered-grape-drink mix, it would be enough to send her grandfather's blood pressure soaring.

"Maggie, can I ask you something?"

"Sure."

"Why has your boss been refusing to take my calls? Is it because I'm a woman?"

Maggie looked genuinely astonished by the question. "Why would you think that?"

"It's just the way some men in business are," Jenna said, thinking of her father.

"Not Bobby," Maggie assured her. "It's just what I've told you on the phone. He's not talking to anybody about the boardwalk yet. Bobby likes to mull things over before he acts. He doesn't rush into anything. Some of that's Southern. Some of it's just

Bobby being Bobby. Don't take it personally. He's refused to talk to any of the men who've called, too.''

Jenna accepted the explanation at face value. "You've been a godsend," she told the young woman as she straightened her skirt, shrugged into her jacket and tried to adjust it. They weren't perfect, but they would do. "Thank you. I couldn't have gotten myself put back together without you."

For the first time, as she started to button up the jacket, she risked a look in the mirror. Her cheeks were still flushed. Her hair, which had started the day in a nice, neat French twist, was hanging down around her shoulders in a tangle of untamed curls.

Of course, that image reflected back at her wasn't nearly as disconcerting as the image of Bobby Spencer's stunned expression right next to it.

A half-dressed Jenna Kennedy was standing in *his* private bathroom. Bobby reluctantly dragged his gaze from full breasts barely covered with scraps of lace to her startled face.

"Seen enough?" she snapped.

He blinked. "Sorry," he said, then shut the door. "Maggie, get out here!"

His secretary emerged from the bathroom. "What the hell is going on?" he demanded.

"Long story, boss. Jenna will be out in a minute. She can explain. I've got work to do."

He shook his head. "Oh, no, you don't. Get back here. Since when are you anxious to get to work?"

"Since five seconds ago," she said with an unrepentant grin. "Go easy on her. She's had a rough morning."

Bobby sighed. "I'm not in the habit of terrorizing people."

"You know that and I know that," Maggie agreed. "She doesn't seem to be so sure. Why is that?"

Bobby had no intention of going down that particular road, not with a female who'd long since declared her intention to find him a woman. Between Maggie and his father, his personal life was doomed. He sure as heck didn't want either of them getting the idea of dragging Jenna Pennington Kennedy into it.

"Never mind," he said. "Go to work."

"I made coffee," she said, looking pleased with herself. "Just in case you didn't have time, what with your early meeting and all. It's instant, but it's better than nothing."

Bobby shuddered. "No, it's not. From now on, leave the coffee brewing to me. Yours tastes like axle grease."

He walked through the yacht center to the restaurant kitchen, prepared a decent pot of coffee, poured two cups, then took them back to his office and sat behind his desk. Jenna still hadn't emerged from his bathroom. He alternately checked his watch and gazed warily at the door as if a restless tiger might be lurking behind it. Finally the knob turned and his pulse kicked up a notch. He deliberately attributed it to annoyance at her tardiness, because anything else was unacceptable.

"You're late," he said, just to emphasize his displeasure.

Those bright patches of color in her cheeks deepened. "No," she said, just as emphatically. "I was right on time. Imagine my surprise when I was told that you *never* come in before eleven. If I'd known that, I could have found a better way to get here than running all the way."

He stared. "You ran? Why?"

"My car ran out of gas. Because you made such a big deal about me being on time, I got out, took off my shoes, hiked up my skirt and ran, which is why you found me in your bathroom looking like a complete wreck, and that was after Maggie and I had repaired most of the damage."

"I see." A dozen questions came to mind, along with quite a few disconcerting images. He would have paid money to see her crosstown race to get here. In fact, he was surprised he hadn't heard about it from someone by now. Then again, maybe that explained a couple of the fender benders he'd spotted along a normally quiet road.

She eyed him warily. "That's all you have to say? *I see?*"

"I'm sorry," he said. "You could have called and explained."

She shook her head. "My cell phone was dead." As if she realized she was making a less than stellar impression, she drew in a deep breath and said, "Maybe we should just forget all this and get straight to my ideas for your boardwalk development. This is just preliminary, of course, to make sure we're on the same wavelength. It can be adjusted and it will have to be fleshed out with architectural renderings."

Bobby sighed. This was what they were here for, though he was no more enthusiastic now than he'd been the day before. "Sure. Why not?" Listening didn't mean he had to agree to anything.

But as Jenna talked about a park setting, about family-style attractions, about picnics and concerts and sidewalk cafés that would become gathering places for a community, he began to see a revitalized area along the riverfront that would be absolutely perfect for Trinity Harbor. Not overwhelming, not unmanageable, but ideally suited for the small town atmosphere he wanted to preserve, even while contributing to the area's economic growth.

"I assume the centerpiece would be an antique carousel," he said.

She blinked as if he'd pulled the idea out of thin air. "How did you know?"

He chuckled at her pretense of amazement. "I might not be the professional cop that my brother is, but that horse you sent was a definite clue."

"Isn't he the most amazing thing?" she said, her eyes lighting up. "You have no idea what I had to go through to find that particular carousel. It's very rare."

"I'm sure," he said. "Thank heavens, though, you got it out of my front yard."

Her mouth dropped open, and she looked as if he'd just revealed that the blasted thing had been kidnapped.

"It's gone?" she whispered in a shocked tone.

"Since a couple of hours ago," he said, watching worriedly as her skin turned pale. "You had it picked up, didn't you?"

She shook her head. "What happened to the overnight guard? My arrangement was that he would stay right there with it until his replacement came this morning."

"I have no idea. He was gone by the time I left the house." He studied her stricken expression. "Are you telling me that someone stole that horse?"

Jenna nodded.

Bobby couldn't believe it. Who would steal a carousel horse? He turned on her suspiciously. "Is this some sort of scam? Or a publicity stunt? I am *not* paying for that horse. It was your bright idea that it was down here in the first place. I was never responsible for keeping it secure."

"I know." She buried her face in her hands. "Oh, God," she murmured. "My father is right. I am the world's worst screwup. That horse is worth a fortune. And the rest of the carousel won't be worth all that much without it. What was I thinking? I should have known something awful would happen. It always does. How am I ever supposed to convince my father that I can handle anything important when I keep messing up the simplest things?"

Her plaintive tone struck a responsive note somewhere deep inside Bobby. He knew a whole lot about judgmental fathers. "Insurance?" he suggested hopefully.

She shook her head. "The guard was cheaper. I used every last penny of my savings to buy that carousel and hire the security company to watch over the horse for a couple of days. Even if they're liable, it will take forever to get paid."

Bobby reached for the phone. "I'll get Tucker over here," he said grimly. He wanted that antique carousel horse found and found fast, because the protective feelings that Jenna Kennedy stirred in him had trouble written all over them.

While they waited for Tucker, Bobby brought Jenna a glass of brandy. It was early in the day, but she looked as if she might go into shock at any second. He did not want her fainting on him. If she did, he'd have to touch her, and he knew exactly how dangerous that could be.

"Drink it," he ordered.

She eyed the glass warily. "What is it?"

"Brandy."

"No, thanks. I have to drive."

"If that horse is missing, you're not going anywhere till it's found, am I right?"

She sighed and reached for the glass. She took one sip and choked on it. "I really don't think I'm the brandy type," she said. "Is there any root beer around?"

It was Bobby's turn to sigh. "I'll get it."

He was on his way back to his office when Tucker arrived, sirens blaring and lights flashing.

"Announce to the world that I'm in the middle of another scene, why don't you?" Bobby grumbled.

"You wanted me here in a hurry, didn't you?"

"Not half as much as I want the woman in there gone," Bobby told his brother.

"So send her home," Tucker said, as if it were a simple matter.

"I would, but there's the issue of the missing horse."

Tucker's lips twitched. "The carousel horse?"

"That's the one," Bobby confirmed. "Gone. Apparently stolen out of my front yard this morning."

Tucker glanced toward Bobby's office. "Think she had anything to do with it?"

"The exact same thought crossed my mind," Bobby admitted. "But no. I saw her face when I told her it was gone. Nobody's that good an actress."

"How much is that thing worth?"

"I'm guessing not much without the carousel," Bobby said. "But then the rest of the merry-go-round isn't worth a heck of a lot without the missing horse, either. Even if she found a replacement, it would be a miracle if it were a perfect match."

"It's quite a dilemma, isn't it?" Tucker said. His expression brightened. "Maybe someone will call and demand a ransom."

"Your wait-and-see attitude toward crime is beginning to get on my nerves," Bobby told him. "Don't try it with Jenna. She's in a fragile state."

His brother looked fascinated by that revelation. "Is that so? And that's a concern of yours because...?"

"Because I want that woman and that horse out of town and out of my life," he said. "I can't believe that twenty-four hours ago I had exactly the kind of peaceful existence I like."

"You were in a rut," Tucker countered. "This is good for you."

Bobby scowled and stalked right past him. He was not going to get into a debate about his low-key lifestyle choice with his brother, not when they had a crisis to resolve.

"Tucker's here," he announced as he walked into his office.

Jenna looked up at him with bright eyes shimmering with unshed tears. His heart did an unexpected flipflop. Probably some sort of fibrillation, he concluded hopefully. He did not want that sensation to be in any way connected to Jenna Pennington Kennedy or her problems or those huge, vulnerable green eyes of hers.

"Thank you for coming, Sheriff," she said politely to Tucker.

"No problem," Tucker assured her. "Why don't you tell me what you know?"

"I don't really know anything," she said, regarding him miserably. "I didn't even know the horse was gone, till Bobby told me just now. I'd paid the security company to keep a guard with it till I picked it up on my way back to Baltimore."

"What's the name of the company?" Tucker asked.

Jenna told him. "They're based in Richmond. They're very reputable. I made sure of that. My father always expects the worst of me, so I was trying very hard to do this right."

Tucker pointed toward the phone on Bobby's desk. "May I?"

"By all means," Bobby said.

His brother called information, got the number for the security company, then called and asked for the owner.

"Mr. Kendrick, this is Sheriff Spencer over in Westmoreland County. I understand you were supplying security for Pennington and Sons at a private home over here.''

Bobby watched Jenna as she listened to Tucker's end of the conversation. She looked increasingly dejected as Tucker nodded, jotted a few notes and murmured quite a few completely unintelligible replies.

''I see,'' he said at last. ''Thanks for your time. I'll be in touch.''

He hung up the phone slowly, then glanced at Jenna, his expression unreadable.

''What?'' she said. ''What did he say?''

''That the guard who was supposed to be on duty this morning just got back to Richmond and left on vacation.''

Bobby stared at his brother. ''What the hell does that mean? Was it sudden?''

''Nope. He'd scheduled it weeks ago. But it could be he stole the horse himself and is anticipating a big payday,'' Tucker suggested. ''Or somebody else has already paid him off to disappear. How much is that horse worth, anyway?''

Jenna named a staggering amount, her voice barely above a whisper. ''The carousel is very rare,'' she added.

''No kidding,'' Bobby said dryly. ''What the devil were you thinking?'' Jenna's face crumpled, and tears slid down her pale cheeks. He felt like he'd just kicked a kitten. ''I'm sorry. I didn't mean that the way it sounded.''

''Of course you did,'' she said, her expression bleak. ''Why shouldn't you say it? My father certainly will.''

''Which is precisely why I shouldn't have,'' Bobby

said. "Believe me, I've been in your shoes more times than I care to count."

"He has," Tucker confirmed. "When it comes to sensitivity, King Spencer missed the classes."

Jenna heaved a sigh. "My father didn't even know there were classes."

Ignoring his better judgment, Bobby gave her shoulder a sympathetic squeeze. "Don't worry. Tucker will track down that security guard and figure out what's going on."

"I don't have time to wait for that," Jenna said. "I have to get home. I have a daughter who wants to dye her hair purple."

Bobby held up his hands. "I don't even want to know about that one. You go on home. Keep the dye away from your daughter. Tucker will be in touch."

She shook her head. "This is my mess."

"Ms. Kennedy, I appreciate your willingness to take responsibility for your actions, but this is *not* your mess," Tucker assured her. "That horse was stolen here in Trinity Harbor. Now it's my mess."

For the first time all day, Bobby managed a grin. "It is, isn't it? Daddy's going to love hearing about a major theft taking place in broad daylight on the supposedly safe streets of Trinity Harbor." He held out his hand to Jenna. "Come on. Let's go to lunch. Maybe by the time we've had dessert, Tucker here will have figured out who the bad guy is."

Tucker frowned at him. "You're giving me an hour to solve this?"

Bobby nodded. "And then I'm going to King and put *him* in charge. You know how Daddy likes to show you up. I'm pretty sure there was a time in his life when he wanted to be Wyatt Earp.''

Jenna laughed, exactly as Bobby had intended. He gave her hand a squeeze. ''We don't have a lot of crime here. A big-time thief won't get far without some nosy person asking a lot of questions. Everything will be all right.''

It had to be, because with her hand tucked into his, he was just starting to realize that he was in very deep water.

4

Harvey Needham was a bona fide, first-class idiot. He'd been the mayor of Trinity Harbor for two terms now, and he still knew next to nothing about managing a town. Oh, he kept the garbage pickups running on schedule and managed to keep the budget in the black, but he was not exactly a visionary, which made him a major thorn in Bobby's side.

If it had been up to Harvey, there would have been condominiums slapped up on every square inch of waterfront property and the public wouldn't set foot in the Potomac River ever again.

His arrival in Bobby's office just as the chaos over the stolen carousel horse was settling down couldn't have been worse timing. He took in Tucker's presence, and a gleam of satisfaction lit his beady little eyes.

"Trouble?" he inquired in a deceptively pleasant tone.

"Already handled," Tucker assured him.

"Good to know the sheriff's office has things under control," Harvey said. "Mind telling me what it's all about?"

"Yes," Bobby said curtly, dragging Jenna toward the door in the faint hope of making an escape before the mayor went off on some tirade.

Harvey blocked his path. "I am the mayor of this town," he said with a huff.

"Something all of us are trying valiantly to deal with," Bobby retorted. Tucker shot him a warning look.

"Now, listen here, young man. If there is crime running rampant in Trinity Harbor—" Harvey blustered. He was about to continue, when Jenna turned on one of her megawatt smiles and stepped in front of him.

"Mayor Needham, I am so delighted to meet you," she said, holding out her hand. "I'm Jenna Kennedy."

Harvey might be an idiot, but he thought of himself as a ladies' man and a Southern gentleman, despite the fact that he'd been born in upstate New York. While Bobby gritted his teeth, the mayor clasped Jenna's hand in his and beamed his best politician's smile.

"I don't believe I've had the pleasure," he said. "Harvey Needham, Ms. Kennedy. Welcome to the town of Trinity Harbor. What brings you here?" It appeared all thoughts of crime had been temporarily forgotten.

"Just getting acquainted with the area," she said with a quick, reassuring glance at Bobby.

Relief flooded through him at her immediate grasp of the situation.

"Perhaps you'd like to have a cup of coffee and tell me all about Trinity Harbor," she suggested, linking her arm through the mayor's. Her Southern drawl, not the least bit pronounced up until now, was suddenly thicker than honey.

Turning her back on the mayor, she winked at

Bobby. "I know you're closed today but can we make that happen?"

"Absolutely," Bobby said at once, leading the two of them to a table in the empty yacht center restaurant and getting them their coffee from the pot he'd brewed earlier. "Just don't let Mr. Needham keep you too long, Jenna. You and I have lunch plans, remember?"

"Of course. The mayor and I won't be long, though I'm sure he has loads and loads of insights to share."

"I do, indeed, Ms. Kennedy," Harvey said with a triumphant look at Bobby.

Shaking his head at the incongruous pair, Bobby walked off and left them alone. He joined Tucker back in his office.

"That was the most amazing display of phony charm I've ever seen," he noted to his brother.

"His or hers?" Tucker asked.

"Both. That female is dangerous," he said, just to remind himself of that fact. For a minute there he'd allowed himself to be impressed by her skillful maneuvering.

Tucker grinned. "Spoken like a man whose hormones have just come out of retirement."

"Go to hell."

"Based on the events of the past two days, seems to me like I might be there already," Tucker said. "What do *you* make of this stolen horse business?"

"*Me?*" Bobby protested. "It's your job to figure it out."

"That business with the guard taking his vacation reeks of a payoff," Tucker said, his expression thoughtful. "Are you sure Jenna couldn't have arranged the theft to garner a little extra publicity? Maybe turned on the waterworks to get your sympathy? Could be the whole thing is a clever business tactic."

"Not a chance," Bobby said with conviction. "She was too upset about it. Besides that, I don't think she has much of a track record at sneaky business tactics. Now if you were to suggest that Harvey had something to do with it, *that* I could believe. You talked to him yesterday. You know how badly he wanted that horse gone. You would have thought it had been sent by the Trojans to wreak havoc on the town."

Tucker bit back a grin. "Yeah, well, Harvey's an idiot, which pretty much rules out his ability to mastermind a theft in plain sight."

"Check his garage, just the same," Bobby suggested. "And, Tucker..."

"What?"

"Do it fast. I'm serious—I want that woman out of town."

A knowing expression spread across his brother's face. "Oh, really? You mean before Daddy gets an eyeful and decides she's a perfect candidate for his latest plot to marry you off?"

Bobby winced at Tucker's quick grasp of one aspect of the problem. "Yes, there is that."

In fact, in his gut he knew that the very last thing he wanted was for King and Jenna ever to cross paths. He could say goodbye to his placid existence if that should happen. Ever since Daisy and Walker's wedding, King had been keeping a close eye on Bobby's social life, asking too many questions, dropping too many less-than-subtle hints about every single female in a twenty-mile radius of Trinity Harbor. Bobby might as well have a target on his back that said, "To marry this man, call 555-6000."

Bobby whirled around and headed for the locked file cabinet in his outer office.

"Where are you going?" Tucker called after him.

"To write her a check. She can name the figure and pay me back whenever she gets the horse back, or collects from the security company. I want her gone *now*."

Tucker's annoying hoot of laughter followed him. "Don't laugh too hard," he warned his brother. "I can always remind Daddy that you're his oldest son. You're the one whose social life he really ought to be worrying about."

Tucker headed straight for the door. "I'll get right on this."

Bobby gave a little nod of satisfaction. "I thought that might motivate you."

Jenna's meeting with Harvey Needham promised to be very enlightening. She had long since picked up on the fact that he and Bobby were sworn enemies, at least when it came to developing the waterfront. That made the mayor *her* enemy, too, but *he* didn't have to know that just yet. So far, he hadn't tried to pin her down about her exact reason for being in Trinity Harbor, and the longer she could keep it that way, the better off she was. He clearly hadn't connected her to the commotion on Bobby's lawn the day before. As long as she kept the attention focused on him, she could keep her own identity and stake in the town's future cloaked in mystery.

She stared across the table and studied him. He was wearing a bright green polo shirt that did little for his washed out complexion. His hairline was slipping, but his round face was virtually unlined, making it difficult to guess his age. He seemed fit enough, though, suggesting he was the kind of man who maintained a rigid control over his diet. She recognized the type. She had one at home just like him. Her father drank to excess when it suited him, but not a single indulgence crossed his lips when it came to food.

"What made you decide to run for mayor?" she asked Harvey.

His chest puffed up as he replied, "Young lady, it is the civic duty of every citizen to give something back to the community in which they live." It sounded like the start of a campaign speech. "When I retired, I finally had the time to serve this town and bring some of my business skills to the operation of the town's services."

"That's a very noble goal," Jenna told him. "Where do you see Trinity Harbor ten years from now? What kind of a community will it be?"

"Quiet," he said at once. "With a sound economic base. The way you accomplish that is to bring in folks with money, good middle-class residents looking for a place to retire. Folks like that want their lives to run smoothly. They want clean shops, good services and low taxes."

"What about entertainment?"

"They've got Fredericksburg and Richmond just up

the road for that," he said dismissively. "The town doesn't need to provide it."

Jenna couldn't believe such a shortsighted view, but she knew she was treading on thin ice. She had to be careful how far she pushed him, or he'd want to know why she cared.

"Don't you think that people with time on their hands want leisure activities nearby?" she inquired cautiously. "A golf course, maybe. Tennis courts. A community center. Things for their grandchildren to do when they visit."

Before he could reply, she added, "What do your grandchildren do when they come, Mr. Needham?"

He blinked at that, looking vaguely disconcerted. "Actually, they haven't come here in some time. Our children prefer that we visit them."

"Why is that?" Jenna asked innocently. She was pretty sure she knew. His children didn't come because they didn't want to listen to a nonstop refrain from his grandchildren about there being nothing to do here. It would be interesting to hear his take on it, though.

"They have their lives. It's less of a disruption if we go to them," he said. "My wife grumbles a bit about how rarely we see them, but I can see the sense of doing it this way."

She decided to press the point. "But Trinity Harbor is such a lovely town. I would think they would absolutely jump at the chance to get away for a while. After all, that is what drew *you* here, isn't it?"

The mayor frowned. "What's your point, Ms. Kennedy?"

"It just occurs to me that if you want to attract the

kind of residents you're hoping to, just putting up places for them to live won't entirely address the situation.''

His gaze narrowed. "Spencer put you up to saying that, didn't he?" he asked suspiciously. "Sounds just like that hogwash he's always spouting around town."

"Bobby and I haven't discussed that precise issue," she said honestly. "Is that what he thinks?"

"You're trying to tell me the two of you aren't in cahoots?" he demanded. "I saw you in his office just now. Why else would you be there?"

"The same reason I'm with you right now," Jenna insisted. "Just getting to know all I can about Trinity Harbor."

"And why would you want to be doing that?" he asked, studying her with a narrowed gaze. "You're a little young to be thinking about moving to an out-of-the-way place like this. There's no nightlife here, Ms. Kennedy."

"Nightlife's not a big priority with me. And more and more people my age are making lifestyle choices, right along with career choices."

He still didn't look as if he believed her. "Where are you from, Ms. Kennedy?"

"Born and raised in Baltimore," she said readily.

"But you want to leave?"

"I'm exploring my options," she told him with complete sincerity. Though she hadn't considered it before, she realized that a part of her had always wanted to live in a place just like Trinity Harbor. She'd always dismissed it as a romantic fantasy, but there was no real reason it had to be, especially if she could nab this job here.

"Well, Trinity Harbor would be glad to have you, I'm sure," Harvey said, though he looked a little doubtful.

Jenna beamed at him. "You'll be the first to know if things work out," she told him. Whether she agreed with his vision for the town or not, she'd have to work with him if she got the contract for the boardwalk development. There was little point in alienating him at this stage.

"I'd better run along," she told him. "Bobby promised me lunch and a tour of the town before I head back home this afternoon."

"You watch yourself with him, young lady. The Spencers are held in high regard around here, but they're a sneaky lot. Never know when one of 'em will stab you in the back."

"I'll keep that in mind," Jenna assured him as she went off in search of Bobby.

She found him in his office, his feet propped up on his desk and a smug expression on his face.

"Enjoy your meeting with the mayor?" he inquired.

"It was illuminating," she told him. "He thinks you're sneaky."

Bobby didn't seem the slightest bit surprised or dismayed by that assessment. "That doesn't hold a candle to what I think of him," he said as he stood up. "You ready for lunch?"

"Can't wait," she told him.

He drove into town and parked down the block from a beachfront diner. "It's not fancy, but Earlene's is the heart and soul of Trinity Harbor. You want to know what's going on around town, this is the place to come. I'd advise you to stay away from the coffee, though. The acid will burn a hole in your stomach.''

Jenna grinned. "What would you recommend?"

"The iced tea and a burger are pretty safe bets."

"I'm surprised you eat here at all. Don't you like the food at the marina?"

He chuckled at that. "I like it just fine. Matter of fact, I cook most of it, but as you noticed, we're closed on Mondays."

"You're a cook? I thought you owned it."

"I do, and I'm a chef," he corrected testily. "But let's not quibble." He led the way to a booth by a window that looked out on the river, then regarded Jenna seriously. "Any plan for the waterfront has to include Earlene's."

"Of course," Jenna agreed at once. Though the interior was a little shabby, the place had an undeniable charm that could only be acquired over time. The wooden floors had been worn smooth by sandy feet. The tunes on the jukebox were oldies. The soda fountain looked as if it came straight out of the set for the old TV sitcom *Happy Days*.

When her iced tea came in an old-fashioned, curving soda glass and her plain white pottery plate came loaded with crispy fries and a burger topped with a bright red tomato slice that looked as if it had just been picked in the garden, Jenna sighed with pure contentment.

Around them there was the steady hum of lively conversation and the occasional burst of laughter. She hadn't missed the speculative looks when she had arrived with Bobby, but the attention had quickly drifted away.

This was the kind of place she looked for in Baltimore and never found. She was sure they existed, but probably in parts of town her father would be appalled if she visited. In her neighborhood there were chic cafés and trendy restaurants, where lingering wasn't condoned, much less encouraged.

"I could really start to like it here," she said, around a juicy bite of hamburger.

"Don't," Bobby said tersely. "There is nothing for you in Trinity Harbor."

She bristled defiantly at his tone and the warning. "Have you made up your mind, then? Are you turning down my proposal?"

He hesitated.

"Well?" she prodded. "Can you look me in the eye and tell me it's not exactly what you would have described, if I'd asked you how you saw the waterfront developing?"

"No," he conceded with obvious reluctance. "But that doesn't change anything. The two of us working together is a bad idea."

"Why?"

"It just is."

"Just what I like," she said scathingly. "A businessman who has solid, rational reasons for his decisions."

"It's my decision to make," he reminded her with exaggerated patience.

"Then don't let it be a bad one," she pleaded. "It's too important. At least say you'll think it over."

"I don't know," he said, his expression troubled.

"Come on. What do you have to lose?"

"My sanity," he muttered.

She chuckled at the plaintive note in his voice. "I swear, I will do my very best not to drive you crazy."

"Too late." He reached in his pocket and pulled out a rectangle of paper and slid it across the table.

Jenna looked at it but didn't reach for it. "What's that?"

"A check."

Hope stirred inside her. Was this the down payment on the deal? They hadn't talked money, but maybe he'd decided on a nominal retainer. She swallowed hard and met his gaze. "For?"

"The horse," he said quietly. "It's the amount you mentioned. It should cover the loss."

Her stomach fell. "You're paying me off to go away?"

He nodded. "That's the idea."

Jenna shoved the check back across the table, spilling her tea in the process. She paid no attention as it ran straight toward her lap. "Forget it," she said fiercely.

She wasn't about to let Bobby Spencer buy her off with a check to cover the cost of the carousel horse. She wanted a contract for the waterfront development *and* her blasted horse. Nothing less would do.

And if she had to pack up Darcy and take up residence right here in Trinity Harbor until she got what she wanted, well, that was what she'd do.

"I'm not going anywhere, Bobby. Get used to it."

He seemed completely nonplussed by her vehemence. "But your daughter—"

"Is out of school for the summer," she retorted. "I can have her down here with me by tomorrow."

"Your job—"

She made a quick decision and met his gaze evenly. "*This* is my job. Getting this contract is my chance to make something happen in my career. I'm not walking away from it without a fight."

The fact that her announcement made Bobby look as if he'd been punched right in the gut was just so much icing on the cake.

"Where's Jenna?" Maggie asked, when Bobby returned to his office after lunch.

"Gone, I hope."

Maggie seemed surprised and a little disappointed. "For good? I thought she was made of tougher stuff than that."

"I should be so lucky," Bobby said with a resigned sigh. "No, I imagine she'll be back."

His secretary grinned. "Good. I liked her."

"That doesn't surprise me. You're cut from the same cloth." He regarded her pointedly and added, "Neither one of you knows when to let well enough alone."

"Okay, I get it," Maggie said agreeably. "By the way, Richard called from the paper. He's on his way over. He heard about the theft."

"Why didn't you tell him to talk to Tucker?"

"How do you think he heard about it?" Maggie retorted.

"Well, hell," Bobby muttered. What good was it being the sheriff's brother, if the man was going to blab your business all over town?

"Think of it this way," Maggie advised. "It could be worse. It could be your father on his way over."

"You have a point," Bobby agreed, but his momentary cheer faded quickly.

Why had King been so silent? Usually he liked to make his opinions known. His silence did not bode well. Either he was sick or he was up to something. Since King was healthy as a horse, it was more likely the latter. Bobby started to reach for the phone, then stopped himself.

"Be grateful," he muttered.

Maggie eyed him curiously. "What?"

"Nothing. When Richard comes, send him over to the kitchen. I'm going to experiment with a new crab recipe." Maybe he could find a spice that would cover the taste of arsenic. The list of people he'd like to serve it to was getting longer and longer.

5

Hiding out in Trinity Harbor for a few weeks began to seem more and more sensible as Jenna drove back to Baltimore. Not only would it give her time to land the development contract, but it would lessen the odds that her father would find out about that missing horse and the money she'd squandered on the carousel. Hopefully she'd recover the stolen horse in the meantime, as well.

And a nice long vacation with Darcy could only be a good thing, too. They needed to spend some quality time together. Maybe Jenna could actually manage to reestablish the fact that she was the mother and Darcy was the kid. Her daughter seemed to be a little mixed up on that point.

The more Jenna considered her plan, the more she warmed to it. By the time she turned into the tree-lined drive at her father's house, she was convinced it was the second-smartest idea she'd ever had. The brightest was going after that development contract in the first place. It was exactly the kind of dramatic gesture that could change the rest of her life. If she made a success of this, her father would have to acknowledge her. He would have to give her more to do than answering phones and typing letters.

After just two days in Trinity Harbor, walking into her father's house reminded her of just how pretentious her lifestyle had been up to now. There was too much of everything. Too many ornate antiques cluttered the rooms. Heavy draperies shrouded the windows. Vases filled with fresh flowers filled all the rooms with an overpowering sweet scent. Her father—or more precisely, his decorators—had access to more money than taste.

Jenna shuddered at the oppressive atmosphere and headed for the one room that was bright and airy, the kitchen that her mother had designed and her father rarely entered.

The housekeeper looked up from the salad she was fixing and smiled. "Welcome home," Mrs. Jamison said. "Did you have a good trip?"

How to describe it? Jenna thought. "It was interesting," she said finally. "And I loved the little town. In fact, I'm going to schedule a vacation for the next few weeks and take Darcy down there until school starts. How is she, by the way? Did she give you any trouble?"

"None at all," Mrs. Jamison insisted, though her tone and the twinkle in her eyes suggested otherwise. Mrs. Jamison doted on Darcy, which meant the girl got away with quite a lot when Jenna or Darcy's grandfather weren't around to forbid it.

"Okay, tell the truth," Jenna said with a sense of foreboding. "What did she do?"

"You'll see soon enough," Mrs. Jamison said mysteriously, that hint of amusement still threading through her voice.

"Please tell me she did not dye her hair purple," Jenna pleaded.

"No, you made yourself quite clear about that," the housekeeper assured her. "But perhaps you should have been a little more inclusive."

A dull throb began behind Jenna's eyes. "Meaning?"

Mrs. Jamison gestured toward the doorway. Jenna turned slowly and found Darcy peeping around the corner. Her hair was shamrock green and had been cut by blunt-edged scissors and gelled so that it poked up in all directions.

"You said I couldn't dye it *purple*," Darcy said, her chin tilted defiantly.

"So I did," Jenna agreed, wondering if this was the payback she was due for her own childhood rebellions. Of course, until Nick, hers had been minor in comparison to this. Keeping her tone level, she beckoned to her daughter. "Come in and let me see."

Despite her defiance, the nine-year-old looked as if she might be harboring some very deep regrets about her impulsive behavior. "I think it looks great!" Darcy said, as if daring her mother to deny it.

"Well, there's certainly no question that you'll stand out in a crowd. Was that what you were hoping?" she inquired, knowing perfectly well that Darcy much preferred to blend in. Usually these little displays were designed solely to drive her mother up the wall. Darcy knew her mother would insist they be corrected by the time she went out in public.

"Yes," Darcy said stubbornly.

"Good." Jenna made a quick decision, one she

hoped might impart a stronger lesson than the usual punishment she doled out, apparently rather ineffectively since the misbehavior kept recurring. "Run on upstairs and pack your clothes."

Darcy's eyes widened. Her lower lip quivered. "You're sending me away?"

"No, I'm *taking* you away," Jenna corrected, her expression as cheerful as if nothing at all were amiss. "We're going on vacation first thing tomorrow."

Her daughter blinked at that. "You're letting me go like this?"

"It is the unique look you wanted, isn't it?" Jenna asked innocently.

"But…"

"But what?"

"You usually take me straight over to Rene's and make her fix it."

Jenna smiled. "Not this time. Besides, you've already cut your hair pretty short. I'm not sure what a hairdresser could do to correct it."

A horrified expression crossed Darcy's face. "You're making me keep it like this?"

"Yep," Jenna said as Mrs. Jamison turned away to hide a smile.

Tears pooled in Darcy's eyes and spilled down her cheeks. "I hate you," she shouted, and ran from the kitchen.

Jenna sighed.

"You're doing the right thing," Mrs. Jamison reassured her. "It's a good lesson in living with the consequences of her actions."

"I know, but you haven't been to Trinity Harbor,"

Jenna said, voicing her one regret about the plan. "Darcy is going to stand out like a sore thumb."

"Then she won't be so quick to do something impulsive like this again," the housekeeper said.

Jenna looked at the woman who'd raised her brothers and done her best to be a mother to Jenna on her rare visits home. "Why does she do things like this? She's only nine. What on earth will she be doing when she hits her teens?"

"Maybe she'll have it all out of her system by then," Mrs. Jamison suggested soothingly.

"Or maybe she'll be in a juvenile detention facility," Jenna said wearily.

"You weren't, were you?"

"I never did anything like this," Jenna insisted.

"Didn't you? Maybe you never touched your hair, but then it was your pride and joy because it was red like your mama's. I do seem to recall that you came close to giving your daddy a heart attack when you came home from school sporting a snake tattoo one year, and that was some years before tattoos were all the rage among respectable people."

"It was temporary," Jenna reminded her.

"Your father didn't know that." The housekeeper grinned and patted Jenna's hand. "Darcy's hair is temporary, too. It will grow and the color will wash out eventually."

"I was really hoping she'd have a good time in Trinity Harbor. How can she if everyone keeps their kids away from her because she looks like a pint-sized member of a grunge band?"

"Is this really about Darcy being accepted, or about you?" Mrs. Jamison asked with her usual insight.

Jenna heaved a resigned sigh. The wise woman had nailed it on the head again. "A little of both," she admitted.

After all, what kind of an impression would Darcy make on uptight Bobby Spencer? He was likely to take one look at Jenna's child and conclude that a woman who had no better control over her daughter couldn't possibly be entrusted with a million-dollar development plan.

"What kind of people make judgments based on appearances?" Mrs. Jamison asked.

Jenna considered the validity of this point and nodded. Bobby hadn't exactly held her disheveled appearance against *her* on the morning of their meeting, had he? Maybe he'd be generous where Darcy was concerned as well.

"You're absolutely right, Mrs. Jamison." Why would she even want to work for someone who held a little girl's appearance against her? "Where's my father, by the way?"

"Out for the evening. He said he'd catch up with you at breakfast."

Jenna didn't bother trying to hide her relief. "Has he gotten a glimpse of Darcy?"

"Not yet. Even she was smart enough to stay in her room when he came back to change for dinner."

"Good. Maybe I can get both of us out of town before he wakes up in the morning."

Mrs. Jamison didn't even pretend to hide her dismay. "You're leaving without talking it over with him? Do you think that's wise, Jenna?"

"I think this might be one of those times when a note is smarter than a direct confrontation," Jenna assured her.

Besides, if she could sneak away, there would be less of a chance that he'd pry her secret mission out of her. She wanted a signed contract in her hand the next time she saw her father. It might mute his disapproval of her underhanded tactics in leaving him out of the loop on this project. She didn't exactly have the authority to commit Pennington and Sons's resources to this deal.

As for abandoning him at the office with no notice, to her very deep regret, she acknowledged that he probably wouldn't even notice.

Bobby looked across his desk into the fascinated gaze of Anna-Louise Walton and winced. "You don't approve of me trying to buy Jenna off, do you?"

"That depends on why you decided to try it," the pastor said, amusement dancing in her eyes. "Care to explain your thinking?"

"No good could come of having her here," Bobby said flatly. "None."

"Because she's a woman?" Anna-Louise asked mildly.

"Watch it," her husband warned Bobby. "Think about your response very, very carefully. You're about to get a sermon on being a sexist pig unless you answer this exactly right."

"Yeah, I can see the trap," Bobby conceded.

Anna-Louise frowned at both of them, then addressed Bobby. "Do you doubt Jenna's qualifications?"

Bobby shook his head. "Her firm has solid credentials, though I got the impression this is her first big presentation. She all but admitted she had something to prove."

"Okay, then," Anna-Louise said approvingly. "And what about the plan itself? Didn't you like it?"

"She didn't have preliminary sketches or anything, but in terms of concept, it was actually right on target," Bobby admitted, knowing that he was digging a very deep hole for himself.

"So you tried to get rid of her just because she's a woman and therefore what? Not in need of a job? Not smart enough?" Anna-Louise pressed.

"Of course not," Bobby denied heatedly. That sort of blatant discrimination was wrong. Even he could see that, though at the moment it was darned inconvenient. Besides, Jenna had made it plain that she was ambitious and smart, both admirable traits in his book.

Anna-Louise grinned. "Then it must be because you were attracted to her and that scared the living daylights out of you. You did swear off relationships after Ann-Marie ran off with Lonnie four weeks before your wedding, right?"

The mention of Ann-Marie and Lonnie still had the capacity to stir up a cold rage in Bobby. Anna-Louise wouldn't have touched that topic if she had a grain of sense in her head, but then she hadn't been here at the time. She hadn't witnessed his humiliation firsthand. She only knew that the prospect of bumping into the two traitors had kept Bobby away from church ever since, and no amount of pressure or cajoling had been able to woo him back.

"I know your heart's in the right place, Anna-Louise, but I do not want to discuss those two with you," he said tightly. "Not ever."

"Or with anyone else, it seems." The minister regarded him with compassion. "Maybe it's time you discussed your feelings about what happened with someone. Until you forgive them and let go of the past, you'll never be able to move on with your life."

"Not going to happen," Bobby insisted. He'd fry in hell first.

"The only person you're hurting is yourself," she said softly.

Bobby sighed. That was probably true enough. He certainly hadn't seen much evidence that Ann-Marie and Lonnie were suffering any pangs of guilt over what they'd done. The only place in town they avoided was the yacht center. Other than that, they paraded around town hand in hand, flaunting the fact that they were madly in love and seemingly oblivious to the fact that they'd betrayed Bobby to be together.

Their children were less circumspect. They turned up on the docks with their friends and invaded the kitchen for snacks whenever they could get away with it. No matter how many times Bobby told Tommy that his restaurant kitchen was off-limits to him and his friends, Daisy's adopted son continued to treat it as if it contained his own personal stash of treats. Ann-Marie's boy, J.C., was usually among the interlopers.

Even so, the yacht center and restaurant were still

about the only places left where Bobby felt reasonably safe from unexpected encounters with the two people responsible for breaking his heart. Not that he intended to admit any of that to Anna-Louise. He just sat there stonily, enduring her expectant stare.

Richard finally took pity on him and spoke to his wife. "Hon, maybe you shouldn't push this. Besides, I'm not sure we're entitled to know why Bobby doesn't want to work with Jenna. It's his project and his money."

"I thought he might feel better if he made a confession about his real reasons for trying to avoid working with her," Anna-Louise said unrepentantly.

"Wrong church," Richard pointed out. "He needs a priest for that."

"I can listen," Anna-Louise protested. "And offer comfort and forgiveness. The mechanics might be different, but the principle's the same no matter which church I belong to."

Bobby chuckled despite himself. "Sorry, Anna-Louise. I'm not in need of either one. I'm perfectly comfortable with my decision. The only thing I regret is that it didn't work. The woman's stubborn as a mule." Spencers knew all about stubbornness, it didn't take much for them to recognize it in others. And Jenna had it in spades.

The pastor's eyes brightened. "Then she *is* coming back? Good! I can hardly wait to meet her. Daisy and I will host a little get-together so she can get acquainted with a few people."

Richard groaned. "You just want a chance to cross-examine her and see how she measures up as a candidate for Bobby's love life.''

"I most certainly do not," Anna-Louise said indignantly. "I'm perfectly content to leave the matchmaking to King. Although the way I hear it, Jenna does look an awful lot like Ann-Marie. Is that so, Bobby?"

The observation seemed to suck the breath right out of him. He hadn't considered it consciously before, but it was true. Jenna did bear a remarkable resemblance to the woman who had broken his heart and humiliated him in the process. Maybe that was why he'd reacted so violently the first time he'd seen her. Maybe it had nothing to do with the commotion on his lawn at all.

"I refuse to answer," he said blandly.

"Which must mean she does," Anna-Louise said complacently. "King is going to be in hog heaven when he hears that little tidbit."

"Not an especially reassuring thought," Bobby noted. He glanced hopefully at Richard. "Can you stop this?"

"Not a chance. My wife is an independent woman. So is your sister. You don't have a prayer, my friend."

Bobby scowled at Anna-Louise. "I could pray about this, couldn't I? And a benevolent God would take pity on me, right?"

She grinned. "Maybe. Maybe not. It all depends on what He has in mind for you. He might have sent Jenna down here in the first place just to shake you out of the doldrums."

"If He did, it was a mean trick," Bobby retorted.

"No, in that case, it was a divine plan," she countered. "Pay attention to it."

Bobby shot a commiserating look at Richard. "And you live with this kind of reasoning all the time? I feel for you."

Richard chuckled and put an arm around his wife's waist as he steered her toward the door. "It has its compensations," he said. "And since we're already married, she doesn't have to meddle in my love life."

Bobby laughed as he watched them leave, but as soon as they were out of sight, his expression sobered. For all of his tart comments, he envied what they had. He truly did.

He just wasn't sure he was ready to take the risks involved in trying to find something like it for himself. And even if he were, Jenna Kennedy would be the last person on earth he'd choose. He liked serenity, and the way he felt around her was anything but serene.

As he always did when he was stressed, Bobby retreated to the kitchen at the yacht center. The dinner rush was only an hour away, and he'd been in the middle of preparations when Richard had come by, ostensibly to get information about the stolen carousel horse. Since he'd come with Anna-Louise in tow, Bobby was a little suspicious of his real motives. Precious little of their time together had been spent talking about the theft. Once the conversation had veered off-course to the topic of Jenna, it had never gotten back on track again.

As he walked into the kitchen, he found the air thick with the spicy scent of steamed shrimp and crabs. The pungent aroma of garlic for the night's scampi special added to his sense of well-being. Based on the aromas alone, he was reassured that the food tonight would be incredible.

This was his milieu. There was nothing he liked better than experimenting with ingredients, adding a dash of this herb or a sprinkling of that one to bring out the flavor of a dish in a whole new way.

For a man who liked his life to be peaceful and calm, the commotion of a restaurant kitchen just before the crowds descended should have been disconcerting, but it suited him. He liked the bustle, the camaraderie, even the temperamental outbursts of his pastry chef, who was a perfectionist and tolerated nothing less from anyone coming into contact with the pies and cakes and light-as-air confections he created. The concept of great meals being orchestrated out of confusion was satisfying to him.

Bobby moved from counter to gleaming counter, from oven to oven, to check on the progress of the night's specials. Everything looked as delicious as it smelled. He clapped his hands and caught everyone's attention.

"We're booked to capacity tonight," he announced. "Let's everybody stay calm and focused and make this a memorable evening all the way around."

Suddenly the eyes that had been trained on him shifted their focus at the sound of a door opening.

"So, this is where you spend your time when you're not trying to bribe people into leaving town," a honey-eyed voice said.

He'd discovered all too recently that only one person had a voice like that, only one had the capacity to make his blood pound, only one had the temerity to invade his space—Jenna. How could she possibly be back already? Bobby had been counting on having at least a few days to mentally prepare for her return. Her overnight return caught him totally off-guard.

As his entire staff feigned a sudden interest in the food preparation that was already under control, he turned slowly. "Back already, Jenna?"

"What can I say? I felt so welcome here, I rushed right back. Can we talk?"

"Not now," he said emphatically. He tucked a hand under her elbow and escorted her back to the dining room. "No one besides staff is allowed back here."

She peered around his shoulder for one last glimpse of the kitchen. "Don't want the customers to see what you're doing to their food? Are you using some preservative that will eventually kill them all?"

He scowled at her. "That isn't even mildly amusing. No one is allowed back here, first, because I say so, and, second, because it's dangerous. They get in the way. They can get burned. Fair warning, Ms. Kennedy."

"Duly noted," she said, not looking the least bit chastened. "When can we talk?"

"Where are you staying? I'll call you tomorrow."

"I meant tonight," she said.

"I'm sure you did. Tomorrow will have to do."

Her gaze met his. "Is everything between us going to be a battle?"

"Pretty much," he said unrepentantly. "It's your choice to be here. I can't ban you from the town, but I don't have to deal with you on your terms."

"But you *do* have to deal with me," she said just

as emphatically. "I'm not going away until you do. What time do you close?"

"On a weeknight, the last of the customers are gone by ten, except at the bar. I'm finished cleaning up in the kitchen about an hour later."

"I'll be here," she said, her gaze unflinching.

Bobby had to admire her grit. Most people would have wilted and accepted his terms. Most would have seen the sense in giving him a tiny, albeit meaningless, victory. Jenna apparently didn't intend to give an inch.

"Whatever," he said, resigned. He headed for the kitchen.

"And don't try sneaking out the back door," she called after him.

Bobby flushed guiltily at that. It was exactly what he had been contemplating. He turned back slowly and, as if the thought had never crossed his mind, said, "I wouldn't dream of it."

She laughed. "Then you aren't half as sneaky as you've wanted me to believe. I'll see you around eleven."

"I wish I could say I'll be looking forward to it," Bobby retorted, then pushed open the kitchen door and retreated.

Safely inside, he leaned for a moment against the counter, drew in a deep breath and prayed for patience.

While he was at it, he added a little prayer for help in resisting temptation, because for the last ten minutes—ever since Jenna Kennedy had appeared in his kitchen—all he'd been able to think about was kissing the annoying woman senseless.

6

Jenna felt triumphant as she went back to the table where Darcy was waiting, her expression sullen.

"There's nothing on this menu I like," Darcy complained as Jenna sat down.

"You love crabcakes," Jenna said, refusing to be goaded into an argument. "And hamburgers and French fries."

"Not anymore," Darcy insisted in the lofty tone of someone twice her age.

"Then sit there while *I* eat."

Darcy stared at Jenna with a shocked expression. "You're going to let me starve?"

"You won't starve if you miss one meal," Jenna said, holding firm for once. "Besides, it's your decision not to eat, not mine."

Her daughter seemed taken aback. "Mommy, what's happened to you? You never used to be like this."

"I developed a backbone," Jenna said, realizing that it was true. For too long she had catered to Darcy's every whim—to say nothing of Randall Pennington's—out of guilt over divorcing Nick. She had paid and paid and paid. Well, no more. It hadn't done any good that she could see, anyway.

Astonishingly, the shift in her thinking had happened after she'd had her first encounter with the impossible Bobby Spencer. He had solidified every ounce of resolve she'd ever possessed. Someday, when he stopped annoying her, she would thank him for that.

"I don't like it," Darcy said, pouting.

Jenna grinned at her. "No, I imagine you don't, but get used to it, because this is the way it's going to be from now on. We're turning over a new leaf while we're in Trinity Harbor."

"What does that mean?" Darcy asked suspiciously.

"It means you don't run the show, I do," Jenna told her. "It'll be a new experience for both of us."

Just then a waitress approached and asked to take their orders. Jenna looked at Darcy. "Are you just having water, or have you reconsidered?"

"I'll have a hamburger," Darcy said meekly. "And French fries."

Jenna hid a smile, then ordered the shrimp scampi for herself along with a salad of arugula, endive, blue cheese and walnuts. "I'll have water to drink for now and coffee after dinner." She glanced at Darcy. "What would you like to drink?"

"A soda," Darcy said at once, regarding Jenna with a defiant look.

Since she'd won the earlier battle over the food, Jenna gave in on the soda. Normally, she restricted her daughter's intake of sodas to one a day, and Darcy was already well over that limit; she'd begged to stop for a drink three times en route to Trinity Harbor.

"Since this is the first night of our vacation, you

can have it," Jenna agreed. "But don't press your luck tomorrow."

As soon as the waitress had brought the drinks, Jenna spotted a woman heading straight toward them, a man and boy in tow. Belatedly she realized the man was the same sheriff's deputy she'd met on Sunday at Bobby Spencer's. He nodded at Jenna.

"Ms. Kennedy, I don't know if you remember me," he said.

"Of course, I do. It's Walker Ames, isn't it?"

"Good memory."

"It was a memorable occasion," she said dryly.

His grin transformed his somber face. "That it was. The impatient woman beside me is my wife, Daisy. And this is our son, Tommy."

As Jenna was about to acknowledge the introduction, Walker held up a silencing hand. "And just so you know, Daisy is a Spencer. She's Bobby's sister."

Daisy frowned at her husband. "You didn't have to say that like she needs to be warned."

"Oh, yes, I did," Walker said with a sympathetic look at Jenna. "Prepare yourself. Daisy has questions."

"A million of them," Daisy agreed. "Will you be in town long?"

"For as long as it takes," Jenna told her.

"Have you considered buying a house and thinking ahead toward retirement?" Daisy said wryly. "My brother can be difficult."

"So I've gathered," Jenna said, her tone just as dry.

Tommy was eyeing Darcy with evident fascination. "Cool haircut," he said admiringly.

"Don't even think about it," Walker said emphatically.

Daisy rolled her eyes. "Long story, but Tommy is actually Walker's nephew. Walker is still adapting to his new role as Tommy's father. He hasn't quite grasped the concept that forbidding something only makes it more alluring."

Jenna laughed and gestured at Darcy. "Sweetheart, tell Deputy Ames what I told you right before you dyed your hair green."

"She told me I couldn't dye it purple," Darcy said, then added with a proud lift of her chin, "and I didn't."

Daisy bit back a smile. "Ah, the loophole defense. I'm a teacher. I hear that one quite often." She tucked an arm around Tommy's shoulders, then added pointedly, "It doesn't work with me."

Tommy shrugged. "I've figured that out." His gaze went back to Darcy. "You want to come by and see my boat sometime? Walker and me have been working on it for a really long time. It's almost ready to go in the water."

Darcy nodded at once, her sullen expression vanishing at the prospect of finding a friend and having an adventure. "Sure. Mom, would it be okay?"

"Please," Daisy said at once. "Jenna, you and I could chat."

Walker groaned. "Agree at your own peril," he warned Jenna. "My wife is not known for the subtlety of her grilling."

Jenna was undaunted by that. "Neither am I," she said at once.

Daisy laughed. "You and I are going to get along very well," she said. "What about tomorrow at noon? We can have lunch."

"I'd love it," Jenna said, already envisioning the million and one tips she could get on handling Daisy's brother. "We'll be there."

"I don't suppose there's any chance at all that Bobby's name won't come up," Walker said in one last display of masculine loyalty.

"None," Jenna and Daisy agreed in chorus.

"Then I'd better go in the kitchen and warn him he might want to consider abandoning any thought of developing the riverfront and concentrate on leaving town," Walker said, heading off in that direction.

Tommy looked up at Daisy. "Why would Uncle Bobby want to leave town?"

"That's just Walker's way of being a smart aleck," Daisy told him. "It is not an attractive quality. Don't even think about emulating him."

Tommy stared at her with a puzzled look. "I don't even know what that means."

Daisy winked at Jenna. "I'll explain it to you back at our table. Nice meeting you, Jenna. You, too, Darcy. I'll look forward to tomorrow."

"Me, too," Jenna responded. Especially if, as Walker had implied, her visiting Daisy was going to drive Bobby Spencer up a wall.

"They're out there, right now, together?" Bobby repeated, staring at Walker with dismay. "Jenna Kennedy and Daisy?"

"Oh, yeah. And they're making plans, big ones

from the sound of it," his brother-in-law warned him. "Some sort of get-together tomorrow for lunch. Just so you know, it was actually Tommy's idea. I don't think he realized what he was setting in motion."

"I'm surprised Daisy let you loose to warn me."

"Oh, I think that's part of her strategy. She wants you nervous."

"Why?"

"Because it will be proof that she's right about Jenna being the woman who can shake you out of your complacency," Walker said. "I'm only beginning to grasp just how devious your sister's mind truly is. If I'd known a few months ago, I might not have been so quick to jump into marriage."

Bobby laughed at that. "As if you had any choice in the matter! You were a goner from the minute you hit town to meet Tommy and try to take him away from her. She had no intention of letting that boy leave with you, even if it meant luring you into falling in love with her."

Walker shrugged. "Let that be a lesson to you. The circumstances might be different, but Daisy sees the same fate befalling you."

"Not a snowball's chance in hell," Bobby insisted, though his denials—which should have been improving with practice—were beginning to lose a little steam instead. Even he could hear the change. He didn't need Walker's prompt grin to point it out.

"Well, consider yourself duly warned," Walker said. "I've done my bit in terms of family loyalty. You know the score. I'm sure you can handle things from here on out."

Bobby sighed. "I wish I were half as confident of that as you are." He picked up the orders that had been prepared for Walker, Daisy and Tommy and handed them to Walker. "Take these with you."

"Hey," Walker protested. "I thought this place was renowned for its good service, as well as its excellent food."

"Like you said, you're family. You can help out."

"See if I ever give you fair warning about any schemes afoot again," Walker grumbled as he left with their meals.

Once his brother-in-law had gone, Bobby went back to work with a vengeance, but nothing he did blocked out the image of his sister and Jenna conspiring behind his back. Just the thought of it made him shudder. The only thing worse would be King getting in on the act.

He could think of only one way to keep the two women apart. He could make Jenna a better offer— maybe dangle the prospect of a noontime tour of the waterfront before her. It was better than leaving her alone with Daisy. At least if *he* was with her, he'd know what she was up to.

He didn't wait until he'd cleaned up the kitchen to execute his plan. The second the last order had been sent to a table, he slipped into the dining room, glanced around until he spotted Jenna and headed her way. His step faltered only when he saw the girl with her. A grin slipped across his face. Green, spiked hair. He had to admire the child's daring. Jenna must be an incredibly liberal mother, or the girl was being taught a lesson. He suspected the latter.

When Bobby reached their table, he pulled out a

chair, turned it around and straddled it. "How was dinner?" he asked.

"Excellent," Jenna conceded.

"It was okay," the girl muttered, her scowl firmly in place.

"Darcy, don't be rude to Mr. Spencer," Jenna chided. "By the way, Bobby, this is my daughter, Darcy."

"I can see the resemblance," he said with a pointed glance at the girl's hairdo.

"It was a little experiment that went awry," Jenna explained.

"I like it," Darcy insisted. She turned to Bobby. "Is there anything to do here?"

Bobby studied her with an assessing look. "How old are you? Ten? Twelve?"

"Nine," Jenna said.

"Then at this hour of the night, there is nothing for you to do," Bobby said.

"Normally she wouldn't be out this late," Jenna said defensively. "But I couldn't leave her at the hotel by herself, and you were the one who refused to talk to me earlier in the evening."

Bobby could have debated endlessly who was at fault for the late meeting, but right now he needed to concentrate on preventing that meeting between Jenna and his sister. "Why don't we get together tomorrow?" he suggested. "Say, around noon. I'll take you on a tour of the waterfront area."

Immediate interest sparked in Jenna's eyes, but faded almost as quickly. "You know I'm supposed to meet your sister at noon, don't you?"

He feigned ignorance. "Really?"

"Oh, don't try that with me. I know Walker couldn't wait to run into the kitchen to warn you."

"So, what's it going to be? Are you more interested in lunch with Daisy or in seeing the land I'm planning to develop?"

"Why does it have to be an either/or proposition?" she asked.

He shrugged. "That's just the way it is. This is a one-time-only offer. Take it or leave it."

Jenna's gaze clashed with his. "Then, unfortunately, I'll have to leave it. It would be impolite to back out on lunch with your sister, now that I've already accepted. Besides, Tommy and Darcy have made plans as well. He wants her to see his boat."

"Your choice," Bobby said, standing up. "Enjoy the rest of your evening."

"Hey," Jenna called after him. "We need to talk."

"We just did," he pointed out.

"You know perfectly well what I mean."

"Call Maggie. Maybe she'll be able to squeeze you in later this month. My calendar's booked pretty tight. All those other developers, you know."

He heard Jenna's gasp and hid a grin before turning back. "Yes?"

"I thought you weren't seeing anyone yet?"

"I hadn't intended to, but once you slipped through the door, I had no choice but to schedule the others. You'd be amazed how many people are anxious for a piece of this project."

She frowned at him. "One o'clock," she said tightly. "I'll cut short my visit with your sister."

He shook his head. "Not good enough. Noon's my final offer."

"Dammit, Bobby Spencer—"

"Careful," he warned with a pointed look at Darcy. She'd been half-asleep, but her mother's muttered curse had gotten her attention. She seemed almost as surprised by it as Bobby was.

Jenna sighed. "Noon. Where shall we meet?"

As far away from Daisy's as possible, he thought. Aloud, he said, "Earlene's. I'll buy you both a sandwich before we head out on the tour."

"Noon at Earlene's," Jenna agreed with obvious reluctance. "But I think you ought to be the one to call your sister and apologize for spoiling our plans."

"Not a chance," Bobby said fervently. He wasn't going to listen to an hour-long lecture on his devious nature and lack of manners.

"I'm not sure you want her to hear my spin on this," Jenna countered.

He frowned at that. "Fine. I'll call and express your regrets."

"My *very deep* regrets," Jenna emphasized. "And do it tonight, before she spends a lot of time preparing lunch."

"Whatever." If it kept those two apart, at least for another day, he would wake his sister from a sound sleep and say whatever was necessary.

Unfortunately, he had a feeling he was only postponing the inevitable.

The conversation with Daisy went pretty much as Bobby had anticipated it would. She didn't buy it for one single second that his offer to take Jenna on a tour of the riverfront property had been a magnanimous gesture.

"You're trying to keep the two of us apart," she had muttered sleepily. "Which only makes me wonder why."

"Jenna is supposed to be here because she wants to land this contract. Don't you imagine that ought to be her first priority?" he had retorted. "It's unfair of you to try to distract her."

Daisy's response to that had been an unladylike snort of disbelief. Then she'd hung up on him.

Given all that, Bobby wasn't the slightest bit surprised when he walked into Earlene's to find his sister and Tommy settled into the same booth as Jenna and her daughter. If he was going to join them and prevent disaster, he was going to have to haul over a chair and sit in the aisle.

Or he could squeeze in beside Jenna, he concluded, studying the situation thoughtfully. Only problem with that was that he couldn't be entirely sure which of them would regret the intimacy the most. Probably him. Jenna had an annoying ability to ignore his best attempts to rattle her. Still, it was worth the risk, just to see a quick flare of heat in her eyes.

"A bit crowded in here," he noted with a pointed glance at Daisy as he nudged Jenna farther along the booth's bench.

"I didn't want Darcy and Tommy to miss out on the chance to spend some time together just because you're sneaky," Jenna said cheerfully. "I called Daisy this morning and suggested they join us." She smiled at him sweetly. "You don't mind, do you?"

"Whatever makes you happy," he said, his own tone sour.

Daisy chuckled, though her expression quickly sobered when Bobby scowled at her.

Lunch went downhill after that. Daisy and Jenna kept up a nonstop barrage of talk about the plague that brothers could be on their lives.

"I'm going to remember every word of this," Bobby told Daisy. "Tucker will find it fascinating, I'm sure. And you'll eventually pay for every disparaging word you said about the two of us."

This time his sister didn't even try to hide her amusement. "Your threats have lost the power to scare me," she told him loftily. "But I will leave you two alone now. Darcy, would you like to come home with Tommy and see his boat?"

Darcy nodded with the first evidence of animation she'd displayed all during the meal.

"Is that okay with you, Jenna?" Daisy asked.

"If you're sure you don't mind. I'll be by in an hour or so to pick her up."

Not if he had anything to say about it, Bobby vowed, at least not without him right by her side to make sure the conversation never veered into the kind of girltalk that would come back to haunt him.

"We'll swing by when we're finished with the tour," he told Daisy. "If you've baked something by then, it will go a little way toward getting you off the hook."

Daisy rolled her eyes. "Will chocolate chip cookies do?"

"As a down payment," he told her.

When Daisy and the kids had gone, he turned and saw that Jenna was studying him with evident fascination.

"You know, for all that talk of Daisy's about how annoying you and Tucker are, you're really very close, aren't you?"

Bobby was surprised she had to ask. He was even more startled by the genuinely envious note in her voice. "Of course. Aren't you close to your brothers?"

Jenna shook her head. "Not really."

"Why not?"

Her expression turned thoughtful and perhaps just a little wistful. "Maybe it was because after my mom died, I was the one sent away to boarding school, while they got to stay home with my dad. I resented it."

Bobby tried to imagine Daisy's reaction if King had tried such a thing with her. Daisy would have fought the move tooth and nail. She might have been her daddy's meek, well-mannered angel most of the time, but Daisy did have a temper and she had taken it upon herself to play mother to Tucker and Bobby. She would never have permitted King to interfere with her self-assigned duty. If he'd actually managed to get her enrolled at a boarding school, Daisy would have turned right around and hiked home the next day, and that would have been that.

Not that King would have considered it in the first place. Keeping Daisy at home had made his life run more smoothly. She'd slipped into the role of hostess at Cedar Hill as if she'd been born to it. Never mind that she'd been barely in her teens at the time. How sad that Jenna hadn't been given the same chance to carve out a niche for herself at home with her family.

Bobby regarded her sympathetically. "That must have been hard."

"It was devastating," she said simply. "Just when I needed the rest of my family the most, I became an outcast."

"How'd you handle that?"

A faint smile touched her lips. "The same way every teenager gets even. I rebelled."

Bobby had no difficulty at all envisioning the woman beside him staging a rebellion that would shake the rafters. Her audacious intrusion into the middle of his life testified to her inventiveness.

"What did you do?" he asked.

"Well, there was the incident of the snake tattoo," she said, her eyes twinkling mischievously.

The thought of a tattoo marring her soft, pale skin made him wince. But, then, curiosity got the better of him. Since no tattoo was visible, this raised some interesting possibilities.

"Where?" he asked, his gaze drawn to the faint curve of her breast exposed by the opening in her blouse.

She elbowed him sharply in the ribs. "Not there."

He feigned an exaggerated sigh. "Too bad. I was hoping to sneak a peek."

"You're too late. It washed off."

He regarded her with disappointment. "It was a fake?"

She chuckled. "Yep, but it did the job. My father almost had a nervous breakdown. Of course, that was nothing compared to the first time I brought home Nick Kennedy."

"Your husband?"

"My *ex*-husband," she stressed quickly. "His tattoo was real, as was the diamond stud in his ear." She glanced pointedly at the one Bobby wore. "I'm pretty sure my father would have left the house and gone straight to his cardiologist's, but he was terrified to leave the two of us alone for a minute."

"But you ran off and married this Nick, anyway," Bobby concluded. His gaze narrowed. "Because you were pregnant?"

Fortunately, she didn't take offense at the blunt, personal question.

"I can see why you'd think that, but no. Darcy might have been a surprise, but for me, she was a happy surprise a full nine months *after* the wedding. And, in my father's view, she's probably the one good thing to come out of that time in my life. In my view, too, for that matter."

"She seems like a handful," Bobby noted, thinking of the green hair.

"You have no idea," Jenna said fervently. "I'm actually hoping our stay in Trinity Harbor will work some magic on her and on our relationship. She's more rebellious at nine than I was at sixteen. It's scary. I'm beginning to understand what I put my father through."

"You're expecting a miracle in a couple of days?"

Jenna met his gaze evenly. "It's going to take more

than a couple of days to complete this waterfront project.''

Bobby's heart began to thud dully. ''You sound awfully confident about getting the job.''

''I am,'' she said without hesitation. She met his gaze with an unflinching look.

Bobby admired the confidence, even if he felt he had to discourage it. ''Jenna, this is not a done deal, not by any means,'' he said, fighting to keep the panic from his voice.

''Of course not,'' she agreed. ''There are all those other developers pouring into town, right? The ones you told me about last night?''

''Exactly.''

''How many, precisely?''

Bobby's gaze narrowed. ''Why do you ask?''

''Just curious about the competition.''

''You've talked to Maggie, haven't you? What did she tell you?''

Jenna grinned. ''No appointments. No developers. You lied to me.''

Bobby was going to kill Maggie...or at the very least explain to her more clearly who her boss was. Not that *that* had ever impressed her before. This was what happened when you hired someone you used to baby-sit. The chain-of-command lines had long since been blurred.

''There will be more,'' he insisted firmly. ''I just hadn't gotten around to telling Maggie to schedule the appointments.''

''Right,'' Jenna agreed with undisguised amusement. ''In that case, we'd better take that tour right now. I want to have my site plans finalized and on your desk before all that competition roars into town.''

''I thought you were just sticking around to make sure Tucker finds your missing carousel horse,'' Bobby said glumly.

''Not entirely,'' she said cheerfully. ''I'm going to be a thorn in your side until you agree to give Pennington and Sons this contract.''

''Why would you work this hard for a company that, by your own admission, is run by men who've made you an outsider in your own family?''

She regarded him as if the answer were obvious. ''To prove they made a mistake, of course.''

In that instant, Bobby knew that not only Jenna's family, but he himself, were seriously guilty of misjudging her. Jenna might look like a pure temptress with little acumen for business, but she had the heart and soul of a shark. It was a frightening—albeit fascinating—discovery.

7

It was killing King that he hadn't yet had a look at the woman who'd been inspired to send that carousel horse to stir up his son. Anyone with that kind of spunk would be perfect for Bobby, so King was prepared to do his part to get the relationship on solid ground, but he felt a little bit as if he were buying a pig in a poke. Still, the fact that she'd come back to town to keep up the pressure did impress him. King was more hopeful about Bobby's future than he had been in some time.

Of course, it wouldn't do to get overconfident. If Bobby thought King approved of this Jenna Kennedy, it would only add to his son's determination to avoid her at all costs. Which meant King had to resort to sneakiness if he was going to wangle an introduction. It had to be casual, unplanned...or at least made to look that way.

The word at Earlene's was that the woman's daughter was visiting with Daisy and Tommy while Bobby showed Jenna the riverfront property he was planning to develop. Sooner or later, that meant that Jenna would show up at Daisy's. If Bobby was still with her, so much the better. King could see for himself if all the reports were right and there was any spark of attraction to be fueled.

He didn't hesitate for a single second before driving over to Daisy's. After all, what was suspicious about a father dropping by to pay a visit to his very own daughter? How was he supposed to know she had company? It wasn't like he kept his ear to the ground about *everything* in Trinity Harbor. Just the important stuff, such as what his kids were up to.

When King arrived at Daisy's, he walked around the house in the direction of all the noise. Tommy and a kid with green hair were engaged in a heated exchange about the best color for that pitiful boat the boy had rescued from the river. Tommy turned to him eagerly.

"Grandpa King, tell her that the boat has to be blue. It can't be pink," he declared with indignation.

"Why not?" the girl asked.

Tommy rolled his eyes. "I'm a guy. Guys don't have pink anything. Right, Grandpa King?"

King grinned at Tommy's earnest expression. The fact that he was even debating the point with a child who'd colored her hair green demonstrated more tolerance than King would have displayed under the same circumstances. But he was being called on here for diplomacy and tact, which, unfortunately, weren't his strong suits. He struggled for a suitable reply. No need to get on the wrong side of a girl who could one day wind up being his granddaughter. At the same time, he didn't want to discourage a boy who was showing suitable respect for King's opinion.

"Well, now, Tommy, pink is a mighty fine color,"

King said, choosing his words carefully. "And there are plenty of places for which it's well-suited."

"See," the girl said triumphantly.

Tommy scowled at her. "He didn't say anything about the boat, Darcy."

King bit back a grin. "That's true. Now it seems to me that a boat ought to reflect the personality of its owner, just the way hair color might reflect the personality of the person choosing it," he said with a pointed look at Darcy's head. She watched him suspiciously, obviously waiting for the rest of what he had to say. "Green hair wouldn't suit just anybody. It takes someone very special to carry it off."

The girl's face lit up. "Thank you."

He patted her on the head. "You're very welcome," he said, and bypassed the pair to get to the back door before he could get drawn into any more tricky discussions.

Daisy met him with a broad grin. "Nice save."

King shook his head. "Damn, why would any mama let her child do something like that?"

"I don't think Jenna *allowed* it exactly," Daisy said. "In fact, I believe she had very firmly told Darcy that she could not dye her hair—unfortunately, she limited that to the original color under debate, which was purple."

King chuckled and eyed the child outside with newfound respect. "Got her mother, did she?"

"Temporarily. I suspect Darcy held out hope that Jenna would force her to dye it back to its natural color. That didn't happen, so now Darcy's facing the consequences of having that hair of hers be the only thing about her that people react to.''

King nodded. ''Clever move. I like this woman already.''

Daisy regarded him knowingly. ''Which I imagine is precisely what brought you by. Did curiosity get the better of you, Daddy?''

King feigned indignation. ''Since when can't a father drop in to see his daughter?''

''That's not the issue,'' Daisy said, regarding him with blatant amusement. ''It's a matter of the timing. You knew Darcy was here and that Jenna would be by to get her, didn't you?''

''I believe I heard something to that effect,'' he admitted with what he hoped was just the right touch of nonchalance. He glanced toward the oven. ''Also heard that you were baking chocolate chip cookies. You know I never could resist your cookies.''

''As flattering as that is,'' Daisy said dryly, ''I imagine the cookies are the last reason you showed up here. Still, the first batch will be out of the oven in a minute. Want some iced tea while you wait?''

''Sounds good,'' King said, settling down at the kitchen table to see what information about Bobby's relationship with Jenna he could pry out of Daisy. But first things first. He had to throw her off the scent.

He studied his daughter as she finished scooping dough onto another cookie sheet, then traded that one for the one in the oven. He'd never seen her looking so radiant. ''You're happy, aren't you, girl?''

The beaming smile she turned on him was answer

enough. "Happier than I've ever been," she told him, leaning down to press a kiss to his cheek.

Satisfied that he hadn't been mistaken when he picked Walker out for Daisy, King nodded. "Tucker says Walker's the best man in the department. Is Walker satisfied with the work? Must seem awfully quiet for a man used to investigating homicides in Washington."

Daisy pulled out a chair and sat down opposite him, her expression thoughtful. "I was worried about the same thing, but Walker says he's content." A spark lit her eyes. "His boys are coming to visit this weekend."

Those two sons of Walker's were fine boys. They'd stayed out at Cedar Hill with King when their mama had brought them up for the wedding. "So you'll have a house crowded with kids. You ready for that?"

"I can't wait," Daisy said at once.

King smiled at her eagerness. His daughter was a born nurturer. She'd pieced this family of hers together despite all the odds against it. When she'd found Tommy hiding in her garage, scared and trying his darnedest to hot-wire her car, she'd seen the boy as the answer to her prayers. King hadn't understood it at the time, but he could see now that Daisy had always known her own heart better than anyone. And the truth was, much as he wanted to claim some credit for her contentment, she was the one who'd first seen Walker's potential. King had been skeptical about a man from a big, crime-ridden city like Washington settling for the quiet life of Trinity Harbor.

"You know how happy I am for you, don't you?" he said gruffly.

"I do," she said, squeezing his hand. Then she grinned. "And now you want to make Bobby just as happy, don't you?"

"Well, of course, I do," King grumbled. "Don't you?"

"Absolutely."

He eyed her intently. "So, what do you think of this Jenna? Will she do?"

"Bobby hasn't let me spend more than a minute alone with her to find out," she said with evident exasperation. "And, trust me, when she comes by here for Darcy, he's going to be right beside her, trying to foil my plans to get to know her."

King grinned at her. "You willing to work with me a bit?"

Daisy chuckled, but she didn't immediately turn him down out of loyalty to her brother. "How?"

"Divide and conquer, that's the ticket. You take Bobby. I'll take Jenna."

"Why can't *I* take Jenna?" Daisy protested.

"Because I'm your father, and if there's any cross-examining to be done around here today, I'm the one who gets to do it." He winked at her. "I *will* share whatever I find out."

Daisy held out her hand. "Deal."

King laughed. "No question you're a daughter after my own heart," he said proudly.

"I'm not sure Bobby's going to consider my inheritance of the meddling gene a valued attribute," she warned.

King shrugged that off. "Who cares what he thinks?

If that boy had found himself a good woman a long time ago, we wouldn't have to get involved.''

"He thought he had," Daisy reminded King, her expression suddenly serious. "Ann-Marie hurt him. I'm not sure he'll ever get past that."

"She wasn't good enough to wipe the dust from my boy's shoes," King said fiercely. "Her actions proved that."

"They surely did," Daisy agreed. "Now, hush. I think I hear a car. I'll go outside and stall Bobby and send Jenna in here to pour the tea. You'll have maybe ten minutes before Bobby gets suspicious. Think you can accomplish anything in that length of time?"

"Can a hound dog hunt?"

Daisy leaned down and kissed him. "There is nobody on earth like you, King Spencer. Nobody." Her grin spread. "Thank the Lord."

The tour of the riverfront had left Jenna more enthusiastic than ever about this project. She'd seen the perfect spot for the carousel in a grove of trees. There was also a sloping hill that would be perfect for lawn seating for outdoor concerts if a bandstand were situated just right to catch the evening breezes off the Potomac. Her mind was literally bursting with ideas she hadn't been able to put on paper. Bobby's wary reaction when she'd reached for the notebook in her purse had made her put off taking notes.

When Daisy had suggested Jenna come inside to fix iced tea for all of them, she'd been eager to comply. It would give her a minute alone to jot down some of her thoughts before going back outside to join the others. She hadn't counted on finding an older man sitting at the kitchen table, the pitcher of tea in front of him and two glasses already poured.

"You must be Jenna," he said at once, gesturing toward a seat. "Join me for a minute. I'm King Spencer."

"Bobby's father?" she guessed.

"Yes, indeed." He seared her with a piercing look. "He's a fine young man, don't you think?"

Jenna wasn't about to report to his father that she considered Bobby to be a little too full of himself, as well as annoyingly stubborn. "I don't really know him that well," she said instead.

King chuckled, evidently seeing straight through the careful evasion. "Giving you a rough time, is he?"

"Let's just say we got off to a rocky start," she said. "It was at least partially my fault."

To her surprise, King frowned. "Don't you go taking any blame on yourself," he scolded. "Bobby's the kind of man who requires firm handling and total confidence. Otherwise he'll bulldoze right over you."

The screen door slapped shut. "Much in the same way my father will," Bobby said, regarding his father with tolerant amusement. "I should have known I'd find you in here. That had to be the only reason Daisy kept trying to ask for my advice about the pests in her garden—because she wanted to distract me from the much larger, more dangerous pest inside. I didn't see your car in the driveway. Where'd you park?"

"Around the corner," King said, looking pleased with himself.

Jenna barely contained a chuckle at the exchange.

She had never once, in all of her twenty-eight years, been able to joke with *her* father like that. If she'd been able to make her points with humor, rather than anger, maybe they would have gotten along better. Maybe her father would have shown her more respect.

"I was just having a friendly conversation," King told his son huffily. "Nothing wrong with that, is there?"

"Has he inquired about your intentions toward me?" Bobby asked Jenna.

Her eyes widened. "My intentions?"

"My father has been looking for a wife for me for some time now. He doesn't think I'm capable of finding one on my own."

Jenna choked on her sip of tea, but one look at the undaunted merriment in King's eyes had her reconsidering the sharp retort on the tip of her tongue. She grinned at him.

"Want to talk terms?" she inquired tartly. "For the right deal, I might be persuaded to let him court me. I couldn't make any guarantees about his success, though."

King hooted at her quick response. "Oh, boy, you're in trouble with this one, son."

"Tell me about it," Bobby muttered, frowning at her. "Jenna, stop encouraging him."

"Okay," she agreed cheerfully. "Let's hear *your* best offer."

Bobby stared at her. "You're playing us against each other?"

"Sure. Apparently you each have an agenda where

I'm concerned. If the price is right, maybe I could be persuaded to ignore your father.''

"What's your price?" Bobby asked, looking resigned.

Jenna didn't hesitate. "Another meeting once I've roughed in some sketches of what we saw today and how I think the land could best be used."

Bobby sighed heavily. "Done," he agreed. He turned on his father. "It's on your head, when Harvey gets his drawers in a knot over the fact that he's getting no say at all in the riverfront development."

"Harvey's drawers are always in a knot about something. I can handle him." King's grin spread. "The question is, can you handle Jenna?"

Bobby's gaze locked with hers. "I'm not even going to try," he said as he turned around and walked away. A minute later, she heard his car start.

Jenna turned back to King to find that he was regarding her with more respect than her own father had ever displayed.

"You'll do, young lady. You will most definitely do."

Jenna wasn't entirely sure that King's stamp of approval was going to get her to her original goal. If anything, his declaration that he wanted her in his son's life might just have muddied the waters.

Jenna was still puzzling over Bobby's parting shot about not even trying to handle her when she and Darcy got back to their hotel later that evening. Darcy was so exhausted by her active day outside with

Tommy that she could barely keep her eyes open. Even so, as she crawled into bed, she gazed up at Jenna.

"Mama, do you think we'll be here when Tommy's boat is done?"

"I don't know. Why?"

"Because he promised to take me fishing."

"And you want to go?" Jenna asked with surprise. "I thought you considered putting worms on hooks to be some form of torture. That's what you told your grandfather when he tried to take you."

"Tommy said I don't have to use worms. He said shrimp work just as good."

And cost a whole lot more, Jenna thought with a sigh of resignation. "We'll see what we can work out. If we're not here, maybe we can drive back down for a weekend."

Darcy yawned sleepily. "I know I didn't want to come, but this isn't a bad place," she said before her eyes slid closed and stayed that way.

Jenna watched as Darcy's breathing slowed into the peaceful pattern of sleep. Sometimes she was awed and a little terrified when she considered the responsibility she had to make sure that nothing bad ever happened to this beautiful, feisty child of hers. Darcy's personality wasn't going to make her job any easier. And Nick wouldn't be any help. He and her father were at opposite extremes. Nick was too indulgent. Jenna's father might adore Darcy, but his strict approach to discipline was only likely to make Darcy even more rebellious than Jenna had been.

A man like Bobby, however... She cut herself off before she could continue the thought. Despite King's high hopes and Bobby's enigmatic remark about not trying to fight her, she would not allow herself to think beyond her goal. That contract was the only thing that mattered. She had to remember that.

She leaned down and pressed a kiss to Darcy's flushed cheek. "I love you, baby, green hair and all."

On Thursday morning Bobby was summoned to Harvey's office. Normally he would have balked at the imperious manner in which the order had been delivered, but it was better to get this meeting out of the way. He found the mayor wearing an expression that was even more sullen and disapproving than usual.

"Explain this," he said, tossing a newspaper in Bobby's direction.

Bobby stared at the headline above Richard's story on the stolen carousel horse:

Who's Behind Theft Of Rare Carousel Horse?

"I believe Richard is asking a question," he said mildly. "The horse was stolen. He's wondering who took it."

Harvey's frown deepened. "Not that, dammit. The story down below."

Bobby's gaze shifted and landed squarely on a picture of Jenna, accompanied by an interview about her views on boardwalk development.

"So?" Harvey demanded.

"So what?" Bobby responded mildly.

"Did you hire that woman without consulting me?"

"Actually, whom I hire is none of your concern, but no, I did not hire her."

Harvey slammed his fist onto the desk so hard it rattled his coffee cup. "As long as I am mayor of this town, I will determine what happens to our waterfront."

Bobby refused to get drawn into a pointless fight. The land belonged to him, not the town. This development was his baby. All the zoning was in place. Unless the town council set out to deliberately thwart him, Harvey Needham could bluster all he wanted. He didn't have a leg to stand on.

Bobby stood up and headed for the door. Just before walking out, he turned back. "I don't think so, Harvey."

"You just try to get around me, Bobby Spencer," he warned. "You won't be able to pull a single permit without running into trouble. You'll be dead and buried before you get this project off the ground."

"Really? How old are you, Harvey?"

Harvey's expression faltered just a little. "Sixty-five, but I don't see what that has to do with anything."

"I'm twenty-eight," Bobby pointed out. "I'm pretty sure I can outlast you." He strolled back across the room and leaned down until he was in the mayor's face. "Don't mess with me, Harvey. The people of Trinity Harbor are on my side on this one. I have a whole drawerful of surveys to prove it. I don't know if you're in bed with some developer or just plain stupid, but this town isn't big enough for some grand-scale project that blocks river access for our residents.

We're a small town with a chance to see that something's done right with our best natural resource. I don't intend to blow that opportunity.''

Harvey's complexion turned pale. "I'll have the land seized for public use."

Bobby's gaze narrowed at the threat. "Just try it," he said quietly.

"I can do it," Harvey insisted.

Bobby shook his head. "You can try," he agreed. "But it will be your last act in public office. And I have a hunch the folks in this community will make your life so uncomfortable, you'll be hightailing it for some retirement village in Florida where the most excitement you'll find is your daily shuffleboard game— assuming you can find someone willing to play with you."

"Typical Spencer," Harvey said disparagingly. "Trying to throw your weight around."

Bobby laughed at that. "You might want to think that one over, Mr. Mayor. I'm not the one who ordered a citizen into my office and started making threats. Wouldn't that look nice in next week's headlines? Maybe I'll stop by Richard's office on my way back to the yacht center."

There was no mistaking the fact that Harvey was seething, but he wisely kept silent. Bobby waited, his gaze locked on the scurrilous jerk, then finally gave a nod of satisfaction.

"Good," he said. "I'll see you around."

He'd barely hit the steps down to the first floor of the town offices when he heard Harvey bellow for his secretary. "Get Mitch Cummings on the phone for me," he shouted. "Now!"

Mitch Cummings? The name sounded familiar, but Bobby couldn't place it. Maybe Richard would know. Instead of heading straight back to work, he swung by the office of *The Trinity Harbor Weekly* paper. He found Richard sitting behind his desk, his feet propped up, reading the latest edition.

"It's a little late to be checking your spelling," Bobby observed as he took a seat opposite Richard.

"Well, if it isn't our own mover and shaker," Richard greeted him. "Did you come by to pat me on the back for the excellent coverage I gave you?"

"Actually, I hardly saw a mention of my name, but that was a nice picture of Jenna. You two in cahoots to pressure me to hire her?"

Richard laughed. "Pressure would be Anna-Louise's turf. I try not to be in cahoots with anybody."

"Well, you certainly did stir up the mayor," Bobby reported. "He's over at Town Hall on the verge of apoplexy. And you realize, don't you, that if Harvey keels over, Tucker will find some way to charge both of us with murder?"

"Oh, all that venting probably keeps the man healthy," Richard said dismissively. He regarded Bobby intently. "If you didn't come by to sing my praises, then why are you here?"

"I've got a name I want to run by you. You ever heard of Mitch Cummings?"

Richard's expression sobered at once. "Where did *you* hear his name?"

"Just now in Harvey's office. The instant I walked

out the door, he yelled at his secretary to call Cummings.''

"Then I suggest you watch your back," Richard said. "Cummings is a retired investigator. Lives down in Richmond. I'm not sure what he's up to these days, but he and the mayor are old pals. My hunch is that he intends to use Cummings to start trying to dig up some dirt on you. If you've got any secrets, now would be a good time to make sure they're buried as deep as you can get them.''

Bobby laughed.

"It's not funny," Richard warned. "It sounds to me like the mayor intends to start playing dirty.''

"Let him knock himself out. My life's so squeaky clean, it could be a testimonial for a detergent.''

"You sure about that?''

"Positive. My sole indiscretion was being stupid enough to ask Ann-Marie to marry me, but she's the one who broke the engagement and ran off with my best friend. Besides, everyone in town knows that story. They could probably also tell you about the time I borrowed Lonnie's bike and he reported it stolen.''

"Well, there you go," Richard said.

"Sadly, when the police came to his house to check it out, they found the bike sitting right smack in the middle of his driveway.''

"Ah.''

"There's nothing for me to worry about," Bobby said. "Not from Lonnie, not from Ann-Marie, not from anyone.''

Richard nodded. "Would Ann-Marie describe your

breakup the same way? For that matter, what about Lonnie? Do either of them have an axe to grind?''

"Are you kidding?" Bobby demanded indignantly. "I was the victim, not either one of them."

"Funny thing about that, though. Over time, particularly if people become outcasts because of decisions they made in the past, they occasionally like to revise history and make themselves into the ones who've suffered."

As Richard spoke, Bobby went absolutely still. His temper, usually slow to build, slipped immediately into overdrive. Nothing could do that to him faster than a mention of Ann-Marie and his former best friend. Add to that the suggestion that somehow *he* had wronged *them* and it made him want to break things. There could be only one reason for Richard to bring up the topic—the Trinity Harbor rumor mill was hard at work.

"What have you heard?" he demanded quietly.

Richard held up his hand in a placating gesture. "Nothing. I'm just saying, I've seen it happen. Keep your guard up."

"You're sure nobody's spreading tales?"

"I haven't heard any. It was just a word of warning."

Bobby nodded. "Okay, then. Thanks."

"Where are you heading now? Want to grab some lunch?"

"Not today. I've got to go see a man about a horse," Bobby said wryly. With any luck, Tucker would have found the blasted thing in the middle of Harvey's living room.

8

Eager to get started on the work that had brought her to Trinity Harbor, Jenna took her sketch pad and a notebook with her to the riverfront the next morning. The day had dawned without a cloud in the blue sky and a welcome breeze to break the midsummer heat. She felt almost as carefree as she had on school vacations years ago, filled with that expectant sense that adventure was right around the corner. If only she could capture some of that anticipation and pass it along to her daughter, Jenna thought with a sigh.

She chose a spot on a decrepit bench, its weathered boards warped and the paint worn away. It gave her a good vantage point from which to study the stretch of land Bobby intended to develop. There was a public fishing pier a few blocks in the distance, as well as a pier where a sightseeing boat docked most days. She'd heard the announcements for the tours when she and Bobby had walked along the waterfront the day before.

There was a tang of salt in the soft morning air and just the faintest whiff of suntan oil from the handful of sunbathers who'd come out early to beat the heat of the day. It was funny how a scent like that could transport her through time, back to the days when her mother had been alive and they'd sat side by side on a blanket on the sand at Ocean City or Rehoboth or any of a dozen other beaches where they'd gone on summer vacations before everything had changed.

In those days, the visits had been business trips for her father. He'd already been building a reputation for seaside development. But for Jenna and her brothers, those times with their mother had been magical. Jenna still had a mason jar at home filled with pale blue and green sea glass collected on those summer outings. Sometimes when she held it up to the sun, she swore she could still smell the beach scents and maybe even a lingering trace of her mother's favorite perfume.

Now she had a chance to create those same kinds of memories for her daughter. Not that it was going to be easy. Darcy sat beside her now, a book from her summer reading list untouched in her lap. She had complained bitterly when Jenna had taken her to the cozy bookstore in town and insisted on something educational, rather than one of the thrillers that kids were crazy about.

Still, though Darcy wasn't exactly exuberant, at least she wasn't pouting. Jenna was learning to be grateful for small favors, even if this one had been accomplished with a bribe. She had agreed to take Darcy and Tommy to the nearby state park after lunch, *if* Darcy finished her required reading.

"You know what, Mom? Tommy says people are always finding shark's teeth and stuff in the cliffs," Darcy told her eventually, her eyes shining with rare enthusiasm. "Isn't that awesome? I can hardly wait to get there. How soon will you be finished?"

Jenna could barely contain a grin. Darcy had been

quoting Tommy nonstop since she'd crawled out of bed that morning. It was an apparent case of hero worship in the making.

"We just got here. And you haven't read the first page of that book yet. Five pages, minimum. That was our deal."

"But I'm ready to go to the park now," Darcy said, scuffing her feet in the sand.

"Too bad. I have work to do. So do you. Now, get busy and read."

Darcy turned her attention to her book. She was a fast reader, and five pages were nothing once she actually started to concentrate.

"Mom, I'm bored," she announced, closing the book. "Can we go? I can't wait to climb the cliffs and look for shark's teeth."

"Forget it. You won't be climbing any cliffs," Jenna warned her. "But I understand there's a public pool there, or you can swim in the river."

"The pool," Darcy said at once. "Tommy says there are jellyfish in the river."

"Well, if Tommy says it, it must be true," Jenna said. "Walk on down to the edge of the water here and check it out. Just stay where I can see you."

"Are you going to be a really long time?" Darcy asked plaintively.

"That depends on whether you leave me alone long enough to get my work done."

Darcy heaved a dramatic sigh and retreated toward the river. Gingerly she stuck one toe in the water, then jumped back. "Mom, a jellyfish almost got me," she squealed.

"Then keep your feet out of the water," Jenna retorted.

"That's no fun. Can we go yet?"

Jenna groaned. Obviously using that outing to the park as a bribe had backfired. Darcy wasn't going to be content until they were in the car and on their way.

"Going someplace?" Bobby inquired, appearing out of nowhere and dropping down onto the bench beside her.

"Where'd you come from?" Jenna asked, cursing the little blip of excitement that rushed through her at the sight of him in a snug pair of jeans and a faded gray T-shirt. Why did he, of all the people in the universe, have to be the one who made her pulse race?

"I just had a meeting with Tucker," he announced, his legs stretched out in front of him. "I was on my way back to the yacht center when I spotted you."

She turned to him hopefully. "Does your brother have any leads on the missing horse?"

Bobby shook his head. "Sorry. Not a one. Nobody saw anything, which means it probably happened before daybreak—my elderly neighbors Sue and Frannie have the neighborhood under surveillance by seven most days. The guard is still among the missing. My hunch is he's taken his family on an extended vacation courtesy of the thief."

Jenna sighed. "That's not good, is it? If there are no leads right after a crime, what are the odds that Tucker will find any as time goes on?"

"Don't worry about that," Bobby said grimly. "Believe me, my brother is highly motivated. I've put his professional reputation on the line. He'll get that horse back." He glanced toward the river, where Darcy was picking up shells and pieces of green and blue sea glass to start her own collection. "What was Darcy saying about going somewhere? You aren't leaving town, are you?"

"Sorry to disappoint you, but no," Jenna said, chuckling at the dismay he didn't even attempt to hide. "Actually, Daisy and I are driving Darcy and Tommy over to the state park this afternoon. I'd hoped that the plan would buy me a little time to get some work done this morning."

Bobby glanced at the sketch pad. "What have you got so far?"

Ruefully, Jenna showed him the blank page. "I got a later start than I'd hoped, and once I sat down, my mind started drifting."

He regarded her intently. "To?"

"A long time ago, when my mother was alive and I was just a girl."

The look he cast at her was filled with understanding. "The same thing hits me when I come out here, too. King wouldn't set foot on the beach, but my mother used to gather Daisy, Tucker and me up and haul us down here or over to the state park for picnics at least once a week. After she died, Tucker and I used to ride our bikes into town and come here, but it wasn't the same."

"How old were you when she died?" Jenna asked.

"Twelve. I remember it like it was yesterday. How about you?"

"I was fourteen."

"A tough age," Bobby said.

"I'm not sure there's any good age to lose your mom," Jenna said, thinking back to how lost and frightened she'd felt. There had been so many questions she'd never gotten to ask, so many dreams she'd never had a chance to share. To make matters worse, only two months later, her father had shipped her off to school, where she'd felt even more isolated and alone. It had created a distance between her and her brothers that had never been breached.

She glanced at Bobby, but his expression behind his sunglasses was unreadable. "You, Tucker and Daisy were lucky," she said. "You all stayed together."

"King would never have considered separating us. For all of his flaws, family is the most important thing in the world to him, and families stick together." A slow grin crept across Bobby's face. "Of course, that didn't apply to his brother who'd managed to get his hands on a prize bull that King wanted. They haven't spoken in thirty years, even though Uncle James lives in the next county."

Jenna laughed. "So that's where the stubborn streak comes from."

Before Bobby could react to that, there was a scream of protest from just up the beach. Jenna recognized that voice. She was on her feet at once, but Bobby was faster. Before Jenna had even fully registered that there were half a dozen kids in their early teens surrounding her daughter, Bobby was in the middle of the crowd, one arm protectively around Darcy's shoulders, his other hand firmly around the scruff of a boy's neck.

"Okay, kids, that's it. Break it up. Go pick on somebody your own size," Bobby said.

His order was far milder than Jenna would have made it. Her heart was still hammering a mile a minute at the image of those bullies ganging up on her baby. She was certain they'd had nothing more in mind than taunting Darcy, but that was terrifying enough.

By the time she reached the small circle, tears were streaming down Darcy's cheeks. She broke free from Bobby and threw herself into Jenna's arms, sobs shaking her shoulders.

"Mommy, they said I looked like an alien," she said, her voice choked. "One of 'em grabbed at my hair and said it wasn't even real, that it was clown hair."

Jenna cursed herself for the decision to force Darcy to live with her green hair. "I'm so sorry, baby. Kids always like to pick on anyone who's different. You know that. It wasn't about you at all."

"But it was mean," Darcy said, hiccupping.

"Yes, it was." Jenna glanced up and saw that most of the kids had scattered, but Bobby still had a firm grip on the apparent ringleader. Engaged in what looked like a very intense conversation with the boy, Bobby finally gave a nod of satisfaction, then nudged the young teen in their direction.

Looking totally chagrined, the boy approached Darcy. "I'm sorry," he whispered, his eyes downcast. "That was really dumb. We didn't mean to scare you."

"Well, you did," Darcy said, clinging to Jenna's hand but staring the boy straight in the eye.

The boy glanced up at Bobby, then back at Darcy. "I'm Pete. I'm a friend of Tommy's."

"You don't act like you'd be a friend of Tommy's," Darcy challenged. "He's nice."

Pete regarded her with an even guiltier expression. "So am I, once you get to know me. We were just goofing around." He risked a glance at Jenna. "We really didn't mean any harm."

Jenna wasn't swayed. In fact, she was having a very difficult time not giving the kid the swat on the behind he deserved. "We appreciate your apology, but I think you should go now."

Pete glanced at Bobby. "I'm really sorry."

"I know," Bobby said. "We'll talk about this later."

After Pete had run off, Jenna looked at Bobby. "You know him?"

"Fairly well, as a matter of fact. He's a good kid."

"Oh, really? Do you find terrorizing a nine-year-old acceptable behavior?"

"Of course not. Look, can we get into this another time?" he suggested, with a pointed look at Darcy. "I think maybe the best thing for Darcy would be a stop at Earlene's for some ice cream." He winked at her. "What do you think?"

"I love ice cream," Darcy said enthusiastically.

Now that the crisis was over, Jenna felt the strength drain right out of her. Sitting down in the air-conditioned chill of Earlene's appealed to her almost as much as it obviously did to Darcy. Sitting there with a man willing to make excuses for a pint-sized bully held no appeal at all.

"I'll take her," she said. "I'm sure you have work to do."

"I'm covered at the restaurant till dinner," he replied, regarding her with amusement. "For a woman who's been pestering me to death for meetings, you suddenly seem awfully eager to get rid of me."

"Because right this second I find you extremely annoying," she shot back.

"Consider it turnabout," Bobby retorted. "You've been irritating me since the day you set foot in town. We can make peace over ice cream."

Jenna sighed. "Fine. Whatever."

Darcy was regarding them both with a troubled expression, but it was Bobby who managed to get a smile out of her. He leaned down with a whispered comment that brought a sparkle back to her eyes.

"What did you tell her?" Jenna demanded as Darcy ran ahead of them to Earlene's.

"I told her she shouldn't pay any attention to her mom's bad manners," he said. "I said it was probably some Yankee flaw in your character."

Jenna whirled on him indignantly. "Excuse me?"

He shrugged, his expression impossibly innocent. "Well, you have to admit you weren't very gracious. A Southern woman is taught from the cradle to be gracious. I can only attribute your attitude to some Yankee gene."

"I was born and raised in Baltimore."

"But where was that school you were sent off to when you were at a very impressionable age?"

"Boston," she conceded.

"I rest my case."

"Do you really want to get into a debate over nature versus nurture?" she asked. "My genes are every bit as Southern as yours, and, frankly, in your case I haven't noticed that those lessons in manners took all that well.''

Bobby looked affronted. ''Don't say that in front of King or Daisy. They did the best they could. Any lapses are my own responsibility.''

''Duly noted.''

He swept open the door at Earlene's with a dramatic flourish that had Darcy giggling and even brought a smile to Jenna's lips. ''You're crazy as a loon, Bobby Spencer,'' she said as she brushed past him.

''But lovable,'' he retorted.

Jenna was increasingly afraid that might be true.

For all of his joking around to lighten the mood, Bobby's heart was still pounding when they reached Earlene's. When he'd seen those kids taunting Darcy, seen the panic in her huge green eyes, he'd felt like banging some heads together.

He'd recognized most of the kids involved, and before the day was out, their parents would hear about how they were spending their summer vacation. The only reason Pete had lingered long enough to apologize directly to Darcy was because at heart he was a decent kid, who'd been through a very rough time himself. When the others had run, Pete had stood fast and faced Bobby.

After they'd finished hot fudge sundaes, Bobby flipped some change to Darcy. ''Darlin', why don't you go to the pay phone over there and give Tommy a call? Let him know you'll be by to pick him up in a half hour.''

Jenna frowned at him. "Planning my schedule?"

"No, buying myself a minute alone with you," he said, regarding her seriously. "I want to explain about Pete."

"You defended a bully," she retorted, her temper clearly escalating all over again. "There's no excuse good enough for that."

"Just listen," he admonished. "Last year when Walker first came to town and joined the sheriff's department, there was a big drug investigation going on. It turned out Pete's father, an ex-marine, was behind some serious smuggling in this region. He was killed the night Walker broke the investigation."

Jenna frowned, but said nothing.

"I don't know if you realize how small towns can be," Bobby continued. "They can pull together in times of tragedy, but they can also heap blame and ostracize. Pete took the brunt of the heat after the story broke about his daddy. Some of his friends weren't allowed to be anywhere around him. Others labeled him a druggie, even though there was no evidence at all that he was using marijuana or in any way involved in his father's crimes. He's withstood his share of bullying and gotten stronger because of it, but he's also struggling to find a way to fit in again."

"Well, he certainly picked a fine way, didn't he?" Jenna said.

Bobby let the comment pass. "Pete and Tommy have remained friends because Walker's determined to see Pete through this with as few scars as possible. But Tommy's a few years younger, and Pete's desperate for friends his own age. He's made some bad choices, like that crew he was with today. He won't make that mistake again."

"How can you be sure?" Jenna's eyes were filled with sympathy, but there was still a hard edge underlying her words.

"Because Walker and I will see to it," Bobby said. "We both try to spend as much time with Pete as we can. He needs some decent male role models in his life. He idolized his father, and discovering what the man was doing really shook him up. It's made him question a lot of the values he was taught. Walker and I are trying to make sure he doesn't confuse the message with the messenger. For all of his father's flaws, he tried to teach Pete right from wrong."

"What about the others? Is this just standard operating procedure for them?"

"If it was, it *won't* be much longer," Bobby said emphatically. "I'll see to that, too."

"So I'm just supposed to leave this in your capable hands?"

"That's one way," he agreed with a grin. "Or you could come along when I talk to their parents."

Jenna reacted with unmistakable surprise. "You intend to do that?"

"You bet."

"You're not just dismissing it as childish mischief?"

"It's never mischief when kids set out to torment other kids. There have been enough school shootings to testify to that," he said grimly. "I don't intend to let things in my town ever get to that stage."

A fleeting grin tugged at her lips. "Your town? A

little proprietary, wouldn't you say? No wonder you make Harvey very nervous.''

"I live here. That gives me a duty to step up when I see things that could undermine a way of life that most of the people around here want," Bobby said. "Once basic civility gives way to lowered expectations and mean-spirited behavior, the slide begins. I don't care if the people involved are adults or kids.''

"You really mean that, don't you?" she said, regarding him with a rare show of respect. "Even though none of the kids involved was yours, including Darcy, you consider this your problem?''

"Somebody has to step up to the plate. You and I were the only adults around, and I'm the only one who knows which kids were involved.''

"You could turn it over to Tucker," she said.

"Why should I? I was there.''

Her gaze narrowed. "Did I slip through some sort of time warp or something?''

Bobby chuckled. "No, why?''

"I didn't think there were any knights in shining armor left.''

"I heard what happened to Darcy," Daisy told Jenna as they sat beside the pool at Westmoreland State Park later that afternoon.

Jenna was surprised. She knew that Bobby hadn't called, and she doubted that Darcy had said anything to Tommy. "How?''

"Pete came by the house. He was close to tears. He was afraid we'd never let him come over again, once we heard what had happened.''

Jenna sighed. Bobby's recitation of Pete's history had touched her, but she had to steel herself against feeling any sympathy for a boy who'd played a part in scaring her daughter.

"I don't want to seem hard-hearted, but what he did was wrong," she told Daisy.

"I know that. You have no idea how it breaks my heart to see the way kids are cruel to one another. It's an everyday occurrence at school."

"Somebody has to stop it," Jenna said, thinking of Bobby's determination to do just that. "Who knows where it could lead?"

"Oh, I think we all know precisely where it can lead," Daisy responded. "We've all had a wake-up call on that score the last couple of years. Stopping it is another issue entirely. Please don't hold it against Pete, though. I know with everything in me that he'll never do anything like that again. He felt terrible, precisely because he'd been through much worse himself and knew how deeply it hurt."

"Bobby's going to talk to the other parents," Jenna reported.

Daisy smiled. "Ah, yes, the avenging angel. Bobby thinks he has to save the world. He always has. If I didn't want him jumping to my defense, I could never tell him about any harmful thing anyone ever said or did to me. My dates were terrified of him."

"Even Walker?" Jenna asked.

Daisy laughed. "The only person on the face of the earth who scares Walker is me," she said proudly. "He's seen my temper. That's one of the reasons I love him. He's completely undaunted by Bobby,

Tucker and King, but a little country schoolteacher like me can make him nervous.''

"Perhaps that's because your means of retaliation can be a bit more, shall we say, personal," Jenna teased.

Daisy gave her an unrepentant grin. "Exactly." She slanted a look in Jenna's direction. "You have the same effect on Bobby, you know."

"I do not," Jenna protested.

"Trust me, you do. And I, for one, think it's wonderful. It's about time my brother took an interest in someone."

"Daisy, don't get any ideas," Jenna warned. "At the moment, Bobby thinks of me more as an annoyance than anything else."

"I know my brother. It may have started that way, but it's changing. I can see a difference in him just in the few days you've been around."

Jenna didn't want to hear that. "I'm just here trying to get a contract for that boardwalk development. That's it," she insisted.

"That's all well and good," Daisy replied. "Having goals is very important, but what's wrong with nabbing a really fine man in the process?"

Put that way, Jenna didn't have a ready answer. But she couldn't allow herself to get distracted from her primary goal. To achieve that, she needed to keep a clear head, and it was already getting harder and harder to think clearly around Bobby Spencer. In fact, when he'd leapt to Darcy's defense earlier, it had taken everything in her to resist the urge to fling herself into his arms and kiss him.

Would that be so terrible? a part of her wondered. Or was that precisely the problem, that it would be incredible, perhaps even unforgettable? Maybe she'd missed the opportunity of a lifetime.

Then again, given Bobby's penchant for rescuing damsels in distress, it was entirely likely that she would get another chance.

9

"You're looking mighty pleased with yourself," Frances noted as she slid into a booth opposite King at Earlene's. "What have you done now?"

King frowned at the smart-mouthed woman. He was awfully fond of her, but she did have an annoying habit of seeing straight through him. He made a probably futile attempt to throw her off the scent. "What makes you think I've done something?"

"History," she said at once, her gaze unflinching.

"If I'd wanted to listen to this kind of abuse, I could have invited one of my kids to lunch," he grumbled.

Her lips quirked with amusement. "Do you think there's one who would have accepted?"

He studied her with a narrowed gaze. She'd done something new with her hair. He couldn't put his finger on it, because he didn't pay much attention to things like that, but she looked younger. Made him think of the spirited girl she'd been. She hadn't taken any guff from him then, either, he recalled with a sigh.

"If you think I'm such all-fired lousy company, why are you here?" he asked.

She laughed at that. "I'll do anything for a free meal, even put up with you."

"As if I believed that for a minute." Getting into

this here and now wasn't something King had planned, but it seemed as good a time as any. "Seriously, why do you put up with me, Frances?"

The twinkle in her eyes faded at his somber tone. "King Spencer, are you asking me what my intentions are?"

"Don't be…" he began to bluster, then sighed. "Yes, that's exactly what I'm asking."

"Oh, King," she said, her expression softening as she reached across the table and patted his hand. "Don't be daft. You know you're good company, at least most of the time."

"Good company," he repeated with a disdainful sniff. "If you can't do any better than that, maybe we're wasting our time. And I, for one, don't have a lot to waste."

She regarded him with obvious surprise. "You're really serious about this, aren't you? I've never known you to be so lacking in self-confidence. Don't you have any idea how much you've come to mean to me over the past few months? We have a lot of history in common. We understand each other. You make me laugh. At our age that means a lot."

King wasn't ready to let it go at that. It sounded as lukewarm and uninteresting as milk left out of the fridge too long. "What about passion, Frances? Do you think we're too old for all that foolishness?"

When color bloomed in her cheeks, he almost regretted the blunt question, but he wanted to know the answer. No, more than that, he needed to know it. They'd been tiptoeing around the subject for months now. King had been resisting the temptation to ask for anything more than a chaste kiss when he took Frances back to her home at night. The polite restraint was wearing on him.

"King, what kind of question is that to ask a lady?" Frances demanded.

She sounded all huffy and indignant, but if King wasn't entirely mistaken, the twinkle was back in her eyes. He risked pushing the point. "An honest one," he said simply. "One that deserves an honest answer."

His gaze held hers as he waited. To her credit, Frances didn't blink once or look away, though he could tell by the way she was clutching her napkin that she was still flustered.

"Okay, then," she said at last. "The thought of more has crossed my mind, but I don't want anybody in town running around behind my back calling me a foolish old woman."

"They wouldn't dare," King said fiercely.

She shook her head. "You, of all people, should know you can't stop gossip, especially in this town."

"Is that the only thing you're afraid of, then? A little gossip?"

"That's enough," she said emphatically. "I have some small measure of standing in this community, as well as a responsible job. I can't just throw all of that away on a whim."

King heard what she was saying, and he was gentleman enough to understand it. An affair could be costly to both of them in terms of the respect they currently enjoyed in Trinity Harbor. And he wasn't ready to offer more. Mary Margaret had died a long time ago, and he'd never been interested in finding a replacement for the woman who'd been the love of his life. Oh, he'd had his share of women friends in the years since, but he'd found those companions elsewhere. Frances was right here in Trinity Harbor, which made the stakes of a relationship entirely different for both of them.

He reached across the table and clasped her hand, liking the feel of the smooth, soft skin against his own rougher hands. "I'll tell you what," he said. "Why don't we take this under advisement?"

"Meaning?"

"We'll both give it some more thought and discuss it again one of these days."

She had the audacity to chuckle at that. "King, you can think it over till the cows come home, but it won't change one basic fact."

He regarded her indignantly. "What's that?"

"You're too blasted selfish to share your life with another human being. If you weren't, you'd have married again years ago."

His heart began to thud, though he wasn't entirely sure if it was caused by panic or irritation. "Who said anything about marriage?"

"No one," Frances said quietly. "Which is precisely my point."

She stood up before King could gather his wits.

"I think I'll skip lunch," she said. "I've lost my appetite."

He started after her, then sank back on the seat. Frances did have her pride. She always had. And right now, she was smarting from a conversation he had insisted on starting with no idea of how he wanted it to end. He was lucky she hadn't snatched up her water glass and tossed the contents in his face.

Glancing out the window, he spotted Frances talking to Daisy, of all people. Judging from her gestures and Daisy's quick looks in his direction, Frances was giving her an earful about what a nincompoop he was. To his surprise, Daisy grinned, then gave Frances a fierce hug.

Two minutes later, his daughter strolled inside and straight over to his table.

"I heard you might be lacking a luncheon companion," she said with blatant amusement. "What did you do to insult Frances? It must have been something, because she's usually incredibly tolerant of your flaws."

"It's none of your business," he said. "What exactly did she tell you?"

"Pretty much the same thing."

"Then what made you think I insulted her?"

"You're in here, looking guilty. She was out there, looking as mad as if someone had stolen one of her prize rose bushes right out of her yard. I can add two and two with the best of them. Don't worry. If you won't tell me, I'm sure I can pry the details out of Earlene."

She probably could, too, King thought with resignation. Earlene might have been clear across the diner, but she saw and heard more than any woman he'd ever had the misfortunate to know.

"If she's smart, Earlene won't tell you a blessed thing," he growled. "I can take my business elsewhere."

"That's an idle threat, and you know it," Daisy said. "You'd be lost if you couldn't come in here to meet your pals and ogle the female tourists in their bikinis and tight T-shirts. You've been in the same rut for thirty years."

"Longer than that, if you must know, but I'm not too old to change," he insisted. In an attempt to get off the topic of his personal life, he regarded his daughter intently. "What are you doing here, anyway?"

"I'm meeting Anna-Louise and Jenna for a late lunch."

King's spirits perked up. "Good. I think I'll stick around. Nobody can wrangle information out of another human being the way Anna-Louise can."

"I doubt she'd consider that a compliment," Daisy pointed out. "Besides, there are no men allowed."

"It's a public place," he said.

"But we're having a private conversation."

"How private can it be in here? You're the one who just finished telling me what a busybody Earlene is."

"Hey, I resent that," Earlene said, slipping up behind him just as he made the comment.

King could feel the color creeping up the back of his neck, but he didn't back down. "If the shoe fits…"

Earlene deliberately tilted the glass of ice water in her hand until it was at a precarious angle. "Frances might be too much of a lady to douse you, but I'm not, King Spencer. Watch what you say to me, or I'll ban you from the premises."

"I'd like to see you try."

Earlene's flashing gaze clashed with his. "As tempting as it is to accept that dare and to soak that hot head of yours, I'm going to resist for the moment. Anna-Louise is on her way in, and she inspires me to try to rise above petty temptations.''

Daisy laughed. ''Daddy, I think that's your cue to leave. You don't want to test Earlene's resolve any more than necessary. And don't hang around over at the counter trying to eavesdrop.''

''You and I had a deal,'' he reminded his daughter as he slid from the booth. ''If you learn anything at all about your brother and this Jenna woman, I expect a full report.''

''Duly noted,'' Daisy said, but her gaze was already shifting to Anna-Louise. ''Daddy was just leaving.''

''Don't let me rush you off,'' his pastor said, greeting him with a grin.

''You're not,'' Daisy said emphatically. ''Daddy needs to get over to the florist's.''

''Oh, really?'' Anna-Louise said, just as King muttered, ''I do?''

''A bouquet of pink roses would go a long way toward making up with Frances,'' Daisy recommended mildly.

''Why do I...?'' he began, then sighed. ''Long-stemmed, I suppose.''

Daisy grinned. ''Exactly. Two dozen, if you're smart.''

This courtship nonsense was for the birds. No wonder Bobby was balking so blasted hard at getting involved in it. King didn't blame him. An image of the smile the flowers would likely put on Frances's face flashed through his mind. Then, again, he thought, courtship did have its rewards.

Jenna was sitting on the end of the fishing pier, Darcy and Tommy beside her. The two of them had their lines lowered into the water and were watching them intently, waiting for any sign of a bite. The sun burned Jenna's shoulders, and she realized that the feeling coursing through her was a lot like contentment…something she hadn't felt in years.

Just then, as if to mock her serenity, her cell phone rang from the depths of her purse. Sighing, she dug through the contents until she found it. Hearing her father's voice when she answered did nothing to restore her fleeting moment of well-being.

"Where are you?" Randall Pennington demanded, his tone imperious.

"Nice to hear your voice, Dad."

He heaved an impatient sigh. "Don't mock me, girl. I came home from dinner and discovered that you'd slipped out of town without a word to anyone."

"That was days ago," she pointed out. "Did you just notice? Besides, Mrs. Jamison knew Darcy and I were going. And I left you a note."

"Which said next to nothing."

"It said I was taking some time off for a vacation," Jenna said defensively, then gathered her resolve and added, "I haven't had one in three years."

"If you wanted time off, all you had to do was ask," her father retorted.

And listen to an hour-long lecture on frittering away

her time, Jenna thought. "You weren't around, and this opportunity came up suddenly."

"Which brings us back to my original question. Where are you?"

Jenna hesitated. She wasn't entirely sure why she hadn't told her father her destination in the original note, but it didn't seem like a good idea now, any more than it had then.

"Jenna?"

"I'd rather not say. Darcy and I are getting some much-needed time together, that's all that counts. If you know where I am, you'll pester me with a dozen details a day until I might as well be back in the office."

"I can do that just as easily by calling your cell phone," her father noted.

Good point, she thought. "Not after today," she said. "Once I hang up, I'm turning it off."

"What if there's an emergency?"

"You mean at work, of course. You, Daniel or Dennis will have to handle it."

"Jenna, I don't like the sound of this. It reminds me of the way you were, you know," he said, his lowered voice making it sound as if he were about to divulge one of the darkest secrets of her life.

"You're going to have to spell it out," she told him impatiently.

"The way you were when you first got mixed up with Nick," he said. "Are you running around with some totally inappropriate man again?"

An image of Bobby Spencer flashed through her mind. Her father couldn't possibly find anything wrong with him, which was yet another reason for her to steer clear of Bobby. She wouldn't want to start accommodating her father's wishes at this late date.

"No," she said mildly. "I'm with Darcy."

"Where is my granddaughter? Let me talk to her," he commanded.

Jenna glanced at her daughter, who was concentrating intently on putting another piece of shrimp onto her hook. She was doing it so gingerly, it was likely to fall off before the hook ever hit the water, which meant there were going to be some mighty well-fed fish in this part of the river.

"She's busy right now," Jenna said.

"Busy? What can a nine-year-old be doing that's more important than talking to her grandfather?"

"She's baiting a hook, Dad." She glanced at her watch. "I've got to go. I have lunch plans and I'm already late."

"Jenna," he protested. "Dammit, Jenna, do not hang up on me."

"I'll have Darcy call you," she promised, then did exactly as she'd threatened: She hung up and turned off the cell phone. That felt so good, she was tempted to chuck it into the river and see if that felt even better, but she resisted the urge. One tiny rebellion for the day was probably all her system could stand.

By the time Jenna had gotten the kids motivated, the fishing gear together and walked to Earlene's, she was a half hour later than the time she'd agreed to meet Daisy and Anna-Louise. Apparently it hadn't mattered, because when she finally walked in, she found the two of them deeply engrossed in a conversation. If it hadn't been for Tommy bolting for the booth, Jenna doubted the two women would have noticed their arrival at all.

"Sorry I'm late. Is everything okay?" she asked as she slid into the booth.

"Everything is fine," Daisy said with what seemed like forced cheer. She grinned at Tommy and Darcy. "Were the fish biting?"

"No," Tommy said, looking thoroughly disgusted. "We didn't catch a single one."

"But they contributed a lot of shrimp to the diet of those swimming by," Jenna said.

"I'm glad we didn't catch any fish," Darcy said. "I think fish are yucky."

Tommy stared at her as if she'd uttered a blasphemy. "What's wrong with *you?* Fishing is so cool! When you catch 'em, you can cut 'em up and clean 'em and they fry 'em for dinner."

"Oh, gross," Darcy said, looking at Tommy as if he'd suggested eating worms.

Jenna bit back a grin. Apparently some of the hero worship was wearing off.

"If you two are going to talk about eating worms and cleaning fish, maybe you should go to the booth across the aisle," Daisy suggested. "There's no point in all of us getting queasy stomachs."

"Awesome," Tommy agreed at once, scrambling from the booth and heading for the other table. "Pete said he'd be by. He can sit with us."

Darcy stopped in the aisle, her expression instantly

troubled. She turned toward Jenna, suddenly hesitant. "Mom?"

Jenna knew that whatever she decided right this minute might make a huge difference, not just for Darcy, but for Pete as well. Daisy had assured her that Pete understood what he'd done and that he was genuinely remorseful. Maybe he deserved a second chance. And they would be right here with plenty of adult supervision.

"It'll be okay," she told her. "I'll be right here. And Pete is Tommy's friend. Nothing's going to happen."

Still looking a bit uncertain, Darcy joined Tommy, but she sat right on the edge of the seat as if she planned to bolt at the first hint of trouble.

"They will be fine," Daisy promised.

Anna-Louise looked from Daisy to Jenna to Darcy and back again. "What am I missing?"

"There was an incident on the boardwalk the other day. A bunch of kids, including Pete, got in Darcy's face. It scared her," Jenna said. "If Bobby hadn't been there to break it up, I'm not sure what would have happened."

"*You* would have handled it," Daisy said with confidence. "These aren't bad kids. They would have listened to you."

Jenna wasn't entirely convinced of that, but she didn't argue the point.

Anna-Louise looked distraught. "I don't like the idea of kids going around bullying other kids. Do you know who was involved besides Pete?"

"I don't," Jenna said. "But Bobby does, and he's

going to talk to the parents. He planned to do it right away, but there was a crisis at the yacht center.''

"Maybe I should go with him," the minister suggested.

"He's already invited me to come along," Jenna told her. "We don't want to gang up on them."

"You mean the way the kids did on Darcy," Anna-Louise said mildly. "No, I'm coming. I'll speak to Bobby and set it up for tonight. Will that work for you?"

"Sure," Jenna said.

"Good. This isn't the kind of thing that should be allowed to drag on. It's best to nip it in the bud. I think a little community service might be a nice punishment. Something that gets all of these kids involved in an activity that teaches tolerance and doesn't leave any time for getting into mischief."

"Any idea what that might be?" Daisy asked.

Anna-Louise shook her head. "No, but I'll have one by tonight." She scooted out of the booth. "I'll call Bobby right now."

Jenna glanced up. "No need. Here he comes now. For a man who has his own restaurant, he spends an awful lot of time in here. Surely he's not looking for recipe ideas?"

Daisy chuckled. "If Bobby's spending a lot of time in here, it's something fairly new. I expect he's been drawn here by the clientele," she said with a pointed look at Jenna.

Jenna felt the heat climb into her cheeks. It only intensified when Bobby slid into the booth right next to her.

"I heard the three of you were here," he said, shooting a look of betrayal at his sister. "Conspiring behind my back, Daisy?"

"Conspiring is such a nasty word," she said. "I prefer to think of it as being supportive of your best interests."

"A convenient spin," Bobby said. He leaned back in the booth and surveyed them all with interest. "So, what's the current topic?"

"Not you, if that's what you're worried about," Anna-Louise chided. "We were talking about that bullying incident involving Darcy. I want to go with you and Jenna when you talk to the parents. And I think we ought to do it tonight, while the incident is still fresh in everyone's minds."

Bobby slanted a look at Jenna. "Did you agree to this?"

"Actually, she pretty much just steamrolled right over me," Jenna said with a grin. "But it's fine."

Bobby nodded. "Okay, then, but it will have to be this afternoon or late tonight. Believe it or not, I do have a restaurant to run."

Anna-Louise grinned at him. "Yet we were just discussing how much time you seem to be spending in here lately. Any particular reason?" she asked, her gaze sliding to Jenna as she spoke.

"I'm sure you have a theory," he retorted.

"But facts are so much more interesting," she shot right back.

Jenna chuckled. She had never known a pastor like Anna-Louise, one who seemed to radiate a certain kind of spiritual calm, yet had a sense of humor and a down-to-earth practicality. For the first time in years, she was actually looking forward to the prospect of going to church on Sunday primarily for the sermon.

Just then Pete wandered in and walked hesitantly up to the booth where Tommy and Darcy were seated. He looked warily at Darcy. "Is it okay if I sit with you guys?"

Darcy seemed surprised that her feelings were being taken into account. She glanced at Tommy, then nodded. "With him, though."

Tommy slid over at once to make room for Pete, and Jenna let out the breath she'd been holding. When Pete said something that made all three of them laugh, she finally let herself relax. Bobby gave her hand a sympathetic squeeze.

"It's a good start," he said quietly. "For both of them."

Jenna nodded. "I know."

"Bobby, who were the other kids involved?" Daisy asked.

He recited several names that Jenna didn't recognize, though the other women obviously did. At the mention of one, J. C. Gates, Anna-Louise and Daisy exchanged a worried look.

"Maybe I should go see J.C.'s parents alone," Anna-Louise said.

For an instant Bobby looked as if he might accept the offer, but then his lips settled into a grim line and he shook his head. Jenna didn't understand the tense undercurrents at all.

"No," he said flatly. "I said I was going to deal with this and I will."

"But, Bobby," Daisy protested, only to be silenced by a harsh look from her brother. "Okay, do what you want to do. Maybe it's for the best."

Anna-Louise's gaze was on Bobby during the exchange, her expression thoughtful. "You know, I think it might be," she said softly.

Bobby scowled. "Don't make too much out of this, you two."

Jenna couldn't stand it any longer. Bobby looked so uptight he might snap. "Would somebody tell me what the deal is with J. C. Gates?"

Anna-Louise and Daisy completely avoided her gaze. Finally Bobby sighed and faced her.

"The reason these two are in such a dither is because J.C.'s mama was once my fiancée and his daddy was my best friend, at least until they ran off together right before the wedding. That pretty much put a crimp in my affection for either one of them." He glanced at the two women across the table. "Did I miss anything important?"

Daisy shot him a defiant look. "You mean besides admitting that they broke your heart?"

"I thought that pretty much went without saying," he said, his expression grim. He slid from the booth without another glance in Jenna's direction. "I'll pick the two of you up at the church at three o'clock. Let's get this over with."

Jenna wanted to rush after him, to tell him how sorry she was, but she could tell from the set of his shoulders that he wouldn't thank her for it.

Earlier she hadn't been especially anxious to confront the parents of the bullies, but now she could honestly say she was looking forward to it. She wanted to get a good look at any woman fool enough to walk away from a man whose heart was as decent and strong as Bobby Spencer's.

10

Bobby would have preferred to eat worms grilled in garlic to walking into Ann-Marie's house to face her and his former best friend, but a deal was a deal. He'd promised Jenna that he was going to speak to all the parents of the kids involved in bullying Darcy. That included Ann-Marie and Lonnie. He'd accepted that before he'd ever made the promise.

Maybe it was time to face the past. He'd caught glimpses of his ex-fiancée over the years, but they hadn't exchanged a single word. As for Lonnie, after one incident when they'd accidently encountered each other outside of Town Hall, his one-time pal steered as clear of Bobby as Bobby did of him. Maybe one bloody nose and a black eye were all Lonnie was prepared to take to have the woman he'd stolen from Bobby.

As if Anna-Louise sensed and understood his unspoken turmoil, she insisted on making the Gateses their first stop after their late start. It was past five by the time they reached the house. Even Jenna was subdued as they went up the front walk and rang the bell of the small home a few blocks away from the river. The unkempt yard was littered with bicycles and toy cars, testimony to the houseful of children Ann-Marie and Lonnie had had in short order after their elopement.

At ten, J.C. was their oldest, a boy who was big for his age, just as Lonnie had been. He was accepted by older boys because of his size and the meanness he'd demonstrated in the incident with Darcy. Bullies tended to congregate, no matter what their ages, especially during the summer months when they all had time on their hands and not enough supervision.

When Ann-Marie opened the front door and found Bobby among the uninvited guests standing on the small concrete stoop, her mouth dropped open. Her stunned, devastated gaze immediately shifted to Anna-Louise, as if the minister had somehow betrayed her by bringing Bobby along. She never looked at Jenna at all.

"Good evening, Ann-Marie. I hope we're not disturbing you," Anna-Louise said mildly. "There's something important we need to discuss."

As if recovering from a trance, Ann-Marie shook her head, then stood aside. "Of course. Where are my manners? Come in, please." She hesitated, then added, "Hello, Bobby. It's been a long time."

"Indeed," he said curtly, his tension no less palpable than his ex-fiancée's.

Anna-Louise stepped in. "This is Jenna Kennedy. Jenna, Ann-Marie Gates."

Despite the circumstances, Jenna politely held out her hand. Bobby couldn't help noticing the contrast. Though the two women were approximately the same age, Ann-Marie looked at least five years older. Her once-vibrant skin was dull. Her cloud of auburn hair had been inexpertly cut into a short style that didn't flatter her at all. Even so, Bobby waited for that once-familiar *ping* of awareness, the little zip of his pulse.

But there was nothing. All these years, even the thought of a chance encounter had filled him with dread, and now, *nothing*. Ann-Marie had lost her power to excite him...or to hurt him. He should have felt an overwhelming sense of relief, but instead all he felt was sorrow for all the years he'd wasted hating her for what she and Lonnie had done to him.

He looked into eyes that had once been as familiar as his own. "Is Lonnie home?"

She shook her head. "He should be here any minute, though. What's this about?"

"It's about J.C.," Bobby said.

Alarm flared in her eyes and her gaze sought Anna-Louise's.

"Sweetie, it's okay. Nothing's happened to him," the minister said at once. "But there was an incident we thought you should be aware of."

"What kind of an incident?" Ann-Marie demanded, her tone turning defensive. She scowled at Bobby. "I don't know what you're accusing him of, but using that boy is a rotten way to get back at me."

Bobby was about to snap that this had nothing to do with their past, but Jenna touched a silencing hand to his arm.

"Actually this has to do with me, or more precisely, with my daughter," Jenna told her.

Ann-Marie looked completely baffled now. "I'm sure J.C. doesn't even know your daughter. Do you even live here?"

"Actually, no," Jenna said. "I'm here on business. Darcy is with me. We were on the boardwalk a couple of days ago. Bobby and I were discussing the development project and Darcy wandered away. A few minutes later she was surrounded by a group of older boys. She was in tears, because they were taunting her."

"J.C. was one of those boys," Anna-Louise said.

Ann-Marie regarded them all with indignation, but she turned the heat of her anger on Jenna. "I don't believe it. How would you know, anyway?" she demanded. "Do you even know my son?"

"No, she doesn't, but I do," Bobby told her quietly. "And it's not the first time I've seen him bullying another kid."

"Kids pick on each other. That's life," Ann-Marie said with a dismissive shrug. She cast a hard look at Jenna. "Your daughter needs to learn to cope with it, instead of running crying to Mommy."

"Oh, really? Would you feel the same way if it were your child being harassed?" Jenna demanded. "What if some older kids cornered J.C. when there were no adults around? How would you like that?"

"Like I said, kids learn to deal with it. Life's not always fair," Ann-Marie insisted stubbornly.

Bobby lost patience with her head-buried-in-the-sand attitude. "How many school shootings have been precipitated by kids bullying a classmate?" he asked bluntly. "You do see the news on TV, don't you? Read the papers? This isn't a joke, Ann-Marie. It's indefensible. If parents don't take it seriously, it can have serious repercussions. We're here because we're trying to nip this kind of stuff in the bud. We need your cooperation, not a litany of excuses.''

"Repercussions? In Trinity Harbor? Don't be absurd,'' Ann-Marie said, refusing to be convinced.

"Ann-Marie, bad things can happen anywhere,'' Anna-Louise insisted quietly. "Kids are kids, no matter where they live. As you've conceded, they can sometimes be cruel. And their victims can just as easily reach the breaking point here as in any other community.''

"I still say you're making a mountain out of a molehill.'' She shot a scathing look at Bobby. "From the minute I married Lonnie, you've been looking for a way to get even. Is this it? You're going to go after my son?''

"Dammit, Ann-Marie, this doesn't have anything to do with you and me.'' Bobby leapt to his feet and began to pace. He paused in front of her and forced himself to meet her gaze with an unflinching look. "It's about a tragedy waiting to happen. I saw the terror on that little girl's face. She's nine years old, Ann-Marie. Was anyone in town allowed to pick on you when you were nine?''

"No, but—''

"And J.C.'s only ten,'' Bobby retorted, cutting her off. "If he's involved in tormenting another kid at ten, what will he be doing a couple of years from now? Setting fire to somebody's pet? Shooting another kid?''

"Like you really give a damn about J.C.,'' Ann-Marie said. "He's the reason I ran off with Lonnie when I did, and you know it. I didn't have any choice.''

Bobby felt the color drain out of his face. "What?" He had been away by the time J.C. was born. He hadn't known the boy's exact birth date and he'd never done the math.

Watching his stunned reaction, shock registered on Ann-Marie's face. "You didn't know?"

"Nope. Afraid not," he said wryly. "So, you see, none of what we're telling you has a blessed thing to do with the past. It's all about the here and now."

Anna-Louise stepped in. "Bobby's right. Let's concentrate on the present. You and Lonnie have to give this some thought and deal with J.C. before the problem gets out of hand. I'll be happy to help in any way I can."

"Keeping him away from the older boys might be a start," Bobby said.

"They're all from good families," Ann-Marie protested, still looking shaken over her inadvertent revelation.

"Even kids from good families need guidance from time to time," Bobby said. "I intend to talk to all the parents tonight. We didn't just target you."

Ann-Marie sighed. "I'm sorry that I overreacted," she said grudgingly. "It was just seeing you after all this time. It was the last thing I expected when I opened the door."

Bobby met her gaze. "Believe me, I can understand that." For just an instant the old chemistry was there. There wasn't anything sexual about it, though. It had more to do with a memory of the way they'd once been able to read each other's thoughts. The silence grew until Anna-Louise cut in.

"There are some groups at church J.C. might enjoy," she said.

Ann-Marie broke eye contact with Bobby and nodded. "I'll speak to Lonnie and to J.C." For the first time, she regarded Jenna with an expression of real regret. "I'm sorry your daughter was scared. But J.C. would never have hurt her."

"But he did," Jenna replied. "Sometimes words and threats can be just as terrifying when you're only nine."

"And alone J.C. might not harm another kid, but if he's being goaded by older, meaner youngsters, there's no telling what he might do to fit in," Anna-Louise warned.

"Trust me, we will deal with this," Ann-Marie said firmly, sounding as if she was no longer in denial.

Bobby gave her a curt nod of satisfaction. "We'll be going, then."

Outside, he forced a smile at Jenna and Anna-Louise. "After this, the rest are going to be a piece of cake."

Jenna regarded him sympathetically. "We don't have to see all of the other parents tonight."

"Yes, we do," Bobby insisted. "Otherwise, J.C. will talk to his buddies, find out no one's been to see their parents, and Ann-Marie will conclude that we did single out J.C. because of past history."

"Bobby has a point," Anna-Louise said.

Jenna's gaze remained locked with his. "You're sure?"

He nodded. "Like I said, after this, the others will be a piece of cake."

Besides, the longer he could postpone thinking about Ann-Marie's revelation about the timing of her pregnancy, the better off he would be. He'd had a whole half hour of being almost over his resentment of what had happened years ago, when she'd dropped that little bombshell. Now he wasn't sure what he was feeling. Maybe nothing. It was as if the part of him that had stirred to life when he'd met Jenna had just died all over again. Of all the things he'd hated Ann-Marie for, it had never occurred to him that she might have gotten pregnant with Lonnie's baby while she was still engaged to him.

Jenna couldn't help slanting worried looks at Bobby for the rest of the evening. He was right, none of the other visits were half as fraught with tension as their meeting with Ann-Marie. They bumped into a lot of denial, but she'd been pleased that not one single parent had reacted with indifference. Once convinced of the seriousness of the problem thanks to Anna-Louise's calm, persuasive statements, each and every one had agreed to separate their sons from the other troublemakers.

As they left the last home, Anna-Louise looked pleased. "Let's keep our fingers crossed that the divide-and-conquer strategy works," she said. "And maybe some of these boys will get involved in other activities that will work off some of their misdirected energy."

"We can always pray," Bobby said wryly.

Anna-Louise grinned at him. "Now you're talking. Okay, you two, I'm exhausted and I have an impatient husband who's probably waiting at home to be fed."

"Daisy said she'd keep something warm until we got there to pick up Darcy. You could call Richard and come along with us," Bobby suggested. "Richard could meet us there."

"Thanks just the same, but I'd like to be alone with my husband, if you know what I mean," the pastor said with a wink.

Jenna chuckled at Bobby's startled expression. "I think we both know exactly what you mean," she said.

"Not that I needed to," Bobby said with heartfelt dismay. "By all means, though, go home. Do you need a ride?"

"Nope. It's only a few blocks, and the walk will do me good."

After she'd gone and they were on their way to Daisy's, Jenna looked at Bobby. "She really is amazing, isn't she? I've never known anyone like her. Not only does she radiate sort of an inner goodness, but she puts herself on the line and gets involved. The church and the community are lucky to have her."

"I can't speak for the church," Bobby said, "but the town surely is. And Richard is making his own kind of contribution by publishing a newspaper that doesn't flinch at taking tough stands on local issues."

"You don't go to her church?" Jenna asked, surprised. "From something Daisy said, I thought your whole family did."

"I haven't been much lately," Bobby said, his expression neutral.

The reason finally dawned on Jenna. "Because of your former fiancée."

He nodded, but before she could say anything more, he held up his hand. "I'm not going to discuss any of that and I would appreciate it if you didn't bring it up around Daisy. My sister will pester me to death about it. In case you haven't noticed, Daisy is a nag."

"I hadn't noticed, but I certainly won't say a word if that's what you want."

"It is," he said flatly.

"Can I say one more thing, though, before we let the matter drop?"

Bobby sighed. "Could I stop you?"

She returned his resigned look evenly. "Yes."

He gave her a disbelieving look, then laughed. "In return for that astounding offer, you deserve to have your say. What is it?"

"A woman who would sleep with her fiancé's best friend is no loss. If she did it before the wedding, she would have done it after. Lonnie did you a favor, Bobby. Try to remember that and keep what she told you tonight in perspective. She only said it to hurt you all over again."

For the longest time, Bobby didn't respond. Jenna thought perhaps she had gone too far, touched an open wound she had no business being anywhere near.

When he finally did meet her gaze again, something had changed. He almost looked at peace.

"Thank you," he said quietly. "Daisy said something like that to me once—she was the only one in the family who even dared to broach the subject—but I dismissed it because she was family and therefore biased. Hearing it from an objective outsider actually helps.''

''I'm glad. I may not know you very well, and we may have our own differences to work through, but I know one thing, Bobby Spencer. You're one of the good guys. Ann-Marie's the idiot.'' She grinned at him and deliberately set out to lighten the mood as they pulled up in front of Daisy's. ''And just so you know, I intend to test your tolerance by pestering you until you agree to look at my complete proposal for the boardwalk. I should have it finished in another day or two. I'm not an architect or an artist, but I think you'll be able to get the idea.''

He cut the car's engine and turned to face her. ''Funny thing about that,'' he said. ''You've been giving me ideas since the moment we met.''

His gaze met hers, and suddenly something between them shifted. Anticipation simmered between them. He reached out and skimmed her cheek with unsteady fingers. A shudder washed through Jenna even before he lowered his head and touched his lips to hers.

The kiss was fleeting, no more than a quick skim of heated flesh across heated flesh. It couldn't possibly have meant anything, yet Jenna's heart thundered; it hadn't been deep or lingering or demanding, but it had been better than all of Nick Kennedy's most dangerous kisses rolled into one.

Bad idea, she thought a little desperately as she reached for the door handle and fled the car. She was still fighting for composure when Bobby joined her on the sidewalk. Kisses were the one sure way to mess up a business proposition. The waters surrounding this project of hers were muddy enough without bringing hormones into play. If—no, when, she thought fiercely—Bobby agreed to let Pennington and Sons have the job, she wanted there to be absolutely no doubt in her own mind about how she'd won the contract.

"That can't happen again," she said staunchly, eyeing him with a determined look.

"It shouldn't," he agreed, though there was amusement lurking in the depths of his eyes as he met her gaze. "But something tells me it will."

Yeah, Jenna thought ruefully. She was pretty sure of the same thing. Something that felt that good, that wicked, was going to beg to be repeated. And her track record for resisting temptation wasn't exactly sterling.

Five pairs of expectant eyes looked up when Bobby and Jenna eventually walked into Daisy's kitchen. Bobby saw his sister take in Jenna's flushed face and could almost read her mind. Daisy was leaping to conclusions faster than King would have if he'd been on the premises. Bobby frowned at her, though he doubted his forbidding expression would dampen Daisy's enthusiasm for whatever theory she'd come up with.

"You two have been lurking around outside for a long time," Walker commented, no doubt echoing his wife's thoughts. "Anything going on we need to know about?"

Bobby's scowl deepened. "We were just discussing everything that happened tonight," he said flatly. "That's it."

"Must have been a lively conversation," Walker noted with a pointed glance at Jenna.

The flush in Jenna's cheeks deepened, but she kept her gaze perfectly level with Walker's. "Indeed, it was," she agreed briskly, turning her back to pour herself a glass of tea at the counter.

"How's everything here?" she asked over her shoulder. "Darcy, have you been behaving for Daisy and Walker?"

"She's been an absolute angel," Daisy said at once. "She, Tommy and Pete helped me fix dinner. Darcy made the biscuits. Sit down and have something before everything gets cold."

Daisy's command forced Jenna to turn around. The bright patches of color in her cheeks had faded, but there was still a hint of guilt in her eyes. Bobby pulled out a chair for her, then took the empty seat beside her.

"Looks good," he told Daisy. "I'm relieved there's some left. I'm starved."

"Can we go outside?" Tommy pleaded. "We've eaten everything on our plates."

Daisy made an elaborate pretense of studying the plates, then shooed the three of them outside. "I'll call you when it's time for dessert." As the screen door slammed behind, she shouted, "And stay away from the river!"

"Yeah, yeah," Tommy shouted back as if he'd heard it a million times before.

"How did the meetings with the parents go?" Walker asked. "Daisy filled me in."

"We ran into some heavy denial," Bobby admitted.

"But I think they'd all come around by the time we left. Just in case, though, alert Tucker and the other deputies to keep an eye out if they see these kids congregating again."

"Will do," Walker agreed at once.

All during the exchange, Bobby noted that his sister's gaze never once left his face. He could practically hear the wheels turning in her head.

"Well?" she prodded finally. "What about Ann-Marie?"

"I included her when I said how all the parents reacted," he said defensively. "And that's all I intend to say on that subject."

"Bobby," Daisy protested.

"Daisy," he mimicked.

His sister heaved a heartfelt sigh. "Okay, I won't pry."

"Ha!" he muttered, but reached for her hand. "Thanks, sis."

"Wait till Daddy hears about this, though," she murmured.

Bobby stilled. "Why would Daddy have to hear a single word about any of this?"

Daisy regarded him with an impatient look. "Because this is Trinity Harbor. Word will leak out that you went to see Ann-Marie. I guarantee you that he'll know about it by morning. I also guarantee that he will be on your doorstep wondering whether you've taken leave of your senses." She grinned. "What do you think, Jenna? Is my brother of sound mind?"

Jenna laughed. "I can see why there might be cause to question it, but in general, I'd have to say yes."

"I agree," Walker said.

Bobby scowled at the lot of them. "Well, thank you for the testimonials. I'll be sure to call you as witnesses when Daddy starts to cross-examine me. Everyone free in the morning?"

"Not me," Jenna said at once. "I'm finishing those sketches."

Walker held up his hands. "I'm on duty tomorrow."

Bobby glanced at his sister. "You? You have someplace better you need to be?"

"Nope. It's summer vacation. I'm free as a bird."

"Good. Then you can meet me at Earlene's for breakfast and we can preempt Daddy's visit to the yacht center. We'll have this whole discussion over and done with by eight o'clock."

"I think you're being overly optimistic," she said. "But I'll be there." She glanced around the table. "Everybody ready for dessert? I baked a strawberry-rhubarb pie and there's vanilla ice cream to go with it."

Walker's eyes lit up. "Now you're talking."

"Should I call the kids?" Jenna asked.

"No," Bobby and Walker said in a chorus. At her startled look, they both grinned.

"More for us," Bobby explained. "You'll understand once you've tasted Daisy's strawberry-rhubarb pie."

Daisy shook her head. "You two men are such pigs. Neither one of you likes to share, which, I might add, sets a very bad example. But that is exactly why I baked two pies. Jenna, call the kids."

Bobby sat back as Jenna stepped outside and hollered for Darcy, Tommy and Pete. The three of them came racing inside, filling the kitchen with the sound of laughter. The commotion could have been overwhelming, but he loved it. He realized just how much he wanted all of this for himself.

Once Ann-Marie had devastated him by turning to his best friend, Bobby had pushed all thoughts of marriage and family firmly aside. He'd run off to Europe to study cooking, burying himself in the excitement and adventure of being on his own in France and Italy, of learning the skills of his trade from a range of international master chefs.

By the time he'd come back to Trinity Harbor, he'd thought his heart was healed, but back then one glimpse of Ann-Marie with her new little family had been enough to tear him apart all over again. From that moment on, he'd shut himself off emotionally. He'd bought the yacht center and buried himself in the work it took to turn it around and make it a successful restaurant and marina. Then he'd begun acquiring riverfront property.

But his workaholic days were over, he thought, watching Jenna move to Daisy's side to help her scoop ice cream onto the pie. She fit in here, he realized with a sense of amazement. He barely knew her. She'd only met his sister a few days ago. And yet right here and now, he could imagine her being in his life forever.

The fact that such a thought had even crossed his mind scared the hell out of him.

He glanced across the table and saw Walker studying him with a commiserating look.

"Goner," Walker mouthed silently, his amusement plain.

Bobby cast a surreptitious glance back at Jenna, then turned back to his brother-in-law with a shrug. Why even bother to deny it?

Still, he leaned in Walker's direction and said in a low voice, "You say one word to my sister and you will live to regret it."

Walker laughed. "My lips are sealed," he said, his grin spreading. "For now."

Daisy paused as she was about to set a plate in front of her husband. "Sealed about what?" she said, eyeing the two of them curiously.

Walker tugged her into his lap and snagged the plate. "It wouldn't be a secret if I told you, would it?"

Heat flared at once in Daisy's eyes. "Oh, I think I know how to get it out of you," she said, then stood up primly and straightened her T-shirt, pulling it just a little tighter across her breasts in the process. "But that can wait till later."

"Hey, you two," Bobby protested. "There are children in the room, to say nothing of the fact that *I'm* here. There are some things a brother does not need to see."

Daisy winked at him. "And some that could be a lesson to him," she teased.

Bobby glanced at Jenna, who was watching the by-play with evident fascination. "Yeah," he said quietly. "I'll definitely keep that in mind."

11

King stared at the headline on the front page of *The Trinity Harbor Weekly* and muttered a curse. There it was again. His family was stirring up talk all over town. It was getting so he was afraid to show his face.

Despite that, he braced himself for a barrage of questions and headed for Earlene's. Right after he had a substantial breakfast, he intended to find his son and ask a few questions of his own, such as why Bobby had gotten it into his head to pay a visit to that trollop who'd humiliated him all those years ago. King had heard all about the social call Bobby had paid on Ann-Marie the night before…while her husband wasn't home, no less. What none of those reporting had seemed to know was why the ice had thawed between those two after all these years.

He spotted Pete and the rest of his buddies in their usual booth by the window, but before he could join them, he was waylaid by his son. King frowned at Bobby, not at all sure he wanted to get into the various private matters he'd intended to discuss right here in public. He'd figured once he'd listened to more of the gossip he'd have time to work up a really good head of steam before having his little face-to-face with Bobby over at the yacht center.

"What are you doing here?" King groused.

"Same as you, I imagine," Bobby retorted cheerfully. "Having breakfast. Daisy's with me. Care to join us?"

Though it had been phrased as a question, King got the distinct impression that Bobby didn't intend to take no for an answer. King cast a longing look at his friends, then shrugged. "Might as well," he said and followed his son.

He frowned at the sight of Daisy's expectant, amused expression. "What's this? Some kind of ambush or something?"

"Consider it a preemptive strike," Bobby said. "I wanted to be the first to tell you that I was over at Ann-Marie's last night."

"Too late," King said succinctly.

Daisy's grin spread. "Told you," she said to Bobby.

Bobby seemed unconcerned. "At least you can't complain that I didn't tell you myself," he said to King.

"Seems to me you're a little late, but I'll let that pass," King said magnanimously. He had other fish to fry. "Mind telling me what possessed you to go scurrying off to her place after all this time? I thought you were finally getting some sense, now that that Kennedy woman is hanging around."

"Leave Jenna out of this," Bobby said, his good humor vanishing in a heartbeat. "I'm not discussing her with you." He cast a pointed look at his sister. "Or anyone else, for that matter."

King took comfort from the fact that Daisy smirked knowingly. He was pretty sure that meant she knew things that King didn't. Positive things. He'd have to find some way to corner her later, but for now he intended to concentrate on getting an explanation about last night's activities.

"Look, son, you know how people in this town talk about everything a Spencer does. You dropping by to visit with your ex-fiancée is big news. If you intend to make a fool of yourself, that's up to you, but remember that what you do reflects on all of us."

"I'm not worried," Daisy said cheerfully.

Bobby scowled at his sister, then turned his attention to King. "Did any of the self-appointed gossips who called you happen to mention that both Anna-Louise and Jenna were with me?"

Now that put an entirely different spin on things, King decided, taking heart. He should have known the callers had left out something that would have rendered the gossip far less juicy.

"No," he conceded.

Bobby regarded him with tolerant amusement. "Feel better?"

King stubbornly shook his head. "I won't feel better until I know what you were doing there. For all I know, Anna-Louise was trying to negotiate a truce between you and Ann-Marie. One of her missions in life seems to be making peace between old enemies. Once she has everyone getting along like a house-afire, this town will be downright boring."

"Actually, that was an interesting by-product of the meeting," Bobby told him.

"Dammit, son—"

"Simmer down," Bobby said, cutting off the tirade

King was about to launch. "That wasn't why we went there."

As Bobby described the bullying incident, King's hackles rose. "Have you spoken to Tucker about this?"

"I mentioned it," Bobby said.

"I should hope so. Those kids have been hanging around down by the river for too long now with no adult supervision. It was bound to take a nasty turn eventually. What about the other parents? Did you talk to them?"

"Every one of them," Bobby confirmed. "Everyone's taking it seriously. And I suspect you'll be hearing a sermon on the topic this Sunday in church. Anna-Louise doesn't intend to let the subject drop."

King turned his gaze on Daisy. "Much of this stuff go on in school?"

"I hear some, but there's probably a lot more I don't hear," she said, her expression thoughtful. "I think I'll recommend that the teachers have some workshops on how to deal with this before school starts in September."

King nodded approvingly. "I imagine Anna-Louise and Frances would both have some valuable things to say."

"Speaking of Frances, are you two still seeing each other?" Bobby asked, leaning back in the booth and feigning innocence. "She hasn't been out at Cedar Hill for Sunday dinner for a couple of weeks now."

"She's been busy," King said, instantly defensive.

Daisy regarded him with alarm. "She didn't break

up with you after that fight the two of you had, did she?"

"What fight?" Bobby asked.

Daisy shrugged. "All I know is that Daddy said something to offend her and she went tearing out of here." She peered at King. "Did you send flowers?"

"Of course I did. I told you I would, didn't I? I went straight from here to the florist. Picked out a real pretty bunch of posies."

"And?" Bobby prodded. "Did you two make up?"

The truth was, King hadn't had the nerve to call Frances after the prickly way she'd reacted to the topic of moving their relationship forward to another level. And she hadn't even called to thank him. Instead, she'd sent a polite little note to the house: *"The flowers were lovely. Thank you. Frances."* Prim and to the point, he thought, still disgusted with the impersonal nature of her response. She hadn't exactly left the door open for further contact.

"Not yet," King said tersely, all but squirming under their attentive gazes.

"Why not?" Daisy demanded. "Daddy, you know that Frances is the best thing to happen to you in years. Don't you dare let her slip away."

"Oh, for goodness' sakes, it's not as if I asked the woman to marry me and she turned me down," King retorted impatiently. "We've just been out a few times. It's no big deal if we go on seeing each other or if we don't."

He realized Bobby was studying him with a thoughtful expression.

"Is that the problem, Daddy? Is Frances expecting marriage?"

King balked at getting into that. It was none of Bobby's concern. Daisy's, either, for that matter. "I am not discussing this with either one of you. It's between Frances and me. We're both adults. We're both perfectly capable of deciding what we do and don't want."

Bobby hooted at the response and grinned at Daisy. "I guess he told us."

"Sure did," she agreed, grinning just as broadly.

"And I, for one, intend to remind you of those precise words the next time you decide to interfere in my love life," Bobby declared.

"As if you even had one," King muttered, not meeting his son's gaze.

"Well, if and when I do, you can be sure that you'll be the last to know," Bobby replied.

King chuckled at that. "Not unless you're carrying on in Richmond or *Baltimore*," he said, deliberately placing a little emphasis on Jenna's hometown. "Anything you do in Trinity Harbor, I'll hear about within the hour."

Bobby sighed heavily in apparent recognition of the truth in King's words. "What ever possessed me to come back here, when I could have stayed in Paris?"

King gaped at the suggestion. "This is home," he said with the indignation of a true believer in the supremacy of the American South. "Anyplace else in this country would come in a poor second. You leave the United States of America, and it's no contest at all."

Bobby met his gaze. For an instant, it looked as if he might make some smart-alecky reply just to annoy King, but he finally shrugged. "Yeah, bottom line, I guess you're right. But there are days when you make being here a real challenge."

"Well, of course, I do," King said proudly. "Any father that doesn't give his children fits to make them better people isn't doing his job."

"Any idea when you'll consider the job done?" Bobby inquired dryly.

King grinned at him. "I'll keep you posted."

The mystery of the missing carousel horse, which was front page news in *The Trinity Harbor Weekly* for two straight editions, got picked up by the Richmond media, then slowly spread around the state. Just when he'd thought he could put the ridiculous incident behind him, Bobby started hearing from classmates he hadn't talked to since they'd moved out of town ten years ago. He was delighted he was able to provide so much blasted amusement for everyone.

It was all Jenna's fault. If she hadn't had the cockamamie idea to send that horse in the first place, none of this would be happening. His resentment of that bubbled up until it was just as heated as it had been on the Sunday he'd found the horse on his front lawn. He determinedly set out to ignore the attraction that had been simmering in the interim.

As a result, he'd flatly refused to see Jenna on any of the occasions when she'd dropped by his office with her completed proposal for the boardwalk. Maggie was fit to be tied.

"I am not lying to her one more time," she told Bobby firmly, scowling at him across his desk. "You promised that woman an appointment and you're going to give her one, or you can kiss me goodbye. Frankly, I can't think of anyone else in town who'd take the job, either."

"Good for you," Daisy said, walking into his office without even bothering to knock.

This was all he needed, he thought with a resigned sigh. It was the first time Bobby had seen his sister since the morning they'd confronted King at Earlene's. He'd been deliberately avoiding her, too, since he knew she'd be an even worse nag than Maggie about his bad manners, to say nothing of the fact that he'd gone back on a promise. In fact, she grinned at his secretary now and shooed Maggie toward the door.

"I'll take over," Daisy said, looking like a woman on a mission.

"Thank you, Lord," Maggie replied fervently, casting a gaze heavenward. "I certainly can't get through to him."

She took her own sweet time about leaving, though, probably because she was hoping to overhear at least the start of Daisy's lecture. Unfortunately for Maggie, his sister kept silent until the door was closed. Then she sat down opposite him.

"Okay, what's going on?" she asked, her penetrating gaze never once wavering from his face.

Bobby refused to flinch. If he'd learned nothing else after all these years of being her brother, he'd learned that it didn't pay to let Daisy know when she had the upper hand.

"I have no idea what you're talking about," he said mildly.

Daisy rolled her eyes. "You're avoiding Jenna. Why?"

"What did she do, come running to you, begging for help?"

"She mentioned that you refused to see her or even to look at her proposals for the boardwalk. Backing out on a promise is not good business, and you know it, Bobby. So something else must be going on. I decided on my own to see what it was."

"*This* is what's going on," Bobby said, picking up a stack of clippings and waving them under Daisy's nose. "This place is the laughingstock of the entire state, thanks to that woman."

"Really?" she said, sounding doubtful. "Because somebody stole a carousel horse from your front lawn?"

The way Daisy phrased it, it didn't sound that bad. "Because it was there in the first place," he muttered. It didn't help that someone in town had sold a snapshot of him in his boxers to one of the state wire services. He pointed to the picture. "I look like an idiot."

"Oh, you do not. You're gorgeous. Women everywhere are probably fanning themselves over their cereal just at the sight of you."

Now it was Bobby's turn to roll his eyes.

"You ought to consider all of this a blessing," Daisy advised. "Every single slip at the marina is filled. Your restaurant hasn't had so much statewide publicity since you opened it. It's been booked solid.

I know, because Walker and I couldn't get a reservation all weekend long.''

That was news to Bobby. He knew they'd been busy, but he'd had no idea his sister had been turned away. "You should have called me," he apologized. "There's always room for family."

She regarded him impatiently. "You're missing my point. You're making a fortune as a result of all this publicity. You should be thanking Jenna, instead of shutting her out as if she ruined your business. And what about Darcy? Ever since you rushed in to save the day, you've been that little girl's hero, and you've been ignoring her, too."

Bobby sighed. Daisy was right. He'd been deluged with customers for the last two weeks. Even midweek, the place was packed.

And every single one of those nights, Jenna with her accusing eyes and her green-haired daughter had been at a prime table where he couldn't miss them as he came and went from the kitchen. Apparently *they* had no trouble getting reservations. That was Maggie's doing, no doubt. He'd had to harden his heart and make himself ignore Darcy's hopeful expression, then pretend he hadn't seen how shattered the kid had looked when he'd passed by without a word. Daisy was right about that, too. He was a complete louse.

"Okay, I'm not being fair," he conceded grudgingly. "What do you suggest?"

"That depends on what you want from Jenna."

"I don't want anything from her. She's the one who showed up here in town."

Daisy regarded him with exasperation. "Oh, get

over it. At the very least, you need to look at the drawings she's done," she told him. "If you hate them, tell her that and send her on her way. That'll be kinder than letting her hang around here for days on end at her own expense."

"This little vacation isn't coming out of her pocket," he retorted. "It's a business expense."

"That's not the way I hear it," Daisy insisted. "She's here without her father's permission or support."

Bobby's gaze narrowed. "Are you telling me this proposal of hers isn't even from Pennington and Sons?"

"That's exactly what I'm telling you—at least not officially, it isn't. This is Jenna's big chance to make an impression on her father. She's taking a huge risk. You ought to be able to relate to that. You, Tucker and I have spent a lifetime trying to prove ourselves to Daddy."

Bobby sighed.

Apparently sensing victory, Daisy added, "There's just one big difference. We've always known that whatever grumbling he might do, Daddy is always in our corner when push comes to shove. Jenna's not so lucky."

"Okay, okay, I get it." He paused, then asked, "Have you looked at the drawings?" He knew perfectly well that the question was a tacit admission that he was curious. Let Daisy make of that whatever she wanted to.

"Yes, and they're wonderful," she said, her eyes sparkling with enthusiasm. "Jenna knows exactly what this town needs, Bobby. She understands Trinity Harbor and what it can be, the same way you do. I've heard you talk about what you envision, and it's as if Jenna's been right inside your head.''

She hesitated, then added, ''Which brings me to another thing. I don't think that's the only thing the two of you have in common. Don't throw away the chance to have someone really special in your life. When the two of you were at my house a couple of weeks ago, it was the first time in years that I've seen you genuinely happy.''

Bobby barely stifled a groan. His sister was right about that, too. He really, really hated admitting that, because it gave her a decided edge that she'd never let him forget.

''I'll consider what you said,'' he finally acknowledged grudgingly.

''Bobby,'' she chided.

''Okay, okay, I'll see Jenna's drawings.''

''And make up with Darcy.''

''Yes, ma'am.''

Her grin spread. ''And since I'm on a roll, take Jenna out on a real date.''

''Don't press your luck.''

She shrugged. ''It was just an idea. Will you be at Cedar Hill for dinner on Sunday?''

''Of course, why?''

''Just wondering,'' she said, feigning innocence.

''I imagine Jenna and Darcy will be there,'' Bobby guessed.

''Could be,'' she conceded. ''Just in case you haven't followed through on your own by then.''

"I can run my own love life," he reminded her.

"So you've said, but I'm with Daddy on this one. Until you show a little more evidence of that, I think I'll help out a little."

"Why aren't the two of you on Tucker's case?" he asked plaintively. "He's the oldest."

"I don't know Daddy's reasons, but mine are easy. Jenna's here. And you've been ready for a new relationship for a long time. You've just been fighting it."

"In other words, you're practicing on me, because you think I'm easy?"

She laughed. "Something like that."

"What if it doesn't work? Is Tucker off the hook indefinitely?"

Daisy regarded him with the same haughty look she'd always used to put him firmly in his place. "As if it's not going to work," she chided.

Bobby sighed as his sister sailed out of his office. He was doomed, all right.

The first that Jenna knew about the extensive media coverage of the missing horse was when the phone rang in her hotel room and her father was on the other end of the line. She was so startled by the sound of his voice that she almost dropped the phone.

"Have you had detectives looking for me?" she demanded indignantly.

"I haven't had to," he retorted. "You're big news in the Baltimore paper these days."

Jenna's heart began to thud dully. "What are you talking about?"

"Daniel handed me a clipping this morning. Pennington and Sons was mentioned prominently in an article about the revitalization of a boardwalk area in Trinity Harbor, Virginia, wherever that is.''

Jenna sank down on the edge of the bed. "Oh, my God.''

"Yes, I can see why you might be upset,'' her father said sarcastically. "Especially since there is no such project on our schedule. Can you imagine what would have happened if the reporter had called me for a comment? What the hell were you thinking, Jenna? Have you completely lost your mind as well as that blasted antique carousel horse? And where did you get the money for that, I'd like to know? You didn't dip into your trust fund, did you? I swear, if you did anything that ridiculous, I will personally see to it that whatever's left of that money is tied up for years so that you can't get a dime of it without my say-so.''

She held her breath during the tirade, then said very quietly, "This is precisely why I didn't say anything, because you never give me any credit at all for knowing the business. I wanted to surprise you with a signed contract.''

"Well, I guess you should be pleased then, because I am surprised. No,'' he corrected. "What I am is shocked that you would betray me and your brothers this way after all we've done for you.''

"Betrayed you?'' Jenna's voice climbed. "How typical of you to think of it like that!'' She didn't even try to hide her fury or her hurt. "I can't discuss this with you now.''

"Well, you'd better,'' he snapped. "I cannot and

will not tolerate you going behind my back and getting involved in things you know nothing about.''

''Oh, you'd be surprised by how much I know,'' she said, reining in her temper. ''That's the problem. I may have given you reasons to doubt my judgment years ago, but you have never once, not in all these years, forgotten that and seen the woman I've become. If it weren't so painful, it would be just plain sad.''

With that, she quietly replaced the receiver on the phone's base. When it promptly rang again, she ignored it.

Only then did she look up and see Darcy regarding her with wide, frightened eyes.

''Mommy, was that Grandpa?''

Jenna held out her arms and Darcy ran into them. ''Yes, it was, baby.''

''Is he mad at us?''

''Only at me.''

''Why?''

Jenna had tried never to say anything bad about the two most important men in Darcy's life—her grandfather or Nick—but the temptation to do so now was overwhelming. She struggled to fight it.

''Sometimes people make mistakes,'' she explained carefully. ''And the people who love them can't forget about it. Whenever anything goes wrong, they drag out all that past history again.''

Darcy looked puzzled. ''Did you make a bad mistake?''

How could it have been a mistake to marry a man who had given her the gift of this child? Jenna couldn't think of her marriage to Nick as anything other than a sad interlude that had left her with a child she treasured more than life itself.

"No, baby. It was the best thing I ever did, because it brought you into my life."

Darcy scrambled into her lap, for once oblivious to her conviction that she was too old for such a show of affection. "I love you, Mommy."

Jenna rocked back and forth holding her daughter. "And I love you, more than anything in the world," she whispered, tensing when the phone rang yet again. She scowled at the offending instrument. "Not now, Dad. Not now."

Darcy gazed at her with pleading eyes. "Mommy, let me answer it. I'll talk to Grandpa and tell him not to be mad at you anymore. Please."

Jenna nodded.

But as soon as Darcy answered, the smile that split her face was way too broad for Jenna's father to be on the other end of the line.

"I thought you'd forgot us," Darcy said. "Want to talk to Mommy?"

She held out the phone.

"Is it your father?" Jenna asked cautiously.

Darcy shook her head.

"Grandpa?"

"No, it's Bobby."

Well, wasn't that fascinating, Jenna thought, as her pulse skipped a beat. She should refuse to talk to him, but she'd been waiting too darned long for some sign that he might deign to meet with her.

"Hello," she said, her tone cool.

"Daisy says your drawings are wonderful," he said, his voice just as cool. "Can you bring them by?"

As badly as she wanted to, she would not play coy about this. There was too much riding on it. Besides, there was no room for emotions in what was essentially a business situation. Never mind that his treatment of her lately had felt a whole lot more like a very personal rejection.

"When?" she asked.

"How about now?"

"Give me thirty minutes," she said, trying to keep the elation out of her voice. "I'll have to bring Darcy along, and she wants to stop by the bookstore and get something to read. I think I can persuade her to choose quickly, since she finally finished her required summer reading and gets to pick whatever she wants."

"Of course," he said. "I'll fix you both a banana split and have 'em ready by the time you get here. Think that will help to make up for me behaving like a horse's behind the last couple of weeks?"

Jenna chuckled. "It'll work on Darcy, that's for sure."

"And you?"

"I could be a tougher sell."

"Name your price."

He said it with a quiet intensity that startled Jenna. "A contract for the boardwalk project," she said without hesitation.

"You drive a hard bargain," he said, but there was a hint of admiration in his tone.

"Tell that to my father," Jenna said wryly.

"You never know. Maybe one of these days I will. See you soon."

Jenna slowly hung up the phone, then picked it up again and dialed Daisy's number.

"Thank you," she said when Bobby's sister answered.

"For?"

"Talking to Bobby. He's seeing me in a few minutes."

"That's fabulous. And don't forget, you'll be seeing him again on Sunday," Daisy stressed. "You and Darcy are having Sunday dinner with the family."

"Let's just see how today goes," Jenna said. She knew what was behind the invitation to Cedar Hill. It was more of Daisy and King's scheming to make something more out of her relationship with Bobby.

"Oh, I have every confidence that it's going to go well today," Daisy told her.

"What did you do, threaten him?" Jenna asked, only partially teasing.

"Didn't have to. The drawings will get his attention, Jenna. They're good."

"You have no idea how much I needed to hear you say that one more time before I go off to face him, especially today."

"Why? What happened?" Daisy asked, instantly concerned.

"We'll get into it another time," Jenna promised. It would take way too long to explain her strained relationship with her father to Daisy. Jenna had a feeling that Daisy—oddly, for someone she'd known only a few weeks—had already figured out much of it on her own. "I promised Darcy we'd go by the bookstore on the way. She's fallen in love with the place."

"Isn't it wonderful?" Daisy enthused. "Gail Thorensen just opened it a few months ago. She's married to Walker's old boss from D.C. It took more time than she'd expected, but she managed to turn an old house into a charming treasure trove of great books and nooks and crannies for browsing. I highly recommend the mystery section."

"I don't have time for browsing today," Jenna said. "I have a meeting with Bobby in a half hour. I can't be late."

As soon as the words left her mouth, Jenna laughed. "Imagine that. I actually have an important business meeting."

"I predict it's the first of many," Daisy said.

With Daisy's confident words ringing in her ears, Jenna set off to prove that her father was completely wrong about her. She was *not* going to screw up this deal. For once in her life she was going to accomplish the impossible.

Then she was going to return to Baltimore in triumph and make her father and her brothers dine on crow for months to come.

12

Bobby waited for precisely thirty minutes, then went to work in the kitchen. He put three scoops of ice cream—chocolate, strawberry and vanilla—into the banana splits, then ladled hot fudge sauce over the top. He was just adding a huge dollop of whipped cream when Jenna and Darcy finally strolled in nearly fifteen minutes late. He got a strange feeling in his chest at the sight of them. Probably indigestion, he decided hopefully.

Darcy was toting a heavy bag of books, which explained their tardiness. Obviously she'd finagled a larger selection than the one book her mother had promised her. Already looking more cheerful than she had in days, she regarded the ice cream with wide-eyed appreciation. "Is that for me?" she asked.

Bobby grinned. "It is if you're sure you can eat it all," he said.

"I can eat lots and lots of ice cream," Darcy assured him, already reaching for the old-fashioned bowl. "Who's the other one for?"

"Your mom." He met Jenna's cool gaze. "Unless, of course, she decides to share it with me."

To his surprise Jenna's reserve disappeared. She grinned at him. His own resolve to keep his relationship with her strictly professional vanished in a heated burst of pure lust.

"Not a chance. Get your own," she said. "Besides, you have work to do."

She handed him a large sketch pad. "If you insist on eating ice cream while you look at these, don't drip all over them," she warned with mock severity.

"Yes, ma'am," Bobby said dutifully, relieved by the release of tension between them. "Maybe I'll put my ice cream on hold. Let's take all of this into the dining room. There's more space." And keeping a whole lot of space between him and Jenna right now was a really good idea.

"Aren't you opening soon?" she asked.

"Worried someone else will see these and steal your ideas?" he teased.

"No. I'm worried that you won't give them your full attention," she said.

"Not a problem. We won't open for another hour. I'll be finished by then." He caught the look of dismay on Jenna's face and guessed the cause. "I'm going to give these thorough consideration, Jenna. I promise. But I will warn you that I won't make a snap decision. You're not going to have my answer when you walk out of here today. There's too much at stake."

There was no mistaking her disappointment, but she managed to nod. "Fair enough."

Bobby guided Jenna and Darcy to one table, then moved to another one nearby and opened the sketch pad. While it was true that Jenna was neither an expert artist nor an architect, she had captured the feel of the setting. He could see that on the very first page, where she'd used discreet splashes of watercolor to give the drawing a vibrancy that made him want to rush to hang it on the wall where everyone entering the restaurant could see it. She had managed with a few brushstrokes to convey the quaintness and allure of Trinity Harbor.

Captivated by that first overview, he was reluctant to move on to the others. What if they disappointed? It was one thing for Daisy to claim the sketches were all wonderful, but quite another to make the financial commitment that would bring the ideas to reality. Besides, a pretty picture didn't necessarily translate into a concrete, profitable plan for developing some very expensive real estate.

He felt Jenna's worried gaze on him and shot a reassuring smile at her.

"You're not turning pages," she said quietly. "Is something wrong?"

"No. This first one is very right."

A slow smile lit up her face and made Bobby's heart lurch unsteadily. Her genuine delight was almost painful to see. Given what he and Daisy both suspected about her uneasy relationship with her father, he understood just how much was riding on whatever he decided. That scared him.

What if the rest of the sketches, which really detailed her ideas, were wildly off the mark? How would he bring himself to tell her? He wanted to plead with her not to get her hopes up, but that would be like snatching something away before it had even been offered. Besides, what was wrong with clinging to hope? It had been a long time since he'd felt that rare emotion. Too long, in fact. And the woman sitting at the next table was responsible for bringing it back into his life. He owed her for that, if nothing else.

With careful deliberation, he turned the page and felt a surprising burst of pure delight. There in a grove of trees, with the water glistening in the background, was a magnificent carousel. Given how all this had started, he shouldn't have been surprised, but he was. The carousel looked as if it had been made for the setting back in the early 1900s.

Even with her inexpert hand, Jenna had managed to create an image that captivated. Bobby could almost hear the music of the pipe organ, the carefree sound of children laughing, the breeze in the trees, the splash of the Potomac lapping against the shore. The carousel was perfect. A roller coaster, even a Ferris wheel, would have been too out-of-scale for the location, but this was charming and right.

Bobby's gaze shot to Jenna. How had she known that when he'd dreamed of this project, this was exactly what he'd seen? *Exactly.* She looked up from her ice cream just then, a dab of hot fudge at the corner of her mouth, and his body went hard. Never in his entire life had he wanted a woman the way he wanted Jenna in that instant. Never had he felt so totally in sync with another human being. It wasn't only the erotic sight of chocolate just waiting to be licked clean or the parting of her lush lips. It was the quick flash of vulnerability in her eyes, a tentativeness she quickly hid behind a brave smile. He understood vulnerabilities like that because he had lived for years with the uneasiness that by not caving in to his father's expectations for him, he would lose King's respect, perhaps even his love.

"Well?" she said, her tone filled with false bravado. "Still on target?"

"Still very much on target," he commended her, then forced his gaze back to the page. Once again, the image grabbed him, moved him.

But a fancy antique merry-go-round wasn't an entire boardwalk project, he cautioned himself. It might be charming and quaint, but it wasn't going to translate into huge income or tax dollars for the town.

The next page demonstrated Jenna's grasp of that. There was a gazebo with picnic tables, also in a grove of trees, and just beyond that were the beginnings of a row of shops with Victorian gingerbread trim.

He turned to the next sketch without hesitation and found that she had included everything from walk-up windows offering ice cream and flavored snow cones to crab cake sandwiches, corn dogs and French fries. Moving along the boardwalk, there were shops selling souvenirs, resort wear, gifts and even a small bed and breakfast hotel with rocking chairs out front. Taking into account the potential for flooding, the entire row of buildings was built several feet higher than flood stage. A porch that stretched across the entire expanse of buildings with appropriate ramps and steps and flowerpots was both decorative and functional. Midway there was a full-scale restaurant with dining on a deck facing the river.

At the far end, closest to the town pier, was one last building, its Victorian facade in keeping with the others. Above the windows, which were open to the breezes, was a sign indicating it was a bingo hall.

He glanced at her sharply. "Bingo?"

She nodded and moved to stand at his shoulder. He could smell the faint scent of her perfume, something vaguely familiar. Lily of the valley, he realized, a scent his mother had worn.

"I checked the papers, and there are bingo games every single night all over this area," Jenna told him. "If the various sponsoring charities could be persuaded to use a central location, there would always be bingo on the boardwalk. That, in turn, would guarantee a nightly crowd."

Bobby was immediately intrigued by the idea. It reminded him of stories he'd heard about Colonial Beach in its heyday. And Frances would be thrilled. King had been taking her all the way to Colonial Beach to play at the rescue squad games on Tuesdays and back again on Saturdays for games at the fire station. Now he could stay closer to home—assuming the two of them ever worked out their differences.

"What would be the benefit to the charities?" he asked.

"More money," she said at once. "Even people who've just come to the boardwalk to take a stroll might be drawn in to play. And for organizations like the volunteer rescue squad and fire department, it would mean not having to move all their equipment to make room for setting up tables and chairs."

"They make some of their money selling food," he pointed out.

"The building would include a kitchen."

He nodded. "Okay, then, what's my incentive to build something that's going to give me no return on my investment? Community service?"

She grinned at that. "No, I wouldn't want to test your charitable instincts. The way I see it, each group would pay a nominal rent, which would be more than offset by the additional players. Added together, those rents would give you a steady income."

It was workable, Bobby thought. And, again, it fit in with his image of a low-key boardwalk that was family oriented. That's what he wanted for Trinity Harbor, a pleasant escape at the end of the day, a weekend retreat for families that stressed low-tech fun.

"Only one thing missing," he said, gazing up at her.

"Oh, really?"

"Miniature golf."

"You're selling me short," she said at once. "Turn the page."

Sure enough, on the next page there was a miniature golf course. "Where would you put it?" he asked.

"My choice would be at the opposite end from the bingo hall, by the carousel," she said without hesitation. "That way you'd have big draws at each end, which would encourage people to stroll along the boardwalk to see all the shops in between."

Bobby had to fight to temper his enthusiasm. There were other bids to consider, dollars and cents issues to be debated. And, then, there was the prospect of working with someone as totally inexperienced—and totally tempting—as Jenna. That part alone had danger written all over it.

But his gut was telling him to buy into this whole

plan right here, right now. Maybe it took someone with a totally fresh view, someone a little hungry for a deal, to pull off what he wanted for Trinity Harbor.

He risked a look at Jenna, and there, once again, was that glint of hope brightening her eyes, the tip of her tongue caught between her teeth as she waited for his decision as if her life depended on it.

In the end, that was what made him cautious, what made him remember all the risks of making a commitment too soon. He needed to work slowly, keep his own emotions on an even keel, be sure he wasn't being persuaded by a desire to bring a smile to this woman's face.

"It's good, Jenna. Really good. You should be proud of yourself," he said. His heart clenched at the slow smile that spread across her face.

"Really?" she said with heartbreaking hesitation.

"Really," he said emphatically. "But—"

The smile fled. "I knew there would be a *but*," she said with a sigh. "It's my lack of experience, isn't it? You don't trust me to pull it off." She regarded him intently, her expression earnest. "But Pennington and Sons is experienced. You'd be dealing with a company with years and years of development background. My father, my brothers—any one of them could do this in their sleep."

Bobby could only guess what it cost her to offer to let them pick up this project that was her baby, her inspiration, something she had put herself on the line to seek.

"I don't want them," he said quietly. "That's not the point, anyway. I simply can't make a decision based on one submission from one company. And these sketches are only the start, anyway. There have to be cost projections, a construction timetable. You know that, Jenna. You must.''

She sank down on the chair next to his, her expression defeated. ''Of course I know that. I just thought…'' She shook her head. ''It was foolish, I know, but I was hoping you'd be so excited about this that you'd want me to continue with the rest.''

''I do want that,'' he insisted. ''I want you to bring me every fact and figure you can put together, so that it's all in front of me when the time comes to make a decision.''

Her eyes lit with another faint spark of hope. ''Then you're not turning me down?''

''Far from it,'' he said.

''I'll have everything ready for you by next week. Is that soon enough?''

''Next week will be fine,'' he said, grinning at her restored enthusiasm. He glanced toward the other table, where Darcy was quietly reading a book based on some teen-oriented TV show. A smile tugged at his lips at the sight of that incongruous green hair. Oddly, for someone who considered himself comparatively straitlaced despite his own pierced ear, the offbeat look was beginning to grow on him…just as Darcy's mother was.

His gaze landed on Jenna's deserted ice cream. ''Your banana split has melted. I owe you another one.''

''I don't care about that,'' Jenna said, beginning to gather up the sketchbook. ''I have work to do.''

"Sure you don't want to stick around?" he asked impulsively. "We could have dinner in a bit. I should be able to sneak out of the kitchen in an hour or so, once all the prep work is done. We could talk some more about your ideas." He knew the latter would be irresistible, and it was. Her expression brightened.

"Sure. I can stay. But Darcy may get bored."

"Call Daisy. I'm sure she'd love to have her come over. And maybe with all those books, she'll be a good influence on Tommy. He's not exactly an avid reader."

Jenna nodded eagerly. "I'll do that. If there's a problem, I'll poke my head in the kitchen and let you know."

There wouldn't be a problem. Bobby knew that. Daisy would leap at the chance to give them some time alone together. In some areas, his sister was entirely predictable. He didn't even need to waste time trying to pave the way.

"Good," he said, letting his gaze linger for just a fraction of a second on Jenna's flushed cheeks and sparkling eyes. What the devil was he doing here? He was asking for trouble, that's what.

But for the first time since he'd found out about Ann-Marie and Lonnie all those years ago, he wasn't moving through life with grim determination. There was actually a faint spark of excitement stirring somewhere deep inside him. And just this once, risky as it might be, he was going to fan it a bit and see what happened.

Jenna almost laughed at the eagerness with which Daisy responded to her request to send Darcy by for a few hours.

"Stop it," she ordered Bobby's sister. "I know exactly what you're thinking, and you can forget it. This is strictly business."

"Are you meeting in his office?" Daisy asked, her tone filled with fake innocence.

"No," Jenna admitted.

"Are food and drink involved?"

"Yes, but a lot of business is conducted over meals. I'll bet even at the school, you and the other teachers confer over lunch."

"Sure we do," Daisy conceded. "Great raucous groups of us, trying to be heard over the noise in the cafeteria. We don't have intimate little tête-à-têtes in a fancy restaurant."

"How intimate can this be? The restaurant is packed."

"If you're half as smart as I think you are, it won't be packed by the time you're lingering over dessert."

"No dessert," Jenna insisted. "We've already had banana splits."

"With all that gooey, sensuous hot fudge," Daisy said in a deliberately suggestive tone. "I love it. You go, girl."

Jenna frowned, then realized that Daisy couldn't see her reaction over the phone. "Enough. If you keep this up, I'm keeping Darcy right here with me to run interference with a man you seem to be implying has lecherous intents."

"Bobby? You've got to be kidding. He's the ultimate gentleman. He won't lay a finger on you unless you invite him to."

"Which I have no intention of doing," Jenna insisted, though now that the thought had been planted in her head, it seemed to be all she could think about. This was definitely not the kind of thinking a professional woman ought to be indulging in.

"I'll drop Darcy off in ten minutes," she said firmly. "If I hear one word about transforming tonight into some sort of seduction, I'll turn right around and go back to the hotel."

"Speaking of which, don't you think you ought to consider renting someplace bigger, maybe even a little more permanent?" Daisy said, shifting gears.

Jenna wasn't reassured one bit by the change of topic. It didn't mean Daisy had given up on her matchmaking, only that she was exploring a new angle. This time it seemed to be about Jenna taking up permanent residence in Trinity Harbor.

"I don't have the contract yet," Jenna reminded her.

"You'll get it. You might as well be ready."

"Thanks for the vote of confidence. Maybe I will start looking around to see what's available," she said, realizing as soon as the words were out that it was an idea that appealed to her on a lot of levels. A home of her own at last. A place where she could raise Darcy without interference. Wouldn't that be something? But *that* was something she'd have to think about in-depth later.

"I'd better get a move on," she said then. "Ten minutes and no meddling, got it?"

Daisy laughed. "I'm afraid I inherited my father's talent for matchmaking, but I'll try my best to keep it in check. And, Jenna, just in case you haven't gotten this part yet, I think it would be wonderful if something happened between you and my brother.''

"So I gathered," Jenna said wryly. "However it's not your vote that counts."

"But it doesn't hurt," Daisy retorted cheerfully.

No, Jenna thought, feeling amazingly contented at the approval she heard in Daisy's voice, it didn't hurt at all. For the first time in years, she felt accepted for who she was, not just by Daisy but, even more important, by Bobby. If she hadn't had so many years of experiencing the opposite—of anticipating that disapproval might be just around the corner—their acceptance might have left her feeling almost giddy.

13

To Bobby's everlasting regret, Maggie had agreed to pinch-hit for his vacationing hostess that night. He'd forgotten about that when he'd suggested that Jenna hang around and have dinner with him. Now his secretary was regarding him speculatively every time he poked his head out of the kitchen.

"Expecting someone special, boss?" Maggie inquired, looking particularly smug.

"Not special," he said a little too quickly, then floundered. "Just someone."

"It wouldn't happen to be Jenna, would it?"

He stared at her. "Why would you ask that?"

Maggie didn't even attempt to contain her amusement. "Because she said to tell you, if you asked, that she'd be back in twenty minutes or so. She was taking Darcy over to Daisy's."

Relief warred with annoyance. "Couldn't you have told me that before?"

"You didn't ask," she reminded him. "For all I knew, you were peering around out here hoping to catch a glimpse of the mayor, who's over in the far corner, by the way."

Sure enough, Harvey, dressed in beige, was seated as far from the kitchen as he could get at a table of six men. All but Harvey were wearing a rainbow of polo shirts, suggesting they'd just left a golf course. Harvey had probably hoped that Bobby wouldn't spot him in his dull jacket amid all those pastels. It must be killing the mayor to have Bobby see that he'd broken his personal resolution never to set foot in the restaurant until Bobby got over his fool notion of putting something other than condos on all that valuable waterfront land.

Bobby grinned at Maggie. "I think I'll drop by and see if they're enjoying the food."

"Are you sure you want to do that?" she asked. "It'll probably give him indigestion, and he'll run all around town blaming it on your cooking."

Confident of his own culinary skills and those of his staff, Bobby replied, "I think I can afford to take my chances. Just last week a Richmond food critic said this place was worth the drive. I believe he described our menu as 'a cut above the usual, bordering on the sensational.'"

"Not that you care what the critics think, right, boss?" Maggie regarded him with another of those annoyingly amused looks.

After casting one last scowl at her, Bobby crossed the packed restaurant, pausing to greet several regular local customers along the way. He noticed that the mayor was looking everywhere except directly at him. He was probably still holding out hope that Bobby hadn't seen him and was simply cruising the room for compliments on the food.

"Good evening, Mr. Mayor," Bobby said, keeping

his tone friendly but impossible to ignore as he stood right smack in the mayor's line of vision.

"Bobby," Harvey said tersely, not quite meeting his gaze.

"I'm surprised to see you in here," Bobby said. "Especially since I'm no closer to putting condos on that property than I ever was."

Fury immediately stained the mayor's cheeks a bright red. "I could tie you up with zoning regulations for years," Harvey blustered before he could catch himself.

"So you've threatened on more than one occasion," Bobby agreed mildly. "But what would that say about you, especially with an election coming up this fall?"

Someone at the table discreetly choked back a laugh, but not before Bobby caught it and gave the man a wink. "It might be especially foolish since I have polling data that suggests people in town like my concept better. They're looking for things for their families to do, attractions to draw more tourists and create more jobs."

The mayor's gaze narrowed. "Polling data?" he repeated suspiciously.

"You know what a poll is," Bobby said. "One of those things that actually asks people what they want, rather than foisting someone else's cockamamie ideas on them."

"Dammit, I knew it all along," Harvey said with an outraged huff. "That's your plan, isn't it, to run for office, because you think you know this town better than I do? Well, Trinity Harbor isn't some major metropolitan area. You can keep your statistics and your poll results. Handshaking's the thing that works around here. Talking to real people and not that highfalutin social set your daddy belongs to.''

Bobby bit back a sigh. There seemed to be little point in defending his egalitarian father, but he did have to try to reassure the mayor about his own non-existent political aspirations. "Harvey, I'm not after your job, at least not for myself. But mess with me on this project, and there's a very good chance I will find someone to oppose you. If I do, you won't stand a chance.''

"Is that a threat? Typical of a Spencer, thinking that just because your family's been around here forever, you get to run things.''

"Force of habit,'' Bobby retorted. "Somebody has to.'' He turned to the others. "Enjoy your dinner, gentlemen. It's on the house.''

"Absolutely not,'' Harvey said at once. "I couldn't. How would it look?''

"Like you'd accepted a bribe from someone you'd just attempted to threaten?'' Bobby inquired. "Sorry. I certainly wouldn't want that. I'll pick up the check for everyone at the table *except* you. How's that?''

He was halfway back to the kitchen when the man who'd tried unsuccessfully to hide his amusement caught up with him.

"Do you think it's wise to antagonize a man who holds the power to ruin your plans for the boardwalk?'' he asked Bobby. "I'm Dave Meltzer, by the way.''

"Of Meltzer Development out of Richmond,''

Bobby said, recognizing the name at once. Big company. Big bucks. No taste.

The man stood a little taller, no easy task since he was only about five-six. "You've heard of us, then?"

"Of course."

"When can you and I meet privately?" Meltzer asked. "I think there are quite a few things we have to discuss."

Bobby knew better than to dismiss Meltzer outright. Even if the developer was a crony of the mayor's, Bobby owed him the same opportunity to make a presentation as anyone else. But since Meltzer built housing, not boardwalks, he pretty much knew they'd both be wasting their time.

"My secretary's pitching in tonight as hostess," he said, gesturing in Maggie's direction. "Speak to her. She'll be happy to set up an appointment."

"What about tonight?" Meltzer pushed. "I'm here. Let's just sit down and see what we have in common. What I have in mind could be extremely lucrative for both of us."

Bobby shook his head. "I'm afraid not. I have another appointment." He spotted Jenna in the foyer. When his pulse picked up, he told himself it was just because he was excited to have an excuse to ditch the developer. He gave the man his phoniest apologetic expression, the one he dragged out when he was most annoyed. "And there she is now. If you'll excuse me."

He moved so quickly that Meltzer was left sputtering to no one. As Bobby passed Maggie, he said, "Over there, the man who's talking to himself. He wants an appointment. Make it tomorrow and make it as inconvenient for him as possible. Something that'll make him get all tangled up with the Richmond rush hour to get here.''

"Sure thing," Maggie said enthusiastically.

Bobby congratulated himself on his good sense in hiring her specifically for moments like this one. There was nothing Maggie liked better than a mission. She was a lot like Daisy and Jenna in that regard.

"Going or coming?" she asked.

"Up to you," he said.

The last thing Bobby heard was Maggie sweet-talking the developer as she led him toward Bobby's office and the appointment book she kept there.

"Very smooth," Jenna said when he approached her. "What would you do without Maggie?"

"Probably live a saner life," he said. "But she is good at a few things, and running interference is one of them."

"So I recall," Jenna said.

"What took so long?" he asked. "I was expecting you back here some time ago."

"Two words. Your sister."

Bobby groaned. "No further explanation necessary. Please tell me she wasn't matchmaking."

"You know perfectly well that she was." She shrugged. "That's okay. She cares about you. She seems to think the fact that you and I have been butting heads since the day we met is a good thing."

Bobby couldn't disagree with Daisy's assessment without lying through his teeth. He had felt more alive the last few weeks. He just wasn't sure about the crash-and-burn letdown that was sure to follow.

"Do you do the same thing with your brothers?" he asked.

Jenna's smile promptly faded. "Are you kidding? I know better. Not only are they married to women I'd never met before their wedding ceremonies, but they would never take or appreciate advice from me."

"I don't appreciate it from Daisy, but that hasn't stopped her," he pointed out.

"That's because you all love each other," Jenna said.

She said it with the same wistfulness that always rocked Bobby back on his heels.

"And your brothers don't love you?"

She looked embarrassed by the question. "In their way, I suppose they do, but mostly it's because it's expected of them. How would it look if the Penningtons didn't get along, at least in public? The sad truth is that they hardly know me. All those years I was sent away to school took a toll. We're more like acquaintances than a real family. My dad and I live in the same house, work in the same place, but we co-exist, we don't really connect. As for my brothers, we don't even have *that* much contact."

"I'm sorry," Bobby said with total sincerity. His family might be annoying, his father impossible, but the bonds between them were strong. Any of them would go to the mat for one of the others, including King, no matter how much he might privately disagree with the actions of one of his children. Publicly the Spencers always stood united.

"Thanks, but it's okay. I just try not to think about it," Jenna said. "It's harder on Darcy. She would give just about anything not to be an only child of a single mom. I think that's why she does such crazy things, like dyeing her hair green. It gets her attention and it makes her fit in with a certain group of kids.''

Bobby shuddered. ''There are more kids in Baltimore with green hair?''

''No, thank goodness, though I've seen some red, blue and purple. The others have body piercing and tattoos. So far I've been able to hold a hard line on that.''

Stunned by the image, Bobby shook his head. ''How old is Darcy?''

''Nine, going on fifteen,'' Jenna said wearily. ''It's payback for the way I was as a teenager. I know it is.''

Imagining Jenna out-of-control made his blood roar in his ears. He couldn't seem to stop wondering just how far she'd pushed the boundaries. He knew about the fake snake tattoo, but had there been more?

''Exactly how rebellious were you?'' he asked.

''By today's standards, not very, but it didn't take much to get my father riled up. I was worse after my mom died, because the only way I could think of to get his attention was to misbehave at school so he'd have to come down to bribe them to keep me.'' The smile that touched her lips seemed sad. ''I'm pretty sure I single-handedly provided funding for a new gymnasium.''

Brave words, but Bobby could hear the hurt behind them. Damn that father of hers for sending her away just when he should have been holding her close. How could a man send his only daughter away right after she'd lost her mother? For that callous act alone, Bobby would have refused to do business with him, but this deal wasn't really about Pennington. It was about his daughter and her struggle for independence and self-respect.

And the more Bobby discovered about Jenna, the more convinced he was that he could never knowingly do anything that would hurt or demean her the way all of the other men in her life apparently had.

Jenna awoke the morning after her dinner with Bobby filled with regret. Why had she spilled all of that personal information about what an irresponsible brat she'd been as a kid? That was hardly the professional, competent image she wanted to project to a man she hoped would invest millions in her boardwalk development plan.

Somehow, though, gazing into his warm, compassionate eyes, she had found herself sharing details about things she'd been trying for years to push out of her mind—old hurts, petty slights, even recent evidence of her father's lack of respect. Once she'd started, she hadn't been able to stop. Bobby had listened to all of it without comment.

"Your father is a horse's ass," he said when she was finally done venting years of pent-up frustrations.

Jenna had grinned. "I've certainly painted him as one, anyway. Sorry. He really isn't a bad person."

"Just thoughtless and cruel, to say nothing of arrogant," Bobby said with a ferocity that startled her.

Jenna hadn't been able to bring herself to contradict

him. At that moment, she hadn't been feeling all that charitable toward the man herself.

Still, it would have been wiser to be more circumspect.

"Mom, what time is it?" Darcy asked sleepily from the next bed. "Why are you up? It isn't even daylight yet."

"My head's spinning," she told Darcy. "I have a lot of things to do."

Always eager for an adventure, Darcy shot up in bed. "Are we going somewhere?"

Jenna had planned to spend the morning at the small desk in their hotel room working the phone and a calculator to come up with the rough figures for her proposed project. One glimpse outside told her it was much too nice a day for that. And Daisy's suggestion that she find a place to rent, at least for the rest of the summer, had been popping into her head all night long, right alongside the image of Bobby's mouth hotly devouring hers. Now *that* would definitely be something worth staying for.

"Darcy, what would you think of staying in Trinity Harbor for a while?" she asked.

"How long?" Darcy asked, instantly cautious. "I thought we were just here on vacation."

"I'm not sure how long," Jenna said. "Till the end of the summer, at least. If we get this deal, maybe even longer."

"Would I go to school here?"

"If we stayed, of course."

Darcy looked hesitant. "I don't know, Mom. Those

kids were pretty mean. I'm not sure I want to go to the same school they do.''

Jenna was alarmed by her daughter's frightened re-action. Had there been further incidents, of which she was unaware? It would be just like Darcy to put on a brave front and keep them to herself if there had been no adult witnesses.

"Those bullies haven't bothered you again, have they?" Jenna asked, studying her daughter's face with a penetrating look. Darcy was many things—impos-sible, smart, funny—but she was a terrible liar. Jenna would know in an instant if she was trying to put a good face on something that had happened.

"No," Darcy admitted. "But we haven't been to the river again, except by Tommy's house. And Pete's been okay since then. I think Walker told him he'd better shape up. Walker's pretty cool. Tommy said at first he wasn't sure how he felt about Walker, since he'd never even known he had an uncle and then this guy shows up and wants to claim him after his mom died. But now Walker's like a real dad to him. He says that's way better than before, 'cause his dad died be-fore he was even born.''

Jenna heard the wistful note in Darcy's voice. "You do know that your father loves you, don't you, Darcy?''

"I guess.''

"Well, he does, but he's never going to be a tradi-tional kind of dad," Jenna said, mentally cursing the fact that Nick refused to take one single thing in his life—including his daughter—seriously. That meant it had been up to Jenna to be the mature adult in Darcy's world, the one person whose love she could count on.

"I know," Darcy said with an air of resignation no child of nine should be expressing. "Dad doesn't like being tied down, and I'm a responsibility."

That was Nick, all right. Darcy had captured his put-upon tone, to say nothing of his attitude, almost precisely. He wanted nothing if it interfered with having a good time.

"You're *my* responsibility, too," Jenna told her. "And that's the best thing that ever happened to me."

"I know," Darcy said matter-of-factly. "But it would be nice to have a dad around all the time." She gave Jenna a speculative look. "Like Bobby. I bet he'd be an awesome dad."

Jenna almost choked. She had thought of Bobby in any number of roles in recent days—some of them even X-rated—but the image of him as a dad hadn't once crossed her mind. Maybe because that was a role in Darcy's life she'd determinedly refused to consider casting after the way Nick had loused up the part.

"Let's not get carried away," she told Darcy. "Bobby and I are potential business partners, nothing more."

"You *could* be more. I'll bet if you asked him, he'd take you on a real date."

"I try to make it a rule not to ask men on dates," Jenna said. "That's a suggestion you might want to keep in mind, too."

"Why shouldn't girls ask guys out?" Darcy asked reasonably. "If you want to go somewhere and you want a boy to come too, what's wrong with asking?"

"There's nothing wrong with it exactly," Jenna said, wondering if her old-fashioned view was completely out of step in today's modern world. "But I don't care how liberated women get, guys still like to do the pursuing in a relationship."

"Then you and Bobby might have a relationship, if he asks you out first?" Darcy wondered.

"That is definitely not what I said," Jenna insisted, fearful that Darcy would get it into her head to meddle. On that score, Daisy was already bad enough. "We've gotten off-track now. All I asked was whether you'd mind if we stayed in Trinity Harbor a while longer."

"I guess it would be okay," Darcy said with what passed for enthusiasm with her these days. Suddenly her eyes lit up. "Could I have a dog if we stayed? Grandpa says all they do is piddle on the carpet, but mine wouldn't. I'd train it real good, and it could protect me, and if we ever go back to Grandpa's, he'd have to let me keep it because it would be a member of the family by then, right?"

Jenna wasn't entirely sure of that. He'd sent *her* away, and she was his daughter. "I'm sure we could work it out," she agreed, suddenly determined to give Darcy something of her own to love and care for. No one knew better than Jenna what it was like to be a scared, lonely kid.

"All right!!!" Darcy exclaimed, bouncing on the bed. "Mom, you're the best."

"For now, anyway," Jenna said wryly. "Okay, get up and get dressed. First things first. Let's check out the real estate situation."

"Call Bobby," Darcy recommended. "I'll bet he knows everything that's for sale in town."

"Leave Bobby out of this. And we're not going to buy," Jenna insisted. "We'll just rent for now and see how it goes."

"Whatever," Darcy said, racing for the bathroom. "I can't wait to get a puppy. Do you think Bobby has a dog?"

"I have no idea."

"I'll bet he does. Guys like dogs. I'll bet there are bunches of them at his father's farm. Tommy says Cedar Hill is so cool. I can hardly wait to go there on Sunday, can you?"

Jenna rolled her eyes at the boundless enthusiasm. "Just get dressed, okay?"

While Darcy was in the shower, Jenna stared at the phone and debated whether to call Bobby or Daisy. Daisy, she decided, then hesitated. Daisy might make too much of her impulsive decision to rent a place to stay. Then, again, Bobby might have a heart attack if he thought she were simply settling in, counting on him to make a decision in her favor. She'd sensed his struggle to keep from discouraging her, but she'd also heard the genuine excitement in his voice over her sketches.

She glanced up and realized that Darcy was peering at her curiously. Her hair was damp and sticking up in green spikes with dark roots. It was quite a look.

"Mom, did you call Bobby?"

"No," she admitted. "I decided we'd go to breakfast and see who we run into. I'm sure there will be someone who can steer us in the right direction."

Naturally, though, because she'd decided against calling him, Bobby was the first person they spotted at Earlene's. He waved them into the booth opposite him.

"Guess what?" Darcy said. "Mom and me are gonna stay here. We're gonna find a house and then I'm gonna get a puppy. I think maybe a golden retriever. What do you think?"

Bobby looked a little dazed. His gaze sought Jenna's. "Oh? When did all this happen? You didn't mention anything about this last night."

"We just decided," Darcy said, not giving Jenna a chance to reply. "Mom asked me what I thought and I said yes, so now we're gonna do it. Do you know a place we can rent? I want one on the beach with a big, fenced-in yard for the puppy."

Bobby's gaze never left Jenna's face. "And you? What do you want?"

"Something that doesn't cost an arm and a leg," she said honestly. "I used up all my spare cash on that carousel."

"So, something cheap in a prime location?" he said. "That could be tricky."

"It doesn't have to be a prime location," Jenna said. "I'll settle for something with running water and no bugs or mice."

He chuckled. "Maybe you could convince Darcy that the mice make better pets than a dog."

"Yuck," Darcy proclaimed. "No way. Mom, I see Tommy coming down the street with Pete. Can I go out and meet them?"

"It's *may I,* and, yes, you may."

When Darcy had gone, Jenna met Bobby's gaze. "I hope this doesn't bother you."

He regarded her with amusement. "What? The idea of you staying in Trinity Harbor? I think the town is big enough for both of us."

"I just don't want you to feel pressured, as if I've set up camp on your doorstep so you'll feel obliged to make a deal with me."

"Sugar, there is very little I feel obliged to do, as my father and Daisy could tell you. When I make this deal with anyone, it will be on the merits of the presentation. Period."

There was no mistaking the warning behind his words. "Don't worry, I won't start counting my chickens before they're hatched," she said.

"I will promise you one thing," he said, his expression grim. "If Tucker hasn't found out anything new about that missing horse by the end of the week, I will pay you for it and for the whole carousel. That will get you out of your financial bind, too."

"You don't have to do that," Jenna protested.

"Yes, I do," he insisted. "No matter what plan I go with, I want that merry-go-round here."

"But what if the horse is never found, Bobby? You'll be stuck."

"No, I won't." He glanced up. "And here's my crime-fighting brother now." He scooted over. "Have a seat, Tucker."

Tucker frowned. "Why do I have a feeling this is a bad idea?" he asked as he slid in.

"That depends on how hard you've been working

to get Jenna's missing carousel horse back," Bobby said.

"I wish I could tell you that I had a lead, but I don't. The security guard is still missing."

"You checked out Harvey?" Bobby asked.

"I didn't have any evidence to get a search warrant, but I did have a chat with him and his wife. I'd stake my badge that they're not involved in this."

"What about a man named Dave Meltzer?" Bobby asked.

"Who's that?" Jenna asked.

"He showed up at the yacht center last night with the mayor. He's a developer out of Richmond. For all I know, he could have ties to that security company. He might use them at his properties all over the county down there. I have an appointment with him this morning. I'm guessing he wants to buy the land outright for condos. Creating a little stir around my ideas for the boardwalk could work to his advantage."

Tucker shook his head. "I just don't see some hotshot developer stealing an antique carousel horse and risking it being traced back to him. Besides, what would he accomplish?"

"You mean aside from making me appear foolish?" Bobby said.

"You're not the one who stole the horse. You're the victim," Tucker reminded him. "Or, rather, Jenna is."

Jenna thought about Tucker's explanation. What if Meltzer knew that she was here without her father's authorization? What if he had somehow figured out that the horse—and the carousel—had tied up all of her funds?

"I want to be there when you talk to Meltzer," she told Bobby.

Both men stared at her, clearly startled by the request. "Why?" Bobby asked.

"What if he took it because he knows I'd be financially strapped, at least long enough to keep me out of the picture? For all I know, my father could have called him and clued him in. Developers might be highly competitive, but it's still a relatively small, tight-knit community. They could know each other. And it would be just the kind of sneaky, underhanded thing my father might do to teach me a lesson."

Tucker looked shocked. "Your own father would do that?"

"And more," Jenna confirmed grimly.

"Then I say we all go to this meeting with Mr. Meltzer," Tucker said, already sliding out of the booth. "You guys coming?"

"Not me," Bobby said.

Tucker paused. "Why not?"

"Because I haven't had my breakfast, and the meeting's not for another hour."

Tucker looked relieved. He sat right back down. "Then by all means, let's eat. Bobby, you buying?"

"I'll buy when you're in my place. In here, you're on your own."

"It's my treat," Jenna said, grinning when both men stared at her in amazement. "It is a business expense, you know."

"Do you actually have an expense account?" Bobby asked.

"No, but I do have a company credit card, and unless my father's cut it off, I haven't even started to max it out."

"Then by all means, you can treat," Tucker said, waving Earlene over.

Bobby shook his head. "You'd think the tightwad didn't have a dime of his own. He's my brother and I'm ashamed of him." He scowled at Tucker. "Letting a woman buy you a meal. What would Daddy say?"

"That he raised me to have good sense," Tucker asserted.

He started to order, but Bobby cut him off. "Just one problem, bro. Earlene doesn't take credit cards."

Jenna sighed. "Sorry. I never thought of that."

"I'll buy," Bobby said. "I can't have the two of you starving to death on my conscience. I've got enough other things on there these days."

His gaze caught Jenna's and held. She trembled at the heat he made no effort at all to hide. The idea that thoughts of her were troubling him was…disturbing. No, correct that. It was exciting, but she couldn't allow him to see that.

"Don't lose any sleep on my account," she said, sounding a whole lot more breathless than she would have preferred.

"Too late for that," Bobby muttered.

Tucker cast a speculative look from his brother to Jenna and back again. "I think I'll go eat at the counter."

"Good idea," Bobby said, without once glancing away from Jenna.

She swallowed hard. "Maybe I should be eating over there, too."

"Now, what would be the fun of that?" Bobby teased.

"This is a bad idea," she said very firmly. "We've discussed that. The timing is atrocious. It's…" She floundered, searching for a word to describe it.

"Unethical?" Bobby suggested.

"Yes," she said at once, seizing on the concept. "It is totally inappropriate and unethical."

"No, it's not," he said. "Unless, of course, you're only interested in seducing me so I'll give you the deal you want."

"I am not…" She sputtered to a halt. Of course, she was. She was very interested in seducing him. It just had nothing to do with the deal.

And that was the problem. The deal had to be the only thing on her mind right now. The *only* thing. Not Bobby's sexy, dimpled smile. Not his amazing, compassionate eyes. Not the way she shivered when he touched her. None of that.

And while she was asking for the impossible, maybe she ought to throw in a request for a few million bucks.

14

Bobby could barely hide his amusement when Dave Meltzer arrived for their meeting and spotted not only Jenna but a uniformed sheriff sitting in his office. To his credit, the man plastered a cordial smile on his face and introduced himself. The smooth manner must have been the result of all the practice he got schmoozing with city officials to get zoning variances for his projects. He was reportedly a master at it, from what Bobby had read overnight in the computer archives of the Richmond paper.

"Sorry to make you deal with the rush-hour traffic to get back here," Bobby said insincerely when they were all seated.

"Not a problem," Meltzer said. "When I told the mayor about our appointment, he invited me to stay over."

Of course Harvey had, Bobby thought. He'd probably been salivating at the thought that this man could make Bobby see reason. Bobby noted Meltzer's well-tailored suit and starched shirt. "Do you always bring a suit along when you're on a golf outing?"

Meltzer chuckled, though there was a hard glint in his eyes at the unspoken suggestion that snagging this meeting had been his plan all along. "I always keep fresh clothes with me. You know how it is—a man in my position often gets caught up in something and winds up staying longer than expected. I never like to show up at a meeting looking anything less than my best."

"Good policy," Tucker said, since Bobby and Jenna were both speechless. "You stay overnight in Trinity Harbor often lately? Seems to me like I've seen your car out around Miller's Pond. Saw it in the lot outside just now. White SUV, right? Tags say something like Liv4Land?"

Meltzer's gaze narrowed. "Something like that. So, are you in on this deal with your brother? I was under the impression that the land was owned under one name."

"It is, and it's not mine," Tucker said at once. "I have enough to do chasing criminals, thanks all the same. Too much politics involved in wheeling and dealing."

"You have a lot of crime in Trinity Harbor? I thought this was a peaceful place," Meltzer said, looking vaguely discouraged.

Bobby saw where Tucker was heading and admired his sneakiness. King would have been proud. A Spencer never asked outright, when a little subterfuge could get the same result.

"Enough," Tucker told the developer. "I've got a case right now that has me baffled."

"Is that so?" the developer said politely.

"In fact, it's beginning to look as if there might be a Richmond connection. I don't suppose you know anybody in the security business down there?"

"I know a lot of people," Meltzer said. "You looking for anybody specific?"

After a few deliberately false starts, Tucker finally mentioned the actual name of the company. TV's deliberately bumbling Columbo had nothing on Tucker.

"Sorry," Tucker said. "You'd think I could remember that, wouldn't you? Anyway, have you ever run across that particular firm?"

Bobby noted that Jenna's gaze was pinned on the man's face as she awaited his reply. If he lied, three people in the room were going to know it and pounce on him.

"I know the name, of course, but I use someone else on all my projects," Meltzer said, his gaze never wavering from Tucker's. "Wellstone Security. Maybe someone there could help you. I'm sure Henry Wellstone knows everyone in the business in Richmond. I'd be happy to give you his number."

He was telling the truth. Bobby knew it. So, apparently, did Tucker and Jenna. They sighed in unison.

"We'll leave you two to your business meeting," Tucker said. "Jenna, could I speak to you for a minute outside?"

She cast a disappointed look in Bobby's direction, then dutifully followed Tucker from the room. Obviously she'd been hoping to linger, to scope out the competition's pitch. Bobby could have told her she had nothing to worry about, at least not from Dave Meltzer.

When Bobby finally dragged his gaze away from her progress, he found Meltzer's gaze on him.

"What the hell was that all about?" the man asked, all pretense of joviality gone.

"I thought Tucker explained it. There's been a crime that's got him baffled. He's looking for leads."

"And my name came up how?"

"Like he said, there's a Richmond angle. I suppose he thought you might be able to help him connect the dots. Believe me, I have no idea how my brother's mind works."

"What's the woman have to do with any of this?"

"She's the victim," Bobby said.

Suddenly Meltzer's expression turned even darker. "Are we talking about that ridiculous stolen carousel horse? That's your big crime wave?"

"Crazy, isn't it?" Bobby agreed. "That sure has stirred up a lot of media attention. It's an oversized kid's toy, for goodness' sakes. How much could it be worth?"

"Quite a lot," Meltzer said. "Assuming the newspaper reports were accurate. Is she holding you liable? It was stolen off your property. Or is she just using it as leverage to get you to support her boardwalk proposal? I hear she has the inside track."

The last was said with a leer and a wink that almost brought Bobby crashing across his desk to bloody the guy's nose. He restrained himself because it hardly seemed worth the energy and the messy repercussions likely when Tucker was forced to come back in to arrest him.

"There is no inside track," he said tersely. "And you've only got another ten minutes for this meeting, so I'd suggest you make the most of them."

Meltzer's expression darkened. "I don't think I like the way you do business, young man."

"Then we're even," Bobby said cheerfully. "You want to forget all about this, it's fine with me."

Bobby could see Meltzer struggling with himself. Pride and arrogance wanted him to spit in Bobby's eyes. The prospect of all that money he could make by plastering the waterfront with condos tempered his response.

"Here's the deal," Meltzer began, then outlined a plan that would have lined both their pockets with a lot of cold, hard cash and forever changed the nature of Trinity Harbor as a peaceful little summer resort. His eyes were shining when he'd finished. "So, what do you think?"

"Give it to me in writing and I'll consider it," Bobby said dutifully. "But I've got to be honest, I'm looking in a different direction."

"I know what that Pennington woman's offering. You won't make a dime," Meltzer said heatedly.

Bobby shrugged. "But I'll be able to live with my conscience. Besides, I like the idea of being able to stroll along the river at night and eat a corn dog and maybe hear the air filled with carousel music and laughter. I'll be candid with you. I don't like the idea that that entire section of riverfront would become private property under your plan. Unless you can work around that, we've got nothing further to discuss."

"I'm confident I can persuade you to reconsider."

Bobby's laid-back demeanor vanished. The look he leveled at the developer was meant to sear him. "And I'm equally confident that you can't."

Meltzer looked taken aback by the harsh tone. "You're a fool," he said succinctly.

"In that case, you probably wouldn't want to do business with me anyway. Let's just call it quits now and save us both a lot of wasted time and energy."

Unfortunately, Meltzer was shaking his head. "I promised Harvey I'd stick with this. He told me you were going to be a hard sell. I can live with that. Of course, I can't compete with a little piece of—"

Booby was on his feet in a shot and leaning across the desk until he was right in the man's face. "You really don't want to finish that."

Meltzer allowed himself a satisfied smile. "I thought so," he said.

"Don't be thinking too hard," Bobby said. "It might fry your brain. As for that written proposal, forget it. I don't do business with people like you."

"You mean someone who understands what it takes to get ahead in this world?"

"No, I mean slime. Tell the mayor I'm sorry, but his boy's going to have to find somebody else's sandbox to play in."

Meltzer regarded him with barely leashed fury. "You're never going to amount to anything more than a small-town operator, you know that, don't you?"

Bobby shrugged. "That suits me fine." A sudden thought occurred to him. "Since you're so well acquainted with the security business in Richmond, do you happen to know a man named Mitch Cummings?"

For a moment, Meltzer looked taken aback, but he covered quickly. "Never heard of him."

This time he was lying. Bobby could read it in the

quick flash of alarm in his eyes. At the very least he was acquainted with the man the mayor had likely hired to investigate Bobby. At worst, he was in cahoots with the two of them.

"Oh, well, it was just a thought," Bobby said, letting the matter drop as he stood up and walked to the door without waiting for Meltzer to budge. "See you. I've got places to go and things to do."

Meltzer regarded him with a stunned expression. "You're walking out on me?"

Bobby grinned. "My, my, you're quicker than I thought."

"Where the hell are you going? Nobody walks out on me," Meltzer shouted after him.

Bobby was already halfway to the dock when the developer came charging out the door.

"Dammit all, I asked you where you were going," Meltzer said, darting onto the dock after him.

"Fishing," Bobby said, stepping down into his boat and casting off in one smooth move.

Not until he was well away from the marina did he consider the fact that he didn't have any bait. Didn't much matter, since he didn't have his fishing pole with him anyway. As soon as he was out on the water and out of earshot of Dave Meltzer or anyone else who might want to talk about something distasteful, he cut the boat's engine, dropped anchor, pulled his baseball cap down over his face and closed his eyes.

For a morning that was only a few hours old, it had been damned annoying. Except for catching Meltzer in a lie and catching a glimpse of Jenna, of course. No question, the latter had been the highlight.

Somehow her announcement that she was considering an extended stay in Trinity Harbor hadn't panicked him the way he might have expected it to. Maybe when he woke up from his nap, he'd think about why that was.

Then, again, maybe he'd just roll with it.

Daisy and Anna-Louise had corralled Jenna within minutes of her exit from Bobby's office.

"I hear you're planning to stay," Daisy said right off the bat. "And I couldn't be happier."

Jenna stared at her. "How on earth did you hear that?"

"It's a convoluted story involving a fair amount of eavesdropping, which I don't normally condone," Anna-Louise said. "But *I* couldn't be happier, either. Have you started looking for a house?"

"Of course she hasn't," Daisy said. "When has she had the time, which brings us to why we're here. Anna-Louise and I are going to drive you around and let you see what's available."

"Shouldn't I work with a real estate agent on that?" Jenna asked.

"You could," Daisy agreed.

"But we know what's coming on the market that hasn't been listed yet," Anna-Louise said.

Jenna grinned. "Let me guess—all that eavesdropping again?"

"Exactly," the pastor said. "As much as I publicly abhor it, it does have its uses. Besides, since Richard and I got married, my ears tend to be sharper when it comes to ferreting out potential news. He says I'm his best source for the paper.''

"Which must be really reassuring to your parishioners," Jenna observed dryly.

Anna-Louise grinned. "To tell you the truth, I'm having a little trouble making it clear where I draw the line. Since there's no confessional in my church, the line gets a little blurry. I tend to err on the side of caution, much to Richard's disappointment and the congregation's relief. Right now, though, there's nothing the least bit indiscreet about me pointing out a few homes that are soon to go on the market.''

"I'm not interested in buying," Jenna cautioned quickly. "Just leasing."

"Take a look and then decide," Daisy said. "There's one on the river about two blocks from me that could change your mind."

That was Darcy's dream house, Jenna realized. The least she could do was take a look. "Let's do it.''

Anna-Louise drove. She had a surprising tendency to speed, Jenna discovered as they raced through town to the collection of old-fashioned cottages along the river. Some, like Daisy's, had been remodeled through the years, dressed up with new siding, fancy backyard decks or freshly painted porches and tidy landscaping. When they turned off of Primrose Lane, Daisy's street, and onto a curving road lined with overgrown hedges of lilacs and picket fences in need of paint, Jenna sat up a little straighter.

These weren't mansions. In fact, the first two houses on the block had been allowed to fall into a sorry state of disrepair. To call them fixer-uppers was being kind.

They were more like candidates for demolition. In other words, they were places she might actually be able to afford.

"How can someone let property like this go to waste?" she asked, regretting the fact that she'd missed the blooming of all those lilacs.

"In some cases, the person owning the house died and the family hasn't wanted to be bothered with coming down here to keep it up," Anna-Louise said.

"Harvey's been pressuring the owners to at least get the yards cleaned up, but he hasn't risked going the extra mile and having the work done and a bill sent to the owner," Daisy said. She pulled to a stop in front of a house halfway down the block. "Here we are."

Uncertain what to expect after the other neglected treasures, Jenna finally dared a look. She discovered a sweet little white cottage with bright blue shutters. The grass had been neatly trimmed, though the old-fashioned twisted metal fence was rusting and the gate listed to one side. Stalks of fading tiger lilies lined the fence. Pots filled with bright pink and purple impatiens hung along the eaves of the porch. A huge dark pink crepe myrtle tree bloomed at the corner of the lot.

The yard was small, but she guessed from having been to Daisy's that it stretched out in back until it reached the narrow strip of sand along the river. She fell in love with it at first sight.

She turned back to find both Anna-Louise and Daisy watching her with grins on their faces.

"She's a goner," Daisy said.

"That's my reading, too," Anna-Louise concurred. "So, do we go inside or not?"

"How much is it?"

"Let's take a look first," Daisy said, already getting out of the car.

Jenna balked. "I don't want to look if it's completely out of my price range. It'll break my heart if I can't afford it."

"You can afford it," Anna-Louise reassured her, exiting the car. "I happen to know the owner very well."

"So do I," Daisy said. "We'll get you a deal you can live with."

Because she trusted them and because she desperately wanted to see if the inside was as charming and ripe with potential as the outside, Jenna followed them from the car.

On the porch, they didn't even knock. Daisy removed a key from her purse and opened the door.

"It's vacant now?" Jenna asked. "Why isn't there a For Sale sign out front?"

"Because the owner hasn't decided whether or not to sell," Daisy told her.

Jenna's gaze narrowed. "Then why are we even here?"

"Because Daisy's convinced he can be persuaded to sell to the right buyer—or even rent, if that's what you'd really prefer," Anna-Louise said. "Our Daisy is scheming again."

Jenna's gaze shot to the other woman. "This house doesn't, by any chance, belong to your brother, does it?"

Daisy beamed. "Sure does."

"And he knows we're here?"

"His idea, as a matter of fact," Daisy said.

"But…" Her voice trailed off. Jenna couldn't imagine how Bobby had gotten word to Daisy. Then again, maybe it was as simple as Spencer ESP. They seemed to be able to read each other's minds, or at least believed they could. Maybe it didn't even matter.

"Why does Bobby own this house?" she asked. "He's not living in it, and it's too far away from the boardwalk to have been part of his plans for that."

Daisy and Anna-Louise exchanged a look that Jenna couldn't interpret.

"Is that really important?" Daisy asked blithely, then unlocked the front door and stepped inside.

"Something tells me it is," Jenna said, refusing to budge until she had a straight answer.

"Bobby used his trust fund from our mother to buy this house for him and Ann-Marie. Then she ran off with Lonnie." Daisy shrugged. "He wasn't much interested in it after that."

Jenna wasn't sure she liked this place, after all, with all of the emotional strings tied to it. "Has he been renting it?"

"No," Daisy said.

"But he has been making sure it was kept up," Jenna surmised, then looked at Daisy with sudden understanding. "Or was that your doing?"

"Mine, though Bobby pays for it," Daisy said. "I'm not sure if he's even driven past it in all these years."

"And you want me to move in here?" Jenna said. "Won't that pretty much assure that he'll never come to visit me?"

"Of course not." Daisy beamed. "You'll chase away the ghosts. Besides, it's a great house. I did a terrific job fixing it up, if I do say so myself. I knew that one of these days the right person was going to come along."

Jenna thought of the large but nondescript house where Bobby currently lived. It could have been in any subdivision across America. This place, though, had a welcoming coziness about it. It had charm.

"Am I supposed to lure him back here?" she asked suspiciously.

"Of course," Daisy and Anna-Louise said at once.

Jenna chuckled. "Well, at least you're honest about it—but what makes you think I can?"

The two women exchanged a look.

"You say it," Anna-Louise told Daisy. "I shouldn't even be thinking such things, much less talking about them."

"My brother has the hots for you," Daisy said, grinning, though her tone was deliberately prim.

Anna-Louise nodded. "That pretty much sums it up, from what I've seen."

If two women who knew Bobby as well as these two did believed that, then Jenna could hardly doubt them. She couldn't help wondering, though, when he was going to get around to doing something about it—or even if she wanted him to. The whole relationship was confusing, a murky mix of desire and ethical considerations that had left her completely out of her depth.

Because she didn't want to think about all of that just now, she marched determinedly across the threshold. "I'm not making any promises," she warned. "But let's at least take a look around."

Every room was filled with sunlight that spilled across polished wood floors. What had apparently once been two separate rooms had been turned into one huge kitchen with room for an old-fashioned oak table big enough for a large family. Jenna could practically hear the laughter around that table or the bickering over a card game. The image was like a dream come true for a woman whose childhood had been filled with lonely meals.

The living room had more of those large windows, which could be opened to the lilac-scented spring breezes. Though the house appeared deceptively small from the street, it was deep. In the back, there were three bedrooms and two baths. The largest of the bedrooms opened onto a wide deck that faced the river. The other access to the deck was from wide French doors at the end of a hall. From the deck there was a magnificent view of the river with a weeping willow along its banks.

Jenna walked through the spacious rooms and sighed. If she'd been able to sketch her dream house, it would have been like this—unpretentious and filled with light.

"You love it, don't you?" Daisy asked, though there was a worried edge to her voice.

"I love it," Jenna confirmed. "But you've put so much work into it. And in this location, it must be worth a fortune."

"It's been sitting here empty all these years. It needs people. And I'm telling you that my brother will make you a deal you can't refuse," Daisy insisted. "All you have to decide is whether you want to buy or rent."

Jenna ran through a mental checklist of pros and cons on buying. Despite Daisy's conviction that Bobby would offer her a good deal, she had no idea if she could afford the place, for one thing. For another, she didn't know how long she would even stay in Trinity Harbor, especially if the boardwalk deal fell through. Was staying here indefinitely even an option? Was she ready to leave Pennington and Sons for the insecurity of trying to make a life for herself and Darcy completely on her own? Too many questions and too few answers.

"I'd better think about renting," she said, not even trying to keep the disappointment out of her voice. "I'll speak to Bobby tonight."

"Maybe you should let me do the negotiating," Daisy said. "I know his weak points."

"But I'm the one who has to learn them, if I ever expect to make a good deal on that waterfront project," Jenna protested. "Besides, I need all the practice in tough negotiating that I can get."

Anna-Louise nodded. "She has a point, Daisy. Let her do it. Something tells me Jenna is one of Bobby's biggest weaknesses, anyway. Let her exploit that."

If only that were true, Jenna thought wistfully. Then that development would be all but in her pocket and her future would be secure.

15

Bobby was in the kitchen at the restaurant making crab cakes for dinner when Jenna marched in, a determined glint in her eyes. He'd been expecting her hours ago. She must have been working up her courage, which made him want to kiss her until she realized he was already close to being putty in her hands.

Instead, he matched her determined look with a tough negotiator look of his own. "You here about renting the house?"

She regarded him with surprise. "Daisy called? I thought she was going to let me handle this."

"Daisy didn't call."

"Anna-Louise?"

"Nope," he said, amused by her confusion.

"What is it with this town?" she asked in obvious frustration. "Is there a radio station that reports all the latest gossip on the half hour?"

"No need," Bobby said. "We have Earlene's. Nothing gets past the crowd in there."

"How discouraging," she said.

"Actually, we find that it serves a useful purpose. We don't have to wait for the weekly paper to come out to know what's going on around town."

"And the complete lack of privacy doesn't bother you?"

"Not me," he insisted. "I'm not a man with a lot of secrets."

"What if you decided you wanted to keep one or two things to yourself—say, a torrid love affair?" Jenna inquired.

Heat immediately shot straight through Bobby. "A torrid love affair, huh?" Interesting that her mind had wandered down that particular path. "Well, in all likelihood, I wouldn't be having it in plain sight, not being much of an exhibitionist."

"But people would know," she said. "You've said it yourself. Nothing gets past the people around here."

He deliberately caught her gaze and held it. "Want to test your theory and see how it goes?"

She blinked as color flamed in her cheeks. "What?"

"I asked if you wanted to experiment with having a torrid affair."

"With you?" Her voice squeaked out the first word, then turned breathless.

"Unless you have someone else in mind," he said, trying to contain his amusement.

"Of course not," she said at once. Her gaze narrowed. "Are you teasing?"

"Not entirely." In fact, in the last ten seconds the idea had grabbed hold of him in a most uncomfortable way. He was rock-hard and aching. It was probably a darned good thing that kitchen island was between them.

She studied him intently, then looked away, muttering something unintelligible.

"What was that?" he asked.

"I was just saying that this whole rental thing is probably a bad idea," she said. "Our dealings are complicated enough without putting a landlord-tenant relationship into the mix."

"Up to you," he said, oddly disgruntled. He'd just been getting used to the idea of having Jenna living in the house he'd bought years ago to please another woman. He'd been looking forward to having Jenna chase away all lingering memories of Ann-Marie standing in the backyard, his arms around her waist, gazing at the river under a moonlit sky. He hadn't set foot in that yard or on that stretch of beach in years.

Jenna scowled at him, or maybe at herself. He couldn't entirely tell, since her gaze seemed to be directed at a collection of stainless-steel skillets hanging above the multiburner gas stove across the room. She finally dragged her gaze away from the pots and pans and looked directly at him.

"I really want that house," she said at last.

Bobby hid a grin. He wondered if she knew she was breaking every rule of how to negotiate to win by admitting such a thing.

"Darcy would love it there," she continued, almost to herself. She drew in a deep breath, and then, as if she'd reached a decision, she asked, "How much a month?"

Bobby named a figure that was half what he could get if he put an ad for the place in the paper.

She stared at him, clearly shocked. "That's ridiculous."

"Too high?"

"Too low, and you know it. Don't do me any favors, Bobby. Charge me the going rate for summer real estate."

He shrugged and doubled the figure. Jenna winced.

"Want to compromise?" he asked, more determined than ever to get her into that house.

"No. I'll pay the going rate, if you'll agree to a month-to-month lease until I know how things are going to go."

"I'm sensing a flaw here," he said. "If I don't hire you to do the work, you won't stay—or you'll stay, but you won't be able to pay me."

"Being a landlord is a risky business," she agreed, grinning for the first time since the negotiations had begun. "Especially when your tenant's employment future is uncertain."

"Yep," Bobby agreed cheerfully. "But I can always deduct the rent from the exorbitant amount you want for that carousel once it's complete again. I'll come out okay in the end."

"I should have known you'd find an angle to work," she retorted.

"Of course. I didn't get to be a small-town real estate mogul without learning a thing or two."

"I thought you considered yourself primarily a chef," she said.

"I do, but all this land just sort of crept up on me. In the greater scheme of things, I own more property than anyone else around here. That puts me in mogul territory."

"Did you buy it so you could prove something to your ex-fiancée?"

Bobby's good humor faded. "That's Daisy's theory. Me, I thought I was in it for the money."

Jenna shook her head. "I'm with Daisy on this one." She regarded him thoughtfully. "You know something, Bobby Spencer? You and I are a lot more alike than I thought."

"Oh?"

"We're both in this waterfront venture for respect."

She had a point, he supposed, though he didn't care to admit it. "Is that so?"

She nodded. "I have to wonder, though, if we're not missing something."

"Such as?"

"Maybe what we both *really* need is a little *self*-respect. Then everybody else's opinion wouldn't matter quite so much."

Bobby considered the idea. "You might be onto something." His gaze locked with hers. "So, do we have a deal on the house or not?"

She crossed the room and held out her hand. "We have a deal."

When Bobby took her slender, smooth hand in his, a jolt shot straight through him. It felt so good, he lifted his hand and cupped her cheek, then rubbed his thumb across her all-too-tempting pouty bottom lip. He felt her tremble at the touch, but she didn't blink and she didn't look away.

"What do you suppose would happen if I kissed you?" he murmured, as much to himself as to her.

"The same thing that usually happens when a virile man and a healthy woman lock lips," she said.

"Which is?"

"An explosion of chemistry that can't be trusted," she replied at once.

He tilted his head and studied her. "You think so?"

"I *know* so," she said emphatically.

"Prove it," he challenged.

She finally blinked at that. "You want me to kiss you?"

"Sure. I'm a liberated guy. Go for it."

"In your dreams."

He shrugged and backed away. "Another time, then."

There was no mistaking the smoldering disappointment in her eyes or the frustration in the set of her lips. Bobby contented himself with that for the moment. She was going to be around Trinity Harbor indefinitely. They could set up the chemistry experiment another time. It might be better not to blow the lid off all this restraint they'd been testing right before the marina's dinner hours anyway. When he finally hauled this woman off to bed, he wanted the leisure to enjoy it.

King glanced around the crowded dinner table at Cedar Hill with satisfaction. There was nothing he liked better than being surrounded by family on a Sunday afternoon.

Then his gaze fell on the chair to his right. Jenna's daughter with her two-toned brown-and-green hair was sitting there. The kid had a lot of spunk and he'd enjoyed talking to her, but there was a sour taste of disappointment in his throat that Frances wasn't the one sitting there.

It was his own blasted fault. Everyone from Daisy to Anna-Louise had made that clear. The only one on his side was Bobby, but given the state of his son's love life, King wasn't especially reassured by that.

Of course, things were looking more optimistic where Bobby was concerned. Jenna was in the process of moving into that house Bobby had bought years ago when he'd wanted to marry Ann-Marie straight out of high school. The money had been his to spend as of his eighteenth birthday, so there hadn't been a thing King could do about it. Besides, owning real estate was always a good investment, though King had thought it a terrible waste that that house had sat there unoccupied, all but tumbling down till Daisy had persuaded Bobby to let her fix it up.

King glanced at Jenna. "Daisy tells me you'll be settled in Bobby's house by the end of this week."

She seemed startled by the comment, or maybe it was his turn-of-phrase that shook her. King took it as a hopeful sign that the mere mention of Bobby's name could put that much color in her cheeks.

"We should be," she said finally. "It's a beautiful house. Daisy did a great job with the renovations."

So, King thought, Jenna was avoiding any mention of Bobby's name. Hadn't looked at him once all during dinner, either. Very promising.

Unless they'd had a fight, he thought, an image of Frances intruding on his concern for Bobby and Jenna's future. Why couldn't he keep the blasted stubborn woman out of his head? It was her choice not to be here. It wasn't like he hadn't called her and asked. He'd swallowed his pride and left a message on that infernal answering machine of hers. She hadn't even had the decency to call him back.

"I hear Frances has gone to Maine," Daisy said, her expression innocent. "How long will she be gone, Daddy?"

"Maine?" King echoed, unable to keep the shock out of his voice. "What the devil's in Maine?"

Daisy regarded him with more of that wide-eyed innocence. "You didn't know?"

"How would I know? She hasn't spoken to me in weeks."

"Whose fault is that?" Daisy asked.

"Not mine, I can tell you that," King insisted, unable to keep the disgruntled note out of his voice. "I've called. I've left messages. I guess she's got better things to do, like gallivanting off to Maine without a word to anyone."

Daisy shrugged. "Apparently so."

King studied his daughter with a narrowed gaze. "Watch yourself, young lady."

"What did I do?"

"You reminded Daddy that he's fallible," Tucker said. "You know how he hates that."

"Amen," Bobby chimed in.

King scowled at the whole lot of them and deliberately turned his attention back to Jenna. He wanted to make sure she was the right woman for Bobby. She had spunk, no question about that, but there were other traits a man liked in a woman.

"Do you cook?" King asked her.

Bobby's smug expression faded at once as he apparently guessed where King was heading. "She doesn't need to, Daddy. *I* cook, remember?"

"How could I forget a thing like that?" King grumbled. He deliberately turned back to Jenna. "You interested in having a big family?"

Again, Bobby jumped in before Jenna could reply. "After being around ours, I imagine she's pretty content with having just Darcy to deal with. Leave her alone."

"I don't know," Jenna said, her eyes twinkling. "This has been fascinating. Is it like this every Sunday?"

"Pretty much," Bobby told her. "The only way to make it better would be to gag Daddy."

"Bobby Spencer, that is no way to speak about your father," she chided him.

Bobby shot a sour look in King's direction, then turned it on Jenna. "I'll remind you of that the next time we discuss your family."

"*My* family is an entirely different story," she said. "Which you would understand if you'd paid the least bit of attention to anything I've said the last few weeks."

"Oh, I've heard you loud and clear," Bobby retorted. "But don't go elevating my father to the top of some pedestal just because *yours* is a jerk."

She frowned at that. "*I* can say that. *You* can't. You've never even met him."

"Consider that a blessing," Bobby shot back.

King leaned back in his chair and listened to the barbs being tossed back and forth, then chuckled. He reached over and patted Jenna's hand. "You'll do, young lady."

"Do?" she echoed, barely containing a grin. "In what way?"

King hadn't expected her to call him on it. "Never mind," he muttered. It was getting harder and harder for a man to control what went on under his own roof, much less get his family settled down the way they were supposed to be.

He glanced at Daisy and Walker, who were looking at each other as if they were still totally smitten after all these months of marriage. Now *there* was a success story. If he could get those two together, then Bobby and Jenna ought to be a piece of cake. The groundwork had been laid, and he'd nudged things along a bit, planted a few seeds today. He'd wait a week or two and see if they took.

If not, he had a few more tricks up his sleeve.

Jenna repeatedly told herself that she was still in Trinity Harbor because she had a job to do, but it was more than that. She didn't want to go home, not with her father in an uproar and her brothers likely to pounce and list every one of her misdeeds and the impact they were having on the company's precious reputation.

Still, if Bobby was serious about Pennington and Sons being in the running for the contract based on her sketches, she needed to go to Baltimore and brief the rest of the family. She'd already delayed the trip by several days so that she and Darcy could get settled in the new house, but she couldn't put it off much longer. She'd been trying to brace herself for the fight that was bound to ensue.

She was ready now, though. In fact, after spending an evening on the back deck listening to the gentle splash of the river, she was about as serene as she'd ever been in her life. She was prepared to deal with anything her family cared to dish out.

If they so much as hinted at taking the deal away from her, she would quit her job and go back to Trinity Harbor and proceed as an independent developer. She knew a whole lot about hiring and firing contractors and subcontractors, thanks to her work during the past few years. She'd learned from the best. For all of his flaws, her father was an excellent businessman, and she'd been watching every move he made for years now. She could pull this off on her own, if she had to. All she needed was to remind herself constantly that she was her father's daughter. The irony of that wasn't lost on her.

After bracing herself for whatever she might have to face, Jenna drove to Baltimore. She deliberately left Darcy behind. Not only did she not want her daughter caught in the cross fire, Jenna needed to have a very firm, practical excuse for going back to Trinity Harbor in case nothing she said to her father worked and he somehow convinced her to give up on pursuing this job on her own. Not that he could. She refused to even consider the possibility that he might win. She just had to stick to her guns through one very difficult hour at most.

Sucking in a deep breath, she marched through the front door of the suite of offices Pennington and Sons had on the first floor of a restored town house near the harbor. There were window boxes filled with bright pink and purple petunias against the brick facade outside, and soothing colors in the offices, all of it her touches. More than one client had said that the quiet, tasteful surroundings had helped to clinch the deal they'd made with her father or her brothers. Several had asked for her to consult on their own decor, but her father had always been quick to point out that she wasn't a licensed decorator, though she would be more than happy to find someone suitable for them. It was just more evidence of the way he diminished her accomplishments.

Since she'd been gone, apparently no one had been hired to fill in at the reception desk she normally occupied. The outer office was completely empty, her desk littered with stacks of correspondence waiting to be opened, answered and filed.

She ignored the mess and sailed straight into her father's office, drawing a startled look that for one instant seemed about to turn into a genuine smile of welcome. But before Jenna could blink, it turned into a more familiar disgruntled scowl.

"Did you finally get some sense in your head and decide to come home?" he asked. "If so, there's a stack of letters on your desk waiting to be answered." He turned back to his computer screen, effectively dismissing her as if she'd just arrived an hour late, rather than after weeks of being AWOL.

"They'll have to go right on waiting," she said calmly.

Her father's head snapped up at that. "I beg your pardon."

"Actually, there are quite a few things for which you should be begging my pardon, but I'll let that pass for now. We need to talk." She sat down across from him, caught his gaze and held it, daring him to try to dismiss her again.

He frowned at her. "Not if you intend to sit there and sass me. I'm still your father."

"Oh, believe me, I'm well aware of that. If any other boss had treated me the way you do, I would have quit long ago."

Shock registered at her harsh words. "What are you saying?"

"I think that's pretty evident. You're a bright man. Figure it out."

He regarded her with evident bewilderment. "Jenna, what has gotten into you? You never used to act like this. What kind of nonsense have you picked up down in Trinity Harbor? Who's been filling your head with wild ideas this time?"

"Maybe I've finally grown up," she retorted.

"If that's the way you see it, you could use a few hard lessons on maturity and gratitude."

"Maybe so," she agreed with rancor. "Look, I didn't drive all the way up here to argue with you. I want to talk to you about the Trinity Harbor project."

His complexion flushed, her father slammed his fist into his desk. "There is no Trinity Harbor project! How many times do I have to say that? Just because you've gotten some crazy notion into your head does not mean that I intend to go along with it."

She refused to flinch. She kept her gaze perfectly level with his. "So that's it? You won't even hear me out?"

"Why should I? You went behind my back on this. You took off without a word to anyone. For someone who claims to be trying to earn the respect she deserves, you have a strange way of going about it."

"I did what I thought I had to do," she said flatly. "Would you have given me the chance to work up this proposal on my own?"

"Of course not!"

"I rest my case."

"Jenna, you're inexperienced. You've gotten yourself into something you know nothing about. Who's going to have to bail you out?" he said in that barely tolerant tone she'd been hearing all her life.

"No one," she said. "It might interest you to know that Bobby Spencer loves the design I came up with."

Her father's mouth dropped open at that. The reaction wasn't very flattering, but it was darned satisfying to see that she could shock him.

"You're kidding," he said finally.

"No. I am not kidding." She tapped the briefcase she'd brought with her. "I have the sketches here, if you'd like to see them."

"Does the man realize that you've never done anything like this before?"

"Yes."

"Does he really? Or is he flattering you, because he wants something else entirely from you?"

Jenna shot to her feet. "That was low, even for you," she said coldly.

Her father had the grace to flinch. "I'm sorry," he said with what sounded like genuine contrition. "It's just that I can't picture a professional buying into the ideas of an amateur."

"Maybe Bobby's as new at this as I am," she said. "Maybe that's why we're on the same wavelength, because we're both looking for something fresh that hasn't been done to death in a hundred other little beach towns up and down the coast."

"You're not giving your brothers and me a lot of credit for being innovative," he said.

"This isn't about you. It's about me being able to make a real contribution to this company, instead of being window dressing in the front office." She leveled a look straight into his eyes. "Are you going to review my sketches or not?"

Tension hung in the air for several minutes as she awaited his decision.

"No," he said finally. "I'm sorry, Jenna, but I'm not going to encourage you in this folly. Come home where you belong before you make a fool of yourself and this company. You don't need to do this. I've always kept a roof over your head, haven't I? Even after you married that ne'er-do-well Nick Kennedy just to defy me, I took you in. Come back, before I regret giving you a second chance."

"Thanks all the same for the gracious invitation," she responded with a heavy dose of sarcasm. "But I'm going back down there this afternoon. I'm staying until I make this deal, and that's that. It's up to you whether I do it for this company or for myself." She stared him down and waited, refusing to blink or to give in.

"Oh, do what you want, but I'm not paying your expenses," he grumbled eventually.

"You would if it were Dennis or Daniel, but fine. That's what credit cards are for."

"Sooner or later, those bills will have to be paid," he reminded her.

She smiled loftily. "Which I'm sure you will be happy to do when I bring in this contract for the company."

"What if you don't?"

"I will," she told him flatly. Not succeeding was not an option. If she hadn't believed that before, she did after this conversation.

Now she just had to convince Bobby Spencer that no one on earth was better qualified to develop his boardwalk.

Unfortunately, despite her brave words just now, Jenna had almost maxed out her company credit card, which meant time was running out. It was time to take the bull by the horns or, to be more precise, the bull-headed man by the scruff of his neck, and get this show on the road.

16

Tonight was the night. Do or die. Win or lose. Go for broke. Jenna ran through a whole list of motivational clichés as she dressed to go to the yacht center for dinner. She'd stopped at the house before leaving Baltimore and chosen a dress that she'd been told in the past could bring grown men to their knees. That was pretty much the effect she was counting on with Bobby.

Now she stood in front of the mirror on the back of her bedroom door in Trinity Harbor and gazed at her reflection in the knock-'em-dead dress. It was a little slip-of-a-nothing dress, just some pale blue silk splashed with exotic flowers that skimmed over curves in a revealing way. It left her shoulders bare and exposed her shapely calves and a good two inches of thigh. Though she wore a strapless bra and bikini panties under it, somehow it managed to look as if she was wearing nothing at all.

"How do I look?" she asked Darcy, who was sprawled across her bed, book in hand.

Her daughter, the fashion critic in baggy jeans and a faded T-shirt, glanced up and shrugged. "Okay, I guess."

Clearly bored, Darcy went back to reading the latest

offering from the *Clueless* series. Was that an omen or what? Jenna wondered. Though she would have walked on hot coals before admitting it to her father, she was playing out of her league. Ignoring the butterflies doing kamikaze nosedives in her stomach, she brushed the silky fabric of her dress smooth, picked up her purse and headed for the door.

"Darcy, come on."

"I want to stay here."

"You can't."

"Why not? I'll be fine. Trinity Harbor is safe. I can call nine-one-one, if anything happens."

"You can't stay here because I'll be worrying about you the whole time I'm out, and I need to stay focused tonight."

Her tense tone apparently caught Darcy's attention. "How come?" she asked.

"Because I'm going to convince Bobby to give me this contract before I leave the yacht center tonight."

Darcy seemed faintly intrigued by that. "And if he says yes, we get to stay, and I get a dog, right?"

Jenna would have agreed to getting Darcy her own jet to get her off that bed and out the door. "Yes," she said tersely.

"Okay," her daughter said, though she took her own sweet time about heading for the door.

By the time Darcy had gathered up enough reading material to get her through the evening, they were already a half hour late for the reservation Jenna had made for dinner. Fortunately, Maggie was working again and had held the table. Her eyes widened when she got a good look at Jenna.

"Whoa! Where did that come from? It has seduction written all over it," Maggie pronounced, then winced when she caught a glimpse of Darcy's startled reaction. "Sorry."

"It's okay," Jenna said. "It's not what you think. I'm not here to…you know. This is all about getting that contract."

"If you say so," Maggie said doubtfully. "I'm not sure Bobby's going to get the distinction, though. I'm pretty certain his mind and his testosterone are going to shoot down the same path mine did."

If that kept him off-kilter, then Jenna would take it. She wanted him agreeable, after all. And men were never more agreeable than when they thought sex might be the payoff.

Because her knees were all but knocking together, though, she wanted to get this over with.

"Is he in the kitchen?" she asked Maggie.

"Yep, but couldn't you wait here and let me get him? I want to see his face when he catches his first glimpse of you."

"I think maybe you'd better stay out here with Darcy," Jenna said. "I don't want witnesses if he laughs me out of the kitchen."

"Trust me, I don't think there's any chance of that," Maggie told her solemnly.

Jenna clung to that thought as she headed for the kitchen—Bobby's turf.

Inside, she plastered a smile on her face and ignored the stunned expression on his. Maggie had pegged his reaction exactly right.

"We need to talk," she announced, marching straight up to him and getting in his face.

His eyes went dark. For a minute she thought it was anger, but then she spotted the flash of heat as his gaze took a leisurely survey from her shoulders to her ankles, then came back to land on her mouth.

Anticipation shot straight through her. Denials aside, that look was exactly what she'd been going for. She could pretend otherwise from now till doomsday, but this outfit wasn't *all* about the deal. It was about seeing that look of purely male appreciation in this man's eyes. She wasn't sure when that had become an issue and she *knew* it wasn't wise, but there it was. Sometimes the truth had bad timing written all over it.

Jenna was about to continue with her planned recitation on the need to get going with this boardwalk project, when she realized that Bobby was moving closer. His gaze locked with hers, and before she could say anything at all, even yes, his lips covered hers and the whole world went spinning.

Apparently Maggie had been right about everything. Bobby's mind definitely was not on business.

And for the moment, with her pulse scrambling, neither was Jenna's.

Evidently he was a whole lot less immune to Jenna than he'd been telling himself, Bobby thought with a sigh as his heartbeat finally began to settle back into a normal rhythm. The woman's mouth ought to be classified as a lethal weapon.

She looked almost as dazed as he felt. Clearly that kiss had taken both of them by surprise. He felt as if he'd been touched by a live wire. He was pretty sure he'd never experienced anything like it before. It had been a fantasy kiss, slow and deep and needy. Just like the other kiss they'd shared, except this time she'd been molded against him, every curve cradled against the heat of his body. Face it, he told himself, he was becoming addicted.

When she'd sashayed into his kitchen in a dress that barely qualified as decent attire, every single rational thought in his head had fled. Lust, never far away these days, had slammed through him with a ferocity that rocked him. If he hadn't kissed her—right then and there—he was pretty sure he would have self-destructed from all the heat.

At least now the temperature was back to an acceptable simmer, though he had a hunch that that wouldn't last long, not unless she covered herself with a blanket. He gulped in some air and tried to act as if kissing a woman senseless during dinner preparations in his restaurant were an everyday occurrence. Never mind the stares they'd drawn from his stunned-into-silence staff.

If he had half a grain of sense in his head, he wouldn't risk a repeat performance, at least not until the matter of the boardwalk contract had been decided once and for all. For both their sakes, he couldn't let the two issues—that deal and his growing feelings for Jenna—become intertwined.

"Sorry," he muttered, backing away and turning his attention to a tray of sour orange tarts he'd made for tonight's dessert special. One quick scowl around the room had the noise level in the kitchen climbing and pots and pans banging once more.

Jenna's voluptuous little body insinuated itself between him and the counter, and she was smack in his face again, all heat and sweet temptation.

"Oh, no, you don't, buster," she declared, eyes blazing. "You don't get to do something like that and then walk away."

"I have work to do," he said stiffly.

"Don't we all," she retorted. "So, I'll make you a deal. I'll let you go back to yours right now, if you agree to see me as soon as the crowd thins out."

"Tonight?" He sounded a little frantic, even to his own ears.

"Yes, tonight."

He shook his head. "Not possible."

"Why not?"

Because he could not spend five minutes alone with her as long as she was wearing that ridiculously skimpy dress without wanting to tear it off and see the body barely concealed underneath. Because he was terrified of the feelings she stirred in him. Just because... Logical reasons weren't coming to him. In fact, his brain seemed to be in a complete fog.

"Because I'm busy tonight," he said finally.

Her expression faltered at his response. "You have a date?"

"No," he said at once, refusing to seize on an even worse lie, no matter how convenient it might be. "Nothing like that."

"Then what?"

"Jenna, I cannot see you tonight. Period."

She studied him intently. "It's the dress, isn't it?" she said, a sense of wonder in her voice. "You're scared of this dress."

"Not the dress, dammit. *You* in that dress. Or out of it." He threw up his hands. "I just know that being alone with you is not a good idea."

"Okay, then, I'll go home and change. How about jeans and a baggy T-shirt?"

Bobby considered the offer, then dismissed it. She could wear a feedsack, and all he'd see tonight would be the image of her in that barely-there dress. It was too dangerous.

"I don't think so. Tomorrow. In my office. With witnesses. Assuming, of course, that this meeting you want is business-related. It is, isn't it? You didn't come here tonight just to drive me crazy, did you?"

She regarded him with evident exasperation. "Yes, it's a business meeting. And we can do it in your office with witnesses, if you're afraid you won't be able to keep your hands to yourself. I'm sure Maggie would be delighted to sit in on our conversation. She was certainly eager enough to be in here when you caught your first glimpse of me in this dress."

"Yeah, I'm sure." Thank heaven for small favors, Bobby thought. Otherwise he'd have been hearing about that kiss for months to come. He still might, if anybody on the kitchen staff blabbed to his secretary. He wondered if generous bonuses or threats would work best in buying their silence.

"So, what's it going to be?" Jenna asked, a glint of amusement in her eyes. "Tonight, right here, or your office, me and Maggie in the morning so you'll be safe?''

"Trust me, I won't touch you again," he said fervently. "Not here. Not there." Once had been too damned disconcerting. More would be taking his life in his hands. He had enough willpower and resolve to stick with that. He didn't need Maggie watching over them and gloating.

"Whatever," Jenna said, studying him intently. "You're going to take the safe route, aren't you? The office? What time should I be there?" She gave him a mocking look. "Ten on the dot?"

He recalled what had happened the last time he'd pulled that on her. "I'll tell you what. Forget the office. Meet me on the dock at seven. We'll go out on the boat. I have crab pots to check."

She looked skeptical. "Seven o'clock in the morning? Isn't that a little early for a man who reportedly is not a morning person? Then there's the idea of you and me alone on a boat. Are you sure you don't intend to toss me overboard?''

He grinned for the first time since she'd walked into the kitchen. "Only if you try my patience."

She nodded, her expression solemn. "Then I'll definitely work hard not to do that."

Jenna hadn't been gone twenty minutes and Bobby's pulse was still in overdrive, when Tucker wandered into the kitchen.

"What the heck are you doing in here? It's not open house night in my kitchen," Bobby snapped.

Tucker grinned. "Feeling a little sexually frustrated, I take it? I heard about Jenna and the dress."

"This is not about Jenna and whatever she was or was not wearing," Bobby retorted, regretting more than he could say that he hadn't killed everyone who'd been witness to their encounter. "I have a business to run."

Tucker snagged a crab leg from a plate Bobby had been about to send into the dining room. "Don't let me stop you. I can wait."

Bobby sighed and set that plate in front of his brother, then fixed another one for the actual paying customer in the other room. As soon as the meals were out the door, he turned back to Tucker.

"Other than tormenting me, do you have a reason for being here?"

"Yep. I got word today that our missing security guard is back in Richmond. I'm off tomorrow, so I was thinking of taking a ride down there. Want to come along? And in case you require an added incentive, it seems that the mayor's pal Mitch Cummings knows this guy."

"This could be the link we need between the mayor and the theft, then," Bobby concluded, his excitement stirring. He thought of the boating trip he was supposed to take with Jenna. It probably wouldn't hurt to let things cool down a little more before they took it.

"I'll have to cancel a meeting," he told Tucker. "But I'll go. What time do you want to leave?"

"Seven-thirty," Tucker told him with a grin. "I figured since you were planning to be up at that hour to meet Jenna, it won't kill you to do it for me."

"How did you know my meeting was with Jenna? Is she still out there? Did she tell you?"

Tucker chuckled. "Man, you are pitiful. No, she is not still out there, but Maggie is. Your secretary is a reliable source of information, especially when it comes to your love life. I'd be careful if I were you. I don't think she's above bugging the place."

"I have no love life," Bobby insisted. "At least not with Jenna Kennedy."

"Yeah, whatever," his brother said, clearly not believing a word of the denial. "I'll swing by and pick you up at seven."

"You said seven-thirty."

"I said we'd leave at seven-thirty. I'm not going anywhere until I've had my coffee. Your house is on the way to Earlene's. I'm not back-tracking to get you."

"Fine."

"Don't look so grouchy. Maybe if you explain what you're doing to Jenna when you cancel on her, she'll come along with us."

"Not a chance," Bobby said grimly. He was *not* going to spend an entire day in close quarters with a woman who could turn him on with a glance. An hour on a boat would have been torment enough. And in his boat, there was no chance of things getting out of hand. In the back seat of Tucker's car, who knew what insane forces of temptation might kick in? There was something about the back seat of a convertible that just begged people to indulge in mischief. "And drive the SUV, just in case I can't talk her out of going."

"Up to you," Tucker said, a knowing grin spreading across his face. He snagged another crab on his way out the door. "These could use a little more spice, by the way."

"As if I'd ever take culinary advice from a man who thinks a peanut butter and mayo sandwich is fine dining."

Tucker winked. "You ought to put it on the menu. You'd bring in a whole new clientele."

"No question about that," Bobby said. "And you'd spend all your time up here arresting them for drunk and disorderly conduct."

As soon as Tucker had gone, Bobby walked over to the phone. If he had to cancel on Jenna, he might as well get it over with. She was going to blast him from here to Sunday. Then he could get indignant and hang up. That would be for the best all the way around, he concluded as he dialed.

When she answered in a sleepy voice, an image of her out of that dress and naked in bed shot his body temperature into the stratosphere and pretty much reduced his resolve to cinders.

"Jenna, I'm sorry if I woke you. It's Bobby." Before she could say anything else in that husky tone, he rushed on. "Something's come up. I have to cancel out on tomorrow. Can we make it the next day?"

"You're canceling on me?" Indignation stripped away the slightest hint of sexiness from her voice.

"Postponing," he corrected. "For one day. It's no big deal."

"It is to me."

And he knew why, he thought, forcing aside the

guilt that swamped him. "One day," he told her. "I swear it."

"You're giving me your word that we will meet day after tomorrow?"

"Yes."

"Okay, then," she said, sounding mollified. "Is everything all right?"

"All right?" he asked, mystified by the question.

"Whatever came up. Is it a problem?"

"No, no, it's nothing like that. Tucker and I just have to run down to Richmond."

There was dead silence on the line, then finally she said, "Richmond? I don't suppose this has anything to do with my case?"

Bobby cursed himself for the slip. He could lie to her, but then he'd feel even worse than he did already. "Yes," he told her reluctantly. "The guard's back."

"And you weren't going to tell me that, were you?"

"I didn't want to get your hopes up."

"You didn't want me going along," she corrected. "Too bad, because I have a right to be there."

"It's official police business," he said, mouthing a phrase that Tucker tossed around whenever an amateur was annoying him.

"You're going, aren't you?"

"Yes, but—"

"Being the sheriff's brother doesn't qualify you for deputy, unless you've been holding out on me. Do you have a badge?"

"No, but—"

"I'm going. What time are we leaving?"

He didn't answer.

"Bobby Spencer, if you don't tell me right this second, I'm going to come over and spend the night outside your front door."

That was probably more temptation than any mere mortal could resist. Bobby told her to meet them at Earlene's at seven.

"You'd better be there," she warned, "or I'll make you regret it."

"Ever since you hit town, I've been living with regrets," he tossed back. "I'm getting used to it."

"Yeah, well, this kind will be painful," she retorted.

Bobby laughed. "Believe me, sugar, so are the ones I've been suffering so far. I'll see you in the morning."

He hung up before she could say anything more. He realized then that his lips were curved in a smile. Apparently he wasn't nearly as distraught by the prospect of being with Jenna all day long as anyone with good sense ought to be.

17

The meeting with the security guard was a total bust from Jenna's perspective. Not only had she had to postpone her best chance yet to discuss the boardwalk contract with Bobby, but the guard swore that he didn't have a clue who might have taken the carousel horse. He also swore that he'd been planning this vacation for months, that there was nothing unexpected about it.

None of her questions or Tucker's had been able to wear him down. They were going over the same territory for a second time, but he maintained that a man he couldn't describe had shown up with a truck and a letter purporting to be from Jenna telling him to release the horse.

"I didn't write a letter," Jenna said with mounting frustration.

"But I got one, ma'am," the guard said apologetically. "What was I supposed to think? And my pay was in the envelope with it."

"In cash, I suppose," Tucker said, not even trying to hide his exasperation.

The man nodded, clearly tired of the repetition.

"Any extra?" Bobby asked, throwing a new twist at him.

Toby Finch regarded him with indignation. "Absolutely not. If there had been, it would have made me suspicious, no question about it. The pay was the exact amount, so it seemed legit to me."

"Do the people usually pay you on the job or do they pay the company?" Tucker asked.

"Depends on the arrangement the boss makes," he insisted once again. "Usually he gives me a heads-up before I go on a job, but this was a last-minute assignment for me. I had to fill in for a fellow who got sick."

Tucker looked at Jenna.

"I hadn't agreed to pay in cash," she said. "I was supposed to be billed. Call the office. Someone there ought to be able to confirm that."

"I'll do that later," Tucker said, turning his attention back to the guard. "Toby, how long have you been in the security business?"

"Ten years, ever since I retired from the police department down here," he said with evident pride.

"So with all that experience, you should have a good eye for details, right?" Tucker asked.

"I'd say so," Toby said, regarding him warily. "What's your point?"

"I'm wondering why you can't recall one single detail about the man or the truck that came that day."

The comment didn't rattle Toby in the slightest. "It was just before daybreak. I couldn't see all that clearly. My eyes aren't what they used to be. That's one of the reasons I retired from the force."

"Then how did you see to read the letter?" Bobby asked.

"Took out my flashlight and put on my reading glasses," Toby responded without hesitation.

"What did you do with the letter?" Tucker asked him.

"Gave it back to the man."

"Shouldn't you have kept it, just in case there was any question later about the change in plans?"

"In retrospect, I can see that that would have been the smart thing to do, given what's happened, but at the time, I couldn't see any reason to hang on to it."

Bobby studied him with a frustrated expression. "Toby, what's your connection to a man named Mitch Cummings?"

"Who's Mitch Cummings?" Jenna asked, bewildered by the new name.

"A friend of the mayor's," Bobby said tersely before turning his attention back to Toby. "Do you know him?"

"Sure I do. Mitch and me were on the force together," he said readily. "What's he got to do with this? He's a P.I. now. I haven't seen him in a couple of years."

"Or talked to him?" Tucker asked, as if the distinction might make a difference in his reply.

"No, sir. I haven't talked to him either. As far as I know, he's got no connection to any of this."

Tucker and Jenna sighed in unison. Bobby's hard gaze never left the older man's face.

"Toby, are you lying?" he asked harshly. "If so, now's the time to come clean. Unless you were in on the theft, you've got nothing to lose by telling the truth and helping us to catch the person responsible. Ms.

Kennedy stands to lose a lot of money unless we can find that antique horse.''

Toby's gaze flew to Jenna. ''I'm real sorry, ma'am. I imagine the company insurance will make it good, if a court holds us liable. Like I said, though, it all seemed on the up and up to me or that man would never have been able to put that horse into that truck without going through me.''

''I'm sure that's true,'' Jenna consoled him. ''It's not your fault. A thief is a thief and this one was obviously very good.''

''Thanks for your time,'' Tucker told him, then handed him a business card with the sheriff's department phone number. He'd jotted his home number on the back. ''You think of anything else, give me a call.''

''Will do,'' the man promised.

Outside of his small house in a middle-class subdivision, Jenna looked at Tucker and Bobby. ''Now what?''

''Now we have some lunch and discuss our options,'' Tucker said.

''It's not even eleven o'clock,'' Bobby pointed out.

''Then we'll have brunch,'' Tucker said. ''Interrogations always make me work up an appetite.''

''I'm glad they're good for something, because that one didn't get us one single piece of information we can use,'' Jenna said.

''Sure, it did,'' Tucker disagreed.

''What?'' she asked, mystified.

''We know whoever took that horse knew that you were the one who sent it,'' he said.

"We do?" Bobby said.

"I'll explain it to you over food," Tucker said, heading for the car. "Until then, you two talk about the weather or something. I need to think."

"In that case, since you deliberately defied me and brought the convertible, Jenna and I will ride in the back," Bobby said, dragging Jenna toward the back seat.

"Just try not to get carried away back there," Tucker warned. "I'm not chauffeuring a couple of naked people around Richmond. Word's bound to get back to Trinity Harbor."

Jenna shot a startled look at Bobby. "Naked people?"

"An interesting idea, but I think I'll have to pass," he said, eyes twinkling. "I have the Spencer reputation to think of. Of course, once we get on the highway heading home, there's nothing stopping us."

She stared at him. "Are you crazy?"

"Only lately." He draped an arm over her shoulders and drew her close.

"I thought you weren't going to touch me ever again," she said, even as she snuggled into his side. Talk about mixed messages. It was a wonder their heads weren't spinning.

"That was last night. This is today. Things change," he said, apparently happy enough with the inconsistency of his plans. "Now hush. I want to see if what they say is true."

"About what?"

"Whether there really is smoke coming out of Tucker's ears when he tries thinking too hard."

"I heard that," his brother said.

Bobby laughed. "I knew you weren't concentrating that hard."

Jenna sighed with contentment and leaned back into the curve of Bobby's arm. She listened to the two brothers bicker all the way to the interstate, despite Tucker's earlier plea for silence. There was so much love behind the teasing. It didn't have the same edge to it that it did when Dennis and Daniel started in on each other or on her. For what seemed like the zillionth time, she wondered why she'd had to grow up in a family that was so blasted dysfunctional. Could anything have changed that?

Maybe if her father had been a different sort of person, she concluded. Someone like King Spencer, for instance. King had lost his wife when his kids were still young, but he hadn't let his family fall apart. He hadn't shipped Daisy off to boarding school because she was more of a bother than her brothers. He'd kept them all under one roof and seen to it that they never once questioned the love of the parent who remained for them.

She glanced up and saw Bobby studying her intently.

"What's going on in that head of yours?" he asked.

"Thinking about how different my life would have been if my dad had been anything at all like yours."

Bobby hooted. "You don't even want to go there."

"Come on. It's plain to everyone how much he cares about the three of you."

Bobby's expression turned thoughtful. "I can't deny that. I suppose Daddy's biggest fault is his tendency to get carried away in trying to do what he thinks is best for us.''

"See?" Jenna said. "That's precisely what I mean."

Bobby kept his gaze level with hers. "Don't you think your father did what he thought was best, too?" he asked quietly. "Even if you think he was flat-out wrong, can't you admit that his intentions were good? In that way, our fathers are pretty much alike. They might be misguided, but their hearts are in the right place."

Jenna considered what Bobby was saying. If being sent away hadn't been so painful, maybe she could have admitted that her father had truly thought she would be better off away from home. But that wasn't the worst of it. It was everything that had happened since, the constant reminders that she wasn't good enough or smart enough to do anything at all mean-ingful at Pennington and Sons, that she was as much of an outsider as if there hadn't been any Pennington blood running through her veins.

"Sorry," she said with a shake of her head. "I don't think I can look at it so generously. Spend a little time with my father and me sometime. You'll see what I mean."

"Then invite him down," Bobby said. "Set up a meeting. If Pennington and Sons is going to be in the running for this contract, then I probably should meet the head of the company."

"No," Jenna said flatly, a sinking sensation in the pit of her stomach. Was Bobby going to snatch this opportunity away from her, after all she'd told him about how important this job was to her?

"Why not?"

"I don't want him here. Not till this is a done deal. I mean it, Bobby. This is my deal or we forget about it."

For an instant he seemed taken aback, but then he nodded. "Yeah, I can see why you'd want it that way. We'll put that topic on the table for our meeting tomorrow."

"Fair enough," she said, just as Tucker parked the car in front of a truck stop that boasted three different fast-food restaurants under one roof. All that cholesterol, plus ice cream for dessert, she thought. It was heavenly, especially since she didn't have to try to explain to Darcy why a high-fat lunch was a really, really bad dietary habit to get into.

Bobby shuddered when they walked inside the packed building. "People actually enjoy this disgusting stuff?" he asked, clearly offended.

"You bet," Jenna said eagerly, heading straight for the pizza with Tucker right on her heels.

Bobby finally uttered an exaggerated sigh and came along with them. "I suppose we might as well all die together."

Tucker frowned at him. "Don't be a snob. Besides, I've seen you wolfing down half a pizza all by your lonesome, remember?"

"It was a sacrifice," Bobby insisted, "to make sure you didn't eat the whole thing."

"Yeah, right," Tucker said. "And the ice cream sundae?"

"I have a sweet tooth."

Jenna grinned. "Good. Then you go stand in that line. I want hot fudge."

"Ditto," Tucker said. "I'll get your pizza."

Twenty minutes later, they were all pleasantly stuffed and destined for indigestion. Jenna faced Tucker. "Okay, tell me again why that meeting with Toby Finch was productive."

"How many people knew you had that carousel horse?"

"Not many," she said slowly. "The dealer I bought it from, the security company."

"Anybody else in Baltimore? Your family?"

She shook her head, beginning to see where he was heading.

"And in Trinity Harbor, who knew?"

"No one at first," she said. "Not until I walked into Bobby's kitchen."

"At which point my brother, Walker and I knew," Tucker said.

"There was a whole yard full of people," Bobby countered. "Any one of them could have figured it out. The mayor could have called the security company to see who'd hired them."

"But he didn't," Tucker said. "I checked. And before you ask, neither did Mitch Cummings. So who else knew for sure?"

"Richard," Bobby said slowly, his gaze on Jenna. "You did talk to him, right?"

"Sure. He was doing a story for the paper. You were the one who gave him my name."

"And once Richard knew, Anna-Louise knew," Bobby continued.

"And given what I've seen of how Trinity Harbor works, ten minutes after that, the entire town knew," Jenna said, discouraged.

"Not necessarily. But I do think a visit to Richard and Anna-Louise should be the first order of business when we get home," Tucker said. "Maybe they can shed some light on who was next in the information-sharing chain."

"Do you honestly think those two will spill the beans? Isn't that a breach of ethics or something?" Jenna asked. "Ministers and journalists both make pretty much the same kind of confidentiality pacts, don't they?"

Tucker shook his head. "We already know their sources. We need to know who *they* told."

"And then we follow the daisy chain straight to the thief?" Bobby said. "Sorry, I think Jenna's right. Even if the paper didn't come out till days after the theft, we're going to end up with everyone in Trinity Harbor on the list of suspects."

"You have any better ideas?" Tucker asked.

"No," Bobby admitted.

"Then we do it my way. We stop by to see Richard and Anna-Louise."

Naturally, Bobby thought, it couldn't be as simple as driving over the see the journalist and the pastor. When they arrived at their house, no one was home. Nobody was at the church office or at the newspaper, either.

"You looking for Richard?" Earlene shouted at them from across the street.

Tucker nodded. "Any idea where they are?"

Earlene cast a worried look toward Jenna, then beckoned Tucker over. Bobby felt a chill all the way down to his bones. Something was wrong if Earlene didn't want Jenna to hear what she had to say. Fortunately, Jenna had been looking in another direction when Earlene had made her surreptitious motion to Tucker.

Bobby waited with a sense of dread until Tucker started back toward them, his expression every bit as grim as Bobby had feared. Instinctively, he reached for Jenna's hand.

"What's up?" Bobby asked his brother.

"We need to get over to Daisy's right away," Tucker said, his gaze on Jenna. "I'm sorry."

All of the color drained out of Jenna's face. "Sorry?"

"Darcy's been hurt. She's going to be fine, but you need to know what to expect. Her arm's broken, and there are some scrapes and bruises. The doc here took X rays and set the break, but he recommends she see an orthopedic doctor in Fredericksburg to make sure he did the job right." His expression turned wry. "Given the state of Doc's eyesight, I'd go along with his suggestion, if I were you."

Jenna regarded him with a shaky expression. "What happened? Did she fall? Get hit by a car? What?" she demanded, her voice climbing.

Bobby squeezed her hand. "Settle down," he said

quietly. "Remember what Tucker said, she's okay. That's the important part."

"Having cuts and bruises and a broken arm is not okay," she said, whirling on him. "I want to know what happened."

"I don't know all the details. Daisy will tell us everything when we get there," Tucker said.

"But you know more than you're saying, don't you?" she said furiously. "Tell me, dammit. She's my daughter."

Tucker glanced at Bobby. "Tell her," Bobby said.

"There was another run-in with those kids."

"She was attacked by those bullies?" she said, her expression incredulous. "What kind of place is this? What kind of parents are those people we talked to? I thought they were going to put a stop to this!"

"They will now," Tucker assured her. "They can't pass this off as a childish prank. Deputies are already rounding up the kids and their parents."

"Let's go," Jenna said, climbing into the car. "I want to see Darcy *now*."

Tucker dragged out his siren, slapped it on the roof and went through town as if he were on his way to a fire, squealing to a stop in front of Daisy's. Jenna was out of the car before he'd cut the engine. Bobby would have been right on her heels, but Tucker latched onto his arm and held him back.

"I've got to arrest Ann-Marie's boy. Word is that J.C. was the ringleader."

"Then do it," Bobby said. "I'm going inside to check on Darcy. Come back when you have him locked up. I don't care what Ann-Marie or Lonnie say, do not let that kid out on bail, not today, or I'll deal with him myself."

Something in Tucker's expression kept him from heading for the house the way he'd intended. "What? Is there something you're not telling me?"

"Maybe we ought to get into this someplace else," Tucker said. "Someplace with a little more privacy than we'll have around here."

"Dammit, Tucker, I am not leaving Jenna. And I want to see for myself how Darcy really is. Just spit it out and be done with it."

"Bobby, don't make me do this, not here. Come out to Cedar Hill with me."

The suggestion completely baffled Bobby. "Why on earth would I want to go to Cedar Hill now? What does Daddy have to do with any of this?"

"I'm not sure. Not entirely, anyway. Please, just come with me. It's past time for you to know about this, even if it's nothing more than some screwball idea Daddy got into his head years ago."

Bobby studied his brother's grim expression and relented. Tucker might be mule-headed stubborn, but he wouldn't be insisting on this if it weren't important. "Give me five minutes," he said finally.

Tucker nodded.

Bobby raced inside and found Jenna sitting in a chair with Darcy curled up in her lap, sobbing as if her heart were broken. For the first time ever, she seemed like the nine-year-old kid she was, instead of nine-going-on-thirty. Bobby knelt down beside them and stroked her hair, smoothing those silly spikes he'd actually come to love.

"Hey, kiddo, you okay?"

Darcy sniffed and turned to face him. Lower lip quivering, she nodded, though huge tears continued to spill down her cheeks. He touched her cast, which already sported a drawing signed by Tommy, as well as Daisy's flowing signature.

"Tough luck," he told her quietly. "I'm real sorry."

"I know. It's not your fault."

"Maybe if I'd been here, I could have stopped it," Bobby said, filled with more regret than she could possibly imagine.

"Tommy and Pete tried, but there were too many of them." Her expression brightened ever so slightly. "I think I gave one of 'em a black eye, though."

Holding her, Jenna shuddered. Bobby grazed Jenna's knuckles with his thumb. "I'm not condoning violence," he told her. "But Darcy had to stand up for herself."

"I know," Jenna said.

"Look, I have to go someplace with Tucker. Will you two be okay here for a while longer?"

"Sure," Jenna said. "Daisy can give us a ride home."

"Of course I will," Daisy said.

"No!" Bobby said vehemently. "Stay right here till I get back."

Jenna regarded him with confusion. "Why? Is there something else going on?"

"No. I just want to be sure the police have all these kids rounded up and everything's settled down. Stay here, please."

Jenna met his gaze and finally nodded. "We'll wait," she promised.

Bobby pressed a kiss to Darcy's damp cheek, then brushed another kiss across Jenna's forehead. Daisy walked with him to the door.

"Where are you going?" she asked, her expression worried.

"To Cedar Hill."

That took her by surprise. "Why?"

Bobby shrugged. "Tucker's idea. He's got some bug up his behind."

Daisy's gaze shot to their brother, who was waiting behind the wheel of his car. "Oh, no," she whispered and took off running across the lawn.

"Now what?" Bobby muttered, trailing along behind. He arrived just in time to hear the end of Daisy's blistering tirade.

Tucker regarded her evenly. "It's time," he said bluntly.

"It is not," she said. "It is exactly the wrong time. Tucker, please, don't do this."

"Okay, that's enough," Bobby snapped. "Whatever you two know that I don't, tell me right here and now."

Tucker sent a see-what-you've-done look at Daisy.

"Don't blame me, you idiot. You're the one who started this," she said. "You finish it."

"Daddy ought to be the one," Tucker began.

"But Daddy's not here and you are," Bobby said. "Spill it, or I swear I'm going to reach in and drag you out here and pummel this big announcement, whatever it is, out of you."

Daisy sighed. "You might as well go ahead, Tucker. It's too late now."

The knot of dread in Bobby's stomach, already as big as Texas, grew even bigger.

"There's a chance," his brother began, "maybe more than a chance, that J.C. is not Lonnie's boy."

The pounding of Bobby's heart was suddenly so loud, he could hardly hear anything else. "Then who's his father?"

Tucker and Daisy exchanged a look. It was Daisy who spoke, her voice gentle. "Daddy believes it's you."

18

The roaring sound in Bobby's head grew louder. Surely he had to have misunderstood. Surely Daisy was not saying that she and everyone else in his family believed that Ann-Marie's son was his child.

"Are you crazy?" he demanded eventually. "Why would you even say something like that? Where's the proof? That boy's the spitting image of his..."

"Of his mother," Daisy filled in. "Not of Lonnie. Daddy claims he put two and two together right after the birth. You weren't here then. You'd already taken off for Europe. Ann-Marie had the baby about seven months after the wedding. Instead of going around town like a proud papa, Lonnie looked as if he wanted to slug anyone who even mentioned the baby. No one was passing out cigars. But it was a long time before Daddy got proof."

"What proof?"

"He wouldn't say, not to me anyway," Tucker said.

"So your theory is what? That Ann-Marie found herself pregnant with my baby, and instead of running to me, she ran to Lonnie and used the baby to trap him into marrying her? Don't you imagine they must have been sleeping together for that to have worked?" Bobby had to make an effort to keep the hurt out of his voice, but he couldn't hide the anger. "Bottom line, she was cheating on me with my best friend. He was the one she wanted to be with, not me."

Tucker regarded him with an unflinching look. "Maybe she wasn't cheating on you until after she found out she was pregnant."

"Then why the hell didn't she come to me?"

"I have a theory about that," Daisy said quietly. "Daddy never approved of her. And he was embarrassed that you'd dropped out of college and taken a fast-food job to earn the money to go to Europe. I think he refused to tell her how to get in touch with you."

"But *you* knew. So did Tucker. Did she ever come to either of you?"

Expressions somber, both of them shook their heads.

"I didn't think so," Bobby said. "Which means she didn't really want to find me."

"Or that Daddy paid her off to find another solution," Tucker said. "I wouldn't put it past him."

Bobby sagged against the side of the car and swiped a hand over his eyes. "No," he said wearily. "Neither would I."

"I just thought you ought to know all of this before I go to pick that boy up and take him in for questioning," Tucker said. "Lonnie's never been a father to that kid, and if Daddy does know the truth, it's little wonder why. But somebody obviously needs to step in before it's too late."

Bobby stared at his brother incredulously. "And you think that somebody ought to be me?"

"Who else is it going to be?" Tucker asked reasonably.

"You don't expect much, do you?" Bobby asked.

"We are Spencers," Daisy reminded him.

"Yeah, right," Bobby muttered. "God help us all."

On the drive over to Ann-Marie's, he couldn't shake the image of J. C. Gates, the defiant expression he wore like a mask, the dark, troubled eyes so like his mother's in recent years. Was it possible the boy was his son? The only way to find out was to ask Ann-Marie a point-blank question. After that, though, things would never be the same. Any pretense that Lonnie was the boy's father would be dashed forever. Who knew what strain it might put on that marriage? Bobby wished there were time to talk to Anna-Louise before he and Tucker went barging into the Gates home. Maybe she would have some ideas about the best way to handle this and cause minimal harm to everyone involved.

One look at Tucker's grim expression pretty much squelched any thought of further delay.

"I can't get into this with Ann-Marie today," Bobby told him. "Things are going to be bad enough."

"Your call," Tucker said. He glanced at Bobby. "Whether it's true or not, I can't go easy on J.C."

"I know that. I wouldn't expect you to."

"What will you do if you find out he is your son?"

"I wish to God I knew," Bobby said. "I suppose a lot depends on Ann-Marie and Lonnie and what *they* want."

"If the boy is yours, you have rights, too."

Bobby nodded. "That's the one thing that doesn't make any sense to me, though. If J.C. is a Spencer, I can't imagine King turning his back on him. He would have been the first grandchild.''

"There are ways of looking out for him without publicly acknowledging him,'' Tucker pointed out.

"Money, you mean.''

"Sure. There could have been a payoff or a trust fund.''

"I suppose,'' Bobby said. "It just doesn't seem like Daddy not to claim what's his, even if it is one generation removed.''

Tucker glanced over at him. "Are you holding out hope that I've got this all wrong?''

Bobby couldn't honestly say how he felt. The whole idea of being a father was brand new to him. And a son who connected him to Ann-Marie turning up at this late date raised a whole string of emotional land mines he wasn't sure he was prepared to tangle with.

"I don't know what I'm hoping for,'' he said candidly. "And even if it turns out to be true, I can hardly waltz into the middle of this mess and say, Okay, guys, you've really screwed things up with this kid. I'm taking over now.''

Tucker sighed as he pulled to a stop in front of Ann-Marie's. "I suppose you're right.'' He regarded Bobby with concern. "You ready?''

"I'm as ready as I'll ever be.''

Bobby followed his brother up the walk, forcing himself not to lag too far behind. When he spotted Ann-Marie in the doorway, her face pale and drawn, he knew she understood why they'd come.

"J.C.'s in his room,'' she said. "I heard about what

happened and sent him up there. I locked the door for good measure.''

Bobby smiled despite the dire circumstances. ''You thinking he can't climb out a window?''

She gave him a weary smile. ''Not since Lonnie sawed off all the nearest branches a month or so ago, when we found out J.C.'d been sneaking out at night.''

''You called an attorney for him?'' Tucker asked.

Alarm flared in her eyes. ''It's that bad?''

''Darcy has a broken arm and other injuires,'' Bobby said fiercely. ''He and those thugs he runs with did that to her. Where's Lonnie?''

''He stormed out when he heard what had happened,'' she said apologetically. ''Said this was my doing and I could handle it.''

Bobby studied her intently. ''Why would he say that? Where's he been all these years?''

Her gaze fell. That alone was enough to tell Bobby the truth. Lonnie had turned his back on J.C. because the boy wasn't his. Though he'd vowed to save that discussion for another time, he couldn't help himself. He tucked a finger under Ann-Marie's chin and forced her to meet his eyes.

''Is J.C. my son?'' he asked bluntly.

He could read the answer on her face even before she spoke. Tears welled up in her eyes.

''Yes,'' she said in a voice barely above a whisper.

''And Lonnie's known all these years?''

She nodded.

''Why, Ann-Marie? You could have told me.''

''I couldn't. I had to think about my family, about

Lonnie and his pride. If anyone else figured it out, it would have killed him."

"So instead you let him take out his hurt pride and anger on my son?"

"He didn't," she claimed, but she couldn't meet his gaze. "It was as if J.C. didn't exist for him, but he never hurt him. Never. He knew I would have left him if he'd laid a finger on that boy."

"There's more than one way to break a child's spirit," Bobby said.

"Look, I know you two have a lot to deal with," Tucker interrupted, "but it's going to have to wait. I need to talk to J.C. If you want a lawyer for him, Ann-Marie, call one now and have him meet us at the station."

"He's your own nephew," she pleaded, pulling out the one trump card she had now that the truth was out in the open. "You can't take him in."

Tucker winced, but Bobby knew he'd never relent. It wasn't in his nature to bend the rules. "Get J.C.," Bobby told Ann-Marie. "We'll go with him."

"No," she said fiercely. "Not you."

"He's my son, dammit. It's a helluva time to find that out, but the bottom line is that I have a duty to be there."

"Please," she begged. "If you're there, everyone will talk about it. It will be the final straw for Lonnie. He'll leave me."

Bobby gazed into her anguished eyes and knew that she was telling the truth. Her family would be irretrievably broken if he stepped into the middle of this today.

There would be time enough to sort things out later in a less public way.

"Does J.C. know about me?" he asked Ann-Marie.

"No. He just knows that he and his father don't get along."

Bobby's heart ached for the boy, but maybe there was time left to repair that damage, too.

"Okay, I'll stay out of this today, but we'll work it out, Ann-Marie. Understood?"

"Yes," she said wearily. "It's past time. I know that."

He glanced at Tucker. "You want me to hang out here till you get him?"

"No. You can take off. Can you get back to Daisy's okay?"

"I'll walk. I need the time to think, anyway."

Unfortunately, there weren't enough miles between here and Daisy's for all the thinking Bobby had to do. For starters, he was going to have to figure out how to keep from killing King for whatever role he'd played in this disaster.

Jenna kept stealing surreptitious looks at Bobby all during a very long dinner at Daisy's. If it hadn't been for Darcy and Tommy's chatter, the meal would have been uncomfortably silent. Walker was still at the station with the bullies responsible for Darcy's injuries. Bobby wouldn't even glance at his sister. Daisy looked more and more miserable. It all clearly had something to do with that family pow-wow that they'd held on the front lawn before Bobby and Tucker had gone off to pick up J. C. Gates.

The instant everyone had finished dessert, Jenna said, "I really do hate to eat and run, but I think I should get Darcy home. She's had a tough day."

"Mom, please," Darcy begged. "Tommy and me were going to see who could catch the most lightning bugs."

As appealing as the harmless activity was, Jenna couldn't imagine spending another hour with Daisy and Bobby when the tension between them was so thick it could be cut with a knife.

"Not tonight, sweetie. Maybe tomorrow."

"But—" Darcy protested.

"I said no," Jenna repeated firmly.

"I'll play a game with you when we get to your place," Bobby offered. "You pick."

"Uno," Darcy said at once. "I'm the grand champion at that."

Bobby grinned for the first time all evening. "Is that so? Then you haven't played with me."

Jenna gave an exaggerated groan. "Just what I need, two people with mile-wide competitive streaks. I think I'll sit this one out."

"Oh, no," Darcy said. "You've got to play. It's more fun with three people." She grinned at Bobby. "Sometimes Grandpa played with us. I beat him, too. He didn't like it."

"Because your grandfather hates to lose," Jenna said. "Doesn't matter whether it's a kid's game or a business deal."

"How about you?" Bobby asked. "Are you a sore loser?"

"Nope," Jenna told him. "But then, between Darcy and my dad, I've had more practice."

He grinned. "Darcy, I think you and I need to throw a couple of games your mom's way tonight, okay? Her confidence needs bolstering."

Jenna frowned at him. "Don't do me any favors, unless, of course, you'd like to throw that boardwalk deal my way."

"We have a date to discuss that in the morning," Bobby reminded her. "Tonight it's all about cards."

When they got to her house, Jenna insisted that Darcy take her bath and get ready for bed before they started the card game.

"Mom, I can't take a bath. I can't get my arm wet," Darcy countered with a triumphant look.

"She's got you there," Bobby said.

"Okay, but you still have to get into your pj's. I'm not struggling to get you into them when you fall asleep in the middle of the card game."

"Okay," Darcy agreed, and ran off to change.

"Brush your teeth and wash your face," Jenna shouted after her.

"I know, Mom," Darcy called back with typical impatience.

Once she was gone, Jenna put on a pot of coffee and poured Darcy a glass of milk. While the coffee was brewing, she turned back to Bobby, who had that faraway expression in his eyes again.

"Want to talk about it?" she asked.

"What?"

"Whatever's been on your mind all night."

He shook his head. "Not yet."

"I'm a good listener. Besides, I owe you. You've listened to me enough the past few weeks."

"This is something I have to sort out for myself," he insisted, his voice tight.

"Sure, whatever." Hurt by the abrupt dismissal, she turned away and started out of the kitchen.

"Jenna." He snagged her hand as she passed him. "I'm sorry. It's a very complicated situation. There are other people involved. I can't talk about it yet. And to be perfectly honest, it could influence things between you and me."

She stared at him. "How?"

"It just could. You'll have to take my word for it."

Her heart began to thump unsteadily. She couldn't lose out on this deal now, not over something he wouldn't even share with her. "Is this about the deal?"

"Not directly, but it could affect you and me working together."

She met his gaze evenly and resisted the longing to reach out and console him. He looked so miserable, but this wasn't about him. She couldn't allow it to be. "If this could affect my future, then I have a right to know," she told him forcefully.

"You do and I will tell you," he promised. "Then it will be up to you to decide what you want to do about it."

"Are you saying this is so big that *I* might pull out?"

He nodded.

"It will never happen," she insisted. "I want this too much."

"That could change. Believe me, I've seen for myself today just how fast your whole life can change."

"But you're not going to explain that, are you?"

He shook his head. "Not tonight, no."

"Then I think you ought to go."

"And disappoint Darcy?"

Jenna sighed. He was right. It wasn't fair to Darcy to ruin the evening she'd been looking forward to, not after the traumatic day she'd already had.

"Okay, fine. But the minute I say the game is over, you walk out of here without another word. Are we clear?"

"Perfectly."

Despite the tension between them, they managed to keep the game lively for Darcy's sake. She didn't seem to notice that anything was amiss. She was too busy playing a cutthroat game of Uno and laughing at Bobby's perplexed expression as she won hand after hand. Even Jenna had to smile when Darcy was the first to slap her last card on the table for the fourth straight game.

"Are you sure you didn't stack the deck?" Bobby grumbled good-naturedly.

Darcy laughed. "I couldn't, silly. You're the one who dealt."

"So I did. I must have given you my cards by mistake."

"Well, I think we should put the man out of his misery and let him leave," Jenna said.

"One more hand," Darcy begged.

Bobby caught Jenna's eye. She flashed him a look of warning that had him on his feet at once.

"Not tonight, kiddo. I've got to get going. Your mom and I have an early morning date to check crab pots."

Darcy's eyes lit up. "You and Mom have a date? A real date?"

Jenna regarded him with exasperation. "No, it's not a *date*. It's a business meeting."

"Call it whatever you want," he said blithely. "It's still at seven o'clock. She needs to get her beauty sleep."

Jenna frowned at the comment.

"Uh-oh," Darcy said. "Even *I* know you're not supposed to tell a girl she needs to sleep to be pretty."

Bobby regarded her innocently. "Is that so? You think I insulted your mom?"

"Pretty much," Darcy said.

"Then I guess I'll have to fix that," he said, his gaze locked on Jenna's mouth. He leaned down. "Even if you don't sleep a wink all night, I'll still think you're beautiful in the morning."

The whispered words sent a shiver racing down her spine, but that was nothing compared to the pulse-pounding effect of his mouth when it settled over hers. The kiss was chaste enough for the nine-year-old in the room. It lasted barely more than a heartbeat, but Jenna's blood turned to liquid fire in her veins.

"Do it again," Darcy pleaded.

Bobby grinned at her. "Once more, then, with feeling," he agreed, and touched his lips to Jenna's.

This time it took everything in her to keep from leaping up and throwing herself into his embrace. She wanted more than that fleeting whisper of flesh on flesh. She wanted more than his breath fanning across her cheek or his heat beckoning to her. She wanted to get lost in touches that seared, in caresses that lingered.

Bobby was nothing at all like Nick. There was no edge of danger, no sense of reckless daring. He was solid and dependable, which should have made him boring, but he wasn't. Far from it. When he kissed her, she felt all of the wicked, dangerous sensations that her ex-husband had stirred in her as a teenager. Only now they came with the added passion of maturity. Jenna could finally admit that she wanted more from this man than a business deal. Much more.

But Bobby was already heading for the door, delivering a smacking kiss to Darcy's forehead, then turning back to wink at Jenna. "Seven o'clock," he repeated.

"I'll be there," she said, her voice far less crisply professional than it should have been.

"I'm counting on it."

And then he was gone, and Darcy was regarding her with the happiest expression she'd worn in a long time. "Bobby's the best, isn't he, Mom?"

"I suppose," she said, careful not to show too much enthusiasm for a man who was keeping a critical secret from her.

"You like him, don't you? You let him kiss you, so that must mean that you like him, right?"

"There are a lot of reasons for people to kiss," Jenna said carefully. "He kissed you good-night, too, remember?"

"Mom," Darcy protested with disgust. "It wasn't

the same. He kissed *me* like a kid. He kissed *you* the way a man kisses a woman.''

Jenna grinned at the impatient explanation. ''Thanks for the play-by-play analysis. How would you know how a man kisses a woman?''

''I see stuff on TV,'' she said at once.

''I'm throwing out our television first thing in the morning,'' Jenna vowed vehemently.

''And I saw the way Walker kisses Daisy,'' Darcy said, clearly unimpressed by the threat. ''That's the way Bobby kissed you.''

Jenna barely resisted the desire to touch her fingers to her still-burning lips. It was, indeed, the way Walker kissed Daisy, a kiss with barely restrained, smoldering heat behind it. It was the kind of kiss Jenna had envied them.

But what were the chances it would ever lead to anything more for her and Bobby? Tonight it had been nothing more than a game played out in front of an impressionable child who was yearning for a dad who'd be more reliable than the one she had.

And all the other times they'd kissed? Jenna couldn't come up with an answer to that beyond the obvious. Just as Darcy had pegged it, Jenna liked Bobby Spencer. Heaven help her.

19

Living on a farm his entire life, King was used to getting up with the roosters, even though it was usually much later by the time he ventured into town for his morning coffee with his pals. Today, though, he had a mission. His phone had rung off the hook the night before with a whole lot of talk about the boys who'd attacked little Darcy Kennedy. The whole incident made King's blood boil, but nothing had stirred him up more than the mention that J. C. Gates was in the thick of it. He intended to see Tucker first thing this morning and demand a few answers.

He was waiting for his son when Tucker walked into Earlene's for his first cup of coffee.

"Over here," King barked in a tone that dared Tucker to defy him.

Tucker slid into the booth opposite King. "You're out early, old man. Something on your mind?"

"As if you didn't know," King shot back.

"You heard about Darcy?"

King nodded. "I heard about what happened to her. Also heard she's going to be fine. Now what I want to know is what's happening with those hooligans who attacked her."

"We'll find out in court today. I have to get over

there as soon as I've had my coffee. They're all being arraigned this morning.''

"Including Ann-Marie's boy?"

"Absolutely," Tucker said without hesitation. "He was the ringleader. The kid has a mean streak. He didn't show the slightest evidence of remorse when I questioned him yesterday. If it were up to me, I'd see him charged as an adult, but the judge is likely to be more lenient since this is the first time his actions have actually landed him in court." His gaze clashed with King's. "But it isn't the first time he's been in trouble, and something tells me it won't be the last. He's a kid with a lot of problems."

King's gaze narrowed. "You say that as if you think *I* had something to do with them. The trouble with you, Tucker, is you have a hard heart. You lack compassion. Other than that, you're a darned fine sheriff, and I'm proud of you, but you need to get a little perspective when it comes to kids. Take Tommy—"

Tucker held up a hand. "Whoa! You were just as opposed to Daisy keeping that boy as I was."

"But I saw the good in him sooner than you did," King said triumphantly.

"I had no idea we were having a contest."

King frowned at the sarcasm. "Bottom line, Daisy was right. Tommy's a good boy, and now she has a fine family. Even Walker's shaping up real nice."

Tucker chuckled. "Thanks to you, I suppose."

"Well, no, I have to give Daisy credit for that," King conceded with some reluctance. "But you've got to admit, they're all happy, and Tommy hasn't been in any mischief lately."

"True."

"Then isn't it possible that with a little guidance, these boys who hurt Darcy will turn out just fine, too?"

"Anything's possible, but I'd rather not take chances," Tucker countered. "The next time somebody could wind up dead, instead of having a broken arm and a few cuts and bruises."

"These are children," King said, appalled by the idea that things would ever go that far.

"Who do you think did the shooting in those school killings in Colorado and California?" Tucker retorted.

King fell silent. He'd come here hoping to exert a little subtle influence to get Tucker to go easier on those boys—all of them, since he could hardly single out J.C. without explaining why. But what Tucker had to say put a different spin on things. He wasn't going to be the one responsible for turning a boy loose to do even more serious harm to another child.

"You do what you have to do," he said at last.

Tucker regarded him with that even, penetrating look that had shaken King, even when his son was just a boy.

"Is this about J.C., Daddy?"

King tried not to let him see just how startled he was by the question. "Why would you ask that?"

"I know you know—or at least think—that he's Bobby's son, your grandson."

Years of keeping the secret to himself lifted off King's shoulders. "You know?"

"Over the years I've heard a few things you've said and put two and two together."

"Dammit. I thought I had a better poker face than that. Does Bobby know?"

"I told him what I suspected yesterday. I thought he had a right to know before I hauled J.C. in for questioning. He confronted Ann-Marie, and she confirmed it."

"Blast it all, Tucker, why'd you go and stir things up?" King demanded. "He didn't need to know, especially not now when there's finally a decent woman in his life."

Tucker frowned at him. "This isn't about Bobby and Jenna, or even about Bobby and Ann-Marie. It's about a boy who's spent his whole life wondering why his dad and he don't get along, a boy who's been acting out to get his father's attention or at least the attention of the man he *thinks* is his father."

Much as he wanted to, King couldn't argue with that. He knew Bobby, possibly better than the boy understood himself. He would step up to the plate and do whatever had to be done to turn J.C. around...even if it meant turning his back on a new relationship for himself.

"Does J.C. know?" King asked.

"Not yet. I imagine Bobby, Ann-Marie and Lonnie will have to sit down and work all that out."

"Lonnie Gates shouldn't have any say in it at all," King said heatedly. "The only reason that man's put up with J.C. all these years is the money I've been sending over there every month."

"You've paid him to keep silent?" Tucker asked, looking disgusted. "I should have known."

"I've paid for J.C.'s support," King corrected.

"Not that a dime of it has been put aside for the boy, I'm sure."

"Daddy, why the hell didn't you let Bobby sort all this out for himself?"

"Because he was little more than a kid himself when this all started. When Ann-Marie came to me with the truth, she was already married to Lonnie. I couldn't see the point of them divorcing and tying Bobby to that woman. I'll make no apologies for leaving things the way they were."

Tucker shook his head. "You never do. Did it ever occur to you that your meddling all those years ago kept Bobby from dealing with the situation and moving on? All this time you've been pestering him to get on with his life, but you were the one responsible for keeping him tied up in knots over losing Ann-Marie to his best friend."

"Some friend," King said with a huff.

"I'll agree with you there, but it wasn't your call, Daddy. Even if he was only eighteen, Bobby had a right to know about that baby," Tucker said. "You taught us all to be independent. Now you turn right around and try to run our lives. You could lose Bobby over this."

"It'll never happen," King blustered, but in his heart he wasn't sure. Had he gone too far this time?

Well, even if he had, he could fix it. Bobby was stubborn, but not impossible. When push came to shove, he was a Spencer. He'd never turn his back on his father or his heritage.

King sighed heavily. Then, again, Bobby had left Cedar Hill and the family cattle legacy quick enough.

He'd never looked back, either. King could see he was going to have to do some fancy footwork to turn things around this time. He could use Frances's advice, but he doubted she was in any mood to give him the time of day.

He drank his last sip of coffee and heaved himself out of the booth.

"Where are you going?" Tucker asked.

"To find your brother. No sense in letting this get any more out of control than it has already, thanks to you."

"Don't blame me, old man. You brought this one all on yourself."

King shot him a sour look. "And you'll take pleasure in reminding me of that all the livelong day, I suppose."

"Longer," Tucker retorted.

But as King headed for the door, Tucker called after him, "Good luck, Daddy."

King tipped his hat. "Thanks, son."

"You'll find Bobby at the marina in an hour or so, I imagine. He and Jenna were going to check crab pots about seven."

"He's with Jenna?" King's spirits brightened. "Well, then, things can't be all that bad."

"You're incorrigible."

"Well, of course I am. I'm a Spencer. When something's worth fighting for, we stick with it. Just wait," he said, leveling a look straight at his son. "It'll be your turn soon enough."

He took great pleasure in walking out of Earlene's

with Tucker's indignant, sputtering protest trailing after him.

The morning Jenna spent with Bobby on his boat was surprisingly pleasant, despite the tension between them the night before. It was difficult to work up to a heated argument when the sky was a cloudless blue, the river calm and a salty breeze kept things cool.

There was a quiet rhythm to the work of motoring slowly from bobbing crab pot to crab pot, checking for succulent crabs, picking out the jimmies and tossing back females and undersized crabs. Bobby wasn't a big-time waterman. He maintained only enough pots to supply the restaurant during the week. For weekends, when demand was higher, he bought bushels of hardshell and softshell crabs from the men who worked the river for a living. He'd told her he did this much work himself, only because he found it relaxing to be on the water.

The catch this morning was paltry compared to a few years ago, he told her. "Supplies are dwindling. There are constant fights between the regulators trying to protect the crabs for the future and the watermen who need to make a living now. It's a delicate balancing act."

"So many environmental issues are," Jenna said, as she trailed a hand in the warm water of the Potomac, her face turned up to the early morning sun. "How could anyone not see the value in keeping this river and the Chesapeake Bay clean and productive for the future?"

"There are a lot of shortsighted people in the

world," he said. "Some are looking for the quick buck, just like the men who would plaster condos along the waterfront, instead of taking the time and making the investment to turn it into something everyone can enjoy."

Jenna should have seized on that as the perfect opening to talk about the boardwalk, but she couldn't seem to do it. Injecting business into this tranquil moment seemed wrong. She was happy just to be on the river with Bobby this morning. She should have found that disturbing, but she didn't.

Her priorities had changed since coming to Trinity Harbor a few weeks ago. She didn't feel nearly the same kind of pressure to accomplish the impossible that she felt in Baltimore. It was a relief to be regarded with approval just for being her. Bobby's sister Daisy seemed to like her. Anna-Louise Walton, who was the kindest woman Jenna had ever met and a minister to boot, seemed to think that Jenna was a worthwhile human being. In fact, she was downright impatient with Jenna's claims to the contrary. The last time she'd quoted her father about her reckless ways, Anna-Louise had used a word that should never cross the lips of a pastor.

As Jenna had begun to view herself in a new light, she was putting less pressure on Darcy. Her daughter's sullen expression was appearing less and less frequently. They hadn't had a rousing battle over tattoos and body piercing in weeks now.

Amid all of this generous acceptance, Jenna had almost ceased to care about her father's criticisms, which still came loudly and frequently. Only his threat to come down to see for himself what was taking so long disturbed her newfound serenity. She had a feeling once he turned up, he would find some way to demean her efforts and take over. It would ruin everything she'd fought so hard to accomplish here—for the company and for herself.

"Hey, are you falling asleep over there?" Bobby teased, nudging her bare foot.

"Not me," she claimed, though she didn't open her eyes.

"How come you're not pestering me with questions or tossing facts and figures at me?"

"Too much like work," she said.

Bobby laughed. "I've done it," he said with satisfaction. "I've turned you into a slug like me."

"Could be," she said. "I intend to hang on to this as long as I can."

"How long do you expect that to be?" he asked.

There was a serious note in his voice that snapped her eyes open. Though he was dragging a crab pot out of the water and checking the contents, she thought she detected a sudden tension in his shoulders.

"What are you asking, Bobby?"

His gaze met hers. "What are your plans? When will you head back to Baltimore?"

"That depends on you," she said, holding his gaze. "You know that."

He nodded. "Okay, say I were to make this deal with you—once the job is finished, what then?"

Jenna resisted the temptation to shout with glee at the promise of a deal. He wasn't really giving it to her, she reminded herself sternly. He was speculating. She was determined to keep the difference in mind.

"I'm not sure," she told him honestly.

"But you do like it here, right?"

She smiled at that. "How could I not? It's a beautiful place." She let her gaze drift slowly over his bare chest. "The company's not bad either."

"Yeah, we'll have to talk about that soon."

"Talk?"

"I'm the kind of man who likes to take things nice and easy. At least that's the kind of man I've become."

"Since Ann-Marie took off with Lonnie."

His expression darkened. "Yeah, since then," he said tersely.

It was the opening she'd been waiting for. "Bobby, what happened yesterday? I know it had something to do with Ann-Marie."

For a long time, he simply kept up the mechanical motions of a man used to working with crab pots. When he found a stubborn knot in one of the ropes, he bent over it with a look of fierce concentration.

Finally, with his gaze still diverted, he said, "I found out that J.C. is my boy."

Jenna moved to an upright position so fast, the boat rocked. "What?"

"I told you you might want to reconsider doing business with me."

She stared at him blankly. "What does one thing have to do with the other?"

"He hurt Darcy."

"Why is that your fault?"

"He's my son."

"Which you didn't know," she pointed out. "Nor could you have controlled the situation, even if you had known."

"You'd feel differently if it had been more than a broken arm."

"But it wasn't," she said. "And, yes, I am furious with him, but certainly not with you, a man who's had absolutely no input into his upbringing at all."

His troubled gaze finally met hers. There was so much torment, she eased over and reached for him. His shoulders were warm from the early morning sun. He smelled of sun and salt water and man.

Jenna slid her hands up his chest, then cupped his cheek. It was rough with dark stubble that felt like sandpaper to the touch. She shivered at the sensation, but she didn't draw away, didn't avert her gaze.

"I'm sorry," she whispered.

"Sorry?"

"That it took so long for you to find out. It must have hurt."

He shook his head. "So far, I just feel numb."

She skimmed a finger across his lower lip, felt him shudder. It brought a smile to her lips. "You don't seem numb to me."

"Inside," he told her. "I'm numb inside."

Jenna drew in a deep breath. She wanted more from Bobby. She'd figured that out last night. Today, though, she wanted to give him something for making her feel alive again.

Recalling a time when she'd been bold instead of

timid, when she'd been reckless instead of safe, she said quietly, "We could change that."

Heat flared in his eyes. "Jenna." The protest was soft and not very vehement.

"I know exactly what I'm saying," she told him. "Exactly."

A rueful grin crossed his lips. "We're in a boat," he pointed out, as if it were a massive obstacle.

"You planning to stay out here forever?"

His gaze stayed steady on hers, unflinching and filled with yearning.

"No," he said at last, emptying the last pot and tossing it back into the river with a rushed, careless gesture. He reached for the throttle and turned back toward shore. One arm slid around Jenna's waist and held her snugly against his chest.

"You've got about fifteen minutes to change your mind." His words were whispered against her cheek.

"Not going to happen," she said, settling back to relish the warmth of his embrace. "Not if we were days away from land."

Of course neither of them were taking into account the possibility of finding King waiting for them at the dock.

"We need to talk," he said to Bobby.

"Not now," Bobby said tersely, not meeting his father's gaze as he tied the boat securely.

"You got something more important going on?" King demanded, then took one look at Jenna. His expression brightened ever so slightly. "Never mind. Call me."

"One of these days," Bobby said, all but dragging Jenna along the dock.

"Today," King ordered.

Bobby looked down into Jenna's eyes and tightened his grip on her hand, then called back to his father, "Don't count on it."

Jenna expected an indignant response, but instead it was a hoot of laughter that followed them to Bobby's car.

20

Bobby drove to his house with one hand on the wheel and the other clutching Jenna's hand. For this one instant in time, she was all that mattered, the only thing that was real. Ann-Marie's duplicity all those years ago, his relationship with J.C., his anger at his father's probable involvement, none of that was important. Not right this second.

When had he begun to count on having Jenna in his life? When had she become the person who could keep him grounded? When had his heart finally healed? Because it had.

Looking at Ann-Marie, even learning about her ultimate betrayal, hadn't shaken him as it once might have. All he felt was sorrow for the lost years with his son and regret for the pain J.C. had experienced living with a man who'd apparently resented him from the beginning.

Bobby glanced over at Jenna and grinned at the soft, feminine smile tugging at her lips. "Pretty proud of yourself, aren't you?"

She turned to face him. "For?"

"Luring me to bed in the middle of the morning."

"Watch it," she warned, amusement sparkling in her eyes. "We're not there yet."

"You thinking of changing your mind?" His tone was light, but fear clutched at him.

"That depends."

"On?"

"Whether you annoy me between now and the time we get to your place."

The words, which echoed his own warning to her about the risk of being out on a boat with him, made him chuckle. "Then I'll definitely try not to do that," he vowed.

Jenna's smile spread. "I was sure you'd see the wisdom of behaving yourself."

Bobby caught her gaze and held it until heat flared and desire darkened her eyes to a deep blue. "Oh, darlin', this has nothing to do with behaving, not if we're doing it right."

He watched with satisfaction as the pulse at the base of her throat began to race, then swerved into his driveway at an angle and cut the engine.

"Let's go," he said, all but dragging her from the car. He was not going to create yet another Spencer public spectacle by making love to her on his front lawn...and the odds of that happening were increasing by the second.

"What's the rush?" she asked, digging in her heels and bringing them both to a halt.

"Do you even have to ask?" Bobby demanded. Unable to hold back a moment longer, he hooked his hand behind her neck and took her mouth with a ferocity that left them both breathless. When he finally released her, she looked dazed and he was hard and aching. He raked a hand through his hair. "I swore I was not going to do this."

"What?"

"Create a public spectacle."

Jenna looked around, seemingly pleased at the discovery that the curtains were drawn back in a telling way in at least two sets of windows across the street. Bobby, however, groaned. Sue Kelly and Frannie Yarborough were getting an eyeful. This little incident would be broadcast far and wide by lunchtime.

"I'm sorry," he said.

"It was a kiss."

"Describing that as a kiss is pretty much like saying that a tiger's a cat," he told her wryly. "There's nothing tame about either one of them."

"Are you really worried about a little gossip?" she asked.

"I am for your sake. If you're going to do business in this town, you don't want people speculating on how you got the job."

His reply clearly flustered her.

"I'm going to get the job?" she asked.

"I didn't say…" He sighed, then conceded reluctantly, "More than likely." He held up a hand. "Don't get carried away just yet. There are details to consider. And I have two more presentations to see, but, yes, unless your figures are out of line or something dramatic comes along to change my mind, you're going to get the job."

The next thing he knew, Jenna had launched herself at him and was plastering kisses all over his face. "Thank you. Thank you. I can't believe it."

"Jenna," he warned.

"I know. All those details and two more presentations. I heard you. But I never thought I'd get this far. You have no idea what this means to me."

"I think I do," Bobby said, peeling her arms from around his neck. "And I still think we really ought to take this inside."

Jenna shook her head. "Oh, no," she said, promptly backing away a few steps. "I can't sleep with you now."

Disappointment slammed through him. Why hadn't he seen this coming? Hadn't he done his own fair share of lecturing about keeping business and personal relationships separate?

"You can't?" he echoed.

"No. It wouldn't be right. We're going to be business partners. You said it yourself. I don't want people to think I used sex to get this job."

Bobby sighed heavily. He had only himself to blame for the fact that he was going to spend the rest of the day tormented by what had almost happened here this morning. He'd planted the idea in her head that people might speculate after seeing the two of them here together this morning. He'd been right to consider it, but for once maybe he should have kept his big mouth shut. Being honorable definitely had its drawbacks.

"Is there any way at all I could change your mind?" he inquired hopefully, even as he prepared to get into his car and head back to the marina. He could all but hear Sue and Frannie's sighs as well. He doubted their regrets could possibly match his own.

Jenna patted his cheek as if she were consoling a

kid. "Not just yet, but think of it this way—I have a really *huge* incentive to get this job done in record time."

Bobby took comfort in the heated promise in Jenna's eyes as he reluctantly made his way over to Ann-Marie's just after five that evening. He'd called earlier, and she'd assured him that Lonnie would be home and the three of them could sit down and talk.

But when Bobby rang the doorbell, he noted that there was no sign of Lonnie's truck in the driveway. Ann-Marie opened the door wearing the skimpiest pair of white shorts he'd ever seen and a tank top that stretched across her breasts in a very revealing manner. No bra. Once, that would have turned him on, but tonight it merely raised all sorts of red flags.

"Where's Lonnie?" he demanded, not setting foot across the threshold. "You said he'd be here."

"He got tied up at work. Come on in. I've got a bottle of wine open. It's the fancy French stuff you like."

Bobby stayed right where he was. "What's going on, Ann-Marie? This isn't a social call, and you know it."

"There's no reason you and I can't talk without Lonnie, is there? I mean this is really between you and me."

"No," he said firmly. "You put Lonnie right smack in the middle of it a long time ago. He needs to be here now. We'll set up another time. In fact, maybe I should make the arrangements directly with him. Did he even know I was coming by tonight, Ann-Marie?"

"What are you suggesting?" she asked, pouting. It wasn't as attractive as when she'd done it to get her way years ago.

"I'm out of here."

"Bobby, don't go," she pleaded. "There's so much we have to talk about."

He regarded her with disgust. "Anything you and I had to say to each other should have been said before you ran off with my best friend. Any conversation we have now involves Lonnie—and maybe a couple of lawyers while we're at it. I'll be in touch."

The door slammed behind him as he walked away. For once in his miserable, meddling life, maybe King had gotten it exactly right, Bobby thought as he got into his car. Maybe his father had known all along the kind of woman Ann-Marie was, when Bobby had been too blinded by hormones to see it.

Since his evening was already pretty much shot, he might as well go for broke and head out to Cedar Hill and get the confrontation with King over with.

He found his father on the porch with a glass of bourbon in one hand and the portable phone in the other. He muttered something into the phone as Bobby approached, then cut it off and all but slammed it down on the table next to him.

"Anything wrong?" Bobby asked.

"That fool woman's still not back from her trip."

Bobby bit back a grin. "You talking about Frances?"

"Who else?"

"Have you told her you miss her?"

"How am I supposed to do that? I have no idea where she is."

"You were mumbling at her answering machine just now, weren't you? Maybe if you said something nice, she'd take it to heart and come home."

"I'll take advice from you when you get your own life straightened out," King shot back.

Bobby dropped into a rocker and set it into motion. "It's getting there," he said.

"About time." He glanced curiously at Bobby. "Jenna?"

"She's a wonderful woman," Bobby conceded.

"That's been my impression," King agreed. "That girl of hers is a real pistol, too."

"She is."

"It's a darned shame, what happened to her."

Bobby sighed. "Which brings us to J.C." He looked his father in the eye. "What were you thinking, Daddy?"

"That there was nothing wrong with the status quo. Ann-Marie would have ruined your life," he said bluntly, not even bothering to pretend not to understand what Bobby was asking. "Can you tell me I was wrong about that?"

"Not after tonight, no," Bobby said honestly. "But I had a right to decide things for myself."

"You were too young to think straight. I'd trust you with a decision like that now, but back then?" King shook his head. "Hormones and common sense just don't mix at eighteen."

"And they do now that I'm almost thirty?" Bobby asked wryly. "Or is it just that now you have a different agenda? You want to see me married and settled down.''

''There's truth to that,'' King said. ''And Jenna's a different sort of woman. She had a rebellious period, same as you, but she's got some maturity on her now. She's got a good level head on her shoulders. Anyone can see that.''

''Then you'd approve if something happened between Jenna and me?''

King's chuckle was deep. ''The way things looked this morning, I'd have bet it already has.''

Bobby glowered at his father. ''I am not discussing that with you.'' He stood up. ''I've got to go.''

''Just one thing before you do,'' King said. ''You gonna leave the past in the past?''

''When it comes to Ann-Marie or to you?''

''Both, for that matter.''

Bobby heard the real worry in King's voice, saw the hint of fear in his eyes. He reached down and gave his father's hand a squeeze. ''You're forgiven, if that's what you're asking.''

King nodded. ''I only did it for your own good.''

''I know that now. A few hours ago, I might not have been so generous.''

''Then I'm grateful to whoever changed your mind.''

''It was Ann-Marie, actually.'' He chuckled at his father's startled, dismayed expression. ''Not the way you think. I just saw what you saw.''

''That's good then. What do you intend to do about J.C.?''

''I'm working on that. I'll keep you posted,'' he said

as he started off the porch. He turned back. "And whatever payments I suspect you've been making all these years can stop. I'm taking over now."

"Your call," King said.

"Yeah, right," Bobby retorted with a snort of disbelief.

Two uncomfortable meetings down, Bobby thought as he drove to the marina. Just one to go. When he reached his office, he picked up the phone and dialed the number for Randall Pennington. As long as he was going to spend the evening mending fences, he might as well get to work on the one between Jenna and her father, though something told him she wouldn't thank him for it.

Jenna sat in Bobby's office and stared at him as if he'd turned into a freak in a circus sideshow. "You did *what?*" she demanded.

"I called your father. He'll be here in time for dinner tonight."

Jenna's stomach rolled over. She couldn't decide if she was more furious with Bobby or more terrified of facing her father. Mostly the former, she concluded, scowling at the man sitting smugly behind his desk.

"What right did you have to do that?"

"Jenna, you're representing Pennington and Sons. It makes sense that I'd want to meet the head of the company," he said reasonably. "He needs to be on board for this."

"Because you don't trust me," she said, trying not to sound defeated. How could he do this to her after everything she'd told him? It was *her* proposal he was buying, not her father's. Her father didn't even want this job.

"I do trust you," Bobby said emphatically. "If I didn't, I would never have made that call. Maybe it's about time you learned to trust yourself."

She frowned at that. "What is that supposed to mean?"

"That the only way to win your father's confidence and approval is to face him and prove to him that you're good at this job."

"So you're doing me some huge favor by giving me that chance?" she asked skeptically.

"Exactly."

"Hogwash! You don't know what you're talking about, Bobby. My father will see this as proof that I'm not doing a good enough job. He'll be convinced that you called him down here to rescue me. He'll think it's because you want his assurances that he'll back me up. In other words, he's going to snatch this chance away from me because he'll be absolutely certain that I'm going to mess it up the way I have every other important thing in my life."

Filled with frustration, she stood up and began to pace. Eventually she paused, leaned down and stared straight into Bobby's eyes. "I'm telling you, the next thing you know, my brothers will be crawling all over Trinity Harbor, checking everything I've already done and probably doubling the costs in the process. By the time they're finished, your mayor will have those condos he wants so badly."

"That's not going to happen," Bobby said calmly.

"You haven't seen Pennington and Sons in action.

I have," she said fiercely. "They're my family and I love them, but those three can rob a person blind and make him like it."

"You're saying I'm no match for them?" he said. "Do you think I'm just some small-town hick who can't play in the same pool as the big-city sharks?"

Jenna hesitated at the cold note in his voice. "No, not exactly."

"Are you or aren't you?"

"I just mean that you don't know them like I do," she said.

"How well do you know me, Jenna?"

"Fairly well," she responded cautiously, not sure where he was heading.

"Have you ever known me to bow to pressure or to go back on my word?"

"No, but—"

He frowned. "If you say that I haven't met your brothers or your father yet, I'm going to toss you out of here."

He sounded so serious that she sank back down in the chair opposite him. "I'm sorry."

"You should be. I did not do this to hurt you. I did it *for* you."

"Well, excuse me for not being grateful," she retorted.

Bobby sighed. "Will you be here for dinner or not?"

"Oh, I'll be here," Jenna said. "Heaven help us all."

After only five minutes with Randall Pennington, every protective instinct in Bobby went on full alert.

He'd thought Jenna was exaggerating her father's attitude toward her, but she hadn't been. Not even a little.

Unlike King, who nagged his offspring to death and tried to manipulate them into doing his bidding, Pennington was an unmistakable bully. It made Bobby's heart ache when he saw the hoops Jenna was willing to jump through to try to get so much as a hint of love, instead of all the harsh words and criticism the man doled out. For all of his faults, King's love had always been freely given.

"I apologize to you for not sending one of my sons down here to handle this," Pennington said right off, after casting a sour look at his daughter. There hadn't been one iota of warmth in the greeting he'd given her, either. "Jenna gets these crazy notions into her head sometimes. I understand that your father raised three of you without a mother in the house. I'm sure he would agree that it's no easy task, especially with a daughter, when there's no female influence around. I'm afraid Jenna has never understood the proper place for a woman."

Jenna all but rose out of her seat at his patronizing words, but a warning look from Bobby settled her down.

"And what place would that be?" he inquired, his own mood turning dangerous.

Clearly, Pennington missed the warning signs, because he said without the slightest hint of embarrassment, "At home, minding her children."

"Not all women have the luxury of staying at home

to care for their children. Some, like Jenna, are single mothers who need to make their own way in life. Some, like my sister, need the challenge of a career for their own fulfillment. Actually, my father is proud of the way all of us turned out,'' Bobby said, making a mental plea for forgiveness for the flagrant lie. ''Especially my sister. She's a lot like Jenna. Strong and independent and smart as a whip.''

Pennington seemed taken aback by the praise for his daughter. So, Bobby noticed, did Jenna.

''What does your sister do?'' the man asked.

''She's a teacher,'' Bobby said.

Pennington beamed. ''Now there's a nice, respectable career for a woman. That, and nursing.''

Jenna started to bristle, then backed down. That left it to Bobby to say what had clearly been on the tip of her tongue.

''Are you saying that working for you is not respectable?'' he asked Pennington, keeping his tone mild.

''Well, of course it is, as long as she stays in the office where she belongs. She shouldn't be out here in the field, though. Not only does she not have the experience for it, but men don't respect women who try to step into an authority role.''

''Is that so?'' Bobby asked. ''Why not?''

Pennington apparently sensed that he was treading on very thin ice, because he backed off at once. ''They just don't. You're a man of the world. I'm sure you've seen it.''

''Not really. Of course, I cook for a living, so maybe I have some gender issues of my own.''

Jenna choked, then quickly covered her mouth. When her gaze met Bobby's, her eyes were twinkling with amusement though. He concluded that she was finally prepared to admit that he could hold his own with this particular shark.

Not that Pennington gave up the fight easily. He spent the entire evening going on and on about what a screwup Jenna was. It took everything in Bobby not to grab him up by his shirtfront, drag him outside and pummel some sense into him.

Finally it was Jenna who brought the dinner to a close. "Dad, I'm sure you've given Bobby a lot to think about. We'll be lucky if he lets us erect a playground swing set after this."

Her father stared at her with a shocked expression, while Bobby silently applauded.

"Let's go," she said. "Before you do any more damage to our chances to get this job."

"But we haven't even discussed the details yet," Pennington protested.

"Bobby and I have covered all of that," she said firmly, tucking a hand under his elbow and practically lifting him out of his chair.

"Without my input?" he asked incredulously.

"Believe it or not," she said, "I didn't need it."

"But—"

"Dad, let's go. We've taken up more than enough of Bobby's time. Where are you staying?"

"Some dump over by the river." He glanced at Bobby. "That's one of the first things we'll need to address. This town needs a first-class hotel, something big enough for all the conventions you'll be drawing once we put this place on the map."

Jenna rolled her eyes at Bobby. "No conventions, Dad. Maybe you and I had better go over the plans Bobby has tentatively approved before our next meeting. You wouldn't want him to think we were squabbling over the proposal, would you?"

Pennington was still protesting as she steered him away. Bobby stared after them and shook his head. If it weren't for Jenna, there was no way in hell he'd deal with that man. In fact, he didn't intend to deal with him now—only Jenna. Wasn't that going to be a rude awakening for the pompous idiot?

Bobby marched into his office the next morning and asked Maggie to find the Pennington paperwork for the boardwalk project.

"You're giving Pennington the contract?" she asked hopefully.

"In a way," he said, tossing the papers into his briefcase, then heading straight for the breakfast meeting he'd arranged during a phone call to Jenna late the night before.

Jenna watched him anxiously as he joined her and her father. He gave her a reassuring wink.

"Here's the deal," he said to her father, holding his pen in hand. "I will sign this on one condition."

Pennington's gaze narrowed. "Which is?"

"That I deal exclusively with Jenna. She stays here to oversee it from start to finish."

Both of them stared at him with openmouthed astonishment.

"You still want me?" Jenna asked, looking far more stunned than any confident, talented woman should have.

He grinned at her. "Oh, yeah, but that's another issue entirely."

"You're making a mistake," Pennington said. "Either one of my sons—"

"Jenna," Bobby said flatly.

"But—"

"Do we have a deal?" Bobby asked.

Her father shrugged. "It's your money you're throwing away."

"Yes," Bobby agreed, "it is my money I'm *investing*." His gaze narrowed. "And one more thing for the record. Your daughter is an extremely talented waterfront planner. If I ever hear you make another remark like that disparaging Jenna's ability, I will strongly suggest to her that she open her own company and whip your sorry butt right into the ground."

21

Jenna was still reeling from the scene with her father. Never before in her entire life had anyone stood up for her like that. In that single instant, she had fallen head over heels in love with Bobby Spencer. Oh, she'd been well on her way weeks ago, but that moment had crystalized everything she was feeling.

Unfortunately, for the past few days, he had been giving her such a wide berth that they might as well have been living in different states. He was acting as if that admission he'd made that he wanted her had been a slip of the tongue or that it referred to something else entirely. It was as if their near-tumble into bed had never happened, either.

The day after the breakfast with her father, Jenna had ducked into Bobby's office, hoping to catch him alone so that she could thank him properly for coming to her rescue, to say nothing of the favor he'd done her by giving her the job. He'd waved off her thanks and scurried out of the office so fast that even Maggie was left shaking her head.

That evening Jenna had gone to the restaurant for dinner, but she hadn't caught so much as a glimpse of Bobby. When she'd finally gathered her courage and poked her head into the kitchen, she'd discovered that he'd left not fifteen minutes earlier after making a lame excuse that no one had bought. She had endured the pitying looks of his staff for a few more minutes, then took off herself.

And so it had gone, day after day, until she was ready to scream in frustration. She refused to be discouraged, though. She knew exactly what Bobby had meant that evening at dinner, knew from solid evidence—so to speak—just how badly he wanted her, and all the denials in the world weren't going to change it. She just had to be patient.

Besides, she had a project to oversee, and she didn't intend to mess it up. Too much was at stake: not only her professional reputation, but Bobby's faith in her. She was not going to disappoint him. The boardwalk in Trinity Harbor was going to be as quaint and charming as the town itself, a peaceful refuge from the stresses of the big city. No one understood those stresses better than she did. In fact, just the thought of having to go back to Baltimore someday was enough to make her jittery.

Proving herself to Bobby was one thing. There was also her father to consider. She didn't intend to do anything to confirm his disparaging remarks about her inexperience. If she had to take a crash course in construction and hammer home every single nail herself, this project was going to come in on time and under budget. She intended to put her brothers to shame on that score. By Memorial Day next spring when it was unveiled right on schedule, the Trinity Harbor boardwalk was going to be the talk of the travel industry in the entire region, and she was finally going to have her father's respect. If she didn't, she was prepared to walk away from the relationship and stand on her own two feet.

Never in her entire life had Jenna been so determined. Okay, maybe when she'd set out to marry Nick, but she wasn't going to linger on *that* mistake. There was no comparison. She might not have understood much about men back then, but she did understand the development business…at least in theory. As a practical matter, she was going to be testing herself, but she could do it. She had to.

"You look grim," Daisy noted, slipping into the booth opposite her at Earlene's the following Monday morning. "What's up?"

"Not grim, determined," Jenna corrected after a weekend of making charts and timetables and enough lists to choke any compulsive overachiever on earth. "I'm going to build this boardwalk project without one single hitch. Not one."

Daisy laughed. "Now there's a surefire way to tempt fate. Mistakes happen. Delays are just part of the real world."

"Not mine," Jenna insisted.

Daisy's laughter faded. "Has Bobby been putting too much pressure on you?"

Now it was Jenna's turn to chuckle. "Hardly. He's not even speaking to me."

"Why on earth not?" Daisy asked, bristling with obvious indignation on Jenna's behalf. "What's wrong with my brother, anyway?"

Jenna really wanted to confide in Daisy, but she hesitated. For one thing, Daisy *was* Bobby's sister. Blood would win out every time…except, maybe, in her family. For another thing, Jenna simply wasn't used to discussing her personal life with anyone. Heck, she wasn't even used to *having* a personal life.

"He's been busy," Jenna said, defending him half-heartedly.

"Like that has anything to do with anything," Daisy scoffed. "Bobby makes time for what he wants to make time for."

"Which should tell you something," Jenna said. "I'm obviously not a priority. And the truth of the matter is, I don't have time for anything personal right now, either. I can't afford to be distracted. He's demonstrated a tremendous amount of faith in me by giving me this contract. I can't let him down. And mixing business with pleasure is probably a really lousy idea."

Wasn't that a conversation they'd had in detail on his front lawn right after he'd kissed her senseless? Even though she didn't like it, it had been her idea as much as his. It was probably better this way. She could focus all her energy on the work that had to be done. Being around Bobby muddled her thinking.

"Since you're staying here to do this job, I assume Darcy will be going to school here," Daisy said, wisely letting the matter of Jenna's relationship with Bobby drop for the moment. "Have you enrolled her yet?"

"I'm going by to do that today, right after I interview contractors."

"Okay, but a word of warning," Daisy said. "Remember that this is Trinity Harbor, not Baltimore.

Things tend to move at a more leisurely pace. Stop by the bookstore and ask Gail Thorensen about that. It took her forever to get everything finished the way she wanted it. Of course, if you've met Gail, you know she was born in a rush, but the bottom line is, don't expect too much, too soon. The work will be excellent, but it might not happen on your timetable.''

Jenna nodded, but dismissed the advice. She didn't have time to waste, not in completing the boardwalk project. Because until then, she wouldn't have a minute to spare for her other project—getting herself into Bobby's bed and, even more important, into his heart.

Bobby found out what job Lonnie was working, drove to the site at the end of the day and waited beside his truck. When Ann-Marie's husband walked out of the house he was wiring and spotted Bobby, his usual sour demeanor worsened visibly. It was hard to believe that at one time he'd been a carefree kid with all the potential in the world. No one had been more surprised than Bobby when Lonnie had given up a basketball scholarship to college and stayed home to apprentice as an electrician. Apparently he'd done it to be close to Ann-Marie—too close, as it had turned out. Bobby tried to work up some sympathy for him, but under the circumstances he couldn't.

''I have nothing to say to you,'' Lonnie said, brushing past him to yank open the truck door.

Bobby latched onto his arm and hauled him around to face him. Even though Lonnie was taller and bulkier, Bobby had always been quicker and stronger.

''Then you can listen,'' he told his onetime best

friend. "I know about J.C. I'm sorry you got caught in the middle, but that's in the past. We need to figure out what to do about the situation now."

"The *situation,* as you describe it, wouldn't exist if Ann-Marie didn't baby that boy the way she does."

"Maybe she's trying to make up for the fact that you ignore him," Bobby said bluntly. "Everybody in town has seen the way you treat him, even if none of them understand why."

Lonnie frowned. "So you intend to spread the word that you're a proud papa? I should have known you'd eventually turn up to claim what's yours. Why didn't you do it years ago, and save us all this misery?"

"If I'd known, I would have, but that's water under the bridge. I want to help now."

"By tossing more money my way to keep me quiet?" Lonnie inquired, his voice heavy with sarcasm.

"No, by providing some guidance to J.C. before he gets into even worse trouble than he's already in—unless, of course, you're prepared to knock that chip off your shoulder and do the job yourself."

Lonnie shrugged. "Kids fight. It's not a big deal."

"Maybe—and I do mean maybe—it's not a big deal when kids pick on other kids their own size. But he beat up on a little girl and left her with a broken arm. If you can't see the problem with that, then there's something wrong with you. You're not the Lonnie Gates I used to know."

"No, I'm not," Lonnie said flatly. "That Lonnie died when I realized my wife was still in love with her ex-fiancé and had given birth to his baby."

The statement and the obvious pain behind it rocked Bobby back on his heels. "I'm sorry," he said, and actually meant it.

"Yeah, well, we get what we ask for, don't we? That's what happens when you marry your best friend's girl."

"Lonnie, I really am sorry, but none of that is important now. Can't we work together to help J.C.?"

"You help him. I want no part of him. He's a constant reminder of everything that's gone wrong in my life," he said bitterly. "I lost my best friend *and* my wife over that kid."

"You can't seriously blame him for that," Bobby said.

"It may not be right, but I do," Lonnie said. "I can't change how I feel. He'll be better off with you as a role model. In fact, he'd be better off living under your roof, if that's the way you want to go."

"Ann-Marie will never agree to that," Bobby said.

"She will if I have anything to say about it," Lonnie said grimly. "It's the only way to save our pitiful excuse for a marriage."

This time when he brushed past Bobby to climb into his truck, Bobby let him go. Ten minutes later he was on Ann-Marie's doorstep. There was no sign of Lonnie.

"Well, well, what brings you by?" Ann-Marie asked, her expression coy.

Bobby frowned at her. "What do you think? I'm here to see my son."

She looked as surprised as if she'd forgotten all

about his relationship with J.C. "I thought we were going to talk and work that out."

"I've spoken to Lonnie. He and I have come to terms. And I'm sure you won't stand in my way," he said, staring her down until she blinked and backed away.

"Come in," she said flatly. "We're telling him together, okay? I'm not leaving it to you, so you can bad-mouth me to my own boy."

"I would never do that," Bobby told her. "But before you get him, there's one more thing. Lonnie thinks that for the sake of your marriage, J.C. ought to live with me, at least for a while. How do you feel about that?"

The color drained from her face. "You're taking him away from me?"

"No. But it might be a good idea for him to spend some time with me. You've had him for ten years. I've never spent ten minutes with him."

Her expression turned resigned. "When?"

"Not today. He needs to get used to the idea that I'm his father, but soon—say in a few weeks?"

"Can we see how it goes?"

Bobby nodded. "Fair enough."

"I'll get him," she said, and went upstairs.

When she returned a few minutes later, J.C. trailed along behind, his expression sullen. When he spotted Bobby, alarm flared in his eyes.

"What do you want?" he demanded. "I didn't do nothing. I been locked in my room for days now."

"J. C. Gates, you have not," Ann-Marie protested.

"But you have been grounded. Staying in your room has been your choice."

He shrugged. "Whatever."

"Have a seat," Bobby suggested. "Your mother and I want to talk to you."

J.C. regarded his mother uncertainly, looking as if he might refuse; but when no one spoke to challenge him, he finally sat.

"Ann-Marie, you want to start?" Bobby asked.

She regarded him gratefully, then swallowed hard and faced her son. "J.C., this isn't easy. I owe you an apology."

Surprise flared in the boy's eyes. "An apology? Why?"

"Because there's something I kept from you, something you had a right to know. I just never knew how to tell you," she said, glancing at Bobby.

Bobby nodded encouragingly.

"Your father," she began, her voice dropping. "Well, he's—"

"A mean son of a gun. Is that what you're trying to say?" he asked bitterly, then dared a look at Bobby as if expecting his disapproval.

"No," Ann-Marie said emphatically, then sighed. "Lonnie…" Again, her voice trailed off.

"Lonnie isn't your biological father," Bobby said quietly, as the boy's mouth dropped open. "I am."

"You?" J.C.'s voice squeaked. "I don't get it."

Bobby glanced at Ann-Marie for permission to continue with the explanation. She nodded.

"A long time ago your mom and I were in love. Then she fell in love with Lonnie and we split up.

What we didn't know was that she was already pregnant with you.''

J.C. absorbed this news with a bemused expression. "Is that why Lonnie treats me the way he does, because I'm not his kid?"

"Someday you'll understand," Bobby told him. "That's a tough thing for a man to handle. He's done the best he could. I'll always be grateful to him for looking out for you."

J.C. snorted. "As if..."

Bobby regarded him sternly. "The point is, I know now that you're my son, and I want to get to know you, to spend time with you."

"Forget it," J.C. said, jumping up. "Lonnie might not be my real dad and he might be mean, but he's been here from the beginning. Where the hell were you?"

"I didn't know," Bobby said evenly.

"Well, who cares? You should have known. I know where babies come from, I'm not a little kid. If I'm ten and *I* know, you should have known."

"Yes, I should have," Bobby agreed, willing to accept his share of the blame, even if it was Ann-Marie who'd kept the secret from him. "But we can't change the past."

"I don't want you for a dad!" J.C. shouted at him. "I don't even need a dad."

He took off for the stairs, but Bobby was faster. He caught J.C. before he hit the first step. Slowly, he turned his son around to face him.

"Every boy needs a father," he said, looking straight into his son's eyes. "I know I'm late stepping up to the plate, but I swear to you that I will make it up to you, if you'll just give me half a chance.''

Tears welled up in J.C.'s eyes, but he didn't relent. "No. I don't need you.''

Bobby felt the pain behind his son's words and fought off the sting of tears behind his eyes. "Maybe,'' he said quietly, "I need you.''

Then he released him. As J.C. fled up the stairs, Bobby called after him, "I'll be back, J.C. No matter how long it takes, I'll keep coming back.''

Something told him, though, it was going to be an uphill battle to get through the rock-solid defenses the boy had built to protect himself from hurt.

"Hi, Grandpa,'' Darcy said excitedly.

Jenna's head shot up from the mountain of paperwork in front of her. She'd gotten architectural drawings for the shops and Victorian bed and breakfast in record time. Bids for the work had come in the day before, and she was sorting through them now. She gestured frantically to Darcy to let her know that she did not want to talk to her father.

"Mom's not here,'' Darcy told him without missing a beat. "She's working. She works all the time.''

Whatever her grandfather said made Darcy frown. "No, she does not leave me by myself for hours on end. Besides, this is Trinity Harbor. It would be okay if she did.''

Jenna tensed when she realized what her father was doing. It almost sounded as if he was trying to find some excuse to suggest she was being a poor mother, so he could snatch Darcy back to live with him in

Baltimore. Given the amount of time and attention he'd paid to her there, the prospect was ludicrous. Fortunately, from listening to Darcy's end of the conversation, Jenna was confident that her daughter could field this problem on her own. Darcy had none of the nagging self-esteem issues with her grandfather that Jenna had had with him when she was Darcy's age. Darcy said whatever was on her mind. And Jenna was just starting to take a page out of her book.

"No, Grandpa," Darcy said with exaggerated patience. "I *like* it here. I'm going to stay. I don't want to go to school in Baltimore. Besides, you're never home anyway, so it wouldn't be any different than Mom working here. Besides, if I want to see her, I can ride my bike to wherever she is."

Jenna grinned and gave her a thumbs-up.

"Bobby's really cool, too," Darcy added with enthusiasm. "He's been teaching me to cook. I can make all sorts of stuff. He says my crab cakes are better than his."

That was news to Jenna. She regarded her daughter with amazement. She knew that Darcy had been dropping by the marina every day to see Maggie, but she'd had no idea that she was spending time with Bobby as well. When Darcy hung up, Jenna regarded her curiously.

"What's this about cooking lessons with Bobby?"

Darcy shrugged. "It's just something we do. One day when I was there with Maggie, his sous-chef didn't show up, so he showed me how to do what needed to be done. Mostly it was cutting stuff up that first time. He didn't let me cook. But the next time he taught me a whole recipe. He says I'm a natural, 'cause I'm not scared of improvising. I couldn't find any tomato sauce one day and I grabbed a thing of tomato paste and asked if that would work. Bobby said it was a great idea. The sauce we were making turned out really, really good. We had compliments.''

Jenna chuckled. "You did, did you?"

"Well, I wasn't there, but Bobby told me the next day.''

"Are you over there every day? I thought you were at Daisy's with Tommy. That's where I've been taking you.''

"Sometimes Tommy wants to do stuff I don't care about, so I ask Daisy if it's okay for me to ride my bike to the marina. Sometimes she drives me over.''

In other words, Jenna thought, sneaky Daisy was doing her bit to create a bond between Bobby and Jenna's daughter.

"Maybe I'd better talk to Bobby about all these visits. I don't want you to wear out your welcome," Jenna said.

"I'm not. He says I'm the best help he has, and the cheapest. He pays me in ice cream.''

Visions of that report getting to some labor advocacy group chilled Jenna to the bone. "Don't repeat that," she warned Darcy. "It could get Bobby—and me, for that matter—into trouble if someone took it seriously.''

Darcy regarded her with confusion. "Why? Because he's not giving me money?''

"And because you're too young to be working at

all. I'll talk it over with Bobby. We'll figure something out.''

"You won't stop me from going, will you?"

"Not if you're not getting in his way,'' Jenna promised.

Confident that she would find Bobby in the restaurant kitchen just before opening, Jenna marched in later that afternoon and found him bent over a pot of seafood chowder. He glanced up when he saw her, picked up a spoon and dipped up a sample.

"Taste this,'' he requested. "It needs something, and I can't figure out what.''

"Hey, I'm not the budding chef in the family,'' she said, but she tasted the chowder anyway. "Maybe a dash of dill?''

Bobby took a sip of the soup, then nodded. He added the herb, then tasted it again. "Better,'' he said happily. "So, what brings you by?''

"A glimpse of your handsome face,'' she said, just to see the immediate rise of heat in his eyes.

"Yeah, right,'' he said, turning his attention back to the soup.

Jenna touched his cheek. "I'm serious. I've missed you.''

He sighed and turned his face to kiss the palm of her hand. "I've missed you, too.''

"You could have solved that problem anytime,'' she told him.

"There's been a lot going on.''

"Then this isn't all about discretion?''

"Absolutely not. I've been trying to work things out

with J.C. Every spare minute I've had has been spent trying to get it through that kid's head that he has a biological father who intends to be a part of his life.''

"Lonnie and Ann-Marie agreed to that?''

He nodded, his expression grim. "Lonnie required a little persuasion, but we worked it out. He's now officially washed his hands of all responsibility for J.C. Imagine what that's done for the kid's already low self-esteem.''

She pulled a stool up to the counter where Bobby was working and sat down. "Are you getting through to your son?''

He sighed. "Not yet. He sits in the same room with me, because Ann-Marie insists on it. I actually got him to go out for ice cream the other night, but he didn't say a single word the whole time except to tell Earlene what flavor he wanted.''

"He's scared,'' Jenna said.

"I know that. What I don't know is how to prove to him that I'm not going anywhere, that I won't turn my back on him, even when he gets into trouble. I'd planned to have him move in with me, but considering how he feels about me right now, I think that would probably be a disaster.''

"Maybe not,'' Jenna said thoughtfully. "Maybe it would prove that you're in this for the long haul.'' She hesitated, took a deep breath, then added, "Maybe I could help.''

He stared at her. "How? And why would you even want to after what he did to Darcy?''

"He's your son,'' she said simply. "And he's ten years old. He deserves a second chance.''

Bobby put aside the knife he was using to cut strawberries to decorate the top of his strawberry-rhubarb pie, wiped his hands on his apron and stepped closer. "You're amazing," he said, then leaned down to touch his lips to hers. "Have I told you that?"

"Not lately," she said, a hitch in her voice as her pulse raced.

"Well, you are. Remind me to tell you that every single day."

"I'll put it on one of my lists," she promised.

"So what's your idea?"

"Why don't we take J.C., Tommy, Pete and Darcy to Kings Dominion?"

Bobby stared at her incredulously. "You want to take all four kids to an amusement park?"

"Why not? It'll be good for them, and it'll be research for me. Maybe we'll get some more ideas for the boardwalk. Daisy and Walker can come along, too."

"Four adults against four kids," Bobby said, his expression thoughtful. "I like the odds."

"We're not going into battle," Jenna chastised.

Bobby grinned. "That's what you think."

22

"**I**'m not going," Darcy said, her arms folded across her narrow chest, a mulish expression on her face. "Not if J.C. is going."

"Nothing is going to happen," Jenna assured her. "I'll be there. Bobby will be there. So will Daisy and Walker. You don't even have to talk to him if you don't want to. You and Tommy can do your own thing."

"Tommy will want to be with Pete and J.C. They're guys."

Jenna beckoned her daughter across the room and looked her in the eye. "Are you scared of J.C.?"

Darcy's lower lip trembled, but the defiant expression stayed firmly in place. "I'm not scared of anything."

"Well, you don't have to be scared of J.C., that's for sure. He's been punished for hurting you. And, trust me, Bobby will see to it that he never does anything like that again—not to you, not to anyone."

Some of the tension in Darcy seemed to ease. "How can Bobby stop it?" she asked warily.

Jenna considered her next words carefully. Though rumors of the relationship between Bobby and J.C. had been racing all around Trinity Harbor for a few weeks now, Bobby and Ann-Marie hadn't publicly confirmed them. Still, there seemed little point in keeping the secret if Bobby intended to play an increasingly important role in J.C.'s life.

"J.C. is his son."

Darcy stared at her in shock. "Get out of here."

Jenna grinned at her reaction. "It's true. No one knew until recently, including Bobby."

"So if you and Bobby get together, that means J.C. would be around all the time? He'd be almost like my..." Her eyes got bigger as she completed the thought. "Like my brother?"

"Bobby and I *aren't* getting together," Jenna said emphatically.

"Like I believe that," Darcy retorted smugly.

"We're not," Jenna felt compelled to insist. "The point is, you like spending time with Bobby. There's a good chance you'll be running into J.C. Why not try to make peace with him now, with both Bobby and me around to supervise?"

"Does he have to apologize to me?" Darcy asked. "Yes."

"Can I tell him what a low-down bully he was?"

Jenna bit back a grin. "You can tell him that once," she agreed. "Then you drop it."

Darcy nodded. "Okay. One more thing, though."

"What's that?"

"Can I please get my green hair cut off before we go? I really, really learned my lesson, and I don't want J.C. to tease me about it ever again."

Jenna gave her daughter a fierce hug. "You can get your hair cut. We'll make an appointment today."

Darcy pumped her fist in the air. "All right! I'll go."

Jenna chuckled at her sudden enthusiasm. "I love you, Darcy Kennedy."

Darcy made a face at her. "Mom, don't get all mushy," she protested. "It's just a trip to an amusement park."

No, Jenna thought, it was more than that. Though Darcy might not realize it, it was her coming-of-age party. Jenna's baby girl was growing up. No doubt there would be a lot more rebellions to come once she hit her teens, but in the last few minutes Darcy had shown a level of maturity—and a capacity for forgiveness—beyond her years. Jenna had to wonder if she was going to be able to be half as understanding as her daughter once she actually saw J. C. Gates face to face. Darcy's bruises had healed. Her arm would be out of the cast in a few weeks, but Jenna would carry with her forever the image of the way her daughter had looked when Jenna had arrived at Daisy's after the brawl in which Darcy had been injured.

That boy is Bobby's son, she reminded herself. And even if he weren't, he would deserve a second chance. Nobody on earth knew more about second chances than she did. She'd just have to keep reminding herself of that.

King was tired of waiting around for his son to get off his duff and propose to Jenna Kennedy. Any man worth his salt would have clinched that deal by now. But it seemed the only deal Bobby had made with her was the one to develop the boardwalk. A business arrangement was one thing, but King wanted something more permanent tying them together.

"Probably making a mistake," he muttered under his breath as he pulled into the parking lot at the marina. He should no doubt let well enough alone. But darn it all, he wanted his family to keep on growing. He wanted a dynasty.

Since none of his own offspring were the least bit interested in perpetuating the cattle business that was their legacy, then he was going to have to count on the next generation. He'd managed to lure Tommy out to Cedar Hill on several occasions for a few lessons, but the boy was more interested in taking apart tractors than he was in cattle. He'd actually fixed an old broken-down John Deere tractor that the mechanics in town had said wasn't worth repairing.

Bottom line, it looked as if King was going to have to look further afield for someone to run Cedar Hill's cattle operation. He needed to get both his sons married off. Since there was no female prospect in Tucker's life at the moment, that meant King needed to concentrate on Bobby.

He strode into Bobby's office, right past a startled Maggie. "Son…" His voice trailed off when he realized he was all alone. He whirled around and scowled at Bobby's secretary. "Where is he?"

"Kings Dominion," she told him, then grinned. "And I'm referring to the amusement park."

King frowned at her sassy remark. "I know that. What the devil is he doing down there?"

"I believe it's a family outing," she said. "Daisy

and Walker went along with Tommy. And Bobby took J.C.''

King paused at that. ''Is that so?''

Maggie regarded him with a sly expression. ''Did I mention that Jenna and Darcy went along, too?''

''Now you're talking,'' King enthused. ''Maybe that boy's not as dense as I feared. Thank you, young lady. You've just made my day.''

He started to leave, but Maggie stopped him. ''Mr. Spencer, Bobby left a message for you.''

''Oh? How'd he know I'd be by?''

She grinned. ''He said it was only a matter of time.''

''What the dickens does that mean?''

''I assume he meant that you have a tendency to meddle,'' she said, her gaze unflinching. ''He's been expecting a visit.''

''Okay, okay, what's the message?'' he grumbled.

''He said you should be concentrating on your own love life,'' she said, grinning broadly.

''Oh, he did, did he?'' King said, unable to keep the indignation out of his voice.

''Yes, sir.''

''Thank you, Maggie. You tell my son this—from here on out, he should mind his own damn business.'' He regarded her with a fierce expression. ''In those exact words.''

She laughed, then covered her mouth and fought for a somber expression. ''Yes, sir. I'll tell him exactly that. If he calls in, can I tell him how to get in touch with you?''

King thought about Frances and this crazy trip she

was on. It was time she got back to Trinity Harbor. Folks around here needed her.

"Tell him I've gone after something I almost lost," King said. "I imagine he'll know what that means."

Now all he had to do was figure out where to start looking. Of course, one of the advantages of having a son who was the sheriff was that there were certain resources at his disposal. All he had to do was march into Tucker's office and declare that Frances Jackson was a missing person.

Five minutes later he was doing exactly that. Tucker stared at him as if he'd gone off his rocker.

"You want to file a missing person's report on Frances?" Tucker repeated, as if King hadn't been perfectly clear on that point.

"That's exactly what I want."

"Why?"

"Because she's missing, dammit!"

"I don't think so," Tucker said.

"Are you telling me you won't do this?" King demanded.

"As a matter of fact, I wouldn't," Tucker told him, grinning. "But that's not what I was telling you. I saw Frances at Earlene's not an hour ago. She didn't look lost to me."

King's heart took the kind of leap it hadn't taken in years. It was a good thing the woman didn't do this kind of thing often. He wasn't sure he was up to it.

"Well, why the heck didn't you say so straight out, instead of letting me go on and on?" he muttered, heading for the door.

"Because it was real nice seeing how worried you

were about her,'' Tucker said. ''A word of advice—
this time don't let her get away. For some reason, the
woman seems to care about you. At your age, I'm not
sure how many more chances you're likely to get.''

''Watch your tongue, boy. I'm still young enough
to whip your butt.''

Tucker grinned. ''If you want to waste time going
a few rounds with me out back, let's go for it. It's
been a slow day. I could use the exercise.''

''Later,'' King said. ''I've got better fish to fry.''
He shot a pointed look at his son. ''Too bad you can't
say the same.''

Bobby glanced in the rearview mirror and felt his
heart turn over. J.C. was sound asleep in the back seat,
his hair tousled, his nose sunburned. For the first time
since he'd discovered that J.C. was his son, he saw
evidence of the innocent kid inside that defensive, sullen boy.

Not that J.C. had been difficult today. With Tommy,
Pete and Darcy around, he'd been on his good behavior, but he hadn't let himself be part of the group. He'd
kept a cautious distance from the others, riding the
rides alone instead of sharing a car, eating his hot dog
or ice cream on another bench. And he hadn't said two
words to Bobby all day long.

Bobby sighed heavily.

Jenna glanced over at him. ''It's going to work
out,'' she reassured him quietly.

''I don't see how. He refuses to get along with anybody.''

''Want to hear my take on today?'' she asked.

"Why not?"

"I think he's scared. The only relationship he's had with a father was with Lonnie, who didn't abuse him but certainly made him feel like he wasn't worthy of a father's love. Now you come along and say you want to be his dad. He barely knows you. All the other kids know you really well and adore you. He's still an outsider. Even tonight, here he is riding back with us, while all of the other kids are with Walker and Daisy."

"I didn't want to shove my responsibility off on them," Bobby said. "Besides, I thought it might give J.C. and me a little time to get to know each other better. I figured we could talk about everything we did today. Then what does he do? He goes to sleep."

"Did it ever occur to you that he might simply be tired?" Jenna asked, smiling. "I honestly don't think he went to sleep to avoid you. It's been a long day. We spent hours in the hot sun, ate too much. I imagine Tommy, Pete and Darcy are sound asleep in Walker's car, too."

"I suppose."

"Bobby, having a relationship with J.C. is not going to happen overnight. Give it time. I thought he did really well today. He apologized to Darcy and to me. He was polite to everyone. Would you have liked it better if he'd picked a fight with somebody?"

"Maybe," Bobby said honestly. "It would have seemed more…I don't know…normal."

"You can't have it both ways. You can't expect him to toe the straight and narrow and then act like a normal kid at the same time. Set the boundaries and give it time. I'm sure he'll start testing them again soon enough, if only to discover if you meant what you said about being in his life to stay.''

"You think he expects me to abandon him?"

"If he misbehaves, yes. I think that's exactly what he expects, what he's most afraid of.''

Bobby sighed again. "God, I hate this. When I think of how messed up that boy's life is, how much I missed out on, I want to strangle Ann-Marie.''

"You're working together to make things right now. That's all that you can do,'' Jenna told him.

He reached for her hand, picked it up and brushed a kiss across her knuckles. "How'd you get to be so smart?"

She laughed at that. "I've had nine years with Darcy, and I'm just now getting a handle on things. You'll get the knack of it, too."

"If nine years is the learning curve, J.C. could be in serious trouble long before then.''

"He won't be,'' she assured him. "I saw him watching the other kids today, even when he was pretending not to care about them. He wants so badly to be one of them. We'll all keep reaching out to him until he is.''

Bobby pulled up in front of Ann-Marie's and cut the engine. He glanced into the back seat where J.C. was still breathing evenly, his eyes closed, his lips parted. Bobby got out of the car and opened the back door.

"Hey, son,'' he said, giving J.C.'s shoulder a gentle nudge.

When J.C. merely moaned and rolled his face away, Bobby shrugged and reached inside to lift him out. He was a big kid, but Bobby had no difficulty carrying him across the lawn. The front door opened, spilling light across the yard. To his surprise, it was Lonnie who was waiting for them.

"Conked out?" he said with a knowing expression. "The boy always did sleep like the dead. I'll take him."

Reluctantly, Bobby transferred his son to Lonnie's arms. "Thanks."

Lonnie met his gaze. "Not a problem."

In that instant, for the first time since this entire mess had been revealed, Bobby felt a ray of hope. "You feel like grabbing a beer one night this week, maybe hanging out for a couple of hours?"

Surprise flared in Lonnie's eyes. "You serious?"

"I think it's time we talked."

"About?" he asked cautiously.

The list was endless—Ann-Marie, J.C.'s childhood, their lost friendship, the future. But instead of mentioning any of that, Bobby grinned. "Let's start with the weather and see how it goes. How does Tuesday suit you? The bar at the marina?"

Lonnie nodded. "I'll be by after work—or is that a bad time for you?"

"I'll make it a good time," Bobby told him.

He was whistling when he went back to the car. Jenna regarded him with surprise.

"Everything okay?"

"It's getting there," he told her. "Lonnie and I agreed to get together to talk things out. I think making peace with him will go a long way toward making things better for J.C."

"You're a smart man, Bobby Spencer."

"Not so smart," he said. "I haven't figured out what to do about you yet."

She grinned at him. "That's okay. I'm not going anywhere anytime soon. I have work to do."

He laughed. "And word on the street is that you're doing an incredible job."

"Do you have people checking on me?" she demanded, regarding him with exaggerated indignation.

"Nope, but this is Trinity Harbor. Reports just keep rolling in. The contractors think you're amazing, and the workers are all in love with you. I'm beginning to think I'd better start hanging around down there to protect my interests."

"Professional or personal?"

"Personal, of course. The professional interests seem to be under control."

"Then drop by anytime. I'll show you around." She grinned as he pulled up in front of her house. "I imagine you'll look incredibly sexy in a hard hat."

"You go for that type, do you?"

"Come on by and we'll find out for sure."

"Best invitation I've had in years. Any of those buildings have locks yet?"

She laughed. "They don't even have doors."

"That could certainly add to the excitement."

It was definitely an image that could keep his hormones stirred up all night long. He gave her a long, lingering kiss and resigned himself to yet another sleepless night.

Jenna half expected to find Bobby waiting for her when she arrived at the site the next morning, but there was no sign of him. Nor was he there the next day or the day after that. She refused to admit just how disappointed she was.

Fortunately, there were a million and one details to see to now that the construction was in full swing. She'd had a temporary shed erected at the site and turned it into a makeshift office that was so cramped it could barely contain her desk, a phone, a file cabinet and one visitor at a time. If she needed to have a meeting with all the subcontractors at once over some crisis or another, they brought folding chairs outside. And it seemed as if there were a crisis every day. Today it was over the requirements of the Chesapeake Bay Preservation Act.

People were hurling regulations at her so fast and furiously, her head was spinning. In the thick of it was one of the mayor's henchmen, as she'd come to regard the town's building and zoning official.

"We're building precisely to the regulations," she told Donald Turner. "We're exceeding the setback requirements."

"But you intend to put paved parking in back of the buildings, correct?"

She nodded slowly, beginning to guess where he was heading with this. "You're about to tell me we're not leaving enough ground surface, correct?"

The Chesapeake Bay Preservation Act was implemented to improve water quality not only in the bay, but in its tributaries. The Potomac River was one of those. Structures and pavement could cover only a certain percentage of the ground near the waterways. The rest had to remain porous to reduce runoff into the rivers.

"That's exactly right," Turner said triumphantly. "You're not in compliance."

"Then we'll use gravel in the parking lots, not asphalt."

"Won't do," he argued. "You could come along later and decide to pour concrete over the gravel."

"Then you could fine me and make me take it up."

"Waste of time and money when I can stop you right now," he said.

"Come on, Donald. Work with me on this."

"You could buy that plot of land out by the road that's vacant. Add it into the project, and you'd have enough green space," he suggested, his expression oddly sly.

Jenna considered the possibility. That land had puzzled her all along. It was the one piece Bobby didn't own. She should have asked him about that at the outset. She'd had a feeling all along that this day might come. She'd known she was squeaking by the requirements as written in the act.

"I'll speak to Bobby," she promised.

"That's fine. Meantime, though, I've got to shut you down."

She stared at him, incredulous. "You can't do that."

"Of course I can. The mayor told me to. If need be, I'll get Tucker over here to enforce it."

"But I'm not in violation of anything until I try to do something with that parking lot."

"It's on the plans," he said, tapping the papers in front of him. "That's enough for me."

Her gaze narrowed suspiciously. "Who owns that land, Donald?"

He seemed startled by the question.

"Come on," she said. "That's not a tough one. Who does it belong to? I know you know."

"I believe it belongs to the mayor."

Well, hellfire and damnation, Jenna thought. She should have guessed.

"I'm not shutting anything down," she told the building inspector. "And unless you've got the whole blasted sheriff's department behind you, I suggest you not try to do it behind my back. I'll get back to you by tomorrow morning."

"But I—"

"Tomorrow, Donald. Same time. Until then, the work continues."

He sighed. "I'll be here with the sheriff."

"Bring the mayor while you're at it," she suggested. "I'm counting on it being the town's first boardwalk fireworks display."

23

Bobby had been expecting something like this. When Jenna told him about the mayor's sneak attack on the boardwalk development, using Donald as his pawn, he was furious enough to march down to Town Hall and knock a few heads together. Instead, Jenna had a far more devious suggestion. He truly loved the way this woman's mind worked.

"I'll make all the arrangements," he promised her. "Work's not going to be delayed for one single minute. Trust me, Jenna. You might want to be sure that Richard is there with his camera. This picture is one he's going to want on the front page of this week's paper."

She grinned at him. "I'm on my way. Anything else you'd like me to do?"

"Nope. I've got the rest covered."

By midafternoon, Bobby had all the pieces in place. Rumors were flying, fueled by a few subtly dropped hints at Earlene's. There was going to be quite a crowd on the boardwalk the next morning, all primed for a big announcement from the mayor. The only one still in the dark, however, was the mayor himself.

The gossip apparently reached Harvey about six o'clock. He stormed into the marina restaurant demanding to see Bobby. Maggie was trying to fend him off when Bobby emerged from the kitchen.

"Are you looking for me?" he asked.

"What the devil do you have up your sleeve?" Harvey demanded. "Everyone in town is talking about some big announcement being made tomorrow morning on the boardwalk." His gaze narrowed. "You pulling out?"

"You wish," Bobby said. "Nope, but I imagine you'll want to be there since it does involve you."

"Me? What kind of announcement are you making that involves me? I'll sue you, dammit."

"For?"

"I'll think of something. Slander for starters."

Bobby regarded him blandly. "You might want to wait till you hear it before you get all riled up."

"You're up to no good. I can see it in your eyes."

"Harvey, that's the first truly intelligent thing I've ever heard you say."

He left the mayor sputtering and went back into the kitchen to report to Jenna.

"Bobby, this could backfire," she said worriedly. "And you're the one who'll be caught in the middle. Maybe I should handle it. It was my idea, after all. Your father..."

"Will be sitting front and center in the morning, cheering us on," he assured her.

"I hope so."

"I know so," he said. Even if he had to hogtie him and drag him there himself. King's presence would lend this little end-run of theirs a certain legitimacy.

* * *

Despite Bobby's reassurances, Jenna looked out over the gathering crowd at the construction site the next morning and felt her stomach twist into knots. She'd been so sure this was a fabulous idea when she'd gone to see Bobby. Now she wasn't so certain.

"Butterflies?" Anna-Louise asked, slipping up beside her.

Jenna regarded her with surprise. "You're here. I wasn't expecting you."

Anna-Louise grinned. "Was that wishful thinking, Jenna? Are you about to do something sneaky and underhanded that you think I'll disapprove of?"

"Pretty much," Jenna said.

"For the good of the town?"

Jenna nodded. "I believe that. I truly do."

"Then don't worry about my opinion. Besides, it's not the one that really counts anyway. I'm not in the judgment business. My boss is."

Jenna regarded her ruefully. "That's what I'm afraid of."

Just then Bobby appeared at her side. "Ready?"

"I suppose so."

"Then let's do it." He pulled her up onto a makeshift stage, which was little more than a wooden pallet. "Ladies and gentlemen, it's nice to see so many of you out here at the crack of dawn for this impromptu event." He surveyed the crowd. "Mr. Mayor, will you come on up here?"

Harvey looked from Bobby to Jenna and seemed about to bolt, but the applause of his constituents finally forced him to join them. "Mitch Cummings has turned up some interesting news during his investigation. Lonnie filled him in about that son you've never acknowledged," he muttered to Bobby. "Consider yourself warned."

Bobby looked as if he might slug the man. Jenna stepped between them. "Indeed, we *have* been warned," Jenna retorted, then regarded him pointedly. "And threatened with blackmail."

The mayor's eyes widened with shock. "I never—"

"Oh?" she pressed, cutting him off. "Yesterday you had Donald do it. Just now you did it yourself. It's beginning to annoy me." She smiled at the crowd and beamed at him, then added in an undertone. "We can talk about that, or we can talk about the generous contribution you are about to make to Trinity Harbor's future."

The mayor turned pale. "Contribution? What the devil are you talking about?"

"Why, the Harvey Needham Park, of course," Bobby said smoothly, his temper evidently under control again. "It's just exactly what this waterfront development needs, several acres of green space."

Harvey's face flushed. "Are you two crazy? That land is worth a fortune."

"Only to me," Bobby said. "And I'll pay you market value for it, which is a helluva lot more than you deserve after what you tried to do here yesterday."

"So, Mr. Mayor, what's it going to be?" Jenna asked, as the crowd turned restless.

There was very little question of the outcome. Harvey could decline and see his chances for reelection go up in smoke, or he could go along with them and be the town hero. Expediency was Harvey's middle name.

"It's a deal," he said sourly.

Jenna felt a huge weight lift off her chest as Bobby made the announcement that the last parcel needed for the waterfront development was being sold to them today by the mayor. In his honor, it would become open space for town events.

As soon as the cheers went up, the mayor came alive. Without a second glance at either Bobby or Jenna, he stepped off the platform and began shaking hands. King was the first in line. He shot a broad wink in Bobby's direction.

"We just launched the mayor's next campaign," Jenna said with some regret.

"It's worth it," Bobby said. "Otherwise, he could have tied us up for months. Besides, despite his paranoia, nobody in town wants the mayor's job more than he does. He'd have been running unopposed anyway."

Richard and Anna-Louise came up to them then, their expressions mystified.

"What did you do to Harvey?" Richard asked. "Cast a spell over him?"

"Not exactly," Jenna said.

"Let's just leave it that he made a generous contribution to the town's future," Jenna said.

"For which I am deeply and profoundly grateful," Bobby intoned solemnly.

Richard regarded them both with disappointment. "That's it?"

"That's our story and we're sticking to it," Bobby told him.

Richard glanced at his wife. "Is that what they told you?"

She grinned at him. "You know better than to ask me that," she chided. "Confession, confidentiality, it's all the same to me."

"A convenient excuse you haul out when it suits you." Richard studied her intently. "They didn't tell you a blessed thing, did they?"

Anna-Louise laughed. "Nope, not a thing."

"You're as frustrated as I am?" he asked.

"Oh, yeah, but something tells me we're better off not knowing the details," the pastor said. "Stop acting like a reporter for once, and act like a citizen of Trinity Harbor. Just be grateful for small blessings."

Jenna glanced at Bobby. Maybe the outcome had been a blessing, but the underhanded way they'd pulled it off was something she would be wrestling with for a long time to come. No matter how much Harvey deserved his comeuppance, she would never feel entirely right about what had happened here today, even though it had been her idea.

"You're not feeling guilty, are you?" Bobby leaned down to whisper in her ear.

Jenna nodded.

"Don't. He's going to be compensated very handsomely for today's 'magnanimous gesture.' Everybody wins."

"You honestly believe that?"

He cupped her chin and looked squarely into her eyes. "I *know* that," he said emphatically. "Now get to work. You're two hours behind schedule."

She laughed. "I think the crew can make it up. Just get all these people out of our way."

"Done," he said.

And like the pied piper, he worked his way through the crowd, herding everyone in the direction of Earlene's. Jenna was left standing on the concrete strip of boardwalk from bygone days all alone. Her workers had already scattered, and soon she heard the buzz of saws and the blast of music from the radios they all insisted on playing at high volume. It was just a taste of the commotion there would be on this site a few months from now. In her head, Jenna could already see it.

The only question was, would she still be here to be a part of it?

The day after the showdown with the mayor, Jenna arrived at the site to find Bobby there ahead of her. For one heart-stopping moment, she was afraid he'd taken yesterday's event and the incident that had led to it as a sign he was going to have to start hovering if this project was going to come in on time.

"Here to keep a closer eye on your investment?" she asked mildly, joining him on a bench facing the river. The sun was a vibrant splash of neon red against the pale gray of the horizon. It would storm before the end of the day, if the old ditty about red sails in the morning held true.

Bobby glanced at her. "Not the way you mean. I trust you."

Jenna gazed into his eyes and saw that he meant exactly what he said. There wasn't so much as a hint of doubt shadowing his gaze. She had a hard time speaking past the lump that suddenly formed in her throat. Time and again, when she'd needed it most, he'd offered his faith in her, something her family had never done. Not even once.

"Then why are you here?" she asked.

"I like to imagine what it's going to be like when it's finished, when the air is filled with the sound of kids' laughter and the scent of cotton candy and corn dogs, when people are sitting on benches like this one eating grape snow cones or ice cream and listening to the announcements for boat rides on the river."

"And the music of the carousel," she added, grinning.

"Assuming we ever find that blasted horse," Bobby said. "Tucker still doesn't have a single solid lead. It's as if the thing vanished. And even I'm convinced now that Harvey had nothing to do with it."

Jenna thought of her own suspicion, formed just recently. One of these days she'd check it out, but not just yet.

"Something tells me it's going to turn up when the time is right," she said.

He regarded her suspiciously. "Meaning?"

"Just that." She moved closer and settled back against his chest. After a shocked intake of breath, he slid his arms around her. "You don't get to control everything in life, Bobby Spencer."

"Hey, I'm not the control freak in the family."

"Couldn't prove it by me," she teased. "You're down here checking on me behind my back, aren't you? Get out of here. I have work to do."

"Not before I do this," he said. "There should be some perks to being the boss." He settled his mouth over hers in a kiss that scrambled her senses.

Eventually he released her, stood up and started to walk away. After a few feet, he turned back. "Go out with me tonight, Jenna. A real date. Just the two of us. A movie in Fredericksburg. Dinner and dancing. Whatever you want."

She met his heated gaze and sighed. "I thought you'd never ask."

Bobby grinned. "Yeah, I was beginning to wonder about that myself."

After all these months, it was their first formal date, but it felt like they'd been going out for about a million years. And Bobby wanted Jenna as desperately as if he'd been waiting that long to have her, too.

All it took was a glance across the table, the brush of her fingers across his knuckles, and he was primed for action. He hadn't been this jittery and anxious since his high school prom, when he and Ann-Marie... Well, that was in the past now, except for the consequences, which were very much with him these days. Every time he looked in his son's eyes, he remembered that night and everything that had happened afterward, everything that had been kept from him.

Since meeting Jenna, though, the memories were no longer accompanied by heartache.

He met her gaze. "You changed my life," he told her, still surprised by just how drastically she had shifted his thinking and how easily she had mended his heart.

"Me?"

He reached for her hand. "You made me want things again, things I've pretty much shoved aside over the years because I didn't want to risk getting hurt again."

"What things do you want?" she asked, the color high in her cheeks.

"You," he said. "I want you."

Under his thumb, he felt her pulse scramble. "You okay with that?"

She swallowed hard, but didn't look away. "I'm more than okay with that. The job's not finished, though. I don't want it standing between us, if something goes wrong. I want to give you your dream for that land."

"Nothing's going to go wrong," Bobby said. "I hired an incredibly competent woman for the job. She has it all under control."

"You really believe that, don't you?" she said, still looking surprised, even after all his reassurances. "It still amazes me."

"Jenna, your father is a fool if he can't see how talented you are."

"I think I'm finally beginning to believe that," she said. "You've given me that."

"So what about what I said?" Bobby asked. "Did you really want to see that movie tonight?"

"Hmm? Sitting in a dark theater holding hands and eating popcorn, when we could be someplace more private doing far more fascinating things? Tough call."

"And?"

Her eyes shone. "It's really my choice?"

"Of course."

"And you don't think it's going to interfere with our business relationship? You can keep the two things totally separate."

"Sweetheart, I've wanted you for weeks now, and I haven't let it get in the way, have I?"

"Not that I've noticed," she admitted.

"Well, then?" He studied her intently. "Or aren't you sure how you feel about me?"

"Oh, I'm sure," she said emphatically. "You make my knees weak, which means that getting up and walking out of here just now could be problematic."

Bobby slapped some money on the table and stood up in one smooth motion. He scooped her into his arms before she could utter a protest and headed for the door. Outside, he gazed into her eyes. "I take it that was a yes. I don't want to get our signals crossed."

"Yes," she said, laughing. "Even if you are crazy. Are you sure you have any business being behind the wheel of a car just now? You seem a little reckless. And word of this is bound to get back to Trinity Harbor."

"We're miles away, and Fredericksburg is a big town now. There wasn't a soul we knew in that restaurant. As for being reckless, trust me, I am not about to risk getting a ticket on the way home. I won't do anything that's likely to keep us from getting there in record time."

It required all of his concentration to keep his promise and resist pressing the accelerator to the floor as they sped through the gathering darkness back toward

Trinity Harbor. He swerved into his driveway at the same careless angle he had the last time they'd been this close to making love. This time, though, nothing was going to stand in their way. Fate wouldn't be that cruel a second time.

Luckily he'd cleaned the house and changed the sheets earlier, all the while telling himself he was not anticipating this precise outcome to the evening.

He would have scooped Jenna into his arms again, but she was already out of the car and striding toward the front door before he had a chance to reach her. Her eagerness inflamed him. It was proof that she was just as desperate for this as he was.

Even so, he warned himself to go slow, not to tear her clothes off the instant the door was closed behind them. He promised himself that he was going to make this night special, that it was going to be memorable. He intended to savor every sweet moment of it.

Unfortunately, all of his good intentions fled when Jenna reached past him, shoving the door shut with a slam. Her gaze clashed with his.

"How far away is your bedroom?"

"Down the hall," he told her.

"Too far," she said, fumbling with the buttons of his shirt. Her knuckles skimmed across his bare chest, then drifted lower and lower as she parted his shirt, then tugged it from the waistband of his jeans.

This was a whole new side of her, Bobby concluded, watching the confidence stir to life in her expression as her caresses turned increasingly daring.

"Are you trying to destroy me?" he murmured, when she released the snap of his jeans.

Her fingers stilled. "Is that what I'm doing?"

"Seems like it to me," he said with a shudder as she skimmed a nail along his zipper. He was already hard as a rock, and he hadn't laid a hand on her yet.

"Want me to slow down?" she inquired, regarding him with a seductive expression.

"Absolutely not. Just let me know when it's my turn."

"Your turn?"

"To drive you over the top."

She had renewed her exploration, but at his words, she paused again. "Good point. This is something we should be doing together."

"Hey, I'm liberated," he said. "You can have your way with me first."

She gave him a sassy grin that made his heart flip over.

"I don't think so," she said. She grabbed the ends of his tie. "Let's find that bedroom of yours."

When they crossed the threshold, Bobby plopped down on the end of the bed and regarded her expectantly. "Okay, kid, let's see what you've got."

For an instant she looked taken aback, and then she laughed. "You should know better than to dare me, Spencer."

"Is that what I was doing?" he inquired innocently.

"You know it was. You're thinking that I don't have the confidence it takes to strip right here in front of you."

"Well?" he challenged.

Her gaze locked with his and her fingers slid under the edge of her blouse. She stripped it over her head in a gesture so smooth, it looked as if she'd had years of practice. Her jeans hit the floor next, leaving her standing before him in her bra and panties which were barely there. Both scraps of lace vanished in the blink of an eye and his breath lodged in his throat.

"You're..." He was at a loss for words. "I don't know what to say."

She grinned. "About my body or about the way I shed my clothes?"

He laughed. "Either one." He shook his head. "I don't get it. You're like another woman all of a sudden." An amazingly, unexpectedly provocative woman.

"Do you want an explanation, or do you want me to crawl into that bed with you?"

"No contest," he said, reaching for her. "We can get back to the rest later."

She relinquished control to him at last, moving into his arms, opening herself to his touches. Her responsiveness was another eye-opener. She came alive for him, arching toward him, moaning when his mouth covered her breast, writhing restlessly when his fingers dove deep inside her. Her skin was on fire and slick with perspiration that made each touch a sensuous journey.

Bobby looked into her eyes and tried to find the vulnerable Jenna who'd come to Trinity Harbor months ago in search of self-respect. There was no evidence of her in this woman who was sharing herself with complete abandon and confidence. Had he given her that? Had she changed so much?

Whatever the cause, the transformation was both remarkable and alluring. He wanted her more than ever, wanted to see that bright spark in her eyes forever, wanted her hands on him, her body seeking his. Most of all he couldn't wait for this, to sink deep inside her, to be surrounded by her heat and taken over the top by the welcoming shudders of her body.

He drove himself deep, felt her muscles clenching to claim him, her fingers digging into his hips, holding him tight as heat and hunger and sensation hit a wicked peak. Then violent shudders were rocking them both, their breath coming in gasps, her cries muffled against his shoulder. Her name, his, their shouts came in unison as the world went spinning.

Bobby wasn't sure he'd ever be able to move again, wasn't sure he'd want to.

The night had been full of surprises. Oh, not the fact that they'd ended up in bed. But the revelation of just how much Jenna had to give, of how eager she was to take. Also, it was a shock to discover that he never wanted to leave this bed, this room, this woman.

When had the last of his defenses crumbled so completely? When had he gone and fallen in love with her?

Once he accepted the reality of his feelings, he could think of a dozen times along the way when he'd been on the verge, but he'd been too blind—too terrified—to see the emotion for what it was. Now that he had, there was only one thing left to do. He had to take the final leap of faith into the future.

He gazed into her eyes. "Marry me," he said before he could stop himself.

Jenna stared at him, looking more pleased than stunned. "You know something, Bobby? You're kind of slow out of the gate, but once you decide on something, you don't waste a lot of time, do you?''

He grinned. ''Last time I waited, I lost. I don't intend to take that chance again. Some things are just too valuable to risk.'' His gaze locked with hers. ''You haven't answered me yet.''

''Oh? I thought I had. Must have been my imagination.''

He regarded her with puzzlement. ''Your imagination?''

She grinned. ''I've been saying yes to you since the night you stood up to my father in my behalf. I've just been keeping it to myself until you caught up.''

24

Frances moved faster than a scared rabbit. King spent two whole days chasing her from one end of Trinity Harbor to another. He always seemed to arrive just as she'd ducked out another door. He was pretty sure she was deliberately trying to exasperate him.

When he spotted her in the back at church on Sunday morning, he began pushing his way through the congregation trying to reach her before she could make yet another escape. Unfortunately, one of the drawbacks to being a Spencer was that everyone had something to say to him. King rudely cut short most of the greetings and kept moving, but by the time he hit the front steps of the church, Frances had vanished yet again.

"Looking for someone?" Anna-Louise inquired, her eyes dancing with merriment.

"What did you do? Stash her in your office? The fool woman can't move that fast."

"Maybe she's highly motivated," the pastor suggested.

"To do what? Drive me crazy?"

Anna-Louise's grin spread. "Is that what she's doing?"

"Well, of course she is. She's avoiding me, and I don't like it one bit."

"Any idea why she might be doing that?"

"Because we had a silly little disagreement."

"Over?"

"None of your business, young woman. You don't get to poke your nose into my personal life."

Anna-Louise laughed out loud at that. "Unlike you?"

"What the devil's that supposed to mean?"

"King, you're the all-time champ of meddlers. Just look at the manipulating you did to get Daisy and Walker together. And you've been working in the wings to see that Bobby ends up with Jenna. They might not know about that, but I do."

"I don't know what you know or think you know, but those two needed a good shove."

"Well, it worked. I suppose you can take some pride in that."

King stopped searching the crowd for signs of Frances and stared at Anna-Louise. "What do you mean, it worked?"

She chuckled. "Don't tell me I know something you don't know."

"Just spit it out, woman. I don't have all day."

"Is Bobby coming to Cedar Hill today for dinner?"

"He hasn't said he isn't. What's that got to do with anything?"

"Ask him what's going on. It's not my news to share."

King's annoyance faded as he realized what Anna-Louise was keeping from him. "They're getting mar-

ried?'' he speculated, keeping a close eye on her reaction. She never even blinked. Damn, but she'd make
a good poker player. Too bad she didn't care for gam-
bling.

"I didn't say a word," she reminded him piously.

"Well, hallelujah!" he said, making the leap all on
his own. "It's about time. Now, if I could just find
that blasted female, my day would be complete."

Anna-Louise shook her head. "Calling Frances a
blasted female is no way to win her heart."

"Coming from me, that's a term of endearment."

She sighed heavily. "Yes, I imagine it is. Check the
choir room. I believe she was going to hide out in there
until you left the premises."

King delivered a smacking kiss to the minister's
cheek. "Thank you. You won't regret this."

"I'd better not," she warned as he took off for the
choir room.

He found Frances sitting on a chair in a corner, her
expression downcast. The last members of the choir
were straggling out. They gave King a knowing grin
and closed the door behind them.

His heart thumped unsteadily. "So," he said finally.
"About time you decided to come home."

She finally looked up and met his gaze. King's
mouth gaped. "Frances? What have you done to yourself?"

A spark of pure fury lit her eyes. "I might have
known you'd say something unflattering right off,"
she snapped. "I don't know why I ever thought there
was a kind or decent bone in your body."

She would have rushed past him, but King blocked

her path. He took her shoulders in both hands. "Now, don't go getting all stirred up. You just took me by surprise. Let me take another look."

Her hair had been cut in a totally new style that made her eyes look bigger. Once almost totally white, it had been tinted to a soft blond shade.

But that was the least of the changes. She'd done something to her face. It seemed less lined, more radiant. And she'd trimmed off maybe twenty pounds, shedding the round figure that he'd totally approved of.

"You through looking yet?" she asked, her tone cranky.

"Why did you go and do all this?" he asked, bewildered.

"Why does any woman fix herself up?" she retorted. "For a man, though I can see it was a waste of effort."

He stared at her. "You did this for me?"

"Of course I did!"

"But why? I liked you just the way you were."

She regarded him sadly, her shoulders slumped in defeat. "Not enough."

"Enough for what?"

"Marriage, you idiot!" She hit him with her purse. "Wake up and smell the roses, King Spencer. Neither one of us is getting any younger. I, for one, do not intend to spend the rest of my life alone. If I'm not good enough to suit you, then I'll find someone who's not too old and decrepit to want a little excitement in his life."

"Frances, excitement to you is a night at bingo. At least that's what you led me to believe."

"Well, I want more, dammit."

"Don't curse in God's house," he scolded.

"Well, you drove me to it," she defended herself. "I think He'll understand. I'm sure you exasperate *Him* all the time. Now let me go."

"I will not. We need to talk about this."

"I think you've said quite enough for one day. Call me in a week...or maybe a month. Maybe by then you'll have figured out why I find you so infuriating. If you haven't, don't bother calling."

She stormed past him then, leaving the room in a swirl of some new scent. King stared after her in bemusement. What on earth had gotten into her? Frances had always been the most sensible woman he'd ever known, just like Daisy.

He halted in his tracks. That was it. Daisy had walked the straight and narrow until the day she'd gotten it into her head she was going to get herself a family by hook or crook. She'd latched onto Tommy and Walker for dear life, reason be damned. Now Frances was acting the same way.

She'd all but said he was the one she wanted, and he'd pretty much thrown it back in her face...again. No wonder she was furious. If his family found out about this—if Anna-Louise found out about it—he'd be hearing about it till he took his dying breath.

There was still time to fix it. It had been a very long time since he'd courted Mary Margaret, but, if he put his mind to it, he could still remember what it took to stir a woman's blood, even one as stubborn as Frances.

But first things first. He needed to get out to Cedar Hill and get a fix on what was going on with Bobby and Jenna. Once he had the two of them settled, he could get to work on winning Frances's heart. Knowing how she liked him to pay for his mistakes, it was likely to take him quite a while to jump through enough hoops to satisfy her.

Bobby chewed on a fried chicken leg and ignored his father's speculative glances. Beside him Jenna was daintily cutting her chicken from the bone and taking tiny bites. The conversation had been lagging for some time now, ever since Tucker had dared to ask his father if he'd ever caught up with Frances. King's terse reply had pretty much silenced all of them, and sent the housekeeper scurrying back to the kitchen.

"How come everybody's so quiet?" Darcy asked eventually.

Tommy shot her a knowing look. "Grown-up stuff. The minute we leave the table, they'll be talking their heads off."

"Then let's go," she said at once. "This is boring."

Jenna frowned at her. "Not till you finish your dinner, young lady."

"Oh, let them go," King said. "Darcy nailed it. This is pretty dull, the way things stand. And Tommy's right, too. There are things we need to get into that shouldn't be said in front of children."

"All the more reason to keep them here, if you ask me," Tucker said.

"Nobody asked you," King shot back. "Darcy, Tommy and J.C., you kids stop in the kitchen and ask

Mrs. Wingate to give you some pie. You can eat it on the porch.''

Tommy didn't wait around for permission from Daisy or Walker. He was out of his chair like a shot, with J.C. on his heels. Darcy cast a quick look at Jenna, who sighed and nodded.

"Now, then," King said when they were gone. "Will somebody tell me what's going on around here?"

"Going on?" Bobby inquired innocently. "We're just having a pleasant Sunday dinner, like always."

"Then why was Anna-Louise acting all smug after church today?" King asked. "What does she know that I don't?"

Daisy and Walker exchanged a mystified look. Tucker sat back and grinned. Jenna's gaze met Bobby's.

"Do you want to put your father out of his misery, or shall I?" she asked.

"I suppose I should be the one," Bobby said. "I'm thinking of putting a new Mexican dish on the menu at the marina."

Jenna elbowed him in the ribs. "Stop it. Tell him."

"Oh, all right, but you're spoiling all my fun. I don't often get a chance to torment my father the way he's always tormenting us."

Daisy regarded him intently, glanced over at Jenna, then grinned. "You're getting married," she said, stealing his thunder right out from under him.

"Hey, that was my big announcement," he protested.

"Then you should have gotten right to it," his sister countered.

"You should have known," Tucker told him without sympathy. "Daisy was always quick to run to Daddy and tattle on us."

"Oh, I was not," she protested.

"Hey," Bobby shouted over them. "Jenna and I are getting married. Could we focus on that?"

He turned to find a smug smile on his father's face.

"About time," King said succinctly, and winked at Jenna. "I can't imagine what you see in my son, but I'm delighted you're willing to take him on. I knew it was a good match the first time I laid eyes on you. Before that, if the truth be known."

Bobby's gaze narrowed. "What does that mean?"

"Nothing," King denied. "I'm real happy for you, son. When's the wedding?"

No sooner had the words left his mouth than three kids skidded to a halt in the doorway. Darcy's mouth gaped. J.C. looked equally stunned.

"Mom?" Darcy said. "Is King talking about your wedding? You and Bobby?"

Jenna flushed guiltily. Now it was Bobby's turn to stare. "You hadn't told her?"

"I thought we'd tell her together tonight. We only just decided," she said defensively.

Bobby regarded Darcy cautiously. "You okay with this?"

"You're not going to be my dad, though, right? I already have a dad."

The color drained out of Jenna's face. Bobby felt a

knot form in his stomach. He hadn't expected resistance on this front. Clearly, neither had Jenna.

"Come over here," he said to Darcy. "You, too, J.C."

She came toward him reluctantly. Bobby took her hands in his. "I know you have a dad. And, no, I am not going to take his place. But I would like to be your stepfather and your friend." He glanced at his son. "It's going to be a little bit of an adjustment for all of us, kind of like the one J.C. and I are making."

"Because you're his biological dad and he already had another dad," Darcy said.

"Yes," Bobby told her. "In a way that means you're both very lucky. You're going to have two fathers, and in J.C.'s case, he's going to have a second mom as well. That's a lot of people to hit up for cash when you want something."

"And a lot of people telling us what to do," J.C. said sullenly. "How are we supposed to know who's in charge?"

"That's something for the adults to work out," Bobby told him. "And we'll make sure you understand all the rules. Whenever you don't, you can ask." He met Darcy's gaze. "How about it? You okay with this?"

"We won't ever go back to Baltimore?" she asked her mother.

"Just to visit," Jenna said.

"But I can go see my dad and Grandpa whenever I want?" Darcy asked, evidently needing to clarify everything.

"Whenever we all agree," Jenna corrected.

"And I can spend all the time I want in the kitchen with Bobby learning to cook, because now I'll be his kid and not just someone who's too young to work?"

Bobby laughed. "Absolutely."

"It'll be so cool," Tommy enthused, piping up now that the details seemed to be ironed out to everyone's satisfaction. "Now we'll all be cousins or something, right, Grandpa King?"

Bobby caught his father's eye and thought he detected the sheen of tears, but King quickly blinked them away. "You've got that right, son. We'll all be family."

"And a damned fine family at that," Tucker said, lifting his glass. "Welcome Jenna and Darcy. You're brave souls."

"Brave, nothing," Bobby retorted. "Jenna's marrying me. I call that smart."

Tucker clinked his glass to Bobby's. "A matter of opinion, bro."

"Just wait," Bobby told him. "One of these days Walker and I are going to get even with you for being so smug while we bit the matrimonial dust."

"Don't hold your breath," Tucker replied. "There's not a woman born who can convince me to give up my peace and quiet."

"Peace and quiet?" Daisy repeated incredulously. "You carry a gun, for heaven's sakes."

He frowned at her. "Not around the house. I walk through that door and my troubles are over for the day. I intend to keep it that way."

Bobby grinned. "Famous last words."

25

Jenna could never in a million years have predicted her father's reaction to the news that she was getting married. She waited until Christmas morning to tell him. It was the one day she could be absolutely certain he wouldn't be racing off to the office five seconds after downing his first cup of coffee.

He heard her out, then nodded once as a look of satisfaction spread across his face. "I thought that was the way the wind was blowing when I came down there a few months ago. I talked it over with King Spencer and decided to let well enough alone. He seemed to have things under control."

Jenna stared at him. "Under control? You and King Spencer conspired?"

Her father flushed guiltily. "Conspiracy is a harsh assessment. We just didn't want to leave anything to chance."

"What exactly did King do?"

"Nothing to get so worked up over. You're happy, aren't you?"

Jenna couldn't deny that, but she still didn't have to like being manipulated. "That's not the point."

"Well, of course it is. I left things to chance with you once before, and look how that turned out. I did a little checking before I came down there, and saw right off that Bobby Spencer was an honorable man from a good family.''

''And then what? You scheduled a meeting with his father to make a deal? How very archaic of you. What did you offer him, a couple of prize bulls?''

''Don't speak to me like that, young lady. I'm still your father. I did what needed to be done, put a few wheels into motion. Bobby did the proposing all on his own. Nobody dragged the words out of his mouth.''

''But from your perspective it was a foregone conclusion,'' she guessed.

''King Spencer does have a way of getting what he wants,'' he agreed.

Jenna thought of Frances, who was still barely speaking to the man. She could sympathize with her at the moment.

''You're lucky I don't walk out of here and never speak to you again,'' Jenna said. ''But since Bobby and I are in love with each other, I don't suppose your meddling matters one way or the other.''

She recalled her suspicions. ''What exactly did King do, by the way?''

Her father grinned. ''I'm afraid I'm sworn to secrecy on that score.''

''I'll find out,'' she told him.

His grin spread. ''Only if and when he wants you to,'' he said. ''The man's sneaky.''

''Which makes you two of a kind,'' she muttered. ''Heaven help us all.''

* * *

Bobby wasn't especially surprised by Jenna's revelation about the conspiracy. All he cared about was getting her to walk down the aisle and say "I do." So far, though, she was holding out for a spring wedding.

"I cannot possibly plan a wedding and finish this project on time," she told him. "Your choice."

"Let Daisy and Anna-Louise plan the wedding." The suggestion was met with stony silence. He concluded she hated the idea.

But a week later, she greeted him at the door with a legal pad and a determined expression. "Here's the deal," she said grimly.

She ran through a list of dates and details that had his head spinning.

"Whatever you want," he said eventually.

She grinned. "Good answer. Now let's talk color scheme for the boardwalk."

"Right after this," he said, pulling her into his arms and covering her mouth. When he finally released her, she looked a little dazed. "Good. Women who can multitask so efficiently make me nervous. It's nice to see I can still ruin your concentration."

"Thank goodness this is a school day. Darcy won't be home for hours. You've pretty much ruined me for getting any work done today at all," she said, giving him a smoldering look and hauling him straight down the hall to her bedroom. "Don't blame me if the wedding and the boardwalk project don't come in on time."

"Any delay will be well worth it," he swore as he stripped off her clothes.

"I'll remind you of that," she said, right before she tumbled both of them onto the bed.

After that, Bobby made absolutely certain that there was only one thing on her mind for the rest of the day.

Jenna's May wedding day dawned with clear skies and a brilliant sun. But an hour before the ceremony, she was still on the boardwalk with a punch list in one hand and a building inspector on her heels. He seemed to be finding dozens of petty details that had to be fixed before he'd approve the buildings for occupancy. With only two weeks to go, time was getting critical. The tenants were chomping at the bit to get in and set up before the official Memorial Day opening.

"Jenna, you're going to be late to your own wedding," Daisy complained when she found them inside the building designated for a small Victorian-style bed and breakfast. "Can't this wait till Monday?"

"We're almost finished," she insisted. "If Donald would stop nitpicking everything, we'd be out of here."

"Rules are rules," he said, his expression rigid.

Daisy planted herself in front of him. "Donnie Turner, you stop messing around right this second. I know the mayor put you up to this just to spoil Bobby's wedding. Well, I'm here to tell you to give it a rest. These buildings are the safest in Trinity Harbor, and you know it. They exceed the fire code requirements, the Disability Act requirements and every petty regulation on the books here in town. Now go home."

"I'm not finished," he protested.

"You are for today," Daisy countered, snagging

Jenna's hand. "Come on. I do not intend to let you walk down the aisle in a pair of jeans and a hard hat."

Jenna couldn't hide the laughter that bubbled up. "Anxious to get Bobby married off, are you? Why? So you can move on to Tucker? You're as bad as your father."

Daisy rolled her eyes. "Please. I don't even come close. I just want today to be special for both of you. If you're distracted, you won't even remember the vows you wrote."

Jenna stared at her. "I was supposed to write my own vows?"

Daisy frowned. "Don't mess with me. I know it's on one of those infernal lists of yours. Did you or did you not write them?"

"Did Bobby write his?" Jenna asked curiously as Daisy shot through the streets of Trinity Harbor with her husband's siren blasting on top of the car. Jenna was pretty sure it was an illegal use of county property, but she doubted Tucker would complain. Walker wouldn't dare.

"How should I know?" Daisy grumbled as she screeched to a stop in the church parking lot. "Tucker's in charge of Bobby. I'm having enough trouble keeping up with you."

Inside the choir room, Anna-Louise was waiting with hot curlers, Jenna's wedding gown and the same kind of militant expression that Daisy wore.

"Let's get this show on the road," the pastor declared. "The groom's been pacing around my office for an hour now, looking more nervous by the second. I don't know how long Tucker, Richard and Walker can keep him away from here. He seemed to have some crazy idea you might not show up.''

"Oh, for goodness' sakes," Jenna protested. "I'm here, aren't I?''

"Only because I went looking for you," Daisy reminded her. "Sit. Let me see your nails.''

"No time," Anna-Louise shot back. "Hair and makeup, that's it, or I will not be responsible for what happens when Bobby walks into the church and Jenna's not walking down the aisle five seconds later.''

"He's waited all these years for the right woman, he can wait a few more minutes so that everything's perfect," Daisy argued.

Just then there was a pounding on the door. "Hey, what's the holdup in there?" King demanded.

"We have twenty minutes, Daddy. Settle down," Daisy commanded.

Anna-Louise was rolling Jenna's hair onto giant curlers when the door burst open. Bobby peered in. "Good. You're here," he said. "All I wanted to know." He backed out and shut the door.

Jenna yelped. "He saw me. That can't be good. Where's Darcy? Has anyone checked to be sure she's ready?''

"Darcy looks like an angel," Daisy assured her. "Tommy and J.C. are complaining about being forced to wear a tux. They're not going to be happy if this wedding doesn't go off on time, either. They've already been in the church hall, eyeing the cake.''

"If one little rosette on that cake is missing, I will personally strangle the pair of them," Anna-Louise chimed in. "Do you know how long it took me to get it looking just right? Why I thought I could bake a wedding cake is beyond me. I should have let you order it from a bakery.''

Jenna stood up and held up her hands. ''Okay, that's it. Will you two settle down before I wind up coming completely unglued? The cake is going to be perfect whether the decorations are snatched or not. I'm going to look…'' She glanced at the mirror and suffered a few qualms. ''I'm going to look okay. Everyone's going to wait till I show up. They can't very well do the ceremony without me. Besides, Anna-Louise, you're in here. Nobody starts without the two of us. Now, both of you, take a deep breath.''

The two women exchanged a look, then laughed.

''Why am I the only one in this room who's not having bridal jitters?'' Jenna demanded.

''Good question,'' Anna-Louise said. ''Maybe I'll bring it up when you actually make it to the front of the church.''

A few minutes later—only ten minutes late, Jenna noted with satisfaction—she was standing at the back of the church with her father. The jitters Anna-Louise had forecast were starting. She was getting married— for the second time. What was she thinking? She was lousy at marriage. She would screw it up, just the way she had last time.

Then she looked down the long aisle and met Bobby's gaze. Her nerves steadied at once. She wasn't a screwup anymore. She was worthy of this incredible man's love. He'd told her that time and again, in a thousand different ways. And even if she made an occasional mistake, so what? He was promising to give her a lifetime to get it right.

Bobby had had a few bad moments when he'd realized that Jenna wasn't at the church. When he'd finally seen her for himself—hair up in curlers, makeup incomplete, wearing a ratty old robe that belonged to his sister if he wasn't mistaken—his relief had been overwhelming. He would have married her right then and there, if he hadn't had to contend with his sister and Anna-Louise. They'd been determined to make this day special, and they were already appalled that he'd seen the bride before the ceremony.

But now, at last, Jenna was at the back of the church, taking her first step in his direction. In mere moments, she would be by his side, where she'd stay forever.

He glanced at his brother-in-law, whose gaze was locked with Daisy's. His misty-eyed sister wore a dreamy expression as she watched Jenna coming down the aisle to the strains of the wedding march. Then he turned to Tucker, who was running a finger inside the tight collar of his shirt and looking thoroughly uncomfortable. Finally he looked out at his father in the first pew. King looked smugly content. And why shouldn't he? He'd gotten his way.

But so had Bobby. Manipulated or not, he'd wound up with a woman who would spend the rest of their lives surprising him. What man could complain about a thing like that? A few years down the road, he'd probably be doing whatever it took to see that his own kids were happy, too.

At last he turned his attention back to Jenna. She reached his side and slipped her hand into his. From that moment on, he had everything in life he'd ever wanted.

The boardwalk was scheduled to open on Memorial Day weekend, two weeks after Jenna and Bobby's wedding. They were postponing their honeymoon until after the opening.

Now it was barely dawn on the day after the wedding and they were standing on the brand-new boardwalk admiring the sunrise. Bobby turned his attention to the development behind them. It was perfect, everything he'd ever imagined. Only one thing was missing.

"We really have to decide on that carousel," he said. "If we're going to bring it in, we need to get it here for the opening whether we have the missing horse or not."

"I have it covered," Jenna said. "Stop worrying. It'll be here soon."

"And the missing horse? I suppose you know something about that, too?"

A grin spread across her face. "I'm almost a hundred percent certain it will be here."

Bobby frowned. "What do you know that I don't? Did Tucker finally track down the thief?"

"Wait and see. I could be wrong."

Two hours later, the magnificent antique carousel was in its place of honor as the centerpiece of the boardwalk. It was even more beautiful than Jenna had described. It was bound to draw people from miles around just to admire it.

There was just one problem. There was a gaping hole where a proud horse had once stood. Bobby shook his head, regretting that he hadn't insisted on a massive search to find a replacement horse weeks ago.

He was about to suggest that they start that search today when a Cedar Hill truck pulled up and his father got out.

Bobby regarded him suspiciously. "Hey, Daddy, what brings you down here?"

"I brought your wedding present," King said, beckoning to Tucker and Walker who were in the back of the truck.

As Bobby stared in amazement, they removed a tarp and the missing carousel horse appeared.

"*You* took it?" he said incredulously. He turned to Jenna, who was grinning broadly. "And you knew?"

"Let's just say I suspected he might have had a hand in it when I began to hear about what a meddler he is and how badly he wanted to get you married off. Then my father said something, and it all pretty much fell into place for me." She looked at King. "You must have been thrilled to discover the guard was going on vacation and wouldn't be around to identify you right away."

King's face flushed. "Let's not get into all that now. The point is, it's here. Puts a finishing touch on things, don't you think?"

It took a little while to get the horse into place, but as soon as it was, King motioned for Bobby and Jenna to climb on the carousel.

"The two of you deserve to have the first ride. Let's see how this thing works." He winked at Jenna. "Who knows, you might even catch the brass ring."

She reached for Bobby's hand. "I've already won the best prize in town."

"Then I'll grab for it," Bobby declared, looking around at his assembled family of clever sneaks. "Something tells me I'm going to need all the luck I can get."

_____ Epilogue _____

Some things in life required drastic measures, King noted as he watched Bobby and Jenna circling around on that magnificent carousel, looking happier than he'd ever imagined when he'd gotten the idea to steal that horse right out from under their noses.

The plan had come to him on Sunday night on the day Jenna had had that horse delivered and set all of this into motion. Walker and Tucker had told him how Jenna had gotten under Bobby's skin straight off. Even Anna-Louise had dropped a few hints about the way the wind was blowing between Bobby and Jenna. King had never been one to look a gift horse in the mouth, no pun intended.

The carousel paused, and Walker pulled Daisy and Tommy on to join Bobby and Jenna for a ride. Darcy scrambled onto a white horse like a princess who'd been born to ride. Tucker stood back, staring at them, looking just a little too lonesome to suit King.

Well, he'd done okay by Daisy and by Bobby, he decided, gazing at them with satisfaction. Now it was Tucker's turn. Tucker had always been the independent type. He was the kind of man who liked to do things for himself, who liked to think it was his job to protect anyone and everyone around him. It had just about killed him when his mama had died. For a time he'd even blamed King for not doing something to save her. Tucker had been too young to understand that there was nothing either one of them could have done to save her. The sorrow of that terrible time was still with Tucker. He'd been keeping a close watch on everyone else he loved ever since.

It was going to take a helluva woman to capture Tucker's interest, King concluded. Somebody with a little spirit, a little daring and a whole lot of heart. She was also going to require a little patience, because Tucker was going to be a hard sell. That was one reason King had saved him for last. He'd wanted his oldest to see Daisy and Bobby settled and happy, so he'd start to believe in the power of love again.

King would start working on settling Tucker's fate first thing in the morning—just as soon as he delivered his daily bouquet of posies to Frances. After all, there came a time when even a stubborn man realized he couldn't take a good woman for granted.

PAMELA MORSI

Doing Good

One more chance...please!

Jane Lofton is so busy rescheduling her next
liposuction, shopping for clothes she doesn't need
and bragging about her latest real estate sale
that she hasn't noticed the callus forming
around her heart. Her husband is cheating on her,
and she talks to her daughter through a therapist.
No, life is *not* perfect.

Very suddenly, Jane's problems become incidental when she is
involved in a traffic accident. She barely escapes a tragic end,
but not before making a solemn promise to "do good" for the
rest of her life.

So how come "doing good" is so complicated?

NEW YORK TIMES BESTSELLING AUTHOR

SANDRA BROWN

HONOR BOUND

Aislinn Andrews didn't know if escaped convict Lucas Greywolf
was a troublemaker who aroused dissidence among Arizona's
Native Americans…or a hero who'd gone to prison for a crime he
didn't really commit. It didn't really matter now, since he'd taken
her hostage. Lucas was going home to the reservation of his birth,
honor-bound to pay his last respects to his dying grandfather. And
Aislinn was his ticket home….

In this classic romance, Sandra Brown explores the myriad emotions
that drive men and women to cross the boundaries of fear,
uncertainty, even hate, to explore the uncharted territory of love.

**"A tour de force reading experience…
explosive, fast-paced and sensational."
—*Romantic Times***

Available the first week of March 2002
wherever paperbacks are sold!

MIRA®

MSB890

SHERRYL WOODS

66815	ABOUT THAT MAN	___ $6.50 U.S.	___ $7.99 CAN.
66600	ANGEL MINE	___ $5.99 U.S.	___ $6.99 CAN.
66542	AFTER TEX	___ $5.99 U.S.	___ $6.99 CAN.

(limited quantities available)

TOTAL AMOUNT	$_____
POSTAGE & HANDLING	$_____
($1.00 for 1 book, 50¢ for each additional)	
APPLICABLE TAXES*	$_____
TOTAL PAYABLE	$_____
(check or money order—please do not send cash)	

To order, complete this form and send it, along with a check or money order for the total above, payable to MIRA Books®, to: **In the U.S.**: 3010 Walden Avenue, P.O. Box 9077, Buffalo, NY 14269-9077; **In Canada**: P.O. Box 636, Fort Erie, Ontario, L2A 5X3.

Name:_____
Address:_____ City:_____
State/Prov.:_____ Zip/Postal Code:_____
Account Number (if applicable):_____
075 CSAS

*New York residents remit applicable sales taxes.
   Canadian residents remit applicable GST and provincial taxes.

MIRA®